Gripping Novels
of Crime and Detection:

SIGNET DOUBLE MYSTERIES

THE
DRAGON'S TEETH

and

CALAMITY TOWN

SIGNET Mysteries You'll Enjoy

THE DRAGON'S TEETH

and

CALAMITY TOWN

By
Ellery Queen

A SIGNET BOOK
NEW AMERICAN LIBRARY
TIMES MIRROR

SIGNET TRADEMARK REG. U.S. PAT. OFF. AND FOREIGN COUNTRIES
REGISTERED TRADEMARK—MARCA REGISTRADA
HECHO EN CHICAGO, U.S.A.

SIGNET, SIGNET CLASSICS, MENTOR, PLUME, MERIDIAN AND NAL
BOOKS *are published by The New American Library, Inc.,
1633 Broadway, New York, New York 10019*

FIRST PRINTING (DOUBLE ELLERY QUEEN EDITION), MAY, 1980

3   4   5   6   7   8   9

PRINTED IN THE UNITED STATES OF AMERICA

THE
DRAGON'S
TEETH

CONTENTS

Part One

Part Two

Part Three

Part Four

Part Five

Part Six

Cast of Characters

Part ONE

I

The Vanishing American

MEET BEAU RUMMELL.

No, not Beau Brummell; he was a London gentleman
of fashion born in the year 1778 . . . Beau *Rummell*. Beau
Rummell was born in Cherry Street, New York City, in the
year 1914.

Never think that Beau took his name meekly. From boy-
hood he was ready to fight the human race, one wit at a
time, in defense of his self-respect. He even tried subter-
fuge. He would change his name to Buck, or Butch, or
something equally manly. But it was no use.

"Rummell? *Rummell?* Say, ya know what? Your first
name oughta be Beau. *Beau Rummell.* Haw, haw, haw!"

Beau's personality was moulded in the crucible of that
bitter name. At the age of twelve, learning by investigation
that his namesake had been London's *arbiter elegantiarum,*
first fop of his time, Beau became a passionate sartorial
rebel; and to this day, if you meet a large young man with
scarred knuckles who looks as if he had slept in all his
clothing for two months consecutively, you may be sure
he is no hungry derelict, but Beau Rummell.

To the despair of his father, Inspector Johnny Rummell
of the Narcotic Squad, Beau was always running away.
He ran away from the intelligent humorists of Columbia
Law School three times—first to shovel sand in a river-
tunnel operation, only to be driven back into the arms of
Contracts when a brawny Lithuanian sandhog discovered
the secret of his shame; then to become press-agent for a
third-rate circus, an episode terminating in a bloody brawl
with Bongo the Strong Man, who thought he could lick
any one named Beau and discovered on being revived that
he had been laboring, as the phrase goes, under a mis-
apprehension; the third time to sling rivets high above
Sixth Avenue. That was the time he almost fell forty stories

11

scrambling angrily after a tormentor; thereafter he chose refuges nearer Mother Earth.

He fled during his summer vacations, too—once to Hollywood, once to Alaska, once to the beckoning southern spheres by way of a freighter Rio-bound. This last was a bad mistake of judgment, for the supercargo was an educated man who delightedly passed the good word around to the crew, so that it became necessary for young Mr. Rummell to punish aspersions upon his Christian name with a whole ocean as his battleground, and no escape except by swimming.

Mr. Ellery Queen heard of him when Inspector Johnny died.

Inspector Queen took the death of his old friend hardly; he wanted to do something for the son.

"The boy's at loose ends," the Inspector told Ellery. "Graduate lawyer, but he's quit and, conditions being what they are, I can't say I blame him. Besides, he wasn't made to grow soft in a swivel-chair. He's a restless sprout, tough as hardtack. Done everything—been to sea, slung rivets, bummed his way around the country, picked oranges in California, dug ditches on WPA projects . . . everything, that is, except find himself. And now, with John gone, he's worse off than ever. Cocky sonofagun, Beau is; thinks he knows everything. Darned near does, too."

"What did you say the name was?" asked Ellery.

The Inspector said: "Beau."

"Beau Rummell?" Ellery began to smile.

"I knew you would. Everybody does. That's Beau's cross. Only don't make fun of it to his face—he goes berserk."

"Why don't you make a cop of him?"

"He'd make a good one at that, except for his blamed restlessness. Matter of fact, he's got a notion he'd like to open a detective agency." The Inspector grinned. "I guess he's been reading some of your terrible detective stories."

"This Peregrine Pickle of yours," said Mr. Queen hastily, "interests me. Let's hunt him up."

They found Mr. Rummell consuming corned-beef sandwiches in *Louie's Grill,* two blocks west of Centre Street.

"Hello, Beau," said the Inspector.

" 'Lo, Pop. How's crime?"

"Still with us. Beau, I'd like to have you meet my son, Ellery."

"Hi, Beau," said Mr. Queen.

The young man set down his sandwich and examined

Mr. Queen with minute attention, concentrating on the eyes and mouth, as suspicious as a hound on the scratch for fleas. But when he found no trace of mirth, but only grave amiability, Beau extended his strife-scarred paw, and bellowed for the bartender, and after a while the Inspector went away smiling—sensibly—in the concealing thicket of his mustache.

That was the beginning of a beautiful friendship. For Mr. Queen found himself drawn irresistibly to this vast, cynical-eyed young man with the air of self-confidence and the broad span of shoulder draped in wrinkled cloth.

Later, when *Ellery Queen, Inc., Confidential Investigations* was born, Mr. Queen often wondered exactly how it had come to pass. The conversation in *Louie's Grill* involved the rotten state of the universe, man's inhumanity to man, Beau's personal ambitions, and suddenly, by a sort of magic, they were talking over an enterprise.

Mr. Queen was astonished to discover that he was about to become Mr. Rummell's partner in a detective agency.

"I've got a few thousand dollars," said Beau, "left by my old man, and I'm lapping 'em up. They'd be better invested in my future."

"I know, but—"

Oh, but he was young, willing, and able. He had legal training, physical courage, the ability to use firearms, a knowledge of the sinkholes of New York and of police methods.

"After all," he grinned, "you can't be a cop's son without getting all that. You ought to know!—and so, how about it?"

"But why me?" asked Mr. Queen in dismay.

"Because you've got a rep. Everybody knows the name of Queen in this town. It's synonymous with detective. I want to cash in on your rep."

"Oh, you do?" asked Mr. Queen feebly.

"Look, Ellery, you won't have to do a lick of work. I'll do it all. I'll run my legs off. I'll work twenty hours a day. I'll sink all my dough. Hell, there's nothing to this detective racket!"

"No?" asked Mr. Queen.

"All I want's your name on the door—I'll do the rest!"

Mr. Queen found himself saying he would think about it.

The next day Mr. Rummell called up and invited him to visit a certain suite in a Times Square office-building.

When Mr. Queen got there he saw his name already gilt-lettered on the front door.

Mr. Rummell, freshly shaved for the occasion, bowed him into a three-room suite. "Some stuff, huh? Meet our new secretary!" And he presented an aged virgin named Miss Hecuba Penny who already, after only an hour's association, was regarding Mr. Beau Rummell with a furtive, prim, but powerful passion.

Mr. Queen surrendered, feeling a little as if he had run several miles. But he liked the feeling, too.

ONE bright day in May Beau telephoned Ellery, demanding his partner's presence immediately. There was such excitement in his voice that even the unemotional Mr. Queen was stirred.

He found Beau rearranging office furniture with one hand and with the other adjusting his disreputable necktie, so he knew that an event of unusual importance had occurred.

"What d'ye think?" Beau roared. *"No* divorce. *No* find-our-dear-runaway-Nellie. *No* insurance fraud. It's a real case this time, my friend!"

"What kind of case?"

"Who knows? Who cares? He wouldn't say. But it's bound to be something big, because he's got all the money there is!"

"Who's 'he'?"

"The Man Nobody Knows. The Ghost of Wall Street. The Vanishing American. Cadmus Cole—in person!"

The great man himself, it appeared, had telephoned for an appointment. He had specifically asked for Mr. Queen—Mr. Queen, and no other. Mr. Rummell had promised to produce Mr. Queen; he would have promised to produce the equestrian statue of General Grant.

"He'll be here in fifteen minutes," said Beau, jubilantly. "What a break! Now keep me out of it. He insisted on you. What d'ye know about him? I buzzed Tom Creevich of the *Herald* and he dug some dope on Cole out of the morgue for me."

They put their heads together. Cole had been born in Windsor, Vermont, in 1873, eldest son in a moderately prosperous family. He had inherited his father's ironworks. He was married in 1901, there had been a scandal involving his wife's fidelity, and he had divorced her in 1903. She married four times more before being shot to death in Italy by a stickler of a husband some years later.

Cole expanded his ironworks. In 1912 he went into South American nitrates. When the World War broke out, he began manufacturing munitions. He made millions. After the War he quadrupled his fortune in Wall Street. It was at this time that he sold out all his holdings and bought the colossal chateau at Tarrytown on the Hudson which he rarely used.

In 1921 the multimillionaire retired and, with his confidential agent, Edmund De Carlos, who had represented him for many years, took to the sea. He had lived aboard his yacht *Argonaut* ever since.

"The *Argonaut* rarely visits the big ports," said Beau. "Puts in only for refueling, supplies, and cash. And when the yacht does drop anchor, Cole sulks in his cabin and this fellow De Carlos—he's still with Cole—manages everything.

"Sort of a plutocratic marine hobo," remarked Ellery. "What's the matter with him?"

"He's wacky as hell," said Beau happily.

"If what you say is true, this must be his first personal appearance in New York City in eighteen years."

"I'm honored," said Beau. "Yes, sir, I'm sorry I didn't put on my other suit!"

Since *millionairus Americanus* is a rare and fine species, it is important to study Mr. Cadmus Cole while we have the opportunity. For Mr. Cole is doomed to an early extinction . . . perhaps earlier than he thinks.

Observe, ladies and gentlemen, that his first act in entering the inner office of *Ellery Queen, Inc.* is to bump into the door-jamb. A curious fact, which it will be instructive to bear in mind. No, he is not drunk.

He then advances to the focus of the beige rug, and pauses. His gait is not so much a walk as a stumping lurch, each foot raised deliberately from the floor and planted wide, as if feeling its way on an insubstantial terrain.

He stares at Messrs. Queen and Rummell with an oddly squinty sharpness. The squint, enmeshed in radial wrinkles, has surely been caused by years of gazing upon the shifting planes of sunstruck seas; but the sharpness, let us suspect, has a deeper root.

The ancient mariner's complexion is redbrown. The shallow pale plinths of pupil visible behind his squint are clear and youthful, if intently focused. His face is a mask,

15

smooth, hollowy, and mummiferous. He is paunchless, erect.

His cranium is innocent of hair; it bulges broadly, a brown and naked bone. And, his pale lips being parted a little, we see that he is as toothless as an embryo.

Clad in a blue, brass-buttoned yachting suit of great age, the millionaire squints from Mr. Rummell to Mr. Queen and back again with all the animation of a tailor's dummy.

"Great pleasure, great pleasure," said Mr. Queen hastily. "Won't you have a chair, Mr. Cole?"

"You Queen?" demanded the great man. He spoke in a strangulated mumble that was difficult to make out. His lack of teeth also caused him to drool and spit slightly when he spoke.

Mr. Queen closed his eyes. "I am."

"Talk to you alone," said Mr. Cole testily.

Beau kowtowed and vanished. Mr. Queen knew he was listening, observing, and engaging in other Rummellian activities from a peephole in the combination laboratory and darkroom adjoining the office.

"Not much time," announced the great man. "Sailing tonight. West Indies. Want to clear up this business. I've just come from Lloyd Goossens's law-office. Know young Goossens?"

"By reputation only, Mr. Cole. His father died about five years ago and he heads the firm now. It's an old, respectable outfit specializing in the liquidation and trustee-ship of large estates. Are you—er—liquidating your estate, Mr. Cole?"

"No, no. Just left Goossens my sealed will. Used to know his father. Good man. But since his father's dead, I've appointed Goossens co-executor and co-trustee of my estate."

"Co-?" asked Mr. Queen politely.

"My friend Edmund De Carlos will share the administra-tive duties with Goossens. Can't say this concerns you at all!"

"Naturally not," Mr. Queen assured the nabob.

"Come to you on a confidential matter. Understand you know your business, Queen. Want your promise to handle this case personally. No assistants!"

"What case, if you please?" asked Mr. Queen.

"Shan't tell you."

"I beg your pardon?"

"Shan't tell you. The case hasn't happened yet."

Mr. Queen looked indulgent. "But, my dear sir, you can't expect me to investigate a case of which I know nothing! I'm a detective, not a clairvoyant."

"Don't expect you to," mumbled the great man. "Engaging your future services. You'll know what it's about when the proper time comes."

"I can't refrain from asking," observed Mr. Queen, "why, if that is the case, Mr. Cole, you don't engage me at the proper time."

It seemed to him that a certain slyness crept over the brown mask of the millionaire. "You're a detective. You tell *me*."

"There's only one reason that comes directly to mind," murmured Mr. Queen, rising to the challenge, "but it seems so indelicate I hesitate to mention it."

"The devil! What's the reason?" And Mr. Cole's nostrils betrayed an oscillant curiosity.

"If you didn't decide to do the normal thing, which would have been to hire an investigator at the time an investigation became necessary, then it must be because you don't expect to be *able* to hire an investigator at that time, Mr. Cole."

"Fiddle-faddle! Talk sense."

"Simply that you think you may be dead."

The great man sucked in a long, snorkly breath. "Ah!" he said. "Well, well!" as if he had not heard anything so astounding in all his sixty-six years.

"Then you do expect an attack on your life?" asked Mr. Queen, leaning forward. "You have an active enemy? Perhaps some one has tried to kill you already?"

Mr. Cadmus Cole was silent. His lids slid closed, like the segmented roof of an observatory. Then he opened his eyes and said: "Money's no object. Always buy the best. Don't haggle. Will you take the case, Queen?"

"Oh, yes," said Mr. Queen promptly.

"I'll send a registered letter to Goossens as soon as I get back to the boat, with an enclosure to be filed with my will in Goossens's possession. It will specify that I've retained you to perform certain services at the stipulated fee. Which is?"

Mr. Queen could sense the mental vibrations of Mr. Beau Rummell imploring him to name an astronomical number. "Since I don't know what or how much work is involved, I can scarcely set a fee, Mr. Cole. I'll set it

17

when, as you say, the time comes. Meanwhile, may I suggest a retainer?"

"How much?" Cole reached into his breast-pocket.

"Shall we say," Mr. Queen hesitated, but only for an instant, "ten thousand dollars?"

"Make it fifteen," said the great man, and he drew out a checkbook and a fountain-pen. "Expenses to be paid. Let me sit down there, young man."

The millionaire heeled round the desk like a clipper in a squall, dropped into Mr. Queen's chair and, sucking in his cheeks, rapidly wrote out a check.

"I'll give you a receipt, Mr. Cole—"

"Not necessary. I've marked it 'retainer against future services.' Good day."

And, rising, the old gentleman set his yachting cap firmly on his naked dome and staggered towards the office door. Mr. Queen hurried forward, just too late to steer his extraordinary client clear of the jamb. Mr. Cole bumped. There was an absent look on his face, almost a majestically absent look, as if he could not be bothered about mere doorways when there were so many important things to think about.

He bounced off the jamb and chuckled: "By the way, just what d'ye suppose I *am* hiring you for, Queen?"

Mr. Queen searched his brain for a reply. The question made no sense. No sense whatever.

But Mr. Cadmus Cole mumbled: "Never mind," and trundled across the reception room and out of Mr. Queen's life.

When Mr. Queen returned, the check was missing from the desk. Rubbing his eyes, he said: "Abracadabra!" but Beau came running in from the laboratory with the slip of paper and said: "I made a photostat of it—just in case. No hairless monkey's passing me a phony check for fifteen grand and getting away with it!"

"You don't seem pleased," said Mr. Queen, alarmed. He sat down at the desk and quickly endorsed the check, as if he expected it to fly away.

"He's either an escaped lunatic," said Beau with disgust, "or else he's one of those eccentric tycoons you read about who like to play. This is a joke. Wait and see. Screwball will stop the check."

The mere possibility agonized Mr. Queen. He rang. "Miss Penny, do you see this scrap of paper?"

"I do," said Hecuba, gazing with love at Mr. Rummell.

18

"Take it down to the bank on which it's drawn first thing in the morning; too late today. If the signature's authentic, deposit the check in our bank."

"Optimist," growled Beau.

Miss Penny made off with the precious cargo of paper. Beau flung himself on the leather sofa and began angrily to chew on a mashed chocolate bar.

"What did you make of friend Cole?" asked Ellery with a remote look. "Didn't anything about him seem—well, peculiar?"

Beau said: "He's hiding something. Like hell."

Ellery sprang from the chair. "But the other thing! His pesky, unreasonable *curiosity*. Why should he be so anxious to find out what *I* think he's hiring me for?"

"He's a nut, I tell you."

Ellery perched on the desk and stared out at Times Square's crenellated skyline. Suddenly he grimaced; he had sat down on something long and hard. He turned round.

"He forgot his fountain-pen."

"Then we're in that much, anyway." Beau scowled at his chocolated fingers and began to lick them clean, like a cat.

Ellery examined the pen. Beau lit a cigaret. After a while he said indifferently: "What ho!"

"What do you make of this, Beau?" Ellery brought the pen to the sofa.

Beau squinted at it curiously through the smoke. It was a large fat pen, its cap considerably scratched and nicked in a sort of arced pattern. Some of the dents were deep, and the whole pen had a look of age and hard use.

Beau glanced at Ellery's face, puzzled. Then he unscrewed the cap and examined the gold nib.

"I make out an old-fashioned black gold-trimmed fountain-pen that's seen plenty of use by somebody that likes a smooth, broad stroke. It's exactly like millions of other pens."

"I have an idea," said Ellery, "that it's exactly like no other pen in the world."

Beau stared at him.

"Well, no doubt all these little mysteries will clarify in time. Meanwhile, Beau, I suggest you take microphotographs of the thing. From every angle and position. I want exact measurements, too. Then we'll send the pen back to the *Argonaut* by messenger. . . . I wish I were sure," he mumbled.

19

"Sure?"

"That the check's good."

"Amen!"

A glorious morrow it proved to be. The sun beamed; their messenger reported that the previous evening he had delivered the pen to the yacht, in its berth in the Hudson, and had not been arrested as a suspicious character; and Miss Hecuba Penny appeared late for work but triumphant with the announcement that the bank on which the fifteen thousand dollar check was drawn had authenticated, promptly and beyond any doubt whatever, the signature of Cadmus Cole.

That left only the possibility that Mr. Cole had been playful and meant to stop the check.

They waited three days. The check cleared.

Beau salaamed thrice to the agency bankbook and sallied forth to drown the fatted calf.

II

Last Voyage

of the Argonaut

THE MORTALITY RATE AMONG SIXTY-SIX-YEAR-OLD MILLION-aires who make out sudden wills and engage detectives for undisclosed reasons is bound to be high.

Mr. Cadmus Cole died.

Mr. Ellery Queen expected Mr. Cadmus Cole to die; to die, that is, under suspicious circumstances. He did not foresee that he himself would come perilously near to preceding his client through the pearly gates.

The blow fell the afternoon of the day the check cleared. Mr. Queen had taken up his telephone to call Lloyd Goossens, the attorney, for a conference of mutual enlightenment. Just as Goossens's secretary told him that the lawyer had left the previous night for London on an emergency business trip, Mr. Queen experienced a pang.

He set down the telephone. The pain stabbed deeply. He said: "Everything happens to me," and rang weakly for Miss Penny.

Within ninety minutes Mr. Queen lay on an operating

20

table unaware that a famous surgeon was removing an appendix which had treacherously burst. Afterwards, the surgeon looked grave. Peritonitis.

Inspector Queen and Beau paced the corridor outside Ellery's room all night, silent. They could hear the Queen voice raised in a querulous delirium. He was haranguing an invisible entity, demanding the answer to various secrets. The words "Cole" and "fountain-pen" ran through his monologue, accompanied by mutterings, groans, and occasional wild laughter.

With the sun emerged the surgeon, and the House Physician, and various others. Mr. Queen, it appeared, had a chance. There was something on his mind, said the surgeon, and it was making the patient cling, perversely, to his life. It had something to do with a fountain-pen and a person named Cole.

"How," said Beau hoarsely, "can you kill a guy like that?"

MR. QUEEN merely lingered in this vale of tears, swinging recklessly on the pearly gate, sometimes in, sometimes out. But when the news came that Cadmus Cole had died, he stopped tetering and set about the business of recuperation with such a grimness that even the doctors were awed.

"Beau, for heaven's sake," implored the patient, "talk!"

Beau talked. The yacht *Argonaut*, Captain Herrold Angus, master, had cleared New York Harbor the night of the day Cole had visited *Ellery Queen, Inc.* She carried her owner, his friend and companion Edmund De Carlos, her master, and a crew of twelve.

"Nobody else?" asked Mr. Queen instantly.

"That's all we know about.

On 13 June the *Argonaut* anchored in the Gulf of Paria, off Port of Spain, and, taking on fresh water and fuel, then sailed north and west into the Caribbean.

On 21 June she spoke a passing cruise liner 100 miles northwest of Port Gallinas. Captain Angus exchanged the usual courtesies of the sea with the liner's master.

At eight bells on the night of 30 June, during a squall, the *Argonaut's* wireless sputtered a general distress call directed to any vessel carrying a medical officer. The message stated that Cadmus Cole had suffered a severe heart-attack and that while Captain Angus had medical equipment in his locker and was capable of administering simple

21

treatment, he felt the serious condition of his owner demanded immediate professional advice.

White Lady, lying some 200 miles northeast, promptly responded. Her chief medical officer radioed for details of pulse, respiration, blood-pressure, and superficial symptoms. This information was supplied him via wireless.

White Lady's physician then advised digitalis injections, applications of ice, and other emergency measures. Captain Angus kept him informed by five-minute radio exchanges of the sick man's condition. Meanwhile, the liner steamed towards the *Argonaut* at full speed.

But she was too late. An hour and fifty minutes after the original distress call, a radio message signed by Captain Angus and Edmund De Carlos announced that Cadmus Cole had passed away. The message concluded with thanks for *White Lady's* assistance and the information that the millionaire's last wish before expiring had been to be buried at sea.

"No, no!" shrieked Mr. Queen. "Stop them!"

"Whoa, Silver," said Beau soothingly. "Cole's been lying at the bottom of the Caribbean in a canvas shroud for a week."

"A whole week!" groaned Ellery. "Is it July already?"

"Wednesday, July fifth."

"Then we've got to speak to De Carlos, to Angus, to the radio operator, the crew! Where are they now?"

"The *Argonaut* showed up at Santiago de Cuba two days after Cole kicked in—that was last Sunday. By Monday Captain Angus and the crew were paid off and discharged."

"De Carlos?" asked Ellery after a profound silence.

"Yeah. De Carlos then put the *Argonaut* in drydock down there, shipping Cole's personal effects to the States, and hopped a plane. He ought to be here tonight or tomorrow morning."

Mr. Queen was ominously quiet. Then he said: "Fee-fi-fo-fum."

"What?"

"A heart-attack in the middle of the Caribbean during a convenient storm, death before a certified medical officer can examine the dying man, sea-burial before an autopsy can be performed—and now the Captain and crew dispersed before they can be questioned!"

"Look at it this way, Master-Mind," said Beau, "because this is the way it's going to be looked at by John Q. Public. Cole's ticker gave out? He was sixty-six. Died at

22

sea? Funny if he hadn't, since he spent his last eighteen years aboard a yacht. Buried fathoms deep? Natural request of a dying man who loved the sea."

"And De Carlos's discharging Captain Angus and the crew in Cuba?" asked Mr. Queen dryly.

"Sure, he could have had them sail the *Argonaut* back north. But a plane is faster, and it would be natural for De Carlos to want to get back to New York as quickly as possible. No, son, the set-up is as smooth as a baby's—"

"Don't like it," said Ellery irritably. "Cole makes out a will, hires us, acts mysterious, dies—some people would use a nasty word, Beau . . . murder!"

"There's an ol' debbil in de law," said Beau dryly, "and his name is *corpus delicti*. I'll be squashed if I see how we'd do it, but suppose we could prove murder. We'd have to produce a body, wouldn't we? And where's the body? Making fish-food at the bottom of the Caribbean. No, sir, all we can have is suspicions, and they don't pay off on those in this racket."

"Just the same," muttered Mr. Queen, "we've got fifteen thousand dollars of Cole's money that say somebody's not going to get away with Cole's murder!"

"We've got it, but not for long. I meant to save the bad news till you were well enough to stand the shock. El, we've got to pay that dough back to the Cole estate."

"What!" exclaimed Mr. Queen. "Why?"

"Because Cole hired you, and you won't be able to investigate whatever it is he wanted you to investigate. The doc tells me you've got to go away for at least six weeks."

"Don't be an ass," snapped Ellery. "You're *Ellery Queen, Inc.*, not I. You'll investigate."

"No can do." Beau was glum. "Cole hired you personally, and you accepted. That constitutes a contract for personal services. A contract for personal services can't be assigned. We're out fifteen thousand bucks and the prospect of being filthy rich."

"The hell you say," scowled Mr. Queen, and he fell into an aggressive reverie. After a time he smiled diabolically. "Beau, whom did Cole say he was appointing executor-trustees of his estate?"

"Lloyd Goossens and this De Carlos."

"Do they know you?"

"No, and the ignorance is mutual. So what?"

23

"They don't know me either." Ellery grinned. "You see?"

"Why, you two-timing pretzel, you!" shouted Beau. "Talk about confidence men!"

"When Goossens asks for Ellery Queen, *you* answer."

"I stand in for you! And neither Goossens nor De Carlos will know the difference." Beau pounced. "Let me shake the hand of a genius!"

"Please, my operation. Of course, you know we're conspiring to commit a crime?"

"Are we?" Beau scratched his head. "Let's see. Well, I guess we are, although I'll be a frosted chocolate if I know what the crime is. And what's more, I don't give a rooty-toot. *Adios*, Mr. Queen!" said Mr. Rummell.

"*Vaya con Dios*, Mr. Queen!" said Mr. Queen.

Lloyd Goossens telephoned the next morning.

Mr. Rummell, alias Mr. Queen, made the subway journey downtown to Park Row in record time.

Goossens was a big, pleasant man in his late thirties, dressed as for the salon. He had a gray and sleepless look. Beau, who read Winchell, knew that Goossens alternated socially between Park Avenue and 52nd Street, with and without his society wife, as suited the occasion. As they shook hands, Beau sighed; it must be swell to be rich, he thought.

"De Carlos just got in on the Florida plane," said the lawyer, waving his fuming pipe towards an inner office. "I suppose you know who he is, Mr. Queen?"

"Mr. Queen" looked around to see where Mr. Queen was, but then, realizing that he was Mr. Queen, said: "Lord Chamberlain, wasn't he? By the way, why all the mystery, Goossens?"

Goossens frowned. "Mystery?"

"Cole wouldn't disclose the nature of the case. He made quite a secret of it."

"I don't see why," said the lawyer, puzzled. "His registered letter to me, in which he outlined the terms of your employment, made it perfectly clear. And then it's down in his will in black and white."

"You mean there's nothing sensational about it?"

Goossens grinned. "It has its points. Come in and meet the Grand Vizier, and we'll go over the whole business."

A moment later Beau was shaking hands with a medium-sized man browned by years of exposure to salt wind and windy sun. De Carlos's hair was a wavy black fur, and he wore a piratical-looking black beard. The eyes behind his silver-rimmed spectacles were widely open, naive—much too naive, Beau thought.

Beau was preoccupied when he left the two executors. At the hospital he told Ellery, who was in a fever of impatience, exactly what had happened, and all about De Carlos.

"He looks like a pirate. Just off the Spanish Main, too!"

"Yes, yes. But how about the case?"

"Oh, the case." Beau stared out the window. "That mysterious case we were all hopped up about. Well, prepare for a shock. Either old man Cole was as nutty as a chocolate bar, or we're up against a real baffler."

"What's the assignment, you aggravating sea-lawyer?"

"Merely to find a couple of missing heirs!"

"Oh, no," groaned Ellery. "That's too much. It can't be. How about the will itself? Did you see it?"

"Yes, and it has its screwy angles." Beau explained Cole's will to Ellery.

"But how is it that Cole didn't know where his heirs were?" demanded Ellery when Beau had finished.

Beau shrugged. Cadmus Cole's unfortunate marital experience in Windsor at the turn of the century had embittered him against the whole institution of marriage. He had had a younger brother, Huntley, whom he had sent to New York to study art. In 1906, in New York, Huntley Cole secretly married his model, a woman named Nadine Malloy. In 1907 a child, Margo, was born; and Cadmus, for the first time learning of his younger brother's marriage, became enraged at what he considered Huntley's ingratitude.

Cadmus stopped sending Huntley money and swore he should never speak to his brother again. Huntley took his wife and infant daughter to Paris, where he painted futilely for two years, living in poverty, his only means of support his wife's meager earnings as a model.

"This Huntley," Beau explained, "was too proud to write to his rich brother. But his wife wasn't, because her brat was starving, and so she wrote to Cadmus pleading for help. Cadmus replied—that's how we know about the Parisian episode of the Huntley branch—saying that his brother had made his bed, and so on—the usual sanctimonious tripe.

"Anyway, Cadmus turned his sister-in-law down cold.

Huntley found out about it, apparently, because right after Cadmus's letter arrived he committed suicide. There's absolutely no record of what happened to Nadine and little Margo. So one of our jobs is to pick up that thirty-year-old trail."

"That makes Margo Cole one heiress—if she's found and if she qualifies under the will. How about the other?"

"Well, Cadmus and Huntley had a younger sister, Monica. Reading between the lines it seems that, hearing about Huntley's suicide in Paris, Monica blamed Cadmus for it and just upped and quit her sourpuss brother cold. Walked out on Cadmus and the Windsor ancestral mansion and disappeared. That was not long after Huntley's death in 1909.

"We know sketchily what happened to her, too, after leaving Vermont. She had a lot of tough luck supporting herself until 1911, when she met a man named Shawn, an accountant or something, in Chicago. Shawn married her. A daughter, Kerrie, was born to Monica in 1918— just about the time her husband died of spinal meningitis in a Chicago hospital.

"Monica was left without a cent. Desperate, she wrote to her brother Cadmus, explaining what had happened and asking for help, just as Huntley's wife had written nine years before. Well, Monica received practically the same answer: she'd put herself outside the reservation by marrying, and she could go take a flying jump at the moon. That's the last record Cadmus had of his sister's— and little Kerrie's—whereabouts. Monica's letter was postmarked Chicago, September eighth, 1918."

"Nothing for Monica, eh?" mused Mr. Queen.

"Not a jit. Of course, she may be dead. Cole left the bulk of his estate, as I said, to his two nieces, Margo Cole and Kerrie Shawn . . . when, as, and if."

"How about insanity?" asked Mr. Queen hopefully.

"No dice. Goossens has already consulted psychiatrists. From the picture, they agree Cole was medically sane. Legally, of course, he had a right to put any cockeyed conditions he pleased on the passing of his estate. De Carlos, who's in the best position to know, pooh-poohs the whole idea, of course. He ought to, since Cole's left him a million bucks in cash and a home for life if he wants it in the Tarrytown mansion!"

"Did you question De Carlos about the circumstances of Cole's death?"

26

Beau nodded. "But he's a cool customer, and he stuck to his yarn. I bawled him out for not holding on to Captain Angus and the radio operator when he scattered the crew of the yacht all over creation."

"What's the point?"

"The witnesses who attested the validity of Cole's signature at the bottom of the will were Angus, the radio operator, and De Carlos."

"What of that?"

"Before a will may be probated, two of the subscribing witnesses must be produced and examined, if they're within the State and are competent and able to testify. In the absence of any witness, the Surrogate at his discretion may dispense with his testimony and admit the will to probate on the testimony of the other. So that in the absence of Captain Angus and the radio operator, we'll have to rely completely on the testimony of De Carlos."

Mr. Queen frowned. "I don't care for that."

"Well, we'll have a check-up, because the Surrogate undoubtedly will insist on better proof of signature than the mere word of a single witness. He'll want proof of the testator's handwriting, and of Angus's, and so on. There must be hundreds of Cole's autographs extant, and they'll all be examined."

"And I have to go to the mountains!" groaned Mr. Queen. "Blast my vermiform appendix!"

BEAU armed two operatives with the names and descriptions of Captain Angus and the *Argonaut's* crew and sent them down to Santiago de Cuba to begin a discreet inquiry. He also set a reliable French agency on the trail of Nadine and Margo Cole, advertised extensively in the French and American papers, and then set off on the Kerrie Shawn trail.

Wrathfully, Mr. Queen departed for the Adirondacks. From this Elba he followed the fortunes of Mr. Edmund De Carlos through the New York gossip columnists and society tattlers. De Carlos, as co-executor of the Cole estate and co-trustee-to-be, had granted permission to himself, as beneficiary, to take up residence at the Tarrytown mansion even before probate of the will.

The house and grounds had been under the supervision of a caretaker until the man died early in 1937. Apparently Cole had never quite got round to hiring another, for the place had been left boarded up and untended. Now De Carlos moved in, hired decorators and servants, and established himself in lone grandeur as lord of the manor.

He promptly set off on a fierce hunt for pleasure. The man's bearded face, menacing teeth, and bushy hair began to appear in newspaper photographs with regularity. Overnight he became New York's premier *bon vivant*, leading benefactor of various lonely ladies of the chorus, lavish spender and frequenter of notorious night clubs and gambling rooms.

"If he keeps up this pace," thought Mr. Queen grimly, "that million-dollar legacy will collapse under the weight of its own mortgages!"

Edmund De Carlos was the son of a Brazilian father and an English mother, born in the Brazilian interior on a coffee plantation in the year 1889. That made him fifty years old, ruminated Mr. Queen from his lofty exile; in his pictures the pirate seemed younger.

Mr. Queen decided suddenly that Mr. De Carlos would bear watching.

Meanwhile, Beau was scampering along a cold spoor.

Beginning with a clue twenty-one years old—the knowledge that Monica Cole Shawn's husband had died in a Chicago hospital—Beau followed a trail that led to a Chicago tenement, then to a secretarial school, where, apparently, the young widow had enrolled to learn a practical means of sustaining her life and her daughter's when Cadmus Cole refused financial assistance.

St. Louis, Minneapolis, New York—cheap rooming houses, small apartments, a draughty theatrical hotel, a dancing and "dramatic" school for children. Eagerly Beau haunted Broadway. Finally, in the curling files of a theatrical agency, he unearthed an old photograph of a beautiful girl-child named Kerrie Shawn. But then he lost the trail.

During his New York investigation Beau learned from Lloyd Goossens that the Surrogate had been satisfied with the proofs of Cadmus Cole's testamentary signature. There were plentiful examples of Cole's handwriting for comparison purposes—on checks, on legal documents, on records in foreign and American banks dating back almost twenty years. Captain Angus's signature was likewise authenticated through the *Argonaut's* log (in which, Mr. Rummell was interested to learn, the details of Cole's last illness and death were meticulously recorded, agreeing to the letter with the verbal account given by De Carlos).

"Almost ready," Goossens told Beau. "Assets, for the size of the estate, are in a very fluid condition. The fourth citation is to be published in a few days, Queen —so where do you stand with the hunt for those two girls?"

Beau dug in again. He found a new clue which led westward. But in Cincinnati he came up against a dead end.

"I can't understand why this femme Kerrie Shawn hasn't answered the personals I've published," Beau complained to Ellery over the long-distance telephone. "Unless she's left the United States, or is dead. As far as that's concerned, there's been enough newspaper publicity to call her back from Africa, or from the dead."

Mr. Queen pondered. "There's a clear record that Monica Shawn was giving her child dancing and dramatic lessons, isn't there? So, working from the professional angle—"

"Listen, Big Brain," snarled Beau, "I've badgered agents and managers in New York so much they're threatening to have me pinched if I so much as show my pan again. That theatrical lead is strictly from hunger, I tell you!"

"Where," inquired Mr. Queen mildly, "does every aspiring American mama with a beautiful child of real or fancied talent eventually, and inevitably, wind up?"

"Am I a dope!" roared Beau, "Goodbye!"

Ten days later Ellery received a wire from Hollywood:

"HAVE FOUND KERRIE WOO WOO EXCLAMATION POINT
BEAU"

III

Mr Santa Claus

AT THE CENTRAL CASTING BUREAU IN HOLLYWOOD BEAU had found no Shawns, but three Kerries. He examined their portraits. Kerrie Acres was a Negro. Kerrie St. Alban was an aged character actress. Kerrie Land was a young girl.

Her face was nice. Light-colored eyes looked straight at him; they fizzed, like champagne. A chin-cleft, a turned-up nose, soft dark rolls of hair . . . nice, nice.

Beau compared Kerrie Land's face with the photograph in his possession of Kerrie Shawn as a child. There was an unmistakable resemblance. But he had to be sure.

He wormed an Argyle Avenue address and telephone number out of a Bureau attendant and called the number.

A woman answered. He identified himself in a raspy voice as "Central Casting" and asked for Kerrie Land. The woman said Kerrie Land had been on location somewhere for two months, and how come? She was expected back within a few days. She slammed the receiver.

Beau returned to his hotel, looked himself over, decided his clothes were shabby enough to lull the suspicions of even a Hollywood landlady, checked out and, carrying one ragged handbag, walked to the Argyle Avenue address.

It was a stucco rooming house which had long since burst its seams—discolored, down at the heel, one of a row of similar dreary, dowdy dwellings.

Beau began to feel like Santa Claus.

He rang the front doorbell and was admitted by a shapeless woman wearing an ancient dinner-gown and carpet-slippers.

"I want a room," he said.

"Extra?" She looked him over without friendliness.

"I'm looking for a job in the movies," Beau admitted.

"Six dollars in advance. Your own soap and towels." The landlady did not stir until he let her inspect the bulging interior of his wallet. "Oh, new in town. Well, I'll show you what I got. Throw parties?"

"I don't know anyone in Hollywood," said Beau.

"With that roll, you'll know plenty soon enough."

"I'm respectable, if that's what you mean, beautiful," grinned Beau.

"See you don't forget it. I run a decent house. Name?"

"Queen. Ellery Queen."

She shrugged and shuffled upstairs. Beau was very critical of the rooms she indifferently displayed. He watched the little cardboard name-plates on the doors. When he saw one that said: KERRIE LAND—VIOLET DAY, he chose the nearest room on the same floor. paid a week's rent

30

in advance, and then settled down to await the return of Cadmus Cole's niece.

That night he stole into the dark bedroom shared by Kerrie "Land" and Violet Day and callously explored it.

It was a mean room, like his own: a rickety dressing table covered by a cheap linen runner smeared in one corner with lipstick and powder; an open closet hung with a faded calico curtain, and inside dozens of flimsy wire hangers; a lame bureau; walls hung with unframed 8 x 10 "still" photographs of Kerrie and a grim blonde with long shanks and an air of world-weariness; two low, lumpy, iron beds.

One bed exhaled strong perfume: Violet Day, Beau decided unchivalrously. The other gave out a sweet, clean odor—obviously Kerrie's.

Poor kid.

Beau mumbled angrily to himself. Getting soft about a perky little brunette with delusions of stardom and come-hither eyes! Why, she stood in line for more dough than he'd see in his whole lifetime!

And he began to look forward to his first sight of Kerrie Shawn with a fierce, insatiable excitement.

He saw her four days later. He heard a taxi pull up outside, a merry voice, light footsteps. Instantly he was out of his room and at the head of the stairs, his heart racing.

The tall grim blonde appeared downstairs, handling two huge pieces of luggage like a stevedore. She was followed by the brunette, who was laughing as she lugged a suitcase. And suddenly there was warmth and happiness in those dingy halls.

"Come on, Vi!" cried Kerrie, flying up the stairs.

At the top there was Beau, staring.

"Oh," said Kerrie, bumping into him in the semidarkness. "Hello!"

"Yourself."

"You're new, aren't you?"

"Absolutely reborn!"

"What? Vi, it's a funny man! My name's Kerrie Sh— I mean, Kerrie Land. This is my roomie, Violet Day."

"Do. Queen. Ellery Queen." Beau stared and stared.

"It talks," said the blonde, peering at him. "Next thing you know it'll touch you for five bucks. Kerrie, come on. My feet are yelling bloody murder."

"It's nice, though," said Kerrie, smiling at him. "What

31

lovely hair, Vi! Looks like Bob Taylor, don't you think?"
And they left Beau grinning in the gloom.

Ten minutes later he rapped on their door.

"Come in!" called Kerrie.

She was in a house-coat. Red flowers and a zipper.
Her small feet were bare. Tousled hair—nice. The suitcase lay open on the bed—the sweet-smelling bed, Beau
noted with an obscure satisfaction—and she was stowing
black panties away in a bureau drawer.

"It's in again," said Violet Day, asprawl on the per-
fumed bed, her naked toes wiggling with ecstasy. "Kerrie,
have you no shame? Giving away all your girlish secrets."

"Hi," said Beau, still grinning. He felt good, he didn't
know why. As if he had had five drinks.

"Go away," said the blonde. "This gal here was born
with the soul of a Girl Scout, and I was placed on earth
just to protect her from hungry-looking hombres who
think they look like the Taylor man."

"Vi, shut up," said Kerrie. "Come in, Queen—we won't
bite you! Got any Scotch?"

"No, but I know where to find some," said Beau.

"Make mine apple. Say! I take it all back," said Vi,
sitting up in bed. "Where?"

"I'm sort of new in Hollywood," said Beau. "You
know. Lonesome."

"It's lonesome!" giggled the blonde. "But it knows
where the Scotch is. Kerrie, it does look like Taylor, you
know that?"

Beau ignored her. "Miss Land, how about joining me
in a little supper with that Scotch?"

Vi shrugged her knees. "Lonesome—supper—Scotch!
What is this, *The Merry Widow?* I bet he'll have you
feeling his muscle before the night's over, Kerrie."

"We'd love to," said Kerrie, stressing the "we" the
least bit. "I know just how you feel, Queen. It's a date!
—the three of us."

"The three of us?" said "Mr. Queen" damply.

"But we pay our own way."

"Utsnay! What do you take me for?"

"Dutch, or you eat by yourself," said Kerrie positively.
"Your bankroll won't last forever—Ellery, was it?—and
we've just had two months of steady extra work being
Hawaiians. Wasn't it Hawaiians, Vi?"

"I dunno," said Vi.

"So give us a half-hour to shower and change," said

32

Kerrie, and as she said it a dimple appeared from nowhere and transfixed Mr. Rummell like an arrow, "and we're your gals, Ellery." And she came and stood close to him at the door, smiling.

Something happened to him. As if he had a sudden heart-attack. What the hell? He found himself in the dark hall leaning against the wall.

He stood there for several minutes, wiping the sweat from his forehead. Whew! Then he ran downstairs to the pay-telephone and sent the telegram to Mr. Queen which ended with EXCLAMATION POINT.

They dined—at Mr. "Queen's" expense—in the Cocoa-nut Grove at the *Ambassador*.

Beau took turns dancing with Kerrie and Vi. Vi just danced. Kerrie floated. She made herself part of him. He actually enjoyed dancing for the first time in his life.

Suddenly Violet Day developed a headache and, over Kerrie's protests, left them.

Kerrie laughed. "You're accepted, Mister. Did you know that?"

"How come?"

"Vi turns her headaches on and off like a faucet. Since she left me to your mercies, it's because she thinks you're a regular guy."

"How about you?" Beau leaned forward hungrily.

"I'm not so naive. You're a nice-looking cover, but what's in the book? I'll know better when you take me home."

Beau looked disappointed. "Tell me about yourself."

"There isn't much to tell."

"Have you and Vi been friends long?"

"I met her in Hollywood." Kerrie turned the glass of vermouth slowly in her long fingers. "Vi took me under her wing when my mother died last year. Just like a hen. And I guess I was a pretty hopeless sort of egg."

"Say, I'm sorry. Your mother, huh?"

"She died of pleurisy-pneumonia. No resistance. She burned herself out trying to make a Garbo out of a cluck." Kerrie said abruptly: "Let's talk about something else."

"You seem to have led a pretty tough life."

"It hasn't been all honey-and-almond cream. Monica—"

"Monica?"

"My mother. Monica Cole Shawn. My real name's Shawn. Monica slaved all her life to see me become some-

33

body, and I'm a little bitter about . . . How did we ever get on this subject, anyway? You see, I have an uncle who's a first-class rat. He's really responsible for my mother's suffering and hardships. But I don't see why you—"

"Monica Cole Shawn," said Beau. "You know, that's funny. Was your uncle's name Cole?"

"Yes, Cadmus Cole. Why?"

"His name's been in the papers. So you're his niece!"

"Papers? I haven't seen a paper in two months. What's he done now—turned a machine-gun on the Marriage License Bureau?"

Beau looked straight at her. "Then you didn't know your uncle just died?"

She was silent for some time, a little paler. "No, I didn't know. I'm sorry, of course, but he treated my mother abominably, and I'm afraid I can't shed any tears. I never even saw him." She frowned. "How did he die?"

"Heart-attack on a Caribbean cruise. He was buried at sea. His own yacht, you know."

"Yes, I read about him occasionally. He was supposed to be a rich man." Kerrie's lip curled. "And all the while he was spending his money on yachts and mansions, my mother was slaving to death, living in hall bedrooms, cooking Sunday breakfasts over gas-burners—if there was anything to cook. . . . I took a job when I was sixteen because I couldn't bear seeing her work her life away for me. But she did, just the same, and when she died last year at fifty-two she was an old woman. Dear Uncle Cadmus could have saved her all that—if he hadn't been a lunatic on the subject of marriage. When Mother married, and my father died, she wrote Cadmus—and I still have his reply." Kerrie's mouth quivered. "Now, look here, Mr. Snoop that's quite enough. I'll be crying on your shoulder, next thing I know."

"Can you guarantee that?" said Beau. "Kerrie, I've got a confession to make."

"This seems to be Aching Hearts night!"

"I'm a heel."

"*Mister* Queen! Thanks for the warning."

"I mean I'm a phony. I'm not an extra. I'm not in Hollywood looking for a job. I'm here for only one purpose—to find you."

She was puzzled. "To find *me?*"

"I'm a private detective."

She said: "Oh."

34

"The Queen agency was employed by your uncle before his death. Our job was to find his heirs when he died."

"His . . . heirs? You mean he died and left—me—money?"

"That's the size of it, Kerrie."

Kerrie gripped the table. "Did he think he could buy me off—pay me conscience-money for having killed my mother?"

"I know how you feel." Beau put one of his paws over her icy hands, and squeezed. "But don't do anything foolish. What's done is done. He's dead, and he's left a lot of money—to you and to a cousin of yours, Margo Cole, your uncle Huntley's daughter, if she can be found. That money belongs to the two of you."

She was silent.

"Part of the money should have been your mother's while she was alive, anyway. Then what's wrong in taking it now? You can't bring her back, but you can enjoy your own life. Do you like Hollywood?"

"I hate it," she said in a low voice. "Because this is a place where only talent counts, and I haven't any. I might work my way up to talking bits, but I'm not an actress. I'm not kidding myself: I face a life like Vi's—cheap boarding houses, a starvation diet, mending the runs in my stockings because I can't afford new ones. . . ." She shivered.

"Do you want to hear more?" asked Beau.

She smiled all at once and withdrew her hand. "All right, Dick Tracy—shoot the works."

"Kerrie, your uncle Cadmus died a multimillionaire."

"A—what?" she shrieked.

"Didn't you know how rich he was?"

"Well, but I thought—"

"His estate is estimated at fifty million dollars."

"Fifty mil—" Her tongue and lips grew stiff.

It was like watching a kid open a Christmas box. Her breath was coming in quick little gusts.

"Take another drink. Waiter! Rye, or Scotch?"

"Oh, Scotch, and lots of it! Tell me more. Did I hear you say fifty million? That's not a slip of the tongue? You don't mean fifty thousand. Fifty MILLION?"

"Whoa! Let's go easy. You're not getting any fifty million dollars."

"But I thought you said— Oh, I don't care! Nobody could spend that much money, anyway. How much *is* it?"

"Let's figure it out." Beau began scribbling on the cloth. "The estate comes to about fifty millions. Your uncle didn't use the cute dodges by which rich men usually cheat the constituted authorities of their death-shares. So inheritance taxes are going to eat up about thirty-five millions."

Kerrie closed her eyes. "Go on. What do I care how I spend money?"

"Fees and expenses will probably come to a half-million. That leaves fourteen million and a half. Invested in safe securities at, say, four percent—that makes an income annually of five hundred and eighty thousand dollars."

"What?" said Kerrie; opening her eyes.

"You don't get the principal. I'll explain why later. Now, there are two of you sharing this income—your cousin Margo and you."

"How do you do, Margo," said Kerrie with a wriggle of delight. "Will you buy a gold-lined tub with me?"

"You mean—? But sure, you never even saw her. Anyway, your half-share annually comes to two hundred and ninety thousand. Income taxes should take a hundred and sixty thousand of that, so you'll have a hundred and thirty thousand a year."

"How much does that come to per week?" murmured Kerrie. "That's the figure I want. I was always rotten in arithmetic."

"It comes," said Beau, scribbling the last figure, "to twenty-five hundred smackers a week."

"Twenty-five hun— Every week? Week in, week out?"

"Yes."

"Why, that's better than being a star!" cried Kerrie. "Twenty-five hundred a week clear! I suppose I'm dreaming. It's a mean one, all right. Pinch me and wake me up."

"It's true. But—"

"Oh," said Kerrie lightly. Then she sighed. "There's a catch in it."

"Well . . . certain conditions. By the way, I'm empowered to finance you—all you want—until you reach New York. Sort of drawing account against that twenty-five hundred per. That is, if you accept the conditions."

"Let's have them," said Kerrie crisply. "I may as well know the worst."

"First," said Beau, "have you ever been married?"

"No, but I'm eligible. Were you considering snaring an heiress this season? What's the point?"

"Never mind me." Beau reddened. "Is there any chance of your being married in the near future? That is, are you engaged, or have you a boy-friend?"

"I'm free, white, and just twenty-one."

"Then you've merely to accept your uncle's conditions and at least half the estate is yours. Now, for the conditions. The first is this: that you agree to live with the other heiress —we're sure now, from the evidence available, that there are only two of you—in your uncle's Tarrytown mansion on the Hudson. The house will be maintained by the estate for one year. You must live there exclusively for that year; after that you're free to live anywhere you like."

"Wow," said Kerrie. "I was really worried. Why, that's not a condition—it's a blessing! Beautiful house, cars, all the clothes in the world, a maid to do my hair, three squares a day and a couple of cooks to prepare them . . . Mister, that's heaven. Bring on your other condition!"

Beau fished a paper out of his pocket. "Let me read you," he said slowly, "a copy of a paragraph from your uncle's will." He read:

"In imposing this second condition upon my heirs, I feel it necessary to warn them against that insidious, degrading, and fatal institution in human relations known as marriage. I was married, and I know. At its best, it is a dull, confining prison. At its worst, it is hell. Since my divorce, I have lived, and I shall die, a bachelor. My only friend, Edmund De Carlos, to whom I have in this testament willed one million dollars and a home for life if he so wishes, is now and has always been a bachelor. We have discussed the subject many times and agree that most of the ills of the world can be traced to marriage, or rather to its effect upon individuals. It has caused men and women to become greedy, it has inspired horrible crimes, it has, historically, bred wars and international treacheries. I am an old man; my heirs, if they still live, will be young. I feel I must impose my experience of life upon them. They are free to reject my advice, of course, but only at the expense of the worldly goods I am in a position to bestow upon them. . . ."

Beau put the paper back in his pocket. "There's more of the same. But I think you get the idea."

Kerrie looked astonished. "He was mad!"

"No," said Beau dryly, "he was perfectly sane—in the legal sense, and we have reason to believe in the medical, too. He was just abnormally bitter and intense on this one subject. I suppose it all dates from the dirty deal his wife gave him 'way back in 1902 or so. Anyway, he felt so strongly about marriage that upon it depends your inheritance."

"I don't quite—"

"The will stipulates that the income payable to any heir shall cease automatically, and that heir from then on forfeits all claim to her share of the estate, *if and when she marries.*"

"You mean," cried Kerrie, "if I accept this legacy I shan't ever be able to get married?"

"Not if you want to keep pocketing twenty-five hundred a week."

"And if I turn the whole thing down now, or accept and then marry?"

"Your cousin Margo, if she's eligible, would become the sole heiress. Your share would go to her. Or if you both become ineligible, the will provides that the income from the estate be donated by the trustees to such organized charities as they may see fit to select, and they continue to be trustees for the estate. Or if the heirs remain eligible, then at the death of one the income goes to the survivor. At the death of the survivor, the income goes to the charities. You see, your uncle Cadmus considered death and marriage practically the same thing."

Kerrie was silent for a long time. The orchestra was playing, and people were dancing under colored lights; her face lay in trombone shadows.

Beau waited for her decision with a curious eagerness. She couldn't turn it down. She wouldn't be human if she did. She was human, all right—he could testify to that, because he had held her in his arms when they danced.

Cole's conditions might have been easy for another girl. But Kerrie wasn't the sort who could take, and give, love except the right way. With her it would be one or the other—the money or her happiness.

He knew what she was thinking. She wasn't in love with any one now. Perhaps she'd never been in love. With her figure, with her face, there must have been men, though—plenty of men, and all the wrong kind. She would be a little cynical about men. So what was she throwing

38

away? Something that didn't exist, probably, for something that you could turn instantly into the delicious good things of life, which she had never had.

Kerrie laughed—a funny, quaking little laugh. "All right, Uncle Cadmus, you win. I die a virgin. Other women have. Maybe I'll become a saint. Wouldn't that be a scream, Ellery? Saint Kerrie. And all the other virgins would put up candles for me, and pray at my shrine!"

Beau was silent.

Kerrie said fiercely: "I can't turn all that money down. I can't! No one could. Could you?"

"It wouldn't be a problem with me," said Beau gruffly.

She looked him in the eye. "It won't be with me, either. But I think we're talking about different things."

"Congratulations," said Beau.

It had to be. And of course she was right. He knew what it meant to go hungry, to be pushed around, to peer up at life from under the eight-ball.

Kerrie smiled and got out of her chair suddenly and came around the table. She leaned over him, so close he smelled her skin. It smelled like clover—Beau had smelled a clover once.

"Mind if I kiss you for being such a swell Santa?"

She kissed his lips. Lightly, in the shadows. He kept his lips deliberately tight, cold, hard.

But his voice was thick. "You shouldn't have done that, Kerrie. Damn it, you shouldn't!"

"On, then you're the keeper of my conscience, too?" She kissed him again, laughing. "Don't worry, Grandpa. I shan't fall in love with you!"

Beau got up from the chair so suddenly it fell over with a clatter and Kerrie stared at him with startled eyes.

"Come on, Miss Millionbucks," he growled. "Let's go tell the good news to your girl friend. I bet she'll die."

IV

Goodbye

to All That

KERRIE AND VI WOUND THEIR ARMS ABOUT EACH OTHER in the dingy bedroom and cried and cried and cried, while Beau sat gloomily in the one good chair and helped himself freely to the contents of a brandy bottle he had thought to buy on the way home.

Kerrie acted like a hysterical child. She threw her wardrobe, one poor dress at a time, all over the room as if they were confetti. Several times she ran over and kissed Beau, and he grinned back at her and offered her a drink.

But she refused. "I'm drunk on good luck. Vi, I'm rich!"

The landlady came up to investigate the noise, but Kerrie poured out the news in a burst, rattling on like a machine-gun, and a cunning look came into the landlady's faded eyes.

"Imagine that!" she said, smacking her lips. "Imagine that—a real heiress! My!"

Beau got rid of her.

"She'll have every reporter in town here by morning," he said. "Kerrie, pipe down. They'll tear you to pieces."

"Let 'em! I love 'em all! I love the whole world!"

"Wet blanket!" shrieked Vi, "Kerrie, he's just jealous!"

"Ellery, you aren't!"

"I guess I am," said Beau. "That's it—jealous. Of the income on half of fifteen million simoleons."

"Oh, darling, don't be! You'll always be Santa Claus to me—isn't he a handsome Santa, Vi? Darling, I won't forget what you've—"

"Damn it," snarled Beau, "don't patronize me!"

"But I'm *not*. It's just that I want everybody to share my wonderful luck!"

That sobered Violet. "Kerrie, you're not going to be a fool? Queen, she'll just throw it away. I know she will. She'll be the softest touch in the universe. Every deadbeat in Hollywood—"

40

"I'll see her through the first pains," said Beau shortly. "It's my job to get her safely back to New York."

"Aren't you the darling?" Kerrie stretched. "Oh, I feel so *swell!* And, Vi, the first thing we're going to do is take your name off the list at Central Casting. No more extra work for you! You're coming East with me, as my—as my *companion.* That's what you're going to do—"

"Kerrie! No!"

"You *are.* At a salary of—of—no salary at all! You'll just share everything with me!"

"Oh, Kerrie." And the blonde laid her head on Kerrie's breast, and wept, and that started Kerrie off, too, and Beau disgustedly finished what was left in the bottle.

It was a mad night, and Kerrie was drunk with the wonderful madness of it. Surveying the disordered room as the sun came up and touched the faces of the two girls, exhaustedly asleep in each others' arms, Beau wondered just how Miss Kerrie Shawn, heiress to the Cole fortune, recipient of twenty-five hundred dollars a week just so long as she remained unmarried, would react to the inevitable hangover.

But it was destined to be a long debauch.

The landlady, true to Beau's prediction, did her joyous work. On the heels of daylight came a rush of reporters and photographers that engulfed the shabby little stucco house like a Pacific tidal wave. They yanked their copy out of Violet Day's arms and, scarcely permitting her to rub the sleep out of her eyes, overwhelmed her. In five minutes the floor was treacherous with blackened bulbs. Beau, roused by the bedlam, had to fight his way through an excited mass of roomers. He spent a busy half-hour then, careful to keep the press from photographing him, evicting them one at a time.

When the room was clear he said: "Well, Cinderella, how do you like it?"

"I'm . . . a little scared," said Kerrie, "but—I think I do!"

"Well, I'll have to tear you away. Get some sleep and then we'll talk about going to New York."

"Is there really a rush?" pleaded Kerrie. "There are so many things I've got to do! Clothes, hair, face—"

Vi winked at him, and he left. But only to nap for another hour, bathe, shave, dress, and sit down outside her locked door.

Vi awoke first. He had a long talk with her, in undertones. There were several things he must do. Establish

41

credit through New York. Corral her proofs of identity, and so on. He would be back as soon as he could. Meanwhile, Vi was to guard Kerrie with her life.

Vi said fervently: "Thank heaven for a man! Queen, I had my doubts, but you're okay. Hurry back, will you?"

He left the house with the brim of his hat far down over his eyes.

He had a long talk with Lloyd Goossens by telephone. Then he called Ellery in the Adirondacks.

"I'm glad it turned out all right," said Ellery. "Get the girl back East, Beau, and go to work on Margo Cole."

"Have a heart," growled Beau. "The kid's in a fever. Give her time. I'll get her back as soon as I can."

"Well, don't bite my nose off," said Ellery. "What's the matter, Beau? You sound strange."

"Who, me?" said Beau, and he hung up. By the time he got round to the bank. Goossens had established an account there for Kerrie Shawn in the name of Ellery Queen.

When he returned to Argyle Avenue the narrow little street was black with people. Beau looked gloomy. He knew what lay ahead.

The next week was the hardest of his life. He was bodyguard, lawyer, big brother, and nuisance-fender all in one. Hollywood was excited. An unknown extra, Cinderella in rags, turned into a wealthy heiress overnight! All the studios wanted her—to sing, to dance, to act; for epics, newsreels, anything . . . but sign here, please, Miss Shawn! The newspaper syndicates offered fabulous sums for her life-story. An army of cameramen followed her wherever she went. Tradespeople sent representatives in all humility, offering their best for nothing—wouldn't Miss Shawn do them the honor of shopping in their establishment? Anything, anything her heart desired. As a gift of the management. If Miss Shawn would only . . . She was offered contracts, silver foxes, imported automobiles; she was deluged with invitations to premieres, to swanky parties, to the castles of Hollywood's great.

In all this madness Beau and Vi moved quietly by her side, hemming her in, Vi practical and cool, Beau silent and with his hatbrim shading his face.

Kerrie moved through events with a vague smile, as if she were floating in a dream. At the party she insisted upon having, she walked among her friends like a shy and happy child. Everyone she knew in Hollywood was there, and they were all the poor, the strugglers, the fringe,

42

the people of the frayed and starched clothes and the starved fixed smiles. But many of them wore new clothes that night, and looked well-fed, and their laughter was real.

"Isn't she grand?" sighed Violet Day to Beau. "Just like Lady Bountiful. She told me today she thinks she ought to do something for Inez. Inez has the bugs, and Kerrie's going to send her to Arizona. And Kerrie's financing Lew Malone's ulcer operation, and goodness knows what else!"

"She's drunk," smiled Beau.

"What? Say, Queen, I don't think you like Kerrie very much!"

"Who, me?" said Beau.

Kerrie refused to move from Argyle Avenue. "I'm going to be in Hollywood just a little while longer," she said firmly, "and I won't have my friends think I'm putting on the dog. Nothing doing, Vi; we stay here."

But they had to take two rooms more to hold all the clothes and trunks she bought. The landlady actually beamed. She raised her rents from six to eight dollars a week; but when Kerrie heard about it she threatened to move out, so back went the rents to six dollars.

It was like that for an incredible week—driving from shoppe to shoppe in the rented Isotta; exciting hours in the beauty emporia patronized by only the starriest of the stars; furs, evening gowns, sport clothes, wraps, jewels; the *Brown Derby*, the *Clover Club*, the *Beverly-Wilshire;* prevues and premieres, until Kerrie's conscience began to bother her.

"Aren't we spending too much money?" she asked Beau.

"There's more where that came from, kid."

"It's a wonderful dream! Like a fairy tale. Magic money. The more you spend, the more you have. Well, maybe not quite . . . Ellery, did I tell you I heard from Walter Ruell? He's back home in Ohio and darned glad of it. Poor kid—"

"Kerrie, I've had three wires from Goossens." Beau did not mention the four from Ellery. "He can't understand what's holding us up here. I tried to explain—"

"Oh, darling, so soon!"

"And don't call me darling!"

"What?" Kerrie was surprised.

"It's a bad habit," muttered Beau. "For a gal who's promised not to tangle with men."

"Oh, but Ellery, I don't say 'darling' to any man but

43

you! You wouldn't sue me for breach of promise, would you?" Kerrie laughed.

"Why pick on me?" said Beau sullenly.

"Because you're my own special darling, my—" And Kerrie stopped short. Very short. Then she said in a subdued voice, not looking at him: "All right, Ellery. We'll go whenever you say."

Kerrie was unusually quiet after that. The vagueness went out of her smile; everything sharpened in her face; most of the time she wore a serious expression. Beau was quiet, too. He bought the tickets and arranged for the luggage and took Kerrie's proofs of identity out of the bank vault and saw the bank manager and wired Goossens.

Then there was nothing to do but wait for the next day, which was to be Kerrie's farewell to Hollywood.

But while Beau was busy with the arrangements for their departure Kerrie shut herself up in one of the rooms and refused to come out, even for Vi.

Vi said worriedly to Beau that last night: "I can't understand her. She says she's all right, but . . ."

"Maybe it's the hangover."

"I guess it's the idea of leaving. After all, her mother's buried here, this is about the only home she's ever had, and now she faces a whole new world. . . . I guess that's it."

"I guess."

"Why don't you take her out for a walk, or something? She's been cooped up here all day."

"I don't think—" began Beau, flushing.

But Vi went into Kerrie's room and remained there for a long time, while Beau fidgeted outside. Finally Kerrie came out dressed in black slacks covered by a long coat, and no hat, Hollywood fashion, and said with a rather pale smile: "Want to take me for a walk, Mister?"

"Okay," said Beau.

They strolled in silence to the corner and turned into Hollywood Boulevard. At the corner of Vine Street they stopped to watch the swirling traffic.

"Busy, all right," said Kerrie. "It's—hard to leave."

"Yeah," said Beau. "Must be."

They walked ahead into the forest of neon signs.

A little while later Beau said: "Nice night."

Kerrie said: "Yes, isn't it."

Then they were silent again. They passed Grauman's

Chinese and soon were strolling through the darkness of the residential district beyond.

Kerrie paused finally and said: "My feet ache. Wouldn't you think shoes costing twenty-two fifty would fit?"

"The curse of gold," said Beau. "It has its advantages, too, though."

"Let's sit down for a while."

"On the curb?"

"Why not?"

They sat down side by side. Occasionally a car flashed by; once a ribald voice shouted at them.

"I really haven't thanked you," said Kerrie in a muffled voice, "for having been so grand this week. You've been like a—like a brother."

"Brother Rat," said Beau. "That's what they call me."

"Please, Ellery. I—"

"I'm getting paid for it," said Beau gruffly. "Fact, it's your dough that's paying. So don't thank me."

"Oh, money!" said Kerrie. "It isn't everything—" She stopped, appalled by what she was saying.

"No?" jeered Beau. "There are a million fluffs who'd give their right arms to be in your shoes—ache and all—this minute."

"I know, but . . . Oh, it's nice being able to do things for people, and to buy and buy without thinking of the price when you've had to watch all your life for basement sales and to make over old dresses, but . . ."

"No buts. It is wonderful, and you're a lucky squirt. Don't spoil it by being—restless."

"I'm not!" said Kerrie quickly. "It's just that I've been thinking about . . ." She stopped.

Beau laughed. "Don't tell me you been regretting that anti-marriage condition already!"

"Well . . . it might be awfully hard on a girl—under the circumstances—if she . . . fell in love."

She screamed, grabbing him. Something wet and cold had touched the back of her neck. But it was only a friendly, night-prowling Schnauzer investigating her scent.

Beau's arms tightened about her. She clung to him, her head falling back. Her lips were parted.

"Kerrie." Beau failed to recognize his own voice. "Don't leave Hollywood. Stay here. Give up the money."

Their lips almost touched as they stared into each other's eyes. He was going to propose. He was! He didn't want her to go East! That could only be because the money

45

stood between him and her. Oh, she didn't care about it! She didn't. She just wanted him. Never to let go. If that was love, she was in love. He was going to propose . . . Oh, ask me, ask me!

He let go of her and got up so suddenly that she cried out again and the Schnauzer whined in alarm and ran away.

"You'd throw away twenty-five hundred bucks a week?"

"Maybe," whispered Kerrie, "I would."

"Then you're an idiot!"

She closed her eyes, all jumpy and sick inside.

"If it happened to me," he shouted, "do you think I'd give it up? Like hell I would! You ought to be examined by Freud!"

"But—but you asked me—told me—"

Beau glared down at her as she crouched, hugging her knees, staring up at him. He was furious with himself, and with her for having made him lose his head. The plea had slipped out under the pressure of her arms, the warmth of her breathing, the joyful yearning and hope in her eyes. He saw her hungry, tramping from studio to studio, one of the thousands of starched, frayed, and fixedly smiling Hollywood job-hunters. . . .

So he sneered: "You dames are all alike. I thought maybe you were different. But you're a pushover like the rest of 'em!"

Kerrie jumped up and ran away.

Just before they left the rooming house for the station the next day, Beau received two telegrams.

One was from Lloyd Goossens.

"MARGO COLE FOUND IN FRANCE"

The other was from Mr. Ellery Queen, and it said:

"MARGO FOUND STOP MORE CONVINCED THAN EVER MURDER IN THIS CASE STOP JOB JUST BEGUN FOR THE LOVE OF MIKE GET BACK ON IT WILL YOU"

Beau glanced at Kerrie Shawn, his eyes a little red, two deep lines running from his nostrils to the corners of his mouth.

But Kerrie sailed past him with Vi as if he didn't exist.

He grinned wryly.

46

Part TWO

Fists Across the Sea

THE INSTANT KERRIE GAZED INTO HER COUSIN MARGO'S eyes, she knew they would be enemies.

In the midst of the hurly-burly of presenting her proofs of identity to Lloyd Goossens and Edmund De Carlos, whom Kerrie immediately disliked, of moving into and exploring the Tarrytown mansion and its broad acres, complete with woods and bridle-paths and hidden streams and unexpected arbors, of selecting personal servants and cars and of refurnishing her own suite of rooms, turning them from gloomy chambers into bright and chintzy places, of shopping and granting press interviews and the whole feverish process of settling down to her new life in the East . . . in the midst of all this, Kerrie had looked forward to her cousin's arrival from France.

It was a peculiar anticipation, touched with sadness, for Kerrie felt as if she had lost something, and she wanted to make up her loss in another way.

But when she saw Margo Cole, she knew she had wished for the moon.

They all went down the bay in a cutter to meet the *Normandie* in quarantine—Kerrie, Vi, Goossens, De Carlos, and Beau. Goossens, brief-case in hand, boarded the liner to meet Margo; they appeared a short time later and descended the ladder to the motor-launch, which ferried them to the cutter.

Margo Cole stepped aboard in a swirl of furs and scent, followed by a pert French maid and a mountain of luggage. She kept chattering gaily with Goossens as her eyes flickered over Vi indifferently, paused on Kerrie, examined her briefly, tossed her aside, and traveled on to De Carlos and Beau. De Carlos's bearded cheeks and toothy grin she greeted with a smile; but her blue eyes, slant, almost Egyptian, narrowed when they came to Beau, and then swept over him from unkempt head to disreputable toe with an astounding relish.

That was when Kerrie decided they were born foes.

"Licking her chops," whispered Vi, pressing Kerrie's

arm. "The flashy type. Don't let her step on you, hon. She'll try."

Margo Cole was a tall, strongly built woman—one of those splendid females who contrive to look vigorous even when they are lolling in a sun-chair. She was beautiful in a cold, majestic way, and she walked with a slow strutting poise that showed off her tightly draped hips.

"Either did a strip-tease or modeled," said Vi. "I don't like her. Do you?"

"No," said Kerrie.

"She's thirty, if she's a day."

"Thirty-two," said Kerrie, who had been absorbing a little family history.

"Look at the so-called men goggle! You'd think they never saw a hip before. It's disgusting!"

They murmured politely when Lloyd Goossens introduced them.

Then Margo slipped her arm through Beau's. "So you're the man who was supposed to find me. How nice he is, Mr. Goossens! If I had known, I should have ignored Mr. Queen's advertisements in the French papers and waited for him to come find me."

"I imagine," grinned Beau, "it would have been fun at that."

"Shall we go to my office?" asked Goossens. "Miss Cole, there are certain formalities—naturally you'll put up at a hotel until we've—ah—checked your proofs of identity. Of course, if you'd rather—"

"No, no. Let's have the dismal scene," said Margo. "Mr. Queen, you'll come?"

"How could I resist a smile like that?"

"Cynic! And—oh, of course, *you*, dear Kerrie! I should feel lost without you. After all, though I was born here, I've lived all my life in France—"

"That was France's hard luck," mumbled Vi.

Kerrie smiled. "I'd be charmed to shield you from the shocks of this rude, new world."

"Ah, no, no," said Edmund De Carlos. "That shall be my special province, ladies." And he bowed first to Kerrie, and then to Margo, licking his bearded lips, meanwhile, with the tip of his red tongue.

The cutter plowed up the bay.

Kerrie developed a headache on shore. She excused herself politely and drove off with Vi in her new roadster.

Margo waved gaily, watching with her cold Egyptian eyes.

Lloyd Goossens examined Margo Cole very sharply when they reached his office, but there could be no doubt of the validity of her proofs of identity.

She accepted a cigaret from the lawyer and a flame from De Carlos. "It seems odd to be called Miss Cole, or even Margo. You see, I've been calling myself Ann Strange ever since 1925."

"How is that?" asked Goossens, filling his pipe.

"Mother died that year. I don't recall my father, of course; we never ran across any one mother'd known in America; she hadn't even a family. We used to travel about from town to town in France—Dijon, Lyon, a few years in Montpellier in the South, buckets of places—while mother taught English to French children and earned enough to keep me in the convent schools.

"I knew nothing about my family; Mother never talked about them. But when she died I found letters, a diary, little mementoes, and they told me all about my Cole heritage. Especially," she laughed, "about dear Uncle Cadmus and how helpful he'd been when Mother, Father, and I had been starving in a Parisian garret. You know, one letter of Uncle Cadmus's drove my father to suicide. So I decided to change my name—wash out everything connected with the past."

"You've brought those letters and things, Miss Cole?"

She produced them from an alligator shopping bag. The handwriting of the diary checked with the handwriting of Nadine Malloy Cole, a sample of which Goossens had from Mrs. Cole's letter to Cadmus Cole in 1909, found among his effects.

There were also some faded old photographs of Huntley Cole and his wife, and one, dated Paris 1910, in which Margo was a chubby three-year-old with blonde hair and staring, frightened light eyes.

And there was Cole's typewritten letter to his sister-in-law, dated 1909, in which he refused financial aid. Goossens and Beau compared it with the typed letter Cole had sent his sister Monica in 1918, preserved by Kerrie. The style and tenor were much the same, and Cole had initialed both in his bold, simple, block-letter script.

"Of course, we'll have everything checked by experts, Miss Cole," said Goossens. "You understand—such a large estate. Matter of form—"

51

"I don't know what else I can say or do to prove I'm Margo Cole, but if you want to hear the story of my life—"

"We'd like to very much," said the lawyer politely; but he glanced at Beau, and Beau's left eyelid drooped. In Goossens's desk there was the copy of a compendious report submitted by the French agency Beau had engaged weeks before.

The report carried Margo Cole's history from infancy in Paris through the year 1925, where—they had been puzzled by this—the trail ended. But now the two men realized what had happened. Margo Cole's change of name in that year to Ann Strange had brought the French operatives up against the back wall of a blind alley. Margo described her life in detail from the time her mother took her from Paris as a baby until her mother's death. After that she had drifted back to Paris and become a mannequin.

Margo looked demure. "I earned enough, and had sufficiently kind and rich friends," she murmured, "to enable me to . . . retire, so to speak, in '32. Since then I've been drifting about—the Riviera, Cannes, Deauville, Monte Carlo, Capri, the usual dull places in Europe. It hasn't been too exciting."

"Then somebody missed a bet," said Beau. "Ever been married, Miss Cole?"

"Oh, no! It's so much more fun having your freedom, don't you agree, Mr. Queen?"

"Mr. Queen" grinned, and Goossens said: "Glad you think so, Miss Cole, because your uncle's will . . . Of course, to complete the check-up, we'll have to cable our French friends to verify your movements since 1925—make sure about your state of single blessedness . . ."

In two weeks everything was complete. The French agency reported that Margo Cole's account of her activities since 1925, under the name of Ann Strange, was true in every detail. She had never been married. The French report also went into corollary matters concerning Miss Strange-Cole's career in "the usual dull places in Europe," but Goossens discreetly ignored them; he was responsible for facts, not morals.

Miss Cole, upon hearing the conditions of her uncle's will, did not hesitate. She accepted, and to the accompaniment of an admiring press and public curiosity moved regally into the mansion at Tarrytown.

"Now that your work is done," she murmured to Beau,

"you won't desert poor little me? I feel so lost in this strange, big country. You'll come to see me—often?"

And she squeezed his hand ever so lightly.

They were in one of the formal gardens on the estate. No one was about, but Beau had caught the flicker of a curtain in a window of Kerrie Shawn's bedroom.

He took the smiling woman in his arms suddenly and kissed her. She was still smiling when he released her.

"And what makes you think, Mr. Queen," said Margo, "that I wanted you to do that?"

"I'm psychic," said Beau. He watched the curtain. It fluttered violently and then was still.

"You clever man," murmured Kerrie's cousin. "And the dear little thing is so jealous. Do come again—soon."

IN the office of *Ellery Queen, Inc., Confidential Investigations*, Mr. Ellery Queen surveyed his partner sympathetically. Back from the Adirondacks, Mr. Queen, while leaner than usual, was browned and fit; but his partner was haggard, and two creases, like quotation marks, separated his gloomy eyes.

"I always knew you were mercenary," said Mr. Queen, "but I didn't think you were a quitter."

"It isn't the dough, I tell you! All right, it wasn't much of a job, and Goossens and De Carlos insist Cole's retainer of fifteen grand, plus expenses, was ample to cover it—"

"Princely," agreed Mr. Queen.

"But the job's over! Our agreement was that we'd find the two women. That's what we were hired to do, we've done it, and we're through. What more do you want?"

"I want," replied Mr. Queen calmly, "to know why Cadmus Cole was so mysterious about the nature of our assignment. I want to know why he didn't tell us the simple truth. I want to know what was at the back of his head."

"Go see a medium!"

"Did he expect to be murdered? Was he murdered? And if so, who murdered him? And why? Cole may have hired us primarily to answer these questions, and for some obscure reason chose not to say so. But if that's the case, we're *not* through—"

"And fifteen grand doesn't begin to pay for the job," growled Beau, "and try to get more out of Goossens and De Carlos. You feeling like John D. these days?"

Mr. Queen said abruptly: "Beau, this isn't like you."

"I don't know what you're talking about."

"There's a reason for your unwillingness to go on with this investigation, and I *don't* think it's money. What is it?"

Beau glared at him. "All right, Master-Mind. There's a reason, and it's not money, it's a dame. So what?"

"Ah," said Mr. Queen. "Miss Shawn?"

"I'm not saying!" shouted Beau. "Anyway, I think she —sort of took a shine to me, and I can't hang around and ball up her life, that's all! She—this girl can't afford to fall in love!"

"Oh, I see," said Mr. Queen. "Deplorable situation. Well, then, make it plain you're not in love with her— or are you?"

"None of your business," snapped Beau.

"Hmm. Well, sir, since you're in love with her, sooner or later you're going to crawl back, you know. So you may as well do it now. *I* can't take over, because you're supposed to be Queen, and exposing our little fraud would mean, for one thing, having to give back that fifteen thousand, for another possibly alarming some one who'd be better off unalarmed."

"But what excuse would I have to keep going back there?" Beau looked sullen. "Goossens and De Carlos gave me the bum's rush yesterday, Kerrie's sore at me. . . . Of course, there's Margo—"

"Of course there is," said Mr. Queen. "A female who apparently enjoys your society. There's no law against a young man calling on a female for social reasons. Just keep your eyes open. Hang around. Watch. I have a compelling feeling," said Mr. Queen reflectively, "that there's going to be trouble."

"Trouble? There's plenty now! Say . . ." Beau looked alarmed. "What d'ye mean—trouble?"

Mr. Queen smiled. "Beau, has it occurred to you that this whole thing arose out of a man named Cadmus?"

Beau stared. "Cadmus? Cadmus Cole? So what?"

"Don't you remember the legend of Cadmus, or Kadmos, King of Sidon, who founded Thebes and brought the sixteen-letter alphabet to Greece?"

"No," said Beau. "I don't."

"Where were you educated?" sighed Mr. Queen. "At any rate, mythology tells us that Cadmus went on a quest— those old mythological boys were always going on quests— and suffered many hardships and perils, and one of the silly things he had to do was sow the dragon's teeth."

"Look, friend," said Beau. "I've gotta amble on up—"

54

"The dragon's teeth," repeated Mr. Queen thoughtfully. "Quite. Quite. Cadmus sowed the dragon's teeth, and out of each tooth sprang—trouble. Trouble, Beau!"

"Oh," said Mr. Rummell quietly.

"Our own Cadmus sowed a few dragon's teeth himself when he wrote that will," said Mr. Queen. "So watch, Beau. Everybody—especially De Carlos."

"De Carlos!" Beau grew angry. "Yeah, De Carlos. I don't like the way that baboon looks at Kerrie. And living in the same house. . . . Maybe you're right. Maybe I ought to stick around."

Mr. Queen smiled. "And now that that's settled, what have you heard from Santiago de Cuba?"

"No progress so far. Angus and the *Argonaut's* crew have simply disappeared. . . . Excuse me," said Beau, preoccupied. "I think I'll mosey on up to Tarrytown to see—Margo."

"Send her my love," murmured Mr. Queen.

THE fairy princess, alias Cinderella, was unhappy. That was against all the rules, and Violet Day told her so emphatically. Vi was a tower of strength and comfort these days. Kerrie didn't know what she would have done without her.

For one thing, there was Margo. Margo had begun to loom large in Kerrie's life. She tried to dominate the house, even that part of it which was exclusively Kerrie's. When she had her own suite redecorated in French provincial, she insisted the whole house be done over in the same style and period. Kerrie defended her maple and chintzes bitterly, challenging Margo's authority. Margo said something in French which sounded unladylike, and Kerrie's eyes flashed fire, and more than feelings would have been wounded had Beau not arrived at that critical moment. Of course, Kerrie instantly withdrew.

"Let her *try*," said Kerrie passionately to Vi. "Just let her! I'll punch her in the nose."

Then there was Beau, or "Ellery," as he was known to that turbulent household. He seemed always to be there. Kerrie tried hard to be polite to him, but her good resolutions broke down and she turned frigid. For he seemed to have become completely infatuated with Margo; he was with her constantly, flattering her, fetching things like a puppy, taking her out.

And Margo's attitude, of course, was nearly impossible

to endure. She was always glancing at Kerrie slyly, and then whispering to Beau, and the two of them would laugh as if they shared some secret, and Kerrie found them so hateful that when she saw Beau she would run away—to the stables for a furious canter, to swim in the big outdoor pool with Vi, to go sailing on the river in the little skiff she had bought, or for a tramp through the woods surrounding the estate.

"If I could only *go* somewhere," she said fiercely to Vi. "Vi, she's deliberately humiliating me! She takes every opportunity to wave him in my face, like a—like a flag!"

"Then why don't you go away?" asked Vi practically.

"I can't! I've asked Mr. Goossens, but uncle's will calls for my remaining on the grounds a full year, and he says there's nothing he can do about it. Vi!" Kerrie clutched her friend. "You don't think she's trying to . . . *drive* me away?"

"I wouldn't put it past her," said Vi grimly. "She's the type. I s'pose if you lived somewhere else this year you'd be cut out of the will and she'd get your share?"

Kerrie's eyes snapped. "So that's what she's up to! Isn't satisfied with twenty-five hundred a week and wants mine, too!"

"Twenty-five hundred a week don't go very far when you're trying to corner the mink and sable markets, the way she's doing."

"Well, she won't chase me away! I'll fight her!"

"Atta girl," said Vi enthusiastically. "Only let me get in a sock once in a while, will you, hon?"

After that, it was interesting. Kerrie no longer fled. She was careful to join them whenever they began to whisper. At other times she permitted herself to be cultivated by Mr. Edmund De Carlos, who had been quietly pursuing her ever since she had moved in. Mr. De Carlos began to glow with a hot, somehow sinister, light. He became insistent. She must go out with him—often. He had discovered New York. He would show it to her. They must be great friends. Once, she accepted—that was the night when Beau, squirming in tropical tails, escorted the beautiful Miss Cole to the summer theatre.

Everything went smoothly, and dully, until they were on their way home in De Carlos's limousine. Then something happened. And after that Kerrie refused Mr. De Carlos's invitations. In fact, she tried to ignore him, finding herself beginning to be terrified.

But Mr. De Carlos's light glowed hotter and more sinister. His wild and reckless excursions into New York's night life almost ceased. He spent most of his time on the estate—watching Kerrie. When she went riding, he followed. When she went boating, he followed. When she swam, there he was on the edge of the pool, a little tense. She stopped tramping in the woods.

Kerrie was thoroughly frightened. Vi suggested slipping poison into his soup, but Kerrie was not to be cheered by jests.

"Then why don't you talk to Ellery about it?" asked Vi. "He's a man, and a detective, besides."

"I'd rather die! Oh, Vi, it isn't just the way De Carlos looks at me. I've handled men with that kind of look before. It's—something else." She shivered. "I don't quite know myself."

"It's your imagination. Why don't you make a few friends? You've been here weeks and weeks and you don't know a soul."

Kerrie nodded miserably.

Vi sought out Beau. "Listen, you. I don't like your taste in women, but I used to think you were a plenty decent guy once. If you're any part a man, you'll keep your eye on this bedbug De Carlos. He's got what they call 'designs' on Kerrie, and I don't mean the kind of designs they put on doilies."

"Seems to me," said Beau indifferently, "She's sort of egged him on."

"How quaint!" said Margo, slipping the strap of her bathing suit back over her magnificent shoulder.

"I wasn't talking to you, grandma!"

"Well," said Beau hastily, "I'll keep my eye peeled."

After that, Beau came even more frequently.

VI

The Knife
and the Horseshoe

SOME ONE STRUCK. BY NIGHT.

Kerrie lay in her four-poster. It was warm, and she was

covered only to the hips by a thin silk quilt. She was reading Emily Dickinson, absorbed in the lovely, piercing cries of ecstasy.

Kerrie's suite lay in an ell of the mansion, one story above the terrace which encircled the house. There were strong vines and trellises of roses on the walls outside her windows.

The windows were open, and through the still curtains the gardens below sounded drowsy with the peaceful seething of crickets. There was an occasional river sound: a splash of oars, the stutter of an outboard motor, once the faint shouts of people being borne upstream by a Hudson River excursion boat.

It was quite late. Kerrie had heard Margo and Beau drive up two hours earlier, laughing intimately over some incident of their evening in town together. She had heard Margo invite Beau to stay the night, and Beau's booming acceptance. They had settled down on the terrace below Kerrie's windows with a portable bar, and after a clink of glasses there had been a silence.

Kerrie would have preferred noise. She had actually slipped out of bed and shut the windows to keep out that silence. But later, when she opened them again—it was so stuffy, she said to herself—and just happened to look down, the terrace was empty again.

Then she had heard De Carlos come home, lurching on the gravel driveway and cursing his chauffeur in a thick, liquorish voice. That was when she had got out of bed the third time and locked the door which led to the corridor.

But the house had settled into quiet since and Kerrie, intent upon the poet's verse, almost forgot she was unhappy. Her lids began to droop; the lines swam. She yawned, saw that it was past three by her bed clock, flung the book aside, and turned off the bedlamp.

And instantly things changed. Instantly.

Instantly she quivered with wakefulness.

It was as if the light had been a thick bright gate, and that turning it off had opened the gate to something that had lain in wait outside, in the thicker darkness. Kerrie lay motionless, straining her ears. But there was nothing to be heard, unless it were the shrilling of the tireless crickets or that slight recurrent creak—like the creak of a slowly swinging shutter. The shutter! Of course.

But there was no wind. Not even a breeze.

Kerrie told herself indignantly she was a fool. She turned over on her right side, drawing her knees up to her chest and pulling the silk quilt up so that her nose and eyes were covered.

That creak.

Abruptly she sat upright in bed. In the darkness she concentrated all her forces of vision on the windows. The darkness was thin and soupy, as if it had been strained through a sieve. She could just make out the curtains.

They were stirring! . . . No. They were not.

There! Again!

This is ridiculous, she thought in panic. It's a sudden breeze that's sprung up on the river. It's a breeze moving the curtains. A breeze . . .

Well, there was a simple way to find out. Just get out of bed and march across the floor to the window, and poke your head out. That's all. Very simple. Then you would know it was a breeze, and that you'd been imagining things like a tot frightened by the dark, and you could go back to bed and sleep.

She slid under the quilt and curled up in a taut ball again, almost smothered.

She could hear her heart clamoring, as if it had slipped out of her chest and taken up a position just above her ear. Oh, this is childish! And she found her legs and arms shaking.

What should she do? Jump out of bed, race across the room to the door that led across the boudoir and into Vi's room. . . .

Her heart stopped clamoring. It seemed to stop altogether.

There was something—something—in the room.

Kerrie knew it. She knew it. This wasn't imagination. This was knowledge.

She followed the steps that could not be heard with ears that could not hear . . . from the window, across the patch of hardwood floor to the edge of the hooked rug, on the rug . . . toward her bed, toward her, where she was lying in a ball under the quilt. . . .

Roll over.

She rolled over and off the bed. In the same instant something struck the bed where she had been lying. There was a hissing sound, like the sound of a snake.

Scream.

Kerrie screamed. Screamed and screamed.

Her nightgown crumpled, her eyes still red from sleep, Vi met Kerrie in the boudoir.

"Kerrie! What on earth—"

"Vi, Vi!" Kerrie lunged for her friend's high bosom and held on for dear life. "Something—somebody—in my bedroom—tried . . ."

"Kerrie, you had a nightmare."

"I was awake, I tell you! Somebody—climbed up the vines—I think—tried to—knife me—"

"Kerrie!"

"When I screamed, he—it jumped back through the window—I saw the flash of the curtains—"

"Who was it?"

"I don't know. I don't know. Oh, Vi—"

"You stay here," said Vi grimly. She grabbed an iron poker from the rack of firetools at the boudoir fireplace and ran into Kerrie'e bedroom. She snapped on the light.

The room was empty.

Kerrie followed to the doorway, looking in, her teeth chattering. The curtains were still moving a little.

Vi looked at the bed; Kerrie looked at it. There was a fresh slash a foot long in the silk coverlet. Vi threw back the coverlet; the sheet and mattress were slashed, too.

She went to the windows and locked them.

"Got away clean. Kerrie, haven't you any idea—"

"N-n-no. I couldn't really s-see. It was to d-dark."

"Kerrie. Hon. You're—"

There was a sharp-and-soft rap on the corridor door.

The two women looked at each other.

Then Vi moved to the door and said: "Who—is it?"

"Queen. Did—Who screamed in there?"

"Don't let him in," whispered Kerrie. "You—I'm not dressed. . . ." She felt calm suddenly.

Vi unlocked the door and opened it to a space of two inches. She looked at Beau coldly. He was in pajamas and his hair was a tumbled log-jam.

"What's wrong?" he demanded in an undertone. "Where's Kerrie? It was Kerrie who screamed, wasn't it?"

"Somebody climbed in from the terrace just now and tried to knife her. She yelped, and whoever it was beat it."

"Knifed!" Beau was silent. Then he cried: "Kerrie!"

"What do you want?"

"Are you all right?"

"Perfectly all right."

Beau grunted with relief. "Who was it?"

"I don't know. I didn't see."

"Knifed, huh," muttered Beau. "Listen. Don't say anything about it. I'll—I'll keep my eyes open. And after this keep your doors and windows locked at night!"

"Yes," said Kerrie.

Vi shut and locked the door. With Kerrie following her closely, she shuffled on her bare soles to the boudoir door and locked that. Then she locked her own bedroom door.

"I guess we're safe now, hon."

"Vi," whispered Kerrie. "Are you—scared?"

"Not . . . much."

"Would you mind if I spent the rest of the night with you?"

"Oh, Kerrie!"

Kerrie fell asleep in Vi's bed, clutching Vi's big warm body desperately. Vi lay awake for a long time, staring into the darkness.

Beau did not sleep at all. He returned to his room, dressed, and began a noiseless tour of inspection. He found the place where the intruder had climbed into Kerrie's room—from the terrace directly under her windows. He climbed the vine like a cat, examining each foot of it in the light of an electric torch. But except for several bruises and, in one place, a snapped piece of trellis-work, there were no clues.

He sought out the night-watchman. But the watchman had seen and heard nothing.

In the house again, he stole into Edmund De Carlos's bedroom. In the heavy half-light the man's beard jutted toward the ceiling, his mouth open and his teeth palely visible as he snored. There was a smell of alcohol about his bed. He was sprawled on it fully clothed.

Beau listened to his snores, eyes on the motionless figure. The snores were regular, too regular. And there was a tension about the supine man which was not like the relaxation of sleep.

De Carlos was shamming.

Beau almost yanked him out of bed by the throat. But then he turned and quietly left the man's room. He spent the rest of the night patrolling the corridor outside Kerrie's suite.

De Carlos absented himself during the next three days. He was reported to be bucking an intimate little poker syndicate somewhere in town.

The morning he returned, livid under his beard and cursing his losses, Beau was not there; and Kerrie felt an overwhelming desire to get away from the house.

She dressed in a riding-habit and went down to the stables with Violet. A groom saddled two horses—*Panjandrum*, Kerrie's white Arabian mare, to which she was passionately attached, and *Gargantua*, the big roan stallion Vi rode.

They trotted into the cool of the woods side by side. The nightmare of three nights before seemed far away, as if it had happened in a world of dark dreams. The sun's rays seeped through the trees like sparkling water, splashing the bridle-path with drops of light.

Kerrie inhaled deeply. "This is the first time in ages I've felt really alive. Trees have an odor, Vi, did you know that? I never realized it before."

"So have horses," said Vi, wrinkling her nose. "Gee up, you plug!"

"You're *so* romantic! I'm going to run for it."

"Kerrie! Be careful!"

But Kerrie was gone, the little white mare skimming down the path, her fine neck extended, her slender legs contemptuous of the speckled earth. They vanished round a turn.

Vi kicked *Gargantua's* vast sides but, turning his massive head in mild inquiry, he continued his lumbering trot. "Come on, you! Shift into high!"

Gargantua stopped altogether, his big ears twitching.

Somewhere ahead there had been a cry, a crash.

"Kerrie!" shrieked Vi. She began to belabor the stallion's ribs so violently that he bounded forward.

She thundered round the turn and there, a hundred yards ahead, made out two figures, one moving, the other still. The white mare's body sprawled on the bridle-path; she was thrashing about, kicking with three legs. The fourth, her right foreleg, was crumpled under her like a snapped twig.

Kerrie lay beside the path in a heap.

Gargantua drummed up and began to nose *Panjandrum* as Vi scrambled off his back and flung herself on Kerrie.

"Kerrie! Open your eyes! Oh, Kerrie, please—"

Kerrie moaned. She sat up, dazed.

"Are you all right, Kerrie? You don't feel—as if—anything's bro . . ."

62

"I'm all right," said Kerrie in a sick voice. "I think I am, anyway."

"What happened, Kerrie? Tell me!"

"*Panjandrum* threw me. It wasn't her fault. She was galloping, and stumbled suddenly. I flew right over her head. Vi, it was a miracle. I mean, ordinarily I'd have broken my neck. But I happened to land in this heap of leaves, and they softened my fall. How is she? . . . *Vi!*"

She saw the mare, writhing in pain on the path.

"Vi! She's broken her leg!"

Kerrie ran over to the mare, sank to her knees, stroked the rigid neck, forced herself to look at the snapped fore-leg. The steel shoe dangled from the motionless hoof.

"Vi," said Kerrie in a horrified voice. "Look—at—this."

"What's the matter?"

"The shoe on her broken leg. It's . . . But it can't be. I watched Jeff Crombie in the smithy only this morning. He shod her fresh—all four—a few hours ago!"

"I don't get you," said Vi slowly.

On hands and knees Kerrie began a feverish examination of the path, pushing leaves aside, flipping twigs away.

"Four of the nails are missing!"

"You mean some one—"

"Here!" Kerrie sat cross-legged on the path, fiercely examining two horseshoe nails. They were bent and scratched.

"Somebody," said Kerrie grimly, "loosened these nails and pried them partly out of *Panjandrum's* hoof with a pair of pliers." And she sat very still, staring at the nails.

"You mean some one loosened the shoe," said Vi, aghast, "so that it would flop free in a gallop and make *Panjandrum* stumble?"

"Except for the miracle of those leaves, Vi, I'd be lying over there with a broken neck this minute, and it would have been put down as an—accident."

Kerrie smoothed the corded, silken neck with her palm. The mare lay more quietly now, her big eyes on Kerrie's face.

Then Kerrie said in a hard voice: "Ride back to the stables and tell them to come for *Panjandrum*, Vi. I'll stay here with her."

"But, Kerrie, you can't! Suppose someone— I won't leave you alone here!"

"Please, Vi. And don't say anything about the nails."

There was something so coldly final in Kerrie's tone that Vi gulped and mounted *Gargantua* and lumbered off.

After dinner that evening Kerrie, on the plea of feeling ill after her accident, excused herself and glanced pointedly at her friend.

Vi followed several minutes later; and Kerrie locked all the doors of her rooms.

"Well, Kerrie? What do you think?"

Kerrie was pale. "I'm the only one who rides *Panjandrum*, and the horseshoe nails were loosened deliberately. Somebody tried to kill me today. The same one who tried to kill me the other night."

"Kerrie. Why don't you call the—police?"

"There'd be no way to prove our suspicions. We've got to *prove* . . . someone did it—the one who did."

"Or Ellery Queen. He's a detective. He—"

"No! He's . . . I just couldn't. I won't crawl to him for help, Vi." Kerrie sat down on her bed and smoothed the spread. "There's only one person in this world who would benefit from my death, Vi." Her voice trembled. "And that's Margo! She's so terribly extravagant. Her weekly checks are mortgaged for months ahead; Mr. Goossens told me yesterday when I—I asked. She wants my share, and if I died, she'd get it. And then—she hates me because of . . . *him*. It's Margo, Vi—Margo who climbed into my room the other night, Margo who loosened those nails this morning!"

"Let's get out of here," whispered her friend. "Give it up, Kerrie. You haven't been happy here, anyway, with all that money. Kerrie, let's go—go back to Hollywood."

Kerrie's mouth set stubbornly. "I won't be chased away."

"It's not the money!" cried Vi. "It's this big he-man of a chippy-chaser who looks like Bob Taylor! Don't tell me!"

Kerrie looked away.

"You're in love with him! And because you are, you're proposing to keep living in the same house with a—a blonde swivel-hips who's tried twice to kill you and won't stop till she has!"

"She won't drive me away," said Kerrie in a low voice.

64

VII

Encounter

on a Siding

BEFORE VI AWOKE THE NEXT MORNING, KERRIE STOLE OUT of the house and hurried down to the stables.

Jeff Crombie, Tarrytown blacksmith, was just getting out of his runabout.

"Oh, Miss Shawn." He removed his hat, twisting it in his permanently blackened fingers. "I was just comin' up to see you. I hear you had a fall yesterday."

"It was nothing, Jeff," smiled Kerrie.

"I sorta feel responsible, Miss Shawn," said the smith. "Your groom told me on the phone the right foreshoe come almost off. I just shod the mare yesterday mornin' with my own hands, and I can't see how——"

"Now, Jeff, it wasn't your fault. Forget it."

"But I'd like to have a look at that shoe, Miss Shawn."

"Such a bother about a little accident! *Panjandrum* must have caught her right forefoot in the cleft of a buried rock, and at the speed she was making the shoe was wrenched almost completely away from the hoof."

"Oh," said the smith. "I didn't want you thinkin' it was any carelessness o' mine, Miss Shawn. You feeling all right?"

"Right as rain, Jeff."

"Sorry about the mare. She was a daisy——"

"Is, Jeff."

The blacksmith was astonished. "Ain't you shot her yet? I'd be thinkin' she'd be better off, poor thing, out of her misery——"

"Dr. Pickens told me about a certain veterinary in Canada who's supposed to be able to mend horses' broken legs. Some new method that gets them over the bad period and makes them good as new. So I'm shipping *Panjandrum* North today."

The smith touched his eyebrow with two soiled fingers and drove off, shaking his head.

Kerrie went into the stable. The mare lay in soft straw,

65

a temporary splint holding her broken foreleg stiff. Dr. Pickens, the local veterinary, had also padded and swathed her other legs from hoof and pastern to above the knees. *Panjandrum's* great moist eyes looked dull and unhappy.

"How is she?" Kerrie asked the groom.

"So-so, Miss. Hasn't done much kickin'. Doc Pickens was here again this mornin' and gave her somethin' to quiet her. But I don't know how long she'll stay that way."

"Poor darling." Kerrie knelt in the straw and stroked the glossy neck. "I'm having that stable car up from the New York yards just as quickly as possible. They'll have it on the Tarrytown siding at eleven o'clock."

"Doc says he's goin' along, Miss."

"Yes, and I want you to go, too, Henry. We've got to save her life."

"Yes, Miss." Henry did not seem too sanguine.

Kerrie rose, brushing her knees. She said casually: "By the way, Henry, have you seen Miss Cole this morning? I wanted to ask her—"

"Why, no, Miss. She told me yesterday, after she brought *Lord Barhurst* in, that she wouldn't ride today."

"Oh, Miss Cole rode yesterday?" murmured Kerrie. "About what time, Henry? I didn't see her on the path."

"She rode before you did, Miss Shawn. Reg'lar horsewoman, Miss Cole is. Even unsaddled *Lord Barhurst* herself when she came in—wouldn't let me touch him."

"Yes," smiled Kerrie, "she's quiet an enthusiast. How is she as a groom—any good?"

Henry scratched his head. "To tell the truth, Miss, I didn't see. She sent me on down into town in her car for something—a new kind of saddle soap. When I got back— that was just before you and Miss Day came down for *Panjandrum* and the stallion—*Lord Barhurst* was unsaddled, right proper, and Miss Cole was gone."

Kerrie's heart leaped. So Margo had been in the stable, alone, before . . . There were plenty of tools about, and she was a powerful woman. It wouldn't have been hard for her to loosen most of the nails in *Panjandrum's* shoe. . . . It had been Margo!

"Henry." Kerrie tried to keep her voice from betraying her. "I shouldn't want Miss Cole to think I'd been—well, you know, checking up on her. You know how women are about things like that." She smiled at him. "So don't mention that I've been asking you questions about her; eh?"

"No, Miss," said Henry, looking puzzled. "Not if you

don't want me to. Only it's funny you should tell me that, just after Mr. Queen told me the same thing."

"Mr. Queen?" said Kerrie sharply. "He's been here this morning? Asking questions, too?"

"Yes, Miss, and about Miss Cole, too. He said not to say anything to her, or to——" Henry stopped, stricken.

"Or to me?"

"Well—yes, Miss. I didn't mean to, but it sort of slipped out." Henry's grip on the five-dollar bill Beau had given him tightened in the pocket of his jodhpurs.

"I'm sure you didn't. Where is Mr. Queen now?"

"He had me saddle *Duke* for him and rode up the path."

Kerrie sauntered out of the stables. She glanced casually over her shoulder after a few yards to see if the groom were watching her. When she saw he was not, she ran like a doe.

Kerrie sped up the bridlepath, her sports shoes making no sound in the soft earth.

So he was spying! He had heard about her accident!

The only one who could have told him was Margo. He hadn't been at the house yesterday, but just before dinner last evening Margo had had a telephone call, and from her dulcet tone and coy air the caller could only have been . . . Kerrie tried not to think his name. Margo had murmured something about calling him back——later. She must have told him then.

And here he was. Furtively.

When Kerrie came to the turn in the path beyond which she had been thrown the previous morning, she stopped, warned by *Duke's* distinctive whinny.

She stole into the woods paralleling the bridle-path and noiselessly made her way to a screen of trees and bushes near the spot where *Panjandrum* had fallen. She peered out through the leaves of a clump of wild blueberry bushes.

Duke was moving slowly along, nosing in the grass and bushes beside the path for succulent tidbits.

And he . . . he was on his hands and knees in the path, nosing, too. Like a bloodhound. He was skimming the surface of the ground with his palms, brushing grains of dirt aside. He knelt sidewise to her, his eyes intent on the earth.

Was it possible he suspected? But how could he? Of course! He knew about the first attempt in her bedroom. That was it. And, learning about her "accident," he suspected at once that it might have been no accident at

all. Or else . . . But Kerrie shut her mind to "or else."
There *was* a horrid possibility—

He growled exultantly, startling her. He was hunched
over the path now, examining two pieces of twisted metal.
The other two horseshoe nails—he'd found them!

He jumped to his feet and glanced suspiciously around.
Kerrie shrank. Then he slipped the two nails into his pocket,
leaped onto *Duke's* back, and galloped off toward the
stables.

Or else . . .

Kerrie came slowly out of the bushes. Or else he knew
it was no accident. Or else . . . he was Margo's confederate
and had sneaked down here early in the morning to get hold
of the telltale evidence of those wrenched nails, to dispose
of . . . to dispose of the evidence!

Kerrie stood still in the path. It couldn't be. He just
couldn't be that . . . But he and Margo were thick as—
yes, thieves! Why not *murderers?* She had seen him kiss
Margo that morning in the garden. They were always together. They were always whispering, running off into dark
corners, hours of it. . . . And later, Margo would look
like a tigress after a full meal. All purrs and claws. Her
white cheeks pink with an inner excitement. That hateful
glitter of triumph in her slanted Egyptian eyes. And *he* . . .

He thought money was everything. He had said so, in a
moment of what must have been unusual honesty for him.
Kerrie thought she understood. There had been a time
when money seemed all-important to her, too. He didn't
have much himself. Kerrie was sure of that. It wouldn't
be so unusual for a poor man under the spell of a ruthless,
beautiful woman like Margo to help her plan the—death—
of . . .

Kerrie cried out: "No!"

The sound of her own voice brought her to her senses.
She became conscious of the woods, and that she was
alone in them.

She started back for the house at once. First she went
slowly. Then her stride lengthened. Then she began to
trot. And then to run. And finally she was sprinting along
the path between the sentinel walls of the woods like a
frightened rabbit pursued by a pack of hounds in full cry.

KERRIE drove her roadster up to the station at a few
minutes past eleven. The stable car she had ordered was

lying on the spur beyond the station. Henry, the groom, was on the platform talking to the agent.

"Is *Panjandrum* all right, Henry? Did you get her into the car without any trouble?"

"She's lyin' in there snug as a bug, Miss Shawn."

"Where's Dr. Pickens?"

"He'll be along in a few minutes. There's still plenty of time for the eleven-fifty. Don't worry about the mare, Miss."

"I think I'll sort of say goodbye to her," said Kerrie slowly. "No, don't bother, Henry."

She trudged along the track to the siding. Outside the stable car she stopped short, frowning. Some one was in the car.

She approached the open door quietly and looked in. Again!

She couldn't see his face; but his wide back was unmistakable. He was squatting on his heels before *Panjandrum*, doing something quickly and powerfully, as if haste were imperative, to the mare's left forefoot. Bandages and packing were strewn about the car's floor.

Kerrie watched in a storm of breathlessness. *What was he up to now?*

Beau grunted with satisfaction and straightened up, and she saw what he had been doing. He had removed the mare's left foreshoe.

He examined it hastily, then thrust shoe and loosened nails into the bulging pocket of his baggy sack-coat. And he bent over again to replace the packing and bandages. The mare lay still, and his big hands worked with rapidity.

Kerrie leaned against the side of the car, miserable. Of course. Margo must have loosened the nails of the left foreshoe as well as of the right. Just to make sure, she thought bitterly. No one had thought to examine it except . . . And how could he have known unless Margo had told him?

Removing the evidence of her guilt again!

Kerrie took command of herself. At least she had one card up her sleeve. He—she—they didn't know she knew. She had passed her fall off as an accident. They thought she didn't suspect. Let them! That was her only protection now.

She stole off a few yards and then approached the car noisily. And she called out in a voice she tried to make unconcerned: "Dr. Pickens! Is that you in the car?"

Beau appeared in the doorway instantly.

"Oh! Hello," said Kerrie. "I thought it was the veterinary in there. What are you doing?"

He jumped to the ground. "I heard about your accident and—"

"Came to pay your respects to the horse?"

He said abruptly: "You all right?"

"Never better, thank you."

"Well." He stood frowning at the ground. "I guess I'll amble along. Hope the mare can be saved."

He strode away. Kerrie did not look after him. She went into the stable car. From there, she looked. He was pacing up and down behind the station—near her car!

She said goodbye to *Panjandrum* a dozen times. Finally, Henry appeared, and Dr. Pickens. They seemed to think her expression of alarm was caused by anxiety over the mare, and kept reassuring her that *Panjandrum* would be all right.

And finally the eleven-fifty rolled in, and she had to get out of the stable car. But she remained to watch the coupling of the car to the northbound train.

When the train pulled out and there was no longer any excuse for lingering on the spur, she trudged back to the platform, trying to appear preoccupied.

"Oh, are you still here?" she said. "I thought—"

He seized her arms. "Kerrie! Listen to me—"

"You're hurting me!"

"You know what happened the other night," he said in a low, hurried voice. "You've got to be—"

"Let—me—go," panted Kerrie. She wriggled out of his grasp and slapped him, hard, on his blue-stubbled cheek. All the bitterness of weeks found expression in that pitiful act of violence. "You're used to manhandling females, I don't doubt," she cried, "but that doesn't mean you can manhandle me!"

His voice was oddly soft. "Kerrie, I just wanted to warn you to be careful. That's all."

"Careful?" Careful. He wanted her to be *careful!*

The miracle of his solicitude, after all her fears, filled Kerrie with joy. Then it wasn't true! He wasn't Margo's confederate after all!

"I mean," he went on, and something in his tone smothered her joy, killing it with a sort of contempt, "you've got one hell of a way of getting into trouble. You're a nuisance!"

Kerrie jumped into her roadster and drove off blindly.

70

She did not therefore see how his shoulders sagged and the lines of his face deepened. She drove into the city.

When the police permit and revolver came, she felt grimly better. It was a pearl-handled .22 of beautiful workmanship, and the ammunition was slick and deadly-looking.

VIII

Woman-Trap

THE GENUINE MR. ELLERY QUEEN SET DOWN THE HORSE-shoe and the twisted nails gently.

"Kerrie's got the finger on her," said Beau.

The tone made Mr. Queen look up. Then Mr. Queen looked down, mercifully. He picked up a nail and turned it this way and that between his fingers.

"Deadly," he remarked. "And a little terrifying. A woman in the grip of a homicidal mania, induced by jealousy and greed, doesn't usually try to commit murder so subtly. Loosening the shoes of a horse!"

"Damn her." Beau turned away.

"A murderess capable of that kind of plot can't be reached through the customary channels. She's probably immune to fear, because she's too far gone in pure cussedness. I'd rather she had tried poison. There's something realistic about poison. This—it's fantastic." He stared at the nail and then flung it aside.

"Just the same," said Beau in his lifeless voice, "I'm not taking that chance, either. I've got an ex-police-woman in the kitchen as assistant to the chef."

"You're convinced it's Margo Cole?"

"I found out from the groom that Margo had managed to be alone in the stable with the mare before Kerrie went riding. It was Margo, all right."

Beau lay down on the sofa and turned his face to the wall.

"How about the other night?" Mr. Queen regarded him with pity. Really an impossible position, he thought. And the girl—

"We'd been in town, the beautiful Miss Cole and I," said Beau without turning. "Having fun. You know, just a couple of innocent kids out on a tear?"

He sat up suddenly. Mr. Queen let him talk.

"We sat on the terrace and hoisted a few, and she got very, very chummy. I guess I wasn't feeling so palsy that night. I tried not to show it, but she's . . . smart."

His eyes were bloodshot, Mr. Queen remarked. And he had a habit these days of working his jaws, as if he were hungry.

"I knew from the way she looked at me that she spotted my trouble. She knew Kerrie was bothering me. From the way she smiled . . . she gave me the shivers," Beau said hoarsely. "I should have known then. But I never thought . . . She said good night as if everything was all right. I sat up a while and then went to bed. I couldn't sleep. When the poor kid let out that awful yell—"

"Yes?" said Mr. Queen gently.

Beau smiled, and there was something cruel and naked in his smile. "De Carlos could hardly have climbed that wall. He was faking when I went in to look him over. Wasn't asleep at all. But he was potted, too. He'd have tumbled to the terrace and broken his damn' neck if he'd tried to climb to Kerrie's room.

"But Margo . . ." He jumped off the sofa and began walking around. "She sleeps in the opposite wing, but it gives out on the terrace, too, and it would have been a cinch for her to slip down at that time of night and climb the vines and trellis. She's an athletic bitch. . . . Maybe what she saw in my eyes that night made up her mind."

Mr. Queen sighed. "How does it feel to be fifty percent of the motive in an attempted homicide?"

"That's not the worst of it, although God knows it's a lousy enough spot for a man to be in!" cried Beau. "It's what I'm forced to do to Kerrie that hurts. Every time I show a spark of interest, her eyes start shining like electric bulbs. She looks like a kid under a Christmas tree. She . . . And then I've got to douse the lights by deliberately acting like a heel. She'll wind up hating my guts, if she doesn't hate 'em already."

"That's what you want, isn't it?" queried Mr. Queen. But he was thinking of something else.

"Yes," said Beau quietly. "That's what I want," he burst out, "but it's more than that, too! She thinks I'm signed up with Margo to put her out of the way!"

"Very natural. The appearance of requited passion, the attempt at murder . . . very natural for her to think so."

"It's easy for you to be calm about it," said Beau bitterly. "You're not in love with her."

"I'm sorry, Beau," said Mr. Queen in a gentle voice. "My specialty is murder, not romance."

"What the devil can I do? I've got to find a way out of this mess somehow!"

Mr. Queen was silent.

"Hell, you're not even paying attention!"

Mr. Queen looked up. "With half a brain. The other half is excogitating a great befuddlement. Beau, what's the connection between these attacks on Kerrie Shawn and the events that preceded and accompanied Cole's death?"

"All I know is that Margo Cole is out for Kerrie's blood. Kerrie's standing between her and me—*she* thinks—but, more important, Kerrie's death means doubling her income. Knowing Margo, I'd say the money motive was the stronger of the two. Not that it makes any difference to a corpse *why* he's been bumped off."

"You think the root of these attempts goes back into the past? The development of a plan made months ago?"

"I think," said Beau savagely, "Margo was responsible for Cole's death!"

Mr. Queen raised his eyebrows. "You believe she was on the *Argonaut?*"

"Why not?" Then Beau growled: "Or she wasn't, and De Carlos did the dirty work for her. It's not impossible those two are working together. They keep away from each other—De Carlos is concentrating on Kerrie, the damn' chaser!—but that doesn't necessarily mean anything. It might be a cover-up."

Mr. Queen looked dissatisfied. "There's so much we don't *know,*" he complained. "Heard anything on the crew and Angus?"

"I had a report this morning. One of my men picked up the trail of three of the crew and the wireless operator. They shipped on a freighter, and they're on the other side of the world by now. Nothing on the others, nothing on Angus. It's just as if—"

"Just as if?" echoed Mr. Queen.

Their eyes met.

"They were dead," said Beau.

Mr. Queen picked up his hat. "Keep watching your light-o'-love. And don't let your suspicions of Margo make you blind to . . . other possibilities."

"What's that supposed to mean?" snapped Beau.

"Merely what it said. There's only one thing about this case I feel sure of. And that is that it's far less simple than

73

it seems. In fact, I've the feeling it's a case of complicated and subtle cross-purposes. You'll have to be very careful, Beau, and I'll help all I can from under cover. Keep your eyes open—to the four points of the compass. The break may come from the least-expected quarter."

"I don't know what you're talking about!"

"That's not strange," said Mr. Queen with a shrug, "since I scarcely know myself."

VI pleaded with Kerrie to run away. "If that she-devil doesn't kill you," she cried, "the suspense will. Kerrie, you're such a—a fool I could shake you. Do you really love him that much? Or this money? A fat lot of good it's doing you! You look like God's wrath. Give it up and let's get out of here—while we can!"

"No," said Kerrie stiffly. "I won't. I won't. They won't drive me away. I won't give in. They'll have to kill me first."

"They will!"

Kerrie trembled. "It's something stronger than I am. It won't let me go. Maybe it's plain stubbornness. I'm scared too—I'm scared, Vi, but I'm more scared of what I don't know. I've got to find out. I've got to."

Vi looked at her with a sort of horror.

"I suppose you think I've gone dotty," said Kerrie with a weak smile. "Maybe I have . . . I *hate* him!"

So it *was* that. Vi shook her head.

And then the enemy struck a third time.

It was a Sunday, and when Kerrie opened her eyes that morning she saw it would be a day of sun and cloudless skies.

"Vi, let's have an old-fashioned picnic, just the two of us!" she cried. "We'll drive into the country somewhere, and camp, and eat pickles and shoo bugs away and swim raw if we can find a stream!"

They found their stream, and gorged themselves on the good things the chef had packed in the bursting hamper, and for the first time in weeks Vi heard her friend's unclouded laughter.

By the time they drove through the gateway to the estate it was dusk, and rapidly growing dark.

Vi yawned. "It's the fresh air. Kerrie, I'm flopping right into bed."

"Sleepy? With such beautiful stars beginning to come out? Here, I'll let you out at the house and you can flop into your old bed if you want to. I'll put the car away."

Vi got out under the porte-cochere and Sir Scram, as she called the butler, opened the front door for her. She disappeared. The butler took the hamper from the car and went back into the house.

Kerrie sat still behind the wheel for a while, mooning up at the darkening sky, her thoughts dream-woven, afloat in a great peace. But soon the brightening stars made her think of what a lovely night it was, and the loveliness of the night led naturally to thoughts of romance, and romance . . .

She drove off abruptly, headed for the garage.

The garage, located behind the stables, was really six garages under one roof. It was a wide shallow brick building with six double-doors, and each car-compartment was separated from its neighbors by brick and plaster walls, making the individual sections complete in themselves.

Kerrie housed her roadster in the second compartment from the right, between the one where the station-wagon was kept and the one reserved for De Carlos's powerful limousine.

In the glare of the roadster's headlights the four double-doors to the left were closed; the two on the right stood open.

Kerrie noticed that the station-wagon was in its garage and wondered why the doors were not closed. But it was the wispiest kind of thought. She drove into her garage, raced her motor, turned off the ignition, withdrew the key, and reached over to switch off her headlights.

Her hand paused in midair. She thought she had heard the slam of a door.

Kerrie twisted in her seat and looked back. The doors of her garage were shut.

"There wasn't any wind," she thought, puzzled. "I guess they just swung shut by themselves after I drove in." And, without turning off her lights, she got out of the roadster and snapped the switch on the wall which operated the ceiling-light.

Then she went to the double-door, pressed down the latch, and pushed. And as she pushed, she heard the click of the lock which was attached to the hook-and-staple on the outside of the door.

Kerrie stood still.

The thought seeped into her mind that, while doors may swing shut of themselves, locks cannot. Her lock required a human hand to slip it through the ring. A human hand

75

to slip the ring through the slit in the staple. A human hand to snap the lock shut.

"You out there!" she called. "You've locked me in! I was just about to—"

There was no answer.

And Kerrie did not finish. She knew it was useless to cry out, and why it was useless to cry out. And her heart catapulted into her throat.

But it was so stupid. To lock her in. Sooner or later some one would come to release her. Even if she had to stay all night. . . .

But another attack, a voice whispered. Vi's gone to bed. The butler won't remember. No one else knows you're here—no one that cares. Another attack. . . .

Kerrie laughed aloud, nervously. That was absurd. For whoever had locked her in had locked himself—or herself, she thought darkly—out at the same time. There was no opening in these walls large enough to admit a mouse. Not even a window. High in the right-hand wall of the compartment there was a radiator-grille; it ran through to the next garage, the one for the station-wagon. But the coils of the radiator were between the two garages, behind the grilles; only a fly or a bug could go from one garage to the other by that route.

"Let me out!" She pounded on the heavy doors. They did not even shake. "Let me out!"

She pounded until her hands were raw.

And then she became conscious of an undertone, a peculiar roaring hum, which seemed to come from the garage on the right . . . where the station-wagon stood.

She stopped pounding to listen.

It was the motor of the station-wagon. Some one had turned it on. And pulled out the throttle. It was roaring away. The penetrating stench of its exhaust came to her nose, floating through the grilles.

"Help!" cried Kerrie. "Whoever's in there!" She raced back and shouted up into the grille. "I'm locked in the next garage! Help!"

There was an answer, but it was not in human accents. The doors of the adjacent garage slammed shut. And over the roar of the racing motor Kerrie heard retreating footsteps.

And now she knew. Now she remembered death, when it was too late.

Some one had imprisoned her in the garage, turned on

the motor of the car in the next compartment, locked the doors, and fled—leaving her to die slowly as the odorless fumes of the deadly carbon monoxide gas being generated next door seeped through the radiator-grilles.

Now that death showed its face again, openly, Kerrie stopped shouting, stopped pounding the door, collected her thoughts with a cold deliberation that astonished the vague, fluttering, helpless part of her that was wilting and crumpling inside.

The garage was far from the house, from the servants' quarters. The sole building within hailing distance was the stable, and only the horses would be there at this time of night. It was useless, then, to scream.

As a matter of fact, she thought, sitting down suddenly on the running-board of the roadster, she had better save her breath. She had better conserve the air in the garage. Mustn't exert herself in the slightest. It would probably help to remain as close to the floor as possible. Didn't gas rise? Or maybe carbon monoxide was heavier than air. If it was, it would sink to the ground. . . . Well, there was only one way to find out. . . .

Kerrie lay down and turned over, pressing her cheek and nose to the cold cement floor.

That wasn't any good. She'd merely live a little longer. Sooner or later the garage would fill with the gas, sooner or later her lungs would exhaust the oxygen supply, and then she would die.

Die!

She sat up, thinking furiously. What could she do? There must be something she could do!

Theoretically, there were two ways to save herself: to stop the flow of the gas, or to get out of the garage. Could she prevent the carbon monoxide from entering her compartment?

She glanced up and discarded that possibility at once. It was conceivable that by stuffing the openings in the grille up there with material torn from her clothing, she might prevent most of the gas from seeping through. But to do that she had to reach the grille. And the wall was so high, and the grille was so high in the high wall, that even if she put up the roadster's top and stood on it, she would still be unable to reach the grille.

Could she get out of the garage?

She couldn't break through the walls. She might scrape through the plaster, but inside there was a core of brick.

No windows. The door. . . . She couldn't break through. It was too thick. If she had an ax, she might; but she had no ax.

Kerrie became aware suddenly of a tightness across her forehead, as if the skin were trying to stretch; of a throbbing at the temples, like the beginning of a bad headache.

So soon!

Think. Think!

She examined the door desperately. And then she laughed aloud. What a fool she'd been! The hinges!

All she had to do was get some tools from the roadster's kit—why, just a screw-driver would do it! Even if she couldn't reach the upper hinges, she could remove the lower ones, push the whole door outward from below, and crawl to the safety of the air outside!

She sprang to her feet and stumbled around the car. She lifted the front seat joyously. . . .

The tools were gone.

Sobbing, Kerrie hurled things out of the seat-compartment—match-packets, slips of paper, scraps of lint, things, things, useless things . . . searching like a madwoman, getting splinters under her fingernails, scratching one finger so that the blood ran in a brilliant stream. Anything would do. A wrench. Anything. . . .

No tools.

Stolen.

She ran back and hurled herself against the door. Again. Again. No. Don't do that. That's silly. Think. Think. . . .

She sank back against the door, exhausted, a severe headache pounding at her temples, the beginning of a dizziness, the beginning of a nausea. . . .

Like a beacon in a foggy sea—the revolver. The revolver! She had slipped it into the side-pocket of the roadster very early this morning. Of course, she had left it for a short time. . . . No. It was there. It was there. She could shoot the hinges off—the lock, the hasp, shoot, shoot. . . .

Crying and laughing, she staggered back to the car, weakly opening the door, weakly thrusting her hand into the pocket on the inside of the door, ready to rejoice at the cold sensation of the metal on her palm, that blessed, loaded revolver. . . .

Every drop of blood in her body stopped flowing.

The little pearl-handled revolver had been stolen, too.

Her last chance, her last hope.

Part THREE

IX

Beau's Gesture

LAST CHANCE. LAST CHANCE. LAST CHANCE.

The two words synchronized with the throb of her temples. A senseless hammering that gradually took meaning, digging through the muck of horror and panic.

Was it? Was it really? The very last?

Kerrie crawled over to the double-doors again, lay down on the floor, pressed her nose as close as she could to the thin line where floor and door met. And she lay still, simulating death in her stillness, struggling to breathe slowly, evenly, quietly, to conserve each precious bubble of oxygen in the garage, in her lungs . . . grudging each breath, doling breath out to her body like a man doling out his last drops of water as he lies dying of thirst in the burning desert.

The cement floor was cold, but she did not feel its cold. Only the taste of death in her mouth and the giant pulse at her temples. Last chance. Last chance.

Was it?

She went over in her mind each physical detail of the garage, taking inventory, a ghastly job of accountancy, before her vision, which already was blurring, should become a jumble of swimming, tumbling, senseless objects, before her head should vibrate like a huge drum, before the nausea should make her so sick that sickness would drive away even the desire to keep living, before she should succumb to unconsciousness and, unconscious, gasp the last bubbles of her life away.

Garage. Three walls—blank, solid. Only that sieve of an opening, the radiator-grille, which she could not reach. The fourth wall—the doors. No tools. Useless to hurl herself against the doors. She would give, her soft tissues her slight weight, her small muscles. She would give, not the doors.

What else?

Herself. No. She had only her hands, her fingers, her nails. What use were they against brick, concrete, hard wood?

If only the butler hadn't removed the hamper from the car. There were knives, forks in the hamper. Tools. But he had. Hamper from the car.

Hamper from the car.

Car.

Car!

The Car!

Kerrie clung to that conception with desperation, turning it over in her mind, searching the flaws in the thought, probing, exploring, testing.

The car. Tool. It was. It could be. Not a puny tool like a screw-driver. A ram. A battering-ram!

She sat up quickly, reckless now of the exertion, her accelerated breathing, staring wildly at the roadster, at the space between her body and the roadster. About four feet. Not much. But it might be enough. And the rear bumper. It was a fairly heavy span of steel. . . . But starting the car. That meant releasing more fumes. More carbon monoxide. It would cut short what remained of her life.

The drums in her head banged louder. She blinked, trying to bring the rear bumper into focus. Her eyes were giving way. Was that what happened? Oh, to die! Here. Don't. Think. Chance. Your last, last chance.

Take it!

She rolled feebly over, managed to steady herself on her hands and knees, crept the four long feet to the car. Around the car. Now. Up. Up into the car. *Up into the car.*

She bit her lower lip with the effort. The pain was remote. She tasted her own blood. Up. . . . The blood dripped from her lip, stained her dress. Up. . . .

How loud the drums were. What was she going to do? Car. Ram. Start the car.

Oh, yes. Key. Where was the key? Key. She had turned off the ignition. What had she done with the key?

Groggily Kerrie looked down at her left hand, felt for it with her right. Both hands swam in a sort of warm and swarming sea of shadow. Key. There it was. In her left hand. She had never let go of it.

She fell forward against the wheel, groping for the

ignition keyhole with the point of the key, scratching, scraping, sliding, key in hole, key in hole. . . . She bit her lip again, deliberately, on the bleeding wound. The pain was sharp this time. Sharper. Bite. Again. She cried out. But her eyes cleared for an instant.

It was in. Now. Turn it. Turn it.

Slowly, slowly. There. It turned.

Now. The starter. Right foot. Bring it up. Drag it, push it up. Oh, it won't move. Damn you. . . . Kerrie took both hands and lifted her right leg from under the knee, carried it forward until the sole of her shoe lay on the starter.

Lean. Press.

The urgent rattle of the starter awakened her a little. She gulped, jerking in an abdominal spasm. The mutter of the motor filled her head. Quickly. Before it's too late. . . .

Left foot, clutch. Right foot, gas. Hand, shift. Shift. Shift!

Now!

The roadster leaped backward. Thud!

Forward. Backward. Thud!

Not hard enough. Stalled. Start again. Harder. Harder. "Oh, the drums!" Thud! Forward. Crash! Forward. Crash! Stall. . . . Start. Forward. *Crash!*

Better. There had been a crackly, splintery sound on that last one. Don't look around. Hang on to yourself. Keep your stomach down. Hold your head up. Right foot, left foot, one going down as the other goes up. *Crash!* Now shift into first, forward, stop, reverse, right foot and left foot, one going down as the other goes up. *Crash!* It's going. Oh, it's going. Think of that. Never stop thinking of that. Maybe just once more. Maybe just. Forward. Reverse. *Crash!*

Her left and right feet were frozen to the clutch and gas pedals as the roadster burst through the double-door, as she lay across the wheel fighting the world of falling shadows, the sickness in her body, the roaring in her head . . . burst through into the black night, rode over the door's defeated, splintered body, careened as the weight of her body shifted the wheel, crashed into a broad and ancient beech yards to the side of the low garage building . . . crashed, snarled, was silent.

As silent as Kerrie who, even as the roadster struck the tree and the shock of the impact jerked her from the driver's seat and threw her out of the car to lie crumpled on the cold grass, even as unconsciousness embraced her fluidly like the arms of the sea, was sucking the sweet clean breath of the world—sucking, frowning, her bleeding lips and throat and smudged nostrils greedy . . . sucking, gulping, savoring, breathing the blessed air.

WHEN Beau drove into the grounds of the Cole estate, it was already dark.

He stopped at the servants' quarters first. His operative, a large stout woman with eyes like steel nailheads, was rocking on the back porch.

"Well?"

"All okay." The woman squinted at him. "You're past due, Mr. Rummell. I was getting worried."

"What happened today?"

"Miss Shawn and Miss Day left early this mornin' on a picnic, just the two of them. Drove out in Miss Shawn's roadster. I handed the chef the eatables meself. No chance for a slip-up, Mr. Rummell."

"Driving off into the country alone!" Beau frowned. "How about Miss Cole? Mr. De Carlos?"

"Miss Cole didn't leave the grounds all day. She entertained a party of newspaper people on the lawn. They left before dark and she had dinner alone and went up to her room. She called your number in the City just after dinner."

"I know, I know. How about De Carlos?"

"Mr. De Carlos threw a water-party in the pool for Mr. and Mrs. Goossens and some free-gin lappers in the afternoon. He got drunk on absinthe at four-thirty and had to be helped to his quarters."

"When did the girls get back from their picnic?"

"Less than an hour ago. Miss Day went right to bed. Miss Shawn drove her roadster round to the garage; butler told me. I guess she's gone on up to her rooms."

Beau drove back to the house. He went upstairs and knocked on Kerrie's door.

He knocked again, listening; then he tried the door and found it unlocked. He pushed it open, went in, snapped on the light, and looked around.

Not there.

He was about to cross to the boudoir door when it opened and Violet Day, in a mauve satin négligé, her hair in two blonde braids down her back, her eyes half-closed

84

in the light, as if she had been in darkness for some time, stood in the doorway.

There was a snub-nosed automatic in her left hand, and it was pointed at Beau's breast.

"Oh, it's you," said Vi. But she did not lower the automatic. "What do you think you're doing, pussy-footing around in Kerrie's bedroom?"

"Where is she?"

"Kerrie? Isn't she here?" A shadow passed over Vi's face; she looked quickly about. "But I thought—"

"Put that pea-shooter down before you hurt somebody!" Vi's arm sank. "Now where is she?"

"I came up here and she drove around to the garage to put the car away."

"When?"

"Almost an hour ago. I was just dozing off when you—"

But Beau was gone.

He drove towards the garage. As he approached, he saw the unmoving shine of two headlights. He jumped out and ran over to Kerrie's roadster. It was backed against a big beech tree, and it was empty.

Puzzled, Beau followed the parallel lines of the roadster's headlights. Then he saw the broken door of the second garage compartment. He ran over and examined it. There was no lock on the fallen door. He rose, sniffing. Exhaust smell. But he could hear no sound of a running motor; and all five of the other garage stalls were closed and silent.

He sprinted back to the roadster. "Kerrie! Kerrie Shawn!"

There was no answer, and he began to circle the roadster. With a flashlight he examined the rear of the car; it was battered, its bumper hanging crazily. Then he went on and saw Kerrie lying still in the grass.

Flying feet made a noise behind him. "Kerrie! Is she— is she—*dead?*" Violet Day stood panting there. She had slipped a squirrel coat over her négligé. Her hair was disordered and her eyes big with fear.

"No. Breathing very fast. Heart's racing. Kerrie!" Beau shook the limp body.

"But—but what—"

"Looks as if she was caught in the garage and had to fight her way out. Kerrie!" He slapped her pale right cheek, his left arm supporting her head. "Kerrie! Wake up. It's—"

Her eyelids fluttered. Her eyes were dull, her brow furrowed, her mouth open to the night air.

"I'm—dizzy," she said with a groan. "Who—I can't see—well—"

"It's . . . Ellery Queen," said Beau, but Vi flung herself beside Kerrie and cried: "It's Vi, hon! What happened? What was it this time?"

"Garage—carbon monoxide—" Kerrie fainted again.

"Carbon monoxide!" Beau shouted: "Get a lot of black coffee!"

Vi flew off.

Beau turned Kerrie over in the grass and straddled her. Her mouth and nose were sucking in the air. His big hands gripped her ribs; his torso worked up and down in a slow rhythm.

She was just coming to again when Vi, accompanied by Margo Cole and half the household, ran up. Vi carried a pitcher of steaming coffee and a glass.

"Vi says—" cried Margo; she was half-dressed. "Vi says Kerrie— Monoxide poisoning—"

Beau did not look at her. He seized the pitcher, poured a glass of coffee, sat Kerrie up and forced her to swallow. She cried out weakly, shaking her head. His fingers clamped the back of her neck; he exerted pressure, and she drank, tears streaming down her dusty cheeks.

When she had swallowed one glassful, he forced her to swallow another. A trace of color began to show in her cheeks.

"Drink it. Breathe in—hard. And drink."

She drank and drank, while the silent group stood about.

"All right," said Beau. "It's as much as we can do now. Anybody call a doctor?"

"I did, sir," said the butler. "Dr. Murphy of Tarrytown.

"All we can do till the doctor comes is put her to bed. Kerrie!"

Her head was against his shoulder, resting heavily.

"Kerrie. Put your arm around my neck. Hang on, now."

"What?" said Kerrie. She raised her eyes; they were still dull with pain.

"Never mind." He picked her up; and after a moment her arm crept about his neck and clung.

Kerrie opened her eyes with a confused recollection of a nightmare. Garage—smell—fight—car—crash—a lot of people and . . . him . . . holding on to him and feeling, through her nausea, through the fog . . . feeling at peace.

And then the scene shifted to her room, like a movie. Windows thrown wide, Vi undressing her and getting her into bed . . . she was sick then . . . and later he was telling her not to mind, not to mind, just close her eyes, breathe deeply, try to rest, to sleep . . . then a strange man injecting something that stung for an instant—the air, the fresh clean sweet air—sleep. . . .

Kerrie opened her eyes and in the hot light of morning saw Beau's face, inches from her own.

She pulled him down to her, sobbing.

"All right. It's all right now, Kerrie," Beau kept mumbling. "You're okay. There's nothing to be afraid of now."

"It was horrible," sobbed Kerrie. "The garage—some one locked me in—I couldn't get out—turned the motor on in the next garage—the fumes came through the radiator-grille—I got sick and dizzy—my tools were stolen, my revolver—I couldn't get out. . . ."

Beau's arms tightened about her. When he had found Kerrie last night the lock was gone from the broken garage door; the motor of the car in the next garage had been turned off. Whoever had tried to kill Kerrie had stolen back, removed the lock, turned off the engine of the station-wagon, and gone away. Had Kerrie not managed to escape from the garage, had she died there like a mouse in a trap, it would have looked like the usual garage accident: the running motor of her own car, the doctors might have said—she fainted and was overcome. There would have been no evidence of a crime. An accident—like the "accident" on the bridle-path.

Kerrie's tears were warm on his cheek. "I thought—*you* were in with her. Please. I was mad. I know you couldn't. Oh, I love you. I do. I've been so miserable. I couldn't leave here and let—her have you. I love you!"

"I know, funny-face. Me, too. . . ."

"Darling." She placed her palms on his cheeks and held his face off, smiling incredulously. Then she hugged him. "Oh, you do!"

The Tarrytown doctor came in and said: "I beg your pardon. Would you mind—?"

Beau stumbled out.

MARGO kept him waiting fifteen minutes. When her maid finally admitted him, Margo was lying graceful-armed on a chaise-longue, her body draped in a dramatic morning gown, every hair in place, and her dead-white cheeks carefully made up.

"How nice," she smiled at him, and then said rapidly to her maid: *"Betise! Vas t'en!"* and the maid fled. As soon as the door closed Margo slipped off the couch and went to him.

He took her in his arms. She put her hands on his chest after a while. "Sit down here with me. You've kept me waiting so long."

"Couldn't get here sooner."

"Oh. Kerrie? It would be." She said it lightly. But she pushed him away a little.

"Sure it would be!"

"And how is the little mousy darling? I suppose you've sat up with her all night?"

"I had to put on an act, didn't I? Somebody had to." Beau made his tone annoyed, even truculent. But he was careful to draw her close to him again.

"You—it was you found her last night, wasn't it?" murmured Margo.

"Lucky for you I did, gorgeous."

"What do you mean?" She opened her Egyptian eyes wide, staring in the innocent-little-girl way she affected.

"You know what I mean."

"But I don't. I was shocked to hear about Kerrie's latest adventure with the fates. She has such foul luck with horses and garages, hasn't she? Is she all right this morning?" Margo sat down on the chaise-longue and patted it invitingly.

"No thanks to you." Beau laughed, stretching out beside her. She leaned on him, chin propped on her long hands, eyes on his face. "Don't you think that was a little raw, baby?"

"Raw?" She looked blank.

"This last stunt of yours." His tone said he was amused.

"This last—" she wrinkled her nose in perplexity. Then she laughed. "You think *I* locked Kerrie in that garage and tried to kill her? I?"

"That's what I mean."

She stopped laughing. "I don't like that!"

"Neither do I. That's why I'm giving you a little friendly advice."

"That, *chéri,* she said softly, "is a very dangerous thing to say. I might sue you for slander—if I didn't like you so much."

"I wouldn't be wasting my time if I didn't have your interests at heart."

"Heart! What do you know about hearts? You're a lump, a stone!"

He grinned at her. "Yeah. Like coal. Hard and black and cold. Till you light a fire under it."

"You're a cinder!"

"Try me and see."

She rose suddenly and went to the window to stare out at the gardens.

"Come here," said Beau lazily.

She turned with reluctance. Then she went back to him, and sat down again, and he took her hands.

"You don't believe me, do you?"

"In what way?"

He put his arms about her. "Don't you know, deep inside, that you're safe with me, baby?"

"Safe?"

"Don't you know you and I can go places together? The only thing is—you're a little foolish."

"What a charming compliment!"

"You're foolish because you take foolish chances. You've let yourself be swept away by your feelings. That's why women's crimes are so easy to spot. For one thing, you think I'm in love with Kerrie Shawn."

"Aren't you?" she asked through her strong white teeth.

"That skinny little thing? When I'm a sucker for your type?"

"Just my *type?*" She was growing arch now.

"For you, damn you! You know it, only you're too damn' suspicious. Does this feel phony?"

He pulled her over until she lay in his arms.

"Does it?" He kissed her.

She closed her eyes, responding slowly. But it was the creep of a rising flood.

"Wait. Wait," she gasped, pushing him away. "You say you don't love her. How do I know? The way you've looked at her. And last night—"

"I tell you she doesn't mean a thing to me!" snarled Beau. "But I'm smarter than you, baby. I put on an act. And you'd be a hell of a lot smarter to put on an act, too, instead of running your neck into a noose!"

"I don't—know what you mean."

"You want her dough, don't you?" said Beau in a brutal tone. "All right. How do you try to get your hands on it?

By putting her out of the way. Dangerous, you fool! It takes finesse. You can get what you want a whole lot more safely."

She did not answer in words. She pulled him down to her and put her lips to his ear.

"You can get it, and me, too," growled Beau.

She whimpered.

"But we split, see?"

She kissed a trail from his ear to his lips.

Later, when Beau left her, he went into a bathroom and spent three minutes rinsing his mouth.

Beau left the grounds early that morning; he was back by the afternoon.

Kerrie was waiting on the terrace. For him. He knew it was for him. By the way she started when she saw him. By the glad look in her eyes—glad, and anxious, too, as if she couldn't make up her mind whether what had happened was a dream or an actuality.

He stooped and kissed her. The book slipped off her lap. "Then it's true!" And she jumped up and kissed him fiercely. "Let's go somewhere!"

"Where's Vi?" asked Beau slowly.

"She had an appointment in town with the hairdresser. Darling. You do love me?"

He held her close.

"That's all I wanted to know." She shivered with joy. "I don't care about anything else."

"Let's take a walk," said Beau.

They strolled into the sweet-smelling woods, his arm about her.

There was something unreal about the afternoon; the sunlight filtering through the leaves had a red cast, so that they seemed to be walking in a place not of earth.

"It isn't," said Kerrie, "as if the future were altogether rosy. It isn't. There are so many thing I don't understand. About you, darling. And *about* the future. But I've made up my mind not to look ahead. . . . Isn't it lovely here?"

Beau sat down on a weatherbeaten stump. Kerrie sank to the ground and rested her cheek on his knee.

"What's the matter, dear? You look—funny."

Beau hurled a twig away. "Kerrie, we've got to face the facts. You're on the spot."

"Please. Let's not talk about that."

"We've got to. You're on the spot, and we've got to do something about it."

She was silent.

"Your uncle paid me to find his heirs. I should have bowed out when I located you and Margo showed up. I've only brought you a peck of trouble." He scowled.

"I'm glad you didn't bow out." She pressed his knee.

"I didn't because—well, I had reason to believe your uncle Cadmus was murdered. I still believe it."

The red light of the sky on her pallor gave her face an eerie violet cast.

She stammered: "But I don't—I don't understand."

"Neither do I." He pulled her up and sat her on his knee, staring at the sky. "Anyway, I've been hanging around trying to find out what it's all about. And who's behind it."

"Margo," whispered Kerrie. "Margo! She's tried to kill me, Ellery. But how could she— Uncle was at sea—"

"There's plenty we don't know. Anyway, funny-face, maybe now you'll realize why I've been paying so much attention to your cousin Margo."

"Darling, why didn't you tell me?" Kerrie sprang off his lap. "Can't we expose her?"

"No proof. She's cute as hell, Kerrie. She's covered her tracks too well. And if we force her hand now, she may become desperate." Beau paused, then said quietly: "Sooner or later, no matter how many precautions we take, one of these little 'accidents' won't fail."

"The police—"

"They'd laugh at you, and you won't have anything to offer them but suspicions. Then the cat will be out of the bag and you'll be worse off than now."

"What do you want me to do, Ellery?" asked Kerrie simply.

"Get married."

Kerrie was silent. And when she did speak, it was in an unsteady voice. "Who would marry me, even if I should be silly enough to give up twenty-five hundred dollars a week for him?"

"I would," muttered Beau.

"Darling!" She flew to him. "If you'd said anything else I'd have killed myself!"

"You'll have to kiss the dough goodbye, Kerrie," he said gently.

"I don't care!"

"Funny kid." He stroked her hair. "I'd have asked you to marry me in Hollywood, but I couldn't bring myself to—not when it meant depriving you of everything money could give you. But now its different. It's no longer a choice between money and me . . . it's a choice between money and—" He drew her closer.

"The money doesn't mean a thing to me," cried Kerrie. "The only one I'm sorry for is Vi. Poor Vi will have to go back—"

"You would think of her," grinned Beau. "Think of yourself for a change! With you married, Margo gets your share of the income automatically. So she won't have to kill you, and you'll be safe."

"But, Ellery." She looked troubled. "She likes you. I know. She likes you a lot. If you marry me, she won't—I mean, a woman can act awfully nasty in a case like that."

"There won't be any trouble with Margo," said Beau quickly.

"But—"

"Kerrie, are you going to trust me, or aren't you?"

She laughed tremulously. "Yes—if you marry me now, today!"

She could hold him against any woman, she thought—once they were married. She had so much love to give. So much more than a woman like Margo could possibly offer, much less feel.

"Is this a proposal?"

"I couldn't make it any clearer, could I? Oh, but I'm delirious, I guess, darling. How can you marry me today? We haven't even a license."

"Didn't I say to leave everything to me?" Beau grinned again. "I took out a Connecticut license last week."

"Ellery! You didn't!"

Kerrie ran all the way back to the house. Beau followed more slowly. Following, with her eyes no longer on him, he stopped grinning. In the deepening crimson light, his face was ghastly, too.

X

The Ring
and the Book

KERRIE WAS FURIOUSLY HURLING THINGS INTO THREE BAGS
when Vi returned. Beau was pacing the terrace downstairs in the dusk; Kerrie could hear the slap of his steps.
She was grateful for them, because they kept him near her.
She felt the need for his nearness when Vi came in, and
that was strange, for Kerrie had never required a defense
against Vi before.

"Kerrie! What's up?"

"Darn it," said Kerrie. "Where are those new nighties?"

"In the bottom drawer. What are you packing for?
Where are you going?"

"Away," said Kerrie, as if it were unimportant. She did
not look at Vi. "This is a heck of a trousseau I'm getting
together."

"Trousseau? Kerrie, are you gaga?"

"I'm going to marry Ellery Queen." From an irresistible
compulsion Kerrie said it lightly.

She heard Vi's gasp and the creak of the box-spring as
her friend sank onto the bed.

"Marry? *Him?*"

"What's the matter with him?" laughed Kerrie. "He's
the most fascinating thing in pants I've ever met, and
I've decided to grab him before he changes his mind."

Vi did not laugh, however. "But, Kerrie— When?"

"Now. Tonight." Despite her best effort, a note of defiance crept into Kerrie's voice.

There was the most peculiar expression on Vi's face.
But then she jumped up and hugged Kerrie. "All the luck,
hon. You've got more guts than I'd have."

Kerrie clung. "Oh, Vi, I know what this means to you.
Back to the old grind—"

"Easy come, easy go," said Vi gaily. "Don't fret yourself about *me*. It's twelve o'clock, and the coach turns into
a pumpkin, and the glad rags become just rags. . . . Well, I
had a few weeks in a fairy tale, anyway." She pressed

Kerrie to her bosom convulsively. "Kerrie, you're sure?"

"What do you mean?" But Kerrie knew exactly what Vi meant. And because she herself had had similar suspicions, she felt herself go hard inside and slipped from Vi's embrace to resume her packing.

"And how about Sister Rat?" asked Vi dryly, after a long time.

"Who? Oh! I don't know. What's more, I don't care."

Vi looked at Kerrie; then she laughed. "So little Kerrie's been snagged by the tough lad who looks like Robert Taylor . . . Quite a triumph. Epic, they'd call it in the movies. Giving up the old boodle for lo-o-ove. He must feel pretty snazzy, that man!"

"Vi. That's hateful," said Kerrie in a low voice.

Vi sat down on the bed again. "I'm sorry, Kerrie; I guess the shock . . . Tell me just how it happened. It's really too thrilling for words."

Kerrie looked her friend straight in the eye. Vi looked away. "Not so long ago, Vi, you were begging me to give all this up, to run away. And now, when I've decided to take your advice, you don't seem . . . well, pleased. Why?"

"*I'm* not pleased? But, Kerrie dear, aren't you a little mixed up? You're the one who has to be pleased, not I. Are you?"

"Very much!" Kerrie tossed her head.

"Then that's all that matters," laughed Vi. "Now are you going to stop being silly and tell me *everything?*"

Yes, Vi was acting peculiarly. Of course, it was natural for her to be—surprised . . . yes, and disappointed, too, over the prospect of Kerrie's marriage. It meant Vi's brief day of bliss was over and that she would have to go back to the old, mean, scraping life. And then for some time Kerrie had had the queerest feeling that Vi had come to distrust *him*. Oh, Vi liked him, all right; Kerrie was woman enough to be sure of that fundamental fact. . . . And, too, Kerrie's marriage meant the separation of the two friends. That much could be remedied!

"Of course, you'll take pot luck with us," said Kerrie quickly. "I couldn't think . . . We won't have much, because Ellery's not well off, and it will probably mean a small apartment in the city. But we'll manage beautifully, Vi—"

"Thanks, Kerrie," said Vi. "But I've been a millstone round your neck long enough."

Kerrie dropped an armful of stockings and ran to the bed. Vi! You're crying!"

"I'm doing no such thing," said Vi, springing up. I'm going right back to Hollywood, where men are rats and all the rats are casting directors, and with the publicity I've had through this little racket of ours I'll get steady work—maybe. Well, I will!"

"Oh, Vi!" And it was Kerrie's turn to sniffle.

"Stop it," said Vi. She picked Kerrie up and deposited her on the bed. "Now you lie there while I finish packing for you. I'll see you through the execution, anyway, and then—"

They finished packing together, in silence.

Pink and blue—that was how Kerrie had always visualized her wedding. She would wear a pale pink satin gown with a short train and a swathing veil of pink tulle. The gown would be princess-lined, with leg-o'-mutton sleeves and a high neckline edged with a narrow pleated ruffle, and the gown would button down the back—one long row of twinkly little buttons from her neck to her waist. Pink satin slippers, long pale pink kid gloves, a wedding bouquet of pink camellias and baby's-breath . . .

There she would stand, a creation in pink among bridesmaids in baby blue, who would be wearing doll hats and little muffs made out of fresh flowers. Of course Vi, as maid-of-honor, would be in powder blue. . . .

That's the way it had always been, a vision of the future. But what was the actuality? Kerrie had hurriedly put on a simple two-piece tailored dress of navy-blue net, with a touch of white at the throat, and a navy-blue hat, white gloves, and navy patent leather shoes and bag. It was all right, but . . . And Vi. Vi had climbed into a white tailored sharkskin suit over a pink sweater.

An even aside from the clothes—just the three of them. That masterful individual who either scowled or grinned had insisted upon secrecy.

"When the papers get hold of this," he had said, "you'll be hounded to death. It's a big story."

"But, darling," Kerrie wailed, "something—anything—a few friends. A woman only gets married once! I mean—"

"So you see what you're getting," said Vi. "A woman only gets married once! Didn't you ever hear of Reno?"

"Lay off my wife," said Beau. "Heiress Gives Up Fortune for Love! They'll play it up bigger than the bundling party at Munich. If you want to enjoy your honeymoon, funny-face, you've got to outsmart the press."

"But how, darling?"

"Leave it to your Uncle Dudley." And he had telephoned a Justice of the Peace he said he knew in Connecticut, upon whose discretion he could rely, and had sworn Margo and De Carlos and the servants to a twenty-four hour conspiracy of silence, and had refused to tell even Kerrie where he was going to take her on their honeymoon.

And Margo—Margo was something of a surprise.

"You mean you're actually giving up Uncle's money?" she asked when she heard the news.

"Yes."

"But why?"

"We happen to be in love," said Kerrie shortly.

"Oh, I see." And Margo smiled slightly at the stiff face of the groom-to-be. "Well, I hope you'll be very happy."

"Thank you."

It was baffling. Margo acted almost *relieved*. Of course, as soon as Kerrie married, Margo's weekly income would be doubled. But Kerrie had been positive Margo was in love with "Ellery"—as much in love as a woman of that sort *could* be. Wasn't there a conflict? Or had Kerrie been altogether mistaken about Margo—in everything?

"You're being married immediately?" murmured Margo.

"We're leaving in ten minutes," said Beau abruptly. "We'll be married before the night's over."

"How romantic!" said Margo; and then she said politely: "Is there anything I can do, Kerrie?"

"No, thanks. Vi's going with me."

"But there must be things you aren't able to do at such short notice—arrangements about your belongings, your bank—"

"They can wait. Goodbye, Margo."

"Goodbye."

They eyed each other inscrutably.

Then Edmund De Carlos stumbled in, drunk as usual.

"What's this I hear?" he shouted jovially. "Getting married to Queen, or some such nonsense, Kerrie?"

"But it's true, Mr. De Carlos."

"True!" He gaped at her. "But that means—"

"I know," snapped Kerrie. "It means I'm giving up twenty-five hundred a week for life in exchange for a big lug who'll probably beat me up for exercise on Saturday nights. Now that *that's* clear—goodbye, everybody."

And they drove off, leaving De Carlos goggling after them, and Margo on the drive in a long white gown which shimmered in the dying sunlight, smiling faintly.

Kerrie found herself thinking about her cousin's smile as Beau's car rattled toward Connecticut. It was a strange quarter-smile, a delicate and subtle exhibition of amusement, and it had persisted throughout their farewells to the silent household staff, the packing of Kerrie's and Vi's bags into Beau's runabout, throughout the exchange with De Carlos.

That smile of Margo's seemed to have cast a pall over all three of them. Beau drove in a shut-in silence, and in the back seat Vi was a mouse.

What's the matter with us? thought Kerrie in despair. This isn't an elopment; it's a funeral. Why is he so quiet? And Vi?

It was that woman back there, dominating the driveway, mistress of all she surveyed—ex-clothes-horse! Gloating over the fine rolling lawns, the big house, the view of the Hudson—visibly gloating over her triumph.

That was it—triumph. Why was she so *triumphant?* Did complete possession of the estate mean so much to her? Or was there something darker and deeper and more hateful in the secret pleasure of that smile?

Kerrie leaned on Beau's shoulder and touched the lobe of his ear with her lips. He grunted something.

"Give the gal a break, Mister," said Vi suddenly from the back seat. "You owe her *something* for making her lose that twenty-five hundred per."

"Vi!" said Kerrie angrily.

But Beau did not take his eyes from the unwinding tape of the road, and both women fell silent, and no other word was spoken until they crossed from Port Chester into Connecticut.

Kerrie burst out at last: "If you'd rather forget the whole thing, this is the time to say so!"

He started at that, looking at her out of the corner of his eye. "Kerrie! What makes you say a fool thing like that?"

"You don't seem very happy over the prospect of marrying me," retorted Kerrie in a small voice.

"Oh." He looked straight ahead again. "Maybe it's because I know what it means to you, Kerrie. What have I got to offer you to take the place of all that dough?"

"If you feel that way about it, then you don't know what getting married means to me!"

"I'm seven different kinds of heel," he said quietly.

"You're marrying me to keep me from being killed!" cried Kerrie. "Oh, I see it all now! You're not in love with me. You never have been! That's what she was smiling—"

"She?"

Kerrie bit her lip. "Never mind."

"Kerrie—"

"Oh, you're being fine and heroic!" said Kerrie scornfully. "Well, thanks, but I want a husband, not a lifeguard. Please turn the car around and take me back to Tarrytown."

And she crouched in her corner, her face turned away.

He drove onto the grass shoulder beside the road, stopped the car, said over his shoulder to Vi, "This woman takes a lot of convincing. Excuse *us*," and, seizing Kerrie by the waist, yanked her to him.

She gasped. After a moment she put her arms about him. When he released her he said: "Any doubts now?"

Kerrie was breathing hard; her eyes were shining. She twisted about and said in confusion: "Never a dull moment, that's us. I think I *am* wacky. Oh, Vi, this is awful. Can you ever forgive us?"

But Vi was—or was pretending to be—asleep.

They pulled up in the yard of a disreputable clapboard house near Greenwich, on the sagging porch of which a mean sign announced:

MARRIAGES PERFORMED
JUSTICE OF THE PEACE
W. A. JOHNSTON

A board was missing from the second step of the wooden stairs leading to the front porch, the plot before the house was a miniature wilderness of weeds and rubbish, and the once-white walls were encrusted with the dirt of decades.

"Cheerful little place to tie the knot," remarked Vi. "So elegant, so refined! What is this, Queen—a haunted house?"

"Johnston isn't very strong on soap and water. Ready, Miss Shawn?"

"Y-yes," said Kerrie.

"She's a little gun-shy," said Vi. "Buck up, darlin'. This is one form of execution that isn't permanent. You can

98

rise from the grave any time you like, if you know the right judge."

"You're—you're sure you've got the license, Ellery?" stammered Kerrie, ignoring Vi's prattle.

"Right in my pocket."

"It's all right? I mean, I always thought the woman had to sign on the license, too, when it's taken out. But—"

"Pull," grinned Beau. "After all, my old man's a somebody in New York, isn't he?"

"Oh, Inspector Queen. And I haven't even *met* him!" Kerrie looked anxious. "But this is Connecticut, darling, not New York!"

"You find more things to worry about," grunted Beau, and he scooped Kerrie from the walk and carried her over the broken step, and Kerrie giggled something about Isn't that premature? and Beau set her down and set off a bell that jangled rustily.

A tall gaunt man wearing thick glasses and an ancient morning coat peered out through the dirty pane at the side of the front door. When he saw Beau his thin features cracked into smiles and he hastened to admit them.

"Come in!" he said heartily. "All ready for you, sir!"

"Mr. Johnston—Miss Shawn—Miss Day."

"So this is the blushing bride." The man beamed down on Kerrie. "This way, please!"

There was something fantastic about the thin, stooped figure that made Kerrie suppress another giggle. What a way to be married, in what a place, by what an agent of the State! The Justice had a head of bristly gray hair, and he wore a mustache of the untrimmed, thicket variety; he looked like a vaudeville comedian. And the house! The front hall was bare, and the parlor he led them into was a cold, dark, sparsely furnished room so full of dust that Kerrie began to sneeze.

Out of the corner of her eye she saw Vi's nose wrinkle with disgust, and laughed aloud. Then Vi laughed, too, and they began to whisper together.

It certainly is a "different" sort of wedding! thought Kerrie as Beau conferred with the Justice at a desk in a corner over the marriage license. He *would* pick a place like this, and a funny man like that to marry them! Always doing the unexpected. "Never a dull moment," she had said to Vi in the car. No, there never would be with him. Perhaps that was why she loved him so much. It would be like being married to a ball of lightning.

Vi whispered: "Scared?"

"I should say not."

"How does it feel to be taking the fatal step, liar?"

"S-simply s-swell."

"No—regrets, Kerrie?"

Kerrie squeezed her friend's hand. "Not even a little one, Vi."

Then the two men came back, and the Justice took up a position in a certain formal way and cleared his throat importantly, and Kerrie was so surprised she said: "But aren't we supposed to have two witnesses, Mr. Johnston?"

"Of course, my dear," said the Justice hastily. "I was about to explain that Mrs. Johnston is unfortunately in Greenwich at the moment, and if you'd care to wait—"

"Miss Day is one," said Beau. "And I don't think we'd like to wait. How about it, funny-face?"

"Certainly not," said Kerrie firmly.

"Naturally, naturally!" said Mr. Johnston. "This occurs occasionally, of course. If you have no objection, Miss Shawn, the only other thing we can do is—er—flag a witness outside, so to speak."

"Pick somebody interesting," giggled Kerrie.

And the tall man hurried out, and they heard him shouting at passing cars, and finally he returned in triumph, like Pompey, towing an inebriated traveller who leered at Kerrie and at Vi and even at Beau, and Beau had to hold him up during the ceremony to avert the total collapse of his rubbery legs.

That was the last straw, and Kerrie was so busy trying to keep a straight face that she scarcely heard one mumbly word of the service. She was actually astonished when Vi giggled: "Wake up! You're a married woman!"

"I'm— Oh, Vi!" And she threw herself into Vi's arms while Beau helped the stranger to a rocker, and paid the Justice, and then approached to claim his bride.

He was actually pale.

"It was the nicest wedding," said Kerrie with a wavery smile. "Darling—aren't you even going to kiss Mrs. Queen?"

He took her in his arms without a word.

XI

Villainy

at the Villanoy

"UP TO NOW," SAID VI WHEN THEY GOT BACK IN THE CAR, "I've been chief mourner. But now that the funeral's over, chickadees, take me to the New Haven and then be gone with the wind—and my blessing."

"No," protested Kerrie. "Ellery, don't you do it!"

"Wouldn't think of it," said Beau. "Where you bound, Blondie?"

"New York."

"Then we'll take you there."

"But that's out of your way!"

"Who told you?" chuckled Beau. "We're headed for the city, too."

"You mean—a honeymoon in New York?" gasped Kerrie.

"Sure. That's the one place the smart boys won't think of looking for us."

"Oh," said Kerrie. Then she said valiantly: "I think that's a gorgeous idea, don't you, Vi?"

"Yes, indeed," murmured Vi. "And just think of all the fun you'll have—a wedding dinner at the Chink's, and you can go roaming the primeval wilderness in Central Park, and all. Such a romantic place to honeymoon!"

"Well, it is!" said Kerrie.

"Sure it is, hon. Anyway, it's your honeymoon—and your husband, thank goodness!"

Kerrie and Vi argued all the way into New York. Kerrie wanted Vi to spend the rest of the evening with them and Vi insisted she was tired and sleepy and had to get settled and all. . . . Beau urged Vi to stick with them, too. Kerrie resented that—just a little. Then she felt ashamed of herself. But she was relieved when Vi remained adamant.

They dropped Vi at a genteel ladies' hotel in the East Sixties. The two women parted with tears and embraces.

"You'll keep in touch with me, Vi?" cried Kerrie.

"Of course, kid."

"Tomorrow—I'll ring you tomorrow."

Then Vi's tall figure was gone, and Kerrie was alone with her silent husband, He was kept busy driving through the midtown traffic, and Kerrie managed to occupy herself for a long time with her lipstick and powder-puff. But even the most careful make-up duty ends at last, and then there was nothing to do but stare straight ahead, feeling hot fires in her cheeks.

"You smell nice," he said in a growly voice.

She laid her head on his shoulder in a spasm of tenderness.

"Where are we stopping?" she whispered.

"The *Villanoy*. Right off Times Square. They won't find us there in a million years."

"Wherever you say, darling."

At the *Villanoy* a doorman took charge of the car, and two bellboys commandeered the luggage—Kerrie flushed when she noticed the initials *K S* on her bags—and Beau registered at the desk, writing "Mr. and Mrs. Ellery Queen" in a firm hand, and the desk-clerk didn't even blink.

Then there was the long ascent in the elevator under the scrutiny of a couple with remarkably inquisitive eyes. The woman whispered something to her escort, laughing, and Kerrie was sure they were whispering about newlyweds, but finally that ordeal was over, and they and their bags and the bellboy were marching down a long corridor to a door marked 1724, and they went in, and the bellboy set down the bags and threw up the shades of the sitting room and opened the windows wide, so that New York flowed into the room in a nice, quiet, above-it-all way.

The boy repeated the chore in the bedroom. Twin beds, Kerrie noticed, recalling that downstairs her husband —husband!—had asked for twin beds. But then she supposed it was because he was accustomed to . . . The bellboy left noiselessly, pocketing a half-dollar with no surprise whatever, and they were alone at last.

"It's a darling suite," said Kerrie in the strained silence. She went to inspect the closets, glorying in the first official impulse of her housewifely existence.

Beau was planted in the center of the sitting room, his hat still on his curly hair, a cigaret forgotten in his fingers—looking rather silly, Kerrie thought with secret amusement as she poked in the closets.

"Aren't you going to stay a while, Mr. Queen?" she called.

"Kerrie." Something in his tone made her come out of the bedroom closet, take off her hat, put it on the bed, strip off her gloves, all slowly. There was that pain again, in her chest. It was a pain she felt through no one but . . . him.

"Yes?" she managed to keep her tone casual. But whatever he was about to say would be—catastrophic. She knew that. It had been coming all afternoon. "Yes, dear?" said Kerrie again in a light tone.

He kept staring at the tip of his cigaret. Kerrie's eyes burned on him. Oh, darling, darling, what is there between us? That comes up even at a time like this? Then he looked up and he was smiling.

"I've got something to do, Kerrie."

"Now?"

"Now. Hungry?"

"Not a bit. What do you have to do?" That was wrong; she shouldn't have asked that. It would make him hate her.

"Business. In all the hurry—" She deserved that. Business! It was almost funny. "I'll send something up for you."

"Don't bother. If I want anything, I'll call Room Service." Kerrie turned her back toward him, stooping over one of her bags. "Will you be gone long?"

"Here, let me do that," he said. He took the bag from her, carried it into the bedroom, returned for the other bags, carried them into the bedroom. She followed slowly. He hadn't answered her question. "While you're waiting, you can unpack—you'd have to unpack, anyway, and you may as well do it now instead of . . ."

"Darling." She ran to him and put her arms about his neck. "Is anything wrong?" She couldn't help it. She couldn't.

He looked blustery, and she knew she had failed. "Wrong? Look, Kerrie. I've just got to go out—"

"Then you've got to," said Kerrie brightly, releasing him. "Don't make such funny faces! Any one would think you were about to leave me forever. You wouldn't desert your bride of an hour, would you, Mr. Queen?"

"Don't be a goop." He kissed first the tip of her nose, then the dimple in her chin, and finally the bow of her lips. "Be seeing you, funny-face." He strode out.

"Ellery! Come—"

She heard the slam of the front door.

Kerrie sat slowly down on one of the beds. Her brains ached. Blank. Void. Nothing. No thinking. Just sit. Or get up and do something. But don't think—

Flowers.

Of course! That's what had been bothering him! He'd forgotten to buy her flowers. He'd felt ashamed of himself. That made him act uncomfortable, and his uneasiness had communicated itself to her, and all the rest was her own imagining. . . . He'd gone downstairs to buy her some. He'd probably be back with boxes of flowers and buckets of champagne, and they'd have a *tête-à-tête* supper high over the city. . . . Mr. and Mrs. Ellery Queen, in love and sitting on top of the world!

She flung herself backward on the bed and stretched luxuriously, yawning and smiling. But it was a yawn of excitement, not sleepiness.

Kerrie undressed quickly, washed in icy cold water, recombed her hair, made up again, and then put on a different dress—the one with the wide red leather belt and the peasant blouse with blue stripes that flattered her eyes so, and heightened her complexion.

It was still early. Perhaps they'd take a walk on Broadway after supper, before returning to the hotel. She'd wear the little straight-brimmed straw with the coque feather. . . .

She unpacked her bags. Her dresses were so wrinkled. But they'd hang out in the closet by morning. As she draped them on hangers she suddenly thought that *he* didn't have a bag at all. It had happened so quickly— their running away, their marriage . . .

She flushed and finished unpacking, stowing her powders and finishing creams and deodorants and perfumes and toilet waters in the bathroom cabinet. *Not* on the vanity. Women ought to keep the machinery of beauty hidden—especially married women. And he wouldn't see her—ever—with her face creamed up and her hair in an unsightly tight net. She'd always be fresh-looking . . . make him wonder . . . Silly. Childish. She wasn't really herself. What difference did it make? If he loved her. They said it did make a difference. She didn't really believe that. Never had. Then why these absurd defensive thoughts? Was it because, deep down, she wasn't absolutely certain he loved her?

When she was unpacked, and all her things had been laid away, and her most beautiful nightgown lay at the foot of one of the twin beds, with her nicest mules, Kerrie realized that it was almost eleven o'clock. He'd been gone over two hours!

She lit a cigaret and sat down in the sitting room by one of the open windows, frowning. After a moment, she took up the telephone.

"This is Mrs. Queen," said Kerrie, thrilling despite herself to the shape of the name on her lips. "Has there been a call, or a message, for me in the past hour, from Mr. Queen?"

"No, Madam."

"Thank you."

She replaced the receiver softly and stared out the window.

The short lace curtains were fluttering in a breeze. Outside, there was a U-shaped court. Their two rooms lay along the right side of the U. The windows on the opposite side were dark. But the room nearest Kerrie's window on the connecting wall of the court was illuminated. The outer wall of that room and of Kerrie's sitting room met in one of the right angles of the court; the adjacent windows of the two rooms were only eight feet apart along the hypotenuse of vision.

Some one was in that room, Kerrie thought idly; the window was open and she could see on the drawn blind the formless shadow of some one crossing the room.

But then the light went out, and after an instant Kerrie noticed the blind flutter.

No use fooling herself longer. He hadn't gone for flowers. He could have bought a whole greenhouse in the time he'd been away. He was up to something else. But what could it be? That made sense? Oh, she could cheerfully strangle him!

But perhaps he was hurt. Perhaps he *had* gone down for flowers, or to arrange for a surprise blow-out, and had been struck by a cab, or had slipped and broken his leg, or—or—

No. That couldn't be it. She'd know if that had happened. Even if nobody notified her, she'd know. It wasn't that kind of accident. It wasn't *any* accident. He had gone away; he was staying away deliberately.

The truth was that he had proposed to her, rushed her to a crummy Justice of the Peace, married her like a —like a Saturday night binge, driven her secretly into New York for a "honeymoon," parked her in a hotel room as if she were a piece of—of luggage, and disappeared.

Kerrie caught up the lace curtains on both sides so that the night air might cool her hot face.

Vi . . . She could call Vi.

No. She'd rather die than do that. Not tonight. Not tonight. Not if she had to sit here by this window like a dressed-up dummy all night, alone! . . .

At midnight Kerrie telephoned the hotel desk. There was no message. She had known there would be none. But it was something to do.

She went into the bathroom to brush her teeth and rinse her mouth; it felt dry and tasted bitter.

As she was coming out of the bathroom there was a knock on the door.

Her heart jumped. He was back! What difference did it make why he had gone away, or where he had been, or to see whom? He was back!

She ran to the sitting-room and pulled it open.

Margo Cole smiled at her across the threshold.

"May I come in?"

Kerrie said: "Go away."

"Now is that nice, Mrs. Queen? Surely you wouldn't keep me out in the passage?"

"Go away, or I'll have the hotel people put you out!"

Margo crossed the threshold and gently closed the door behind her.

"I don't believe you'd fancy a scene just now."

"What do you want?"

"Are you really married?"

"Yes! Will you go now, please?"

"As soon as I've said my little piece."

"If you don't go," cried Kerrie, "I'll call my—my husband!"

"Do that," smiled Margo.

They faced each other in a keen, hostile silence.

Then Kerrie said: "You knew," in a shocked, faint voice.

"Of course I knew, darling! And since the groom isn't here, I thought I'd console the bride."

"Where is he?" whispered Kerrie.

Margo walked past her, stalking about the room, staring insolently at the stylized furniture, the cheap prints on the walls, the tinny decorations.

"How did you know he left me? How did you know

we were in New York? How did you know we were at this hotel?"

"It was all arranged, my dear," drawled Margo.

Kerrie went over to the armchair by the window and sat down, fumbling for another cigaret.

"I suppose," she said calmly, "this is another of your little jokes." The room was whirling.

"Poor dear," sighed her cousin. "So brave. Such a good show. Just the same, darling, you're an ass! You *actually* married him. I didn't think even you would be ass enough to do that. But his plan worked!"

Kerrie choked over the smoke and flung her cigaret out the window. "His—plan?"

"Oh, you didn't know that. Such a pity. Why, yes, dear, it was. Do you recall last night? After your little accident in the garage? When he found you and took you to your room? He remained with you all night—he's so very clever. But this morning, when your doctor came, your husband-to-be came to see . . . me."

"That's not true!"

"Ask him. He came to see me, and it was his plan you've been following today." Margo laughed. "I knew about your marriage and where you would stop on your 'honeymoon' before you did!"

"Get out of here!"

"Not yet, dearest." Margo rested her gloved hands on the back of Kerrie's chair. Kerrie could hear her breathing, but she did not look up and around. "Not until I've made you see just how *big* a fool you've been. That's my revenge, darling. You were willing to give up a fortune because you love him. And so you married him. But why do you think he married you? Because he loves *me!*"

"No," said Kerrie with a rising nausea. "No . . ."

"Then where is he on your wedding night?"

"He had to go out somewhere—he'll be back soon—"

"He didn't have to go out. I told him to. Men are weak," Margo smiled, "and I wasn't taking a chance on your husband's showing weakness at the wrong moment. You *are* attractive in a wishy-washy sort of way, you know. So I made him promise he'd marry you and ditch you—yes, the very first night; and he has, you see."

"I don't believe—a single word," whispered Kerrie.

"All the rest was his idea—to marry you so that you forfeited your share of Uncle Cadmus's estate and it would pass to me. As it has. So you've nothing at all, darling—

107

no money, no husband. The money is his and mine now, and you may get a divorce if you like. Not that it will do you the least good—you've forfeited your inheritance by marrying! Don't you agree you've been a fool? Such an empty-headed, trusting, ridiculous fool?"

And Margo's voice sharpened until it hissed through the ache in Kerrie's head, and without looking up Kerrie knew that her cousin's white face and Egyptian eyes were hateful with triumph.

And Kerrie said: "I want you to stay here, Margo. I shan't let you go. You'll stay here until Ellery gets back—"

"He won't be back," drawled Margo. "You may as well pack up and get out."

"I want to see your face when he denies your lies. I want you to stay—"

"I'd be glad to, my dear, except that I've more important things to do, and it would all be so useless, wouldn't it?"

"If—that were—true," said Kerrie in a remote voice, "I think—I'd kill him."

"That *would* be gratitude!" laughed Margo. "Kill him! You ought to thank him. Don't you know you owe him your silly life?"

Kerrie barely heard the mocking words.

"You're a lucky miss. He's saved you that by marrying you. And if you hadn't been lucky, you'd have been a dead pigeon long before this. Or didn't you know that, either?"

What was she saying? thought Kerrie dully.

"Do you think that little visit to your room was a joke? Or that your mare stumbled by accident? Or that what happened in the garage last night happened by chance, or some one's blunder? Do you?"

"No!" cried Kerrie. "I knew! All along. I knew it was you. You. You!"

"You did?" Margo laughed again. "Clever girl! But it wasn't only I who planned those attacks. You didn't know that, did you? It was I—and somebody else."

"Somebody else!" cried Kerrie, sitting up straight in the armchair.

"I and—"

The world exploded over Kerrie's head. She fell back in the chair, half-deafened, half-blinded by three incredible flicks of fire.

Behind her she heard a gasp, a gurgling cry, and then

the sound of a sliding, slipping body. And finally a hollow thud on the carpet.

Kerrie gripped the arms of the chair and blinked into the moonlit court, and saw the flutter of the blind in that window diagonally across from where she was sitting, only eight feet away, and a hand . . . a hand, reaching out, holding something, making an odd tossing motion . . . and something hurtled past her head and landed with another thud on the floor.

And Kerrie got out of the chair and stumbled over Margo's body lying still on the floor, and mechanically picked up the object, turning it over and over and over.

It was a little pearl-handled .22, and smoke was still curling from its muzzle.

Her revolver. Hers. The one that had been stolen from the pocket of her roadster. Smoking . . .

Only then did eyes and brain coördinate—only then, as she knelt beside Margo, holding the .22 in a cold clutch, holding it and staring down at the mushroomed splash of red at Margo's throat, at the red ruin of Margo's left eye, at the red crease across Margo's right cheek.

Margo was still. Margo was dead.

Some one had shot Margo three times across the angle of the court from that room with the fluttering blind.

Margo was dead.

There was a sound at the door. Kerrie turned, still on her knees, the revolver still in her hand.

Margo was dead.

And there was her husband in the doorway. So purple-eyed and haggard. Staring at the bloody dead woman on the floor. At the revolver in his wife's hand.

Part FOUR

XII

Silence, Please

BUT KERRIE DID NOT SEE HIM. SHE WAS STILL BLIND from the brilliance of those three red flashes over her head into the throat and eye and cheek of Margo. Blind, deaf, stunned with the three sounds of a world tumbling.

"She's dead," Kerrie said in a clear voice. "Margo's dead. Her eye is dead. Blood on her neck. She has one eye. See how funny she looks. See how funny—"

Beau stood in the doorway trying to speak.

"One moment she was alive. Then she was dead. She died over my head. I heard her gurgle her life away. I heard her die behind me." Kerrie began to laugh.

Beau stumbled in. "Kerrie!"

He dropped beside her. He could think of nothing to do but put his arms about her and press her face against his chest. He couldn't bear to look at her face. It was white, fixed, a plaster-of-Paris mask made by a crude workman. Her eyes were shiny with something not fear, not panic, not horror; something inscrutable and dead, like the eyes of a wax-works figure.

At his touch she stopped laughing. "She came to laugh at me. Said you and she had planned the whole thing. Our elopement. Marriage. She said you told her where you were taking me. That's how she knew where to find me. Your plan. You didn't love me, she said. You loved her, she said. This was your scheme to get hold of the money Uncle Cadmus left me. To share it with her. The two of you. . . ."

"Kerrie, stop."

"She began to talk about the attacks. She admitted she had made them. She and some one else—"

"Some one else!" muttered Beau. "Who?"

"She didn't get a chance to tell me. She began to. But then the three shots from the window . . ."

The window. Beau got to his feet, walked stiff-legged to the window by the armchair. Open. The blind blowing.

113

Kerrie in the chair, Margo standing behind the chair—direct line of fire—in the throat, the eye . . . Revolver.

"Revolver," he said hoarsely. "What happened?"

"It's mine," said Kerrie, as in a dream. "Mine. I bought it. When you—warned me to be careful. It was stolen from the pocket of my car. Must have been some time yesterday, because I missed it when I was locked in the garage."

"Yours!" Beau took a forward step, and stopped. "But if it was stolen—"

She looked up at him in a dumb way. "Hand. Or fingers. Threw it from that window. In here. Right after the shots." She looked down at her own hand in the same way, the hand which still gripped the pearl-handled .22.

Beau jumped at her. Her head flapped on her shoulders as he shook her.

"Don't you see?" he cried. "It's a frame-up! Some one shot her and is trying to frame you with the gun! Get up! We're getting out of here."

"What?" She didn't understand. She was trying to, her face twisted with the effort.

He lifted her to her feet, slapped her cheeks hard. "Kerrie! For God's sake get a grip on yourself. I've got to get you out of here before—"

"Stand still."

Beau stood still, Kerrie limp in his arms, the revolver dangling from her fingers.

Hadn't even taken the gun out of her hand. Couldn't do anything now. Her gun-hand was in full view of the doorway. You dope. You damned dope. Hadn't even shut the door.

"I've got you covered."

They were blocking the doorway. One was the hotel manager—Beau recognized him by the tuxedo, the aster, and the half-moon sacs under his eyes. Suspicious-looking guy. Husky. The other was the house dick. Big boy with an iron hat and a .38 in his fist.

No dice. Think of something else. The windows. . . . Seventeen floors from the street. Escape. Screwy idea, anyway. They were registered. Think. You've been a prize poop so far. Think this through.

The house detective came in on a straight line, his eyes on the revolver in Kerrie's hand. His right hand trained the cannon on them, his left went into his pocket and came out with a handkerchief.

He knew his business. He didn't try to take the gun from her himself.

"Drop that heater."

Kerrie looked blank.

"Drop it," said Beau in her ear. "The gun."

"Oh." She dropped it.

"You. Big guy." The detective shifted his eyes from Kerrie's hand to Beau's hands now. "Just push it with your toe. Gentle, Mister. In my direction."

Beau pushed it. It slid three feet across the rug and stopped by the detective's large feet. He stooped without looking at it and spread the handkerchief over it, fumbling.

Beau whispered in Kerrie's ear: "Kerrie, you listening?"

Her head against his breast stirred slightly. She held on to him.

"I'm going to make a break for it. Understand?"

Her arms tightened about him in a convulsive rebellion.

"Say nothing. Not a syllable. Whatever they ask you, say you don't know. The cops'll be here in a few minutes. But you don't know anything till I come back and say it's all right to talk. Savvy?"

He felt her head wag over his heart, faintly.

"What you two whisperin' about?" demanded the detective. He was on his feet again, the .22 swathed in his handkerchief.

"Is it all right to move now, Commissioner?" asked Beau. "I'm getting stiff standing still like this."

"Come here. Leggo the dame. Hold your hands up." Shrugging, Beau obeyed. Kerrie stumbled over to the armchair and fell into it. The hotel manager moved over quickly and shut the window beside her; he stood there looking down at her.

The house detective slapped Beau all over, grunted. "Okay. Stand over there and be a good boy."

He dropped to his knees beside Margo's body and put his ear to her chest. "I guess she's dead, Mr. O'Brien. You better 'phone Police Headquarters while I—"

The door to the hall slammed. Both men whirled. Beau was gone.

The detective cursed and leaped for the door, while the manager put his hands on Kerrie's shoulders and held her down with all his strength, as if he expected her to try to escape, too.

"Please," said Kerrie. "You're hurting me."

The manager looked abashed. He grabbed the telephone and shouted a description of Beau to the hotel operator. "Don't let that man get out of the hotel!"

Kerrie hugged herself. She felt cold and hungry.

Beau took the emergency stairway four steps at a stride, going up. They would expect him to go down.

He scaled his hat into a corner of the twentieth floor landing and slipped into the main corridor. No one in sight. He walked over to the nearest elevator and pressed the *Down* button. The operators coming down couldn't have heard the alarm.

An elevator stopped, and he got in. There were three passengers in the car, looking sleepy. The operator paid no attention to him.

He got off at the mezzanine floor.

From the balcony he could see the lobby seething. The house detective was down there yelling to a patrolman. The cop looked startled and ran out into the street.

Beau slipped into a telephone booth and dialed a number.

"Yes?" said a sleepy voice.

"Ellery! This is Beau."

"Well?" Mr. Queen's voice became alert.

"Can't talk. I'm at the *Villanoy*, with the whole hotel on my tail."

"Why? What's the trouble?"

"Murder—"

"Murder!"

"Margo's been shot to death."

"Margo?" Mr. Queen was speechless, but only for an instant. "But how did she— Who shot her?"

"Don't know." Tersely Beau recounted the story of the evening, and how he had found Kerrie, and what Kerrie had told him before they were interrupted by the manager and the detective.

Mr. Queen muttered: "Where's Kerrie now?"

"Upstairs in 1724. In a daze. El, you've got to come over."

"Of course."

"Nobody knows about that other room except you, Kerrie, me, and the killer. And I told Kerrie to keep

116

her mouth shut. We've got to search that room before the cops!"

"What's the number of the room?"

"It's just around the corner of 1724, in the transverse corridor. I think it's 1726. Can you get into the hotel without being collared?"

"I'll try."

"Step on it. I think they're searching the mezzanine now—"

"How are you and Kerrie registered?

"As Mr. and Mrs. Ellery Queen."

Mr. Queen the First groaned. "Do you realize that an old gent by the name of Queen is going to have to take charge of this homicide?"

"My God," said Beau. He hung up slowly.

After a moment he stepped out of the booth and strolled over to the marble railing, lighting a cigaret. The house detective and the partolman Beau had seen dart out of the lobby were hurrying from writing desk to writing desk, scanning the startled features of the correspondents. They were on the opposite side of the mezzanine. Beau sauntered towards them and said: "Can I be of service, gentlemen?"

The detective's heavy jaw dropped. He screeched. "That's him, Fogarty!" and the two men jumped on Beau.

He stiff-armed the policeman and caught the house man's gun-hand at the wrist. "Why the rough stuff? I gave myself up, didn't I?"

They looked baffled. A crowd had collected and Beau stood there grinning at them in an apologetic way.

"All right, wise guy," panted the detective, shaking his hand free. "What was the idea of lamming?"

"Who, me?" said Beau. "Come on, boys. We mustn't keep the lady waiting."

"Who're you? What's your name?"

"Queen. Ellery Queen. Want to make something of it?"

"Queen!" The policeman gaped at him. "Did you say Ellery Queen?"

"That's the ticket, Officer."

Fogarty looked awed. "Sam, you know who this is? Son of Inspector Queen of the Homicide Squad!"

"Mistakes will happen, boys," said Beau grandly. "And now, shall we return to the scene of the crime?"

"Inspector Queen's your old man?" demanded Sam.

"You heard Fogarty."

"Well, I don't give a damn," said Sam doggedly. "Fogarty, this is the guy was in 1724 with the dame when O'Brien and me busted in. She was holdin' the rod, but how do we know he ain't a, now, accomplice?"

"Inspector Queen will identify me," said Beau.

"Suppose he does? Suppose he does?" said the house detective hotly. "I don't care who you are, Mister; you were caught in that room—"

"What's the argument about?" asked Beau. "Sam, you're making a spectacle of yourself. Wow, look at those laws pour in! Come on upstairs before the press gives you the razz. Are you coming, or do I have to go up alone?"

"Don't worry," said Sam, taking a fresh grip on his .38. "I'm with you, baby."

They took a special elevator up to the seventeenth floor. Outside Room 1724 a policeman held back a crowd of pushing people. Inside, there were two radio-car officers and a detective from the West Forty-seventh Street precinct. They were all asking questions at the same time.

Kerrie was still seated in the armchair, in the same position.

"This him?" said the precinct man.

"Yeah," said Sam. "In person."

"Well, the girl gives him an out. She says he wasn't even here when the shots were fired. He came in right after."

"Kerrie," growled Beau. She had answered questions. He had told her not to.

She glanced at him in a calm, remote way.

"She admit givin' the other dame the business?" asked Sam eagerly.

"She don't admit nothin'."

Beau shook his head warningly at Kerrie. She placed her hands, palms up, in her lap and stared out the window.

"Lucky stiff," said Sam to Beau with a scowl.

"Yeah," said Beau, looking steadily at Kerrie's profile. "Am I lucky."

When the call came from Centre Street, Inspector Richard Queen was in Doc Prouty's office playing a hot game of two-handed *klabiatsch* with Sergeant Velie. He was waiting for the Medical Examiner's autopsy report on Hunk Carnucci, the nation-wide search for whom had ended that very evening at the bottom of the East River.

"*What?*" said the Inspector into the telephone; and

118

Sergeant Velie saw his superior's gray mustache quiver and his little bird-like face blanch. "Yes. Yes. All right. Now listen. No reporter gets into that room, see? Grab the registration card, too. I'll have your scalp if there's a leak. . . . Right away!"

He hung up, looking ill.

"What's the matter?" asked the Sergeant.

"Plenty." Inspector Queen rose. "A woman's been knocked off at the *Villanoy*."

The Sergeant looked puzzled. "So what?"

In the squad car, rushing towards Times Square with the siren screaming, the Inspector told him so what.

"I don't believe it," protested Velie. "It's a gag."

"They're registered as Mr. and Mrs. Ellery Queen, I tell you!" snarled the old man.

"But who's the dame? And the one that was shot?"

"I don't know. Nobody knows yet."

"When'd you see Ellery last?"

"This morning. He didn't say anything to me about his getting married. I thought he acted funny, though." The Inspector gnawed his mustache. "To do a thing like this to me! Step on her, will you?"

"Boy, the papers," groaned Velie.

"Maybe there's a chance to keep it quiet," said the old man feverishly. "Step on it, you baboon!"

The Sergeant looked at him pityingly.

At the *Villanoy* the Inspector shook off reporters, had the lobby cleared, listened to several reports, nodded to one of his squad, who was waving a registration card, and commandeered an elevator.

In the elevator he surreptitiously examined the fateful card. "Mr. and Mrs. Ellery Queen." His eyes narrowed even as he sighed with relief. The handwriting was not Ellery's. But it was almost as bad—it was Beau Rummell's.

"What's the bad news?" whispered Sergeant Velie.

"Stand by, Thomas," muttered the old man. "There's something queer going on. It's Beau Rummell, not Ellery; he's using Ellery's name."

"The nervy sprout!"

"We'll play along for a while. Pass the word along to the squad. No cracks about who Beau is."

The instant Inspector Queen entered 1724 Beau seized his hand. " 'Lo, Dad! How's the old man? I'll bet you never expected to find sonny-boy in a spot like this!" He winked.

119

The Inspector deliberately took a pinch of snuff. He glanced at the body, and then at Kerrie, and then at Beau.

"I'll bet I didn't," he said dryly, and turned to one of the precinct men. "All right, Lieutenant. Clear the room. Witnesses outside till I call." Then he took Beau by the arm and steered him into the bedroom.

"Thanks, Pop!" said Beau, grinning. "That was fast thinking. Thanks a million. Now look, I've got to scram out of here—"

"You do?" The Inspector eyed him coldly. "What's the idea of using Ellery's name and who's the brunette?"

"It's a long story. Too long to tell now. She's my wife—"

"Your *what!*" gasped the old man. "I thought that 'Mr. and Mrs.' business was—"

"With her? Say, we were married late this evening. There was a reason—I mean, why I couldn't use my own name."

"Ellery know?" snapped the old man.

"Yes."

He was silent.

"I've got to get out of here for a half-hour, Pop!"

"Where do you think you're going?"

"I won't leave the hotel."

"Beau." The Inspector looked him in the eye. "Did you have anything to do with that woman's murder in there?"

Beau looked back and said simply: "No, Pop."

"Did your wife?"

"No."

"How d'ye know?" asked the old man in a flash. "I'm told you walked in on her after the murder—your wife said so herself."

"I can't tell you how I know," muttered Beau. "For Pete's sake, Pop, let me go now, will you? It's important!"

"I'm a fool," snarled the Inspector.

"Pop, you're a prince!"

Beau strolled back into the sitting room, which was cleared except for the Inspector's squad. He sauntered over to Kerrie and whispered into her ear: "I've got to go now, kid, for a little while. Remember what I said. Don't talk. Not a word. Not even to—my old man."

"What?" Her eyes were swimming in tears. "I mean . . ."

Beau swallowed. She looked so helpless he felt like jumping through the window. He had to do something! Get into that room from which the shots had come.

After that . . . improvise. Keep going. It was toughest on her.

"I'll be back soon."

He kissed her and went out.

With him went the *Do Not Disturb* placard which had been hanging by its chain on the inside of the sitting room door. He thrust is casually into his pocket.

Outside, a group of hotel employees and police looked at him curiously. Detective Flint, at the door, said it was all right. He went to the elevator and rang the *Down* bell. An elevator stopped. He got in and said: "Sixteen."

He got out on the sixteenth floor and bounded up the steps of the emergency stairway to the seventeenth floor. The exit gave on a different corridor. He stole out. Clear sailing.

He made his way on tiptoe to Room 1726. Around the corner he could hear the group before 1724 talking excitedly.

Beau set his ear to the door of 1726. Then he slipped the *Do Not Disturb* sign over the knob and tried the door noiselessly. It gave. He pushed the door in quickly and softly, stepped inside, and closed the door again, careful to make no sound.

When the door was shut he turned the catch sidewise, locking the door from the inside.

Only then did he heave a sigh and turn round.

He crouched.

Some one was smoking a cigaret in the darkness of the room.

The murderer!

He rasped: "Don't move. I've got you covered!"

"Really?" drawled Mr. Queen from behind the glowing tip of the cigaret. "Bluffer."

XIII

Mr. Queen and Mr. Queen
in Room 1726

"NERVES," SAID MR. QUEEN. "FROM WHICH I GATHER you've been having a rough time of it."

121

"Damn you," said Beau. "How'd *you* get in?"

"As you see, in one piece. Oh, you don't. Then let's have some light. We both seem to need a lot of that." Mr. Queen groped, found the light-switch, and snapped it on.

They blinked at each other, and then about the room.

"Don't worry," said Mr. Queen, noting the object of his partner's scrutiny. "I shut the window at once, and of course the blind was drawn when I got here."

"Prints?"

"I'm wearing gloves. As for you, don't touch anything. When we're through, there's still the law."

"You'd never know it," grunted Beau. "Maybe with the light on, though—it's only a few feet across the angle of the court to the window of the sitting room there—"

"No danger," said Mr. Queen cheerfully. "This room is reserved, did you know that?"

Beau stared.

"Oh, you didn't. Well, it is."

"How d'ye know?"

"I asked."

"You mean you just walked into the hotel—"

"Certainly. Always carry a badge or two. Detective What-You-Call-It, of H.Q.—at your service. I got in all right, and even made a few 'official' inquiries at the desk. Beat all around the mulberry bush to find out what I wanted to know without tipping my hand. At any rate, some one reserved Room 1726—"

"Man or woman?"

"No information. Reserved this room at about a quarter to nine this evening."

"A quarter to nine? Why, Kerrie and I only checked in around half-past eight!"

Mr. Queen frowned. "That's fast work. Followed you, do you suppose?"

"I don't see how it's possible. El, there's been a leak!"

"Who knew you were coming to the *Villanoy?*"

"Only Margo. You know how I pretended to cook up that scheme with her. She fell for it, but insisted on knowing just where I was going, because she wanted to make sure I didn't doublecross her. She even made me promise I wouldn't spend the night with Kerrie—jealous as hell. Only Margo knew—so she's the one who talked."

"To whom?"

"To the same one she gave Kerrie's gun to! How was the reservation made?"

"By wire, in an obviously false name—L. L. Howard. Of course, 'Howard' didn't show up to claim the room —officially. Simply made sure the room would be unoccupied by reserving it, then let himself in with a skeleton key, I suppose, the way I did. How's Kerrie?"

"Never mind," said Beau miserably. "Let's go."

"You're sure she didn't bop Margo herself?"

"I told you what she told me! Don't badger me. If we find evidence that some one was in this room, it's a confirmation of her story, isn't it?"

"It won't mean much legally. Not a terribly inspiring room, is it?"

It was an ordinary single room-and-bath, with a bed, a dresser, two chairs, and a writing-table. The bed was prepared for the night, its spread neatly folded at the foot, and blankets turned down at one corner; but the pillows were plump and unwrinkled and the blankets smooth.

"Those ashes—" began Beau, pointing to the rug.

"Mine," said Mr. Queen. "Also that butt in the tray on the desk. The other trays are clean, I see. Well, let's begin with the bathroom. Look, but don't touch."

They went to work in silence. The bathroom was speckless—fresh towels laid out, clean bath-mat, paper-wrapped soap, shower-curtain, wash-rag. Nothing in the medicine chest. Nothing in the hamper. The washbowl was dry.

"That's one," said Mr. Queen, and they went back into the bedroom.

"Closet's as clean as the bathroom," announced Beau. "Not a sign. How you doin'?"

Mr. Queen crawled out from under the bed, "Remarkaby efficient cleaning women in this hotel! Beau, start at the door and work towards the window. I'll start at the window and work towards the door."

"What on?"

"The rug."

They crept towards each other in a weaving route— from one side of the room to the other. When they met in the middle of the room they glanced at each other and then rose.

"This," remarked Mr. Queen, looking about, "is going to be tough."

He went through the writing-desk and the dresser, not because he hoped but because he was thorough.

"That's that," he said. "Beau, what have we missed?"

"The window? Shade?"

"I went over them while you were in the closet. The only evidence that might be there is fingerprints, and while I can't be sure, I've a feeling friend 'Howard' wore gloves."

"But there must be something," scowled Beau. "This guy was in here at least an hour, maybe more. You just can't occupy a room for that length of time without leaving some trace of yourself."

" 'Howard' seems to have done it, though."

"Well, let's go. It's a washout." Beau turned disconsolately to the door.

"Wait, Beau. My fault!" Mr. Queen whirled.

"What's your fault?"

"I overlooked something on this side of the room."

"What?"

"The radiator."

Beau joined him at the window. The cold steamradiator stood directly beneath the sill.

Mr. Queen stooped over the coils, trying to peer between them. Then he lay down on the rug, twisting so that he might see clearly the narrow patch of rug just beneath the coils.

He stiffened. "Here's something!"

"Hallelujah! Fish it out, Brother Queen!"

Mr. Queen reached in and, after a moment, delicately, between gloved thumb and gloved forefinger, drew out a longish slender object which tapered to a point.

It was black and made of a hard rubber composition. An automatic pencil. The gold clip was loose.

"Simple enough to reconstruct what happened," observed Mr. Queen after examination. "Whoever fired those shots at Margo Cole had to shoot through this window. So he was standing at the window—perhaps for a long time, watching from behind the drawn shade in the dark. At some point during that vigil, he stooped; and, the clip being loose, the pencil dropped from his pocket.

"By a miracle it missed both the sill and the radiator, falling through the space between them to the rug without making a sound. And it rolled several inches under the radiator. He had no reason to use a pencil, consequently he left without discovering his loss. Very considerate of him."

"That's all true the way you say it," argued Beau. "But suppose it was dropped by some one who occupied this room yesterday, or last week, or last year?"

"Improbable. The room was prepared for occupancy late this evening, after the wired reservation. We know that, because the bed's made up for the night. That means a maid cleaned up in here later than 8:45 tonight. And a maid who left not a speck of dust under a bed would scarcely have overlooked a pencil under a radiator. No, Beau, this pencil was dropped by 'Howard,' whoever *he* is.

"Not much of a clue," growled Beau. "Just a plain, ordinary, garden variety of automatic pencil. He might just as well have dropped nothing."

"Well, now, I don't know," murmured Mr. Queen. "Doesn't anything about this pencil strike you as familiar?"

Beau stared at it. "Not guilty."

"You've never seen one like it before?"

"I've seen thousands like it before," retorted Beau. "That's just the trouble."

"No, no, not a pencil. Don't you recall another writing implement of hard black rubber composition, with a gold clip?"

"Cole's fountain-pen?" Beau laughed shortly. "That's quite a deduction. Are you trying to tell me that, just because Cole's pen was hard black rubber stuff and had a gold clip, this pencil was part of Cole's pen-and-pencil set?"

"I'm trying to tell you exactly that," said Mr. Queen, "but not for the reason you give, although the similarity of construction and appearance are striking. Where are your eyes?"

He held the pencil up. Beau looked it over without touching it—from its leaded point, where Ellery was gripping it, up it's body to the eraser-cap.

And just below the cap he saw something that made him exclaim. The hard rubber was considerably scratched and dented in a sort of arced pattern; some of the nicks were deep.

"Those nicks looks like the ones in Cole's pen. . . . But that's impossible!"

"Disregarding philosophical considerations," said Mr. Queen with a certain excitement, "I think we may prove or disprove the theory by completely material means."

125

He laid the pencil carefully down on the rug between them and produced his wallet. From an inner pocket of the wallet he extracted a series of tiny squares of film.

"The microphotographs of the nicks in Cole's pen I asked you to take," he explained.

"But I thought they were in the office."

"Too valuable to be left lying about. I've been carrying them in my wallet ever since." Mr. Queen compared the photographs with the pencil on the rug. Then he handed the films to Beau.

When Beau looked up there was an expression of incredulity in his eyes. "The same!"

"Yes, the marks on this pencil and the marks on Cole's pen were created by the same agency. Consequently this pencil *is* a companion of Cole's pen."

"Cole's pencil," mumbled. Beau. *"Cole's."*

"Without a doubt."

Beau got to his feet. Mr. Queen squatted on his hams Buddha-like, musing over the photographs and the pencil.

"But it can't be," Beau said.

"There's the evidence."

"But—Cole's been dead for nearly three months! Unless the pencil's been lying here—"

"I explained before," replied Mr. Queen with a trace of impatience, "why that's probably not so. But if you insist on confirmation, run your hand over the rug and patch of flooring under the radiator and between the radiator and wall. You'll find it completely free of dust. Indicating that the rug and floor have been cleaned very recently. No, this pencil was dropped tonight by the person who shot Margo Cole."

"By Cole, I suppose?" Beau laughed shortly. "You'll be asking me to believe in the boogey man next!"

"There are other possibilities," murmured Mr. Queen. "But if you insist on being argumentative—why not by Cole?"

"What?" cried Beau.

"Well, why not?" Mr. Queen stared at his partner impassively. *"What proof have we that Cole is dead?"*

Beau looked groggy. "It's beyond me. Cole not dead?"

"I'm not asserting a fact, I'm posing a question. We have only one person's word for the alleged fact that Cole died—Edmund De Carlos's. Captain Angus, the crew—every one who could possibly substantiate De

Carlos's story is gone. No body was produced—'buried at sea,' wasn't the report?"

"But . . ."

"Is the reason Cole hired us three months ago beginning to emerge? Has Cole been hanging around all this time under the cloak of the perfect disguise—death and burial?"

"It's true," muttered Beau, "that we wouldn't know him even if he were alive—no, that's not true. We did see him. In our office. So that doesn't wash. Then that would mean he's hiding out somewhere. But why?"

"I can think of at least two reasons," replied Mr. Queen, "either of which is perfectly sensible and makes the theory very attractive—very."

"You mean you think Cole's behind the whole business—the attacks on Kerrie, the murder of Margo? Then why did he hire us in the first place? Or, if he's alive, where do the heirs fit in? Heirs can't inherit from a living man; if they do, if that's what he planned . . ." Beau shouted: "I'm going nuts!"

Mr. Queen said nothing.

"Wait! We're both crazy. Of course there's the simplest explanation! Cole *is* dead. This *is* his pencil, all right, but somebody else got hold of it and has been using it. Whoever that was is our man. Phew! For a few minutes there you had me going."

Mr. Queen still said nothing. He wrapped the pencil in his breast-pocket handkerchief and tucked it away. Then he rose.

"Here! What are you doing?" demanded Beau. "Hand over that pencil."

"I think not," said Mr. Queen, buttoning his coat.

"But it's our only evidence that someone was in this room. We've got to give it to your old man, Ellery."

"We shan't even tell him about it yet."

"But—for the love of Pete, why not?"

"The trail's a little too involved for the regular police mind," said Mr. Queen egotistically. "Acute as Dad is. And we're not destroying evidence—we're merely suppressing it temporarily. By itself it means little; we've got to make it mean more. And handing it over to the police means inevitably publication of its discovery. We can't afford to warn off our man before all the cards are in our hands."

"But—Kerrie!" stormed Beau. "Where's the poor kid

127

come in? At least that pencil establishes that some one was in this room tonight. To that extent it bolsters her story of the shots having come from this window."

Mr. Queen looked grave. "If I really thought the pencil would clear her, Beau, I'd tell Dad myself. But it won't, and you know it won't. She's in a tight spot; the circumstances under which she was found are so damning by contrast with the tenuous reasoning from the pencil that she's bound to be held. Let her tell her story by all means, truthfully; exactly as it happened. Dad will examine this room and find"—he grinned—"a burnt match-stick and the ashes and butt of my cigaret. That's even better evidence than the pencil that the room was occupied tonight—the maid would certainly have removed *those* if they'd been present when she cleaned up."

"You mean we don't even tell him we've been in here?"

"He'll probably guess it," said Mr. Queen comfortably. "And then there's the light in here. But he can't prove it's my butt if we don't talk, can he?"

Beau stared at him. "You'd doublecross yourself, I swear, if you thought some good would come of it!"

"Dad and I have been on opposite sides of the fence before," said Mr. Queen in a thoughtful way, "although I will admit this business tonight is in the nature of a dirty trick."

"My God! He's actually got a conscience!"

"So long, Beau. Let me know in the morning exactly what happened."

XIV

Inspector Queen Inspects

WHEN BEAU STEPPED PAST THE DETECTIVES ON GUARD IN 1724 he found Kerrie gone from the sitting room and the door to the bedroom shut.

Inspector Queen was alone. He was seated in the armchair by the window, a sheaf of reports before him. The débris of flash-bulbs cluttered the floor.

The body of Margo Cole was gone.

"Where's Kerrie?" asked Beau, alarmed.

The Inspector looked at him. "Why don't you stick around and find out?"

"Where is she?"

"In the bedroom in charge of the hotel doctor and a nurse. And one of my men. And a friend of hers, a Violet Day."

Beau blinked. "Vi! How did she get here?"

"Your wife kept calling for her, told us where Miss Day was stopping . . . No, don't go in yet. I want to have a talk with you."

"But if Kerrie's sick . . . Let me see her for a minute!"

"She isn't sick; she just fainted. She's all right now."

Beau was silent. Then he said: "Did she talk?"

"You told her not to," said the old man dryly, "so she didn't. She must like you a lot, Beau, because she's in one big kettle of fish."

"She's in no spot she can't explain! Do you know who she is?"

"Sure. Kerrie Shawn. And the dead woman was her cousin, Margo Cole."

Beau sat down suddenly. "Look, Pop. Let's not spar around. What have you got?"

The Inspector sneezed over a pinch of snuff, and then regarded Beau unwinkingly. "Your wife's own admission establishes the fact that you weren't here when the Cole woman arrived. In fact, that you didn't get here till after the shooting. That lets you out for the record.

"Your wife was the only one in this room with Margo Cole—unless," said the Inspector, "she can produce a third person. Point number one."

"She can produce me," said Beau quickly. "I tell you I was here. She said I wasn't because she didn't want to involve me."

"Nothing doing. I've got a witness who saw you leave the hotel, Beau, and one who saw you come back. I know the exact times you went and returned. You couldn't have been in this room when it happened. The elevator boy who landed you on the seventeenth floor says he heard the shots just as you stepped out of his elevator."

"I tell you—"

"No, not you, Beau," said the old man patiently. "Somebody else—if there was somebody else. But I'm pretty sure there wasn't."

"There was!"

"Who?"

"Beau looked down. "I don't know—yet."

"I see." Inspector Queen paused. "Well, let's go on. Point number two: The house dick and O'Brien, manager of the hotel, both saw your wife holding the revolver which shot Margo Cole—holding it over the dead body. The house man says the barrel was still warm when he wrapped the gun in his handkerchief. Doc Prouty, who's been here and gone, dug one of the three bullets out of the body. The slug came from a .22. The revolver your wife was holding is a .22. I'm having comparison tests made downtown right now, but I'm pretty sure without the report that those slugs came from the same weapon."

"There were three bullets fired from the .22?"

"Yes. And, of course, your wife's fingerprints are on it, too. *And no others.* That's point number three." The Inspector waited, but when Beau said nothing he went on. "Four: A quick check-up with the pistol-permit records has established that the .22 *belongs to your wife.*"

"But it was stolen from her," protested Beau.

"Exactly when? Under what circumstances?"

Beau drooped. "Never mind. We can't prove when or where. She only missed it yesterday."

"Why didn't she report the theft?"

"She hasn't had time! She missed it yesterday, I tell you."

The Inspector shook his head. "Thin, Beau. The picture looks—well, good. Her weapon, sole opportunity, caught red-handed a matter of minutes after the shooting, caught over the body with the proved weapon in her hand. . . . The only thing we've got to fill in is motive."

"Yeah, motive," exclaimed Beau. "You say Kerrie killed Margo. Why should she?"

"That's what I asked De Carlos."

Beau sprang to his feet. "You talked to that— Where is he? What did *he* have to say, the hairy ape?"

"I notified De Carlos and Goossens by telephone of the murder; they'll both be here soon. I asked De Carlos about a possible motive, and he was very helpful."

"I'll bet," growled Beau. "What did he say, damn him?"

"Oh, you don't like him? Why, several things. He said if you and Kerrie Shawn hadn't run off to be married tonight, he could think of a dandy motive. At Margo's death

130

Kerrie would inherit the dead woman's share of the income from the Cole estate, you see."

Beau nodded gloomily.

"But, of course," continued the Inspector, "he explained—and Goossens confirmed it when I asked him later—that Kerrie's marriage automatically cut her out of all participation in the estate—her own share as well as Margo's. So that motive's out."

"So what are you battin' about?" grumbled Beau.

"But he mentioned something," drawled the old man, "about some 'accidents' to your wife in the past few weeks which didn't quite come off—a horse that threw her and almost broke her neck, that little business in the garage last night. . . ."

"What? What's that? What about it?"

"And then I had a little chat with Miss Day a few minutes ago," replied the Inspector mildly. "And she told me they weren't accidents—something about nails having been loosened in the horse's foreshoe, and the locking in of your wife in that garage having been deliberate, and something about some one having climbed into Miss Shawn's bedroom not long ago during the night for a little exercise with a knife—"

"That blabbermouth," said Beau hoarsely.

"And Miss Day also said it was both her opinion and Kerrie's that all those 'accidents' had been staged by Margo Cole."

Beau sat down again. "I don't get you." Then he rose.

"No? Then I'll explain it to you." The Inspector leaned back. "If your wife thought Margo Cole was trying to kill her—whether Margo Cole was or not, mind you!—then wouldn't it be natural for your wife to buy a gun—as she did—and wouldn't it be natural for her to shoot Margo Cole when Margo showed up in this room tonight and the two of them were alone? Yes, sir, that sounds like a motive to me."

It's an out, thought Beau desperately; a possible out. "Even if that's so," he shouted, "it's self-defense, isn't it?"

"My job is to get the facts. It's the D.A.'s job to put them together." The old man eyed Beau. "By the way, don't you think it's time you hired a good criminal lawyer?"

Beau began to race around the room.

"It's as strong a circumstantial case as I've ever seen, Beau," said the Inspector soberly.

"You've got it all wrong, I tell you. When you hear Kerrie's story, you'll see!"

"It will have to be more than a story, I'm afraid." The Inspector rose. "Beau, you know how friendly your father and I were. And I've always looked on you as a sort of second son. Why don't you tell me what you know, so I can help you?"

"I don't know anything about it," snapped Beau. "Nor does Kerrie!"

"There's something else behind this. Where did you go a while back? What were you looking for? Who'd you see? Beau, you can trust me—"

Beau was silent.

"You're putting me in a rotten spot," said the Inspector gently. "You registered here in Ellery's name and, even granting it was with El's permission, that drags in a lot of personal considerations. I may even have to step out of the case because you did that. I've suppressed facts myself tonight. I've taken possession of the registration card and threatened all sorts of extra-legal punishments to those in the hotel who know the name you registered under. The newspaper boys are still in the dark about that. But they won't be for long. At least tell me why you used my son's name, so I'll be prepared with an explanation."

"Pop, I can't," said Beau hoarsely. "Pop . . . did you tell Kerrie?"

"Your wife?" The Inspector's eyes narrowed. "Do you mean to stand there and tell me your own wife doesn't know who you are?"

"She thinks I'm Ellery Queen," confessed Beau. "Ellery knows about it. In fact, it was his idea."

Inspector Queen stared at him; then, shaking his head, he went to the bedroom door.

Kerrie lay on one of the twin beds holding on to Violet Day's hand. A nurse and a doctor stood by. There was a pungent odor of ammonium carbonate in the air. Leaning against the wall was Sergeant Velie.

Kerrie was the first to move. Her head swivelled, froze. But a moment later she sat up eagerly.

"Darling, you were so long." She sounded tired.

Beau started for the bed, but the Inspector touched his arm. "No."

Kerrie remained in a sitting position.

132

"Doc, would you mind waiting in the next room?" said the Inspector. "You, too, Nurse."

They left the bedroom, Sergeant Velie carefully closing the door behind them.

"Well, I'm waiting," said Inspector Queen.

Kerrie moistened her dry lips.

"It's all right, Kerrie," said Beau in a low voice. "It's all right to talk now. Tell just what happened."

Her glance was grateful. Vi took her hand again. Inspector Queen nodded to the Sergeant, who took a notebook and pencil out and prepared to write.

Kerrie told simply of the attempts to murder her, her suspicions of Margo, her purchase of the revolver, her discovery in the garage when she was trapped that the revolver had been stolen from the pocket of her roadster. She told of Beau's proposal, and of their elopement.

"One moment." The Inspector glanced at Beau.

"You thought the Cole woman was behind these attacks, too?"

"I know she was."

"How do you know?"

"She told me so."

"What!" The Inspector was incredulous.

"I made love to her," said Beau flatly. "I pretended to be on her side . . . for a price. I told her I was going to marry Kerrie, so that Kerrie's share of the estate would be lost and would revert to Margo. We made a deal in which Margo was to kick back a certain part of Kerrie's share to me."

"Why?" demanded the old man. "Why'd you do this?"

"Because my chief concern was to save Kerrie's life. Margo hated her, because of me and because of the money. If I could put the dough in her hands and convince her I loved her, not Kerrie, Kerrie's life would be safe."

Kerrie's eyes were on his lips.

"The only thing I didn't know," continued Beau, "was that Margo was working with some one else. Go on, Kerrie."

Kerrie went on. She told about their arrival at the *Villanoy*, how Beau left her, and how Margo came.

"I was sitting in the armchair by the window and she came over and stood behind me, still gloating over the trick she said she and Ellery"—the Inspector winced—"had played on me. Somehow she got round to talking about the attacks on my life—"

"Yes? What did she say, exactly?"

"As far as I remember, she said Ellery saved my life by marrying me. 'If you hadn't been lucky,' she said, 'you'd have been dead long before now.' And she went on to say that the visit to my room that night, the accident to my horse, my being locked in the garage and nearly gassed, were not accidents at all. When I said I suspected all along she was responsible, she laughed and said: 'But it wasn't only I who planned those attacks. It was I—and somebody else.' And just as she was about to tell me who the other one was—the shots . . ."

She stopped, her chin quivering.

"Ah, the shots," said the Inspector politely. "But I thought you two were alone in the sitting room."

"We were," she said in a faint voice. "The shots came across the court, through my window, over my head, striking Margo who was standing behind my chair. That other window, my window, I, Margo, were all in one straight line."

The Inspector glanced pityingly at Beau. But Beau was lighting a cigaret with shaking hands.

"Suppose you show me just how it happened," the old man sighed.

Beau jumped forward to help Kerrie off the bed. Her fingers coiled tightly in his. The Inspector looked away, and Sergeant Velie opened the door for them. They all went into the sitting room.

Inspector Queen spent some time over Kerrie's story. He had her sit in the armchair as she claimed to have sat at the moment of the shooting. He checked the position of the body. He made Kerrie retell her story four times.

"A hand threw the gun in through my window, I tell you!" moaned Kerrie. "Why won't you believe me?"

"But you don't seem to know whether the hand was a man's or a woman's."

"I was in the light, and the court and that room there were in darkenss. I could hardly see. But I made out the flash of a hand. How could I tell whether it was a man's or woman's?"

The Inspector grunted. The doctor gave him a warning look and insisted on Kerrie's returning to the bedroom to lie down again. The old man nodded and, glancing at Sergeant Velie, who winked, went outside without explanation.

But Beau knew he had gone to examine Room 1726. He went back into the bedroom with Kerrie and sat down on the bed, and she curled up in his arms and closed her eyes. Neither said anything.

Lloyd Goossens arrived shortly after the Inspector went out, and considerably later, Edmund De Carlos marched in.

Goossens was smoking his pipe with nervous embarrassment, rubbing his unshaven cheeks; he had apparently been roused from his bed by the Inspector's summons. De Carlos's skin was leaden, his beard gaunt. But there was a queer sparkle in the wide eyes behind his spectacles. The Sergeant kept them in the sitting room, where they occupied themselves chiefly in endeavoring to avoid the blood-stained spot on the rug as they paced in aimless circles.

Beau came out of the bedroom and the two men bombarded him with questions. He told them what had happened and then took Goossens aside, to De Carlos's annoyance. "What do you think?"

Goossens shook his head. "It looks bad, Mr. Queen. A hard story to believe. Especially without evidence to confirm it. If I were you, I'd engage the best lawyer in New York. In fact, if you'd like me to suggest counsel for Mrs. Queen—"

"Thanks. Don't you think it's a bit premature?" said Beau curtly.

When the Inspector returned, he conferred with De Carlos and the lawyer for some time in the sitting room. Finally they all went into the bedroom.

It was a bad moment, De Carlos and Goossens hanging back, avoiding Kerrie's staring eyes. But the Inspector was brisk.

"I'll be frank with you," he said to Kerrie and Beau. "There's no evidence of 1726 having been occupied tonight except a cigaret butt, a burnt match-stick, and some ashes. The maid on duty says she prepared the room late this evening, and there's a record of a wired reservation. But the maid isn't sure she mightn't have overlooked the cigaret, and there's a clear record that no one showed up tonight to occupy the room. "Beau."

"Well?"

"There was a light in 1726 this evening. Is that where you went? Is that your cigaret butt in there?"

Beau said: "Who, me?"

The Inspector shrugged. "Anyway, the evidence doesn't begin to bolster the story."

"But it's true," said Kerrie slowly. "I tell you—"

Beau shook his head at her.

The Inspector stroked his mustache with an agitated forefinger. "I'll have to hold you," he said.

XV

The De Carlos Entente

WHEN THE INSPECTOR HAD LEFT, HURRIEDLY AND WITH a murderous glance at Beau, Goossens coughed and said: "Mrs. Queen, as—as co-executor of the Cole estate it's my duty to inform you that your marriage today eliminates you from further participation in the income from your uncle's estate. There are certain matters, papers . . . If there's anything I can do in the way of legal advice, of course . . . Dreadfully sorry . . ."

He left, like the Inspector, in a sort of flight.

Kerrie was sobbing on Beau's shoulder, and Vi was tearing a handkerchief methodically to pieces by the window.

"What are you hanging around for, pop-eyes?" demanded Beau, eying De Carlos with angry dislike.

De Carlos smiled nervously. "I'd like—I'd like to speak to you alone, Mr. Queen."

"Scram."

"I must. It's a private matter—"

"It'll have to wait. Beat it, will you?"

De Carlos said in a soft voice: "But it's quite urgent."

Beau glared at him. The man made a weird picture with his brushlike hair, his beard, his glittering teeth and spectacles, a certain air of mingled intentness, triumph, and anxiety.

"Meet you in my office in Times Square in half an hour," said Beau on impulse. "I'll leave word with the night man to let you in."

"Thank you." De Carlos bowed to Kerrie, smiling or seeming to smile in his beard, and scurried out.

"Ellery. Don't go," said Kerrie tiredly. Her arms were dead weights about his neck.

"I've got to, funny-face." Beau signalled to Vi over Kerrie's head. "Vi won't leave you. Will you, Vi?"

"What do you think I am? Of course not!" said Vi with an attempt at cheerfulness. "I don't like the dump I'm in, anyway."

"You get the doc to give you a shot of something," Beau told Kerrie gently. "You need a pocketful of sleep."

She hung on to him, whimpering.

"Kerrie. You know I love you, don't you?" She hugged him. "You don't believe a single word of what—she told you tonight, do you?" Kerrie shook her head violently. "You know I'm in there batting for you a thousand per-cent, don't you?" She nodded, empty of words. "Then leave everything to me, and don't worry."

He kissed her and rose. Kerrie twisted her body on the bed and buried her face in the pillow. Beau cracked his knuckles in a sort of baffled agony. Then he kissed her again and ran out.

Beau stopped on the sidewalk outside the hotel to cup his hands around a cigaret.

He glanced swiftly about. The street was deserted. An occasional cab cruised by. By his wristwatch it was almost four o'clock. He tossed the match away and began to walk briskly towards Broadway. The night air had a chilly touch; he turned the collar of his jacket up.

He slipped into an all-night drug store, went into a phone booth, shut the door tightly, and called Mr. Ellery Queen's home telephone number.

Ellery answered almost at once.

"It's Beau. Weren't you in bed?"

"I've been thinking. What's up?"

Plenty. Listen, El, De Carlos showed up at the *Villanoy* and says he's got to have a private chin with me. I played a hunch and told him to meet me at the office right away. You want to sit in?"

"Oh, yes, indeed," said Mr. Queen with a certain grimness. "Any idea what's stirring?"

"No. Grab a cab and get down here fast as you can."

"I'll be there in time. How's Kerrie?"

Beau hung up.

He strode to Times Square, crossed the street, pounded on the door of his office-building.

A yawning watchman admitted him. "Hey, Joe. I

137

expect a man by the name of De Carlos to blow in soon. Let him in. He'll ask for Mr. Queen. Take him up to our office."

"Sure thing, Mr. Rummell. Say, don't you ever sleep?"

"Don't answer any questions. Get me?"

"Yes, sir."

Beau let himself into the Queen office, switched on the lights, threw open the windows, and took a bottle from a desk-drawer.

Ten minutes later there was a knock at the reception-room door. He put the bottle down and went out.

The knocker was De Carlos, alone.

"Come in," said Beau. He locked the door. "You're early. I've telephoned my partner to come down; he'll be here soon."

"Your partner?" De Carlos did not look pleased.

"Yes. Uh—guy by the name of Beau Brummell—I mean, Rummell. We're like that." Beau rubbed his eyes and led the way to the inner office. "Have a snifter."

"But I wanted to speak to you privately."

"No secrets between Beau and me," growled Beau. He waved towards the bottle as he lit a cigaret. De Carlos licked his red lips, looking about for a glass. There was none in sight, and Beau did not offer one. De Carlos tilted the bottle. Beau watched him cynically. The man drank and drank. When he set the bottle down his gray cheek-bones had turned pink.

He smacked his lips and said: "Now—"

"*Not* now," said Beau. "Have another."

De Carlos waved gaily. "Don't mind if I do."

He picked up the bottle again.

De Carlos was drunk when Mr. Queen unlocked the front door and entered the inner office.

The bearded man lay sprawled in the "client's chair," waving the bottle and leering glassy-eyed at Beau.

"Ah, the pardner," said De Carlos, trying to rise. He fell back in the chair. " 'Do, Mis'er Rummell. Lovely night. I mean sad. So sad. Have seat, Mis'er Rummell."

Ellery glanced at Beau, who winked. "This is Mr. Edmund De Carlos, Rummell," said Beau to Ellery in a voice loud enough to pierce the clouds of alcohol on Mr. De Carlos's brain. "One of the trustees of the Cole estate, you know."

"Siddown, Mis'er Rummell," said Mr. De Carlos cordially, waving the bottle. "Pleasure, 'm sure. Siddown!"

Ellery sat down behind the desk. "I understand you've something important to say to us, Mr. De Carlos."

De Carlos leaned forward confidentially. "Impor'nt an' worth money, Mis'er Rummell. Pots o' money, y' un'erstan'."

"Go on, spill," said Beau.

"We're frien's. We're all frien's here. An' we're men of the worl', hey?" De Carlos giggled. "Know what it's all about. Now I know de—de-tec-tive a'ncies, gen'l'men, an' I know de-tec-tives. Bought—can all be bought. Jus' a madder o' price, I say, Jus' a madder o' price . . . tha'sh all."

"Do I understand that you want to engage us to investigate a case for you, Mr. De Carlos?" asked Ellery.

De Carlos stared at him owlishly, then burst into laughter. "Very good, Mis'er Rummell. I wanna 'ngage you *not* to inveshtigate a cashe!"

Beau and Ellery exchanged glances. Then Beau said: "You want what?"

De Carlos grew immediately serious. "Now look, Mis'er Queen. Le's shpread cardsh on table, huh? I know you married li'l Kerrie tonight 'caush you wash in a deal wi' Margo. You marry Kerrie, she loshes income from eshtate, Margo gets it, you share with Margo—nishe work, Mis'er Queen, nishe work. But wha' happensh? Your wife goesh and shpoilsh it all. Putsh three bulletsh in Margo. Woof! Margo'sh dead." He wagged his head solemnly. "An' then where are you, Mis'er Queen? Holdin' the bag, Mis'er Queen, hey?"

"You can that kind of talk," said Beau in a hard voice. "You might get hurt. You heard the story!"

"Nishe shtory, Mis'er Queen," leered De Carlos, "but it won't go. No, shir, it'sh fan—fantastic. Sure she killed Margo—she'sh guilty ash hell, Mis'er Queen. Whadda you care, anywaysh? Tha'sh not the point. Tha'sh—"

Beau spanned the space between him and De Carlos in a split second. He grabbed De Carlos by the throat.

Ellery said: "Hold it, Brains," and Beau relaxed his grip sheepishly. De Carlos stared up at him, frightened.

"No sense in going off half-cocked," said Ellery smoothly. "You'll have to excuse my partner, Mr. De Carlos. He's had a trying night."

"Got no call shtrangling people," muttered De Carlos, feeling his Adam's-apple.

"You were about to say?"

139

De Carlos struggled out of the chair, eying Beau warily. "You gen'l'men been jockeyed out of a lot o' money by Kerrie—by shome one killing Margo." He shook his forefinger at Ellery. " 'S a shame, I shay. Y'oughta be recom—recompenshed, I shay. An' Edmund De Carlos's the man to do it! Good frien's huh? I make it up to you, huh?"

"Huh," said Beau. "The piece of cheese. And we're the rats. I didn't get it, and I still don't. What's the gag, Blackbeard?"

"No gag, gen'l'men! Oh, coursh if I do somethin' for you, you gotta do somethin' for me. Tha'sh on'y fair, hey?" He peered anxiously at them. "Hey?"

"Hey, hey," said Ellery, with a warning glance at Beau. "I should say. Now, as I understand it, you're worried over our loss in the Margo deal, and you'd like to make it up to us financially. In return for your little contribution to our agency account you want *us* to do something for you in return. And what might that be, Mr. De Carlos?"

De Carlos beamed. " 'S a pleasure to do bushiness with you, Mis'er Rummell. Why, you gotta do nothin', shee. Tha'sh what I shaid before. I'm payin' you *not* to inveshtigate a cashe! You shtep out. 'Way, way out. You forget you ever heard of Cadmush Cole, or the Cole eshtate, or —or anything. Shee what I mean?"

Beau growled deep in his throat, but Ellery rose quickly and came forward to step between the two men. He kicked Beau's shin not gently with his left heel and took De Carlos's arm.

"I think we understand, Mr. De Carlos," he said with a leer to match their visitor's. "You feel we've been snooping about a bit too freely, and you'd breathe more easily if we directed our agency energies elsewhere. How much did you say our stepping out was worth to you?"

"I didn't shay." De Carlos peered up at him with a bleary shrewdness. "Shall we shay—ten thoushand dollars?"

"Come, come, Mr. De Carlos. We'd have made a good deal more than that in the Margo Cole deal."

"De Carlos boy'sh bein' held up, held up," De Carlos grunted. "Now don' hol' me up up, gen'l'men. Fifteen."

"Now you're bruising my feelings, Mr. De Carlos."

"Aw ri'," grumbled De Carlos, "shall we shay twen'y thoushand?"

"Shall we rather say twenty-five, Mr. De Carlos?"

De Carlos muttered to himself. Finally he growled: " 'S a deal. Twen'y-fi' thousand. Robbersh!"

"Just business," Ellery assured him. "Now how is this little payment to be made? Cash, I trust?"

"Cash! I don't carry that mush cash aroun' me," said De Carlos irritably. "Give you a sheck."

"Checks bounce," reflected Mr. Queen.

"Well, thish one won't! An' if it doesh, you're protected. You don't have to go through with our 'greement."

"Before that logic we bow. A check it shall be. Chair, Mr. De Carlos?"

He helped the reeling man around the desk and sat him down in the swivel-chair, reaching over to switch on the powerful desk-lamp.

De Carlos fumbled in his clothes and brought out a checkbook. He opened it, stared at the last stub morosely, then groped in his pockets again. Finally his hand emerged with a fountain-pen.

He unscrewed the cap, pushed it onto the other end of the pen, leaned over and, tucking his tongue in one cheek, began laboriously to write out a check.

If he had taken a bomb from his pocket Mr. Queen and Mr. Rummell could not have been so startled.

Their eyes fixed in a fascinated amazement at the pen in De Carlos's lax, blundering fingers.

It was a black hard-rubber fountain-pen, fat and scarred, and it was trimmed in gold.

On the cap, etching-sharp in the bold light of the lamp, there were certain curious scratchy marks and dents in an arced pattern—a familiar pattern, a pattern Messrs. Queen and Rummell had seen twice before . . . once earlier that evening in Room 1726 at the *Villanoy* on the pencil they had found behind the radiator, and once months before in that very office, at that very desk.

The identical pen. Under the identical circumstances.

It was Cadmus Cole's fountain-pen!

Part FIVE

XVI

The Empty Mouth

Cadmus Cole's fountain-pen! What was it doing in De Carlos's possession?

Ellery raised his eyebrows to Beau. They drifted off to a corner of the office as De Carlos, at the desk, struggled to control his hand.

"You're sure it's the same one?" whispered Beau.

"Positive, although we've always got a check-up against those microphotographs."

"Cole's pen!" mumbled Beau. "The same pen he used to write out that check for fifteen grand when he originally hired us. It might have a simple explanation, El. Maybe De Carlos just appropriated it after Cole cashed in."

Ellery shrugged. "There's one way of finding out. De Carlos is just drunk enough to be off guard, and if we asked him he's apt to tell the truth. Let me handle this."

He went back to the desk and rested his palms on it, smiling down at the writing man.

"There!" said De Carlos with a bubbly sigh. "Twen'y-fi' thoushand dollarsh, Mis'er Rummell." He sat back limply in the swivel-chair, waving the check like a flag to dry the ink. "Shay! How'd I know you'll keep your wor', gen'l-men?"

"You don't," replied Ellery with a smile.

"You doublecrosh me," said De Carlos furiously, reeling to his feet, "an' I'll—I'll—"

Ellery took the check gently from the man's slack fingers. "Is that friendly? We're a reputable agency, Mr. De Carlos. Word's our bond. Yes, twenty-five thousand, signed Edmund De Carlos—correct, Mr. De Carlos, and thank you!"

" 'S all ri'," said De Carlos, forgetting his suspicions and trying to bow. He almost fell on his face. Beau caught him and straightened him up none too carefully.

145

"Thanksh, Mis'er Queen. 'S mighty rocky weather we're having. An' now I'll be on my way."

He put the black fountain-pen back into his pocket. Beau watched it disappear with the expression of a fox watching a rabbit vanish in a hole.

Ellery grasped De Carlos's other arm and he and Beau began to steer the bearded man to the door.

"By the way, Mr. De Carlos," said Ellery respectfully, "you're just the man to help me out."

De Carlos stopped short, weaving. "Yesh?" he said, blinking at Ellery.

"Mr. De Carlos, I have a hobby—you know, hobby? I collect little personal mementoes of famous people. Not expensive things, you know—the homelier and more personal the better I like them."

"*I* like t'collect the ladies, bless 'em," chuckled De Carlos. "Blon's, brunettes—any kind, I shay, 's long's they're beau'ful."

"Every man to his own hobby," smiled Ellery. "Well, I've often thought no collection of the sort I own would be complete without some memento of Mr. Cadmus Cole."

"Should think sho," said De Carlos warmly. "Great man, Mis'er Cole. Great man. Gen'l'men, give you Mis'er Cole!"

"I meant to ask him for some little thing when he hired us a few months ago, but he was in such a hurry that I thought I'd wait for a more propitious time. And then," Ellery sighed, "he passed on, and I'd missed my chance. Do you think you could help me out, Mr. De Carlos? I mean, you were probably the closest friend he had."

"On'y frien'," said De Carlos. "Give you my wor'. On'y frien' he had in the worl'. Lemme think. Le' shee. Pershonal—"

"What happened to his personal belongings after his death, Mr. De Carlos—his clothing, fob, studs, things like that? Anything of that nature, you see—"

"Oh, they were all packed in a bunsh o' trunksh, an' I shipped 'em North from Cuba," said De Carlos, waving his hand. "They're in the housh in Tarrytown ri' now, Mis'er Rummell. I'll shee what I can fin'—"

"I shouldn't want to put you to all that trouble. Didn't he give *you* anything before he died? Or perhaps you took something from his effects to remember him by—

146

his watch, his ring, his fountain-pen, something like that?"

"Di'n' take a thing," said Mr. De Carlos sadly. "Honesht shteward—tha'sh Edmund De Carlos, gen'l'men. Give you my wor'. Di'n' take so much as a shteel pin!"

"Oh, come," protested Mr. Queen. "You must have taken something, Mr. De Carlos. Some little thing. His fountain-pen, for instance. Didn't you take that?"

"I beg your par'on," said De Carlos, offended. "Di'n' take his fou'n'-pen, di'n' take anything!"

"Such epic honesty," said Mr. Queen with a gleam in his eye, "deserves a substantial reward." He snatched off Mr. De Carlos's spectacles suddenly, leaving the man blinking.

"Mis'er Rummell . . ." began De Carlos with a gurgle.

Ellery waved the silver spectacles at Beau. "Give the gentleman his reward."

"Huh?" said Beau.

"Mr. Queen," said Mr. Queen, "the floor is yours. I suggest you stretch Mr. Edmund De Carlos out on it."

Beau's mouth closed. "It would be sort of taking advantage, wouldn't it? He'd fall apart."

De Carlos stood gaping and squinting from one to the other.

"That," said Mr. Queen, "is the idea."

Beau stared at him and then began to chuckle. "Come and get it," he said to Mr. De Carlos.

The bearded man shrank against Ellery.

Beau's paw flashed. It clamped about the nape of Mr. De Carlos's neck.

Mr. Queen stepped back and watched with a detached and scientific interest.

De Carlos squealed and flailed at Beau like an agitated crab. Beau grinned and began to shake him up and down, and from side to side, as if De Carlos had been a cocktail shaker. De Carlos's head flopped back and forth, his eyes popping, his glittering teeth rattling with a peculiar, mechanical rattle that awakened another gleam in Mr. Queen's eye.

And suddenly an astonishing thing happened. Mr. De Carlos's teeth, that shining ivory army, that perfect and beautiful string of dental pearls, detached themselves in one piece from Mr. De Carlos's gaping mouth and flew halfway across the room to land at Mr. Queen's feet. De Carlos began to mumble curses, his cheeks sunken in magically, his gums nakedly forlorn.

Beau shouted: "So *that's* the way it is!" and grasped the man's beard with his other hand, yanking viciously, already triumphant, as if he did not doubt the beard was as false as the teeth. But De Carlos only howled with pain; the beard refused to part from his cheeks.

Cursing, Beau released it and plunged his fingers into the bush of Mr. De Carlos's hair. This time he was not foiled. Mr. De Carlos's black hair came away from Mr. De Carlos's scalp with a sucking, reluctant sound, in one incredible piece, leaving an almost nude dome behind—almost, for there was a sparse fringe of gray-black hair on his head in the general shape of a horseshoe.

And then Mr. De Carlos ceased howling, ceased struggling, as he felt the top of his head and his hand encountered naked flesh. He grew limp.

"Desist," said Mr. Queen.

Mr. Rummell desisted, looking rather dazed at the unexpected result of his handiwork. Immediately Mr. De Carlos dropped to all fours and began to grope about the rug. He found his wig by chance and hastily—and askew—clapped it back on his pink gray-fringed skull. Then he began hunting for his teeth.

Mr. Queen stooped and picked them up. "You may rise," he said gravely, "we have them," and he inspected them curiously as Mr. De Carlos scrambled to his feet. They were set in their pink shell in perfect alignment—superbly regular teeth disposed with superb regularity . . . so perfect, so superbly regular, Mr. Queen told himself, that he should feel ashamed for not having suspected their falseness before. And he did feel ashamed.

He returned teeth and spectacles to their owner, and their owner swallowed the one and clapped the other on his nose and at once, with a surprising dignity, went to the desk and reached for the telephone.

Mr. Queen sighed. "I beg your pardon," he said, "but apparently the effects both of my partner's whisky and his seismic treatment have not yet worn off, Mr. De Carlos. The hour is late, and if I am not mistaken I detect the dawn's early light. You will not be able to stop the check you wrote out a few moments ago for some few hours yet."

De Carlos replaced the telephone, made an attempt to brush himself off, thought better of it, set his hat on his tilted wig, and calmly went out into the anteroom.

"Mr. Queen," said Mr. Queen, "show the gentleman out."

"But—" began Beau hoarsely.

Mr. Queen shook his head at his partner with violence. Beau shrugged and let Mr. De Carlos escape into the friendlier world.

When Beau came back, he said sharply: "What was the idea of letting him go?"

"Plenty of time, plenty of time," said Ellery. He was examining the twenty-five thousand dollar check De Carlos had written out—examining it with an intentness that puzzled Beau.

"That's easy for you to say," muttered Beau. "How about Kerrie? Hey!" Ellery looked up. "You're not even listening. What's so interesting about that check? You may as well tear it up. He'll stop it as soon as the bank opens in the morning."

"This check," remarked Mr. Queen, "has more than a monetary value to us. It's so valuable, I suspect, that I shan't entrust it even to the office safe. I'm going to carry it about with me, as I've been carrying these microphotographs."

"You think somebody'd try to crack us open?" demanded Beau, making two fists.

"It's not improbable."

"I'd like to see 'em try! Say, why didn't you take the pen from him, too?"

"No hurry, and we don't want to flush our rabbit too soon."

"It's all mixed up," growled Beau, flinging himself on the leather sofa. "How the hell did De Carlos get Cole's pen, if Cole didn't give it to him? He must have been lying about that. And if he has Cole's pen . . ." Beau sat up on the sofa suddenly. "If he has Cole's pen, why couldn't he have had Cole's automatic pencil, too?"

Ellery felt absently in his pocket to see if the pencil were still there. It was. He stowed De Carlos's check carefully away in his wallet.

"It's important to check up on De Carlos's story about Cole's personal effects. He said they were in some trunks at the Cole house in Tarrytown. You'd better make sure De Carlos told the truth about that."

"Yeah, but the pencil! I tell you—"

Ellery frowned. "I have the feeling we oughtn't to jump at conclusions, Beau. There's a good deal to weigh and

149

examine and mull over. Meanwhile, I want you to dig into De Carlos's past. Question old-timers in the Street. Find out as much about him as you can. There must be some people who remember him from the days—1919, 1920, or whenever it was—when De Carlos was running Cole's market operations, before Cole retired to his yacht."

"But why?"

"Never mind why," said Mr. Queen. "Do it. And—oh, yes. One thing more—perhaps the most important of all."

"What's that?"

"Find out if De Carlos has ever been married."

"Find out if De Carlos has ever been married? Of all the cock-eyed assignments! What's the point?"

"It may *be* the point."

"You're too much for me. Say! Cole's will actually stated that De Carlos was a bachelor, so there's your answer."

"I'd rather have it from a more objective authority," murmured Mr. Queen. "Check it."

"I wish you'd taken that pen away from him!"

"Yes, the pen." Mr. Queen's tone was damp. Something about the pen seemed to trouble him. Then he shrugged. "Let's forget remote considerations and discuss things nearer home. What happened tonight after I left you at the hotel?"

Beau told him.

Ellery began to walk about. "I don't like one thing. I don't like the spot we've put Dad in with your use of my name. He's done too much already in the way of suppressing facts. Beau, we've got to spill the truth before the newspapers get hold of it by themselves and ride Dad out of the Department."

"Damn the mess!" roared Beau, jumping up. Then he sat down again, looking foolish. "It's getting too involved for me. You're right. I'll have to face the music. Kerrie—"

"You've got to tell her, Beau. And about the other thing—"

"No!" Beau glared. "That's the one thing I won't tell. And you keep your mouth shut, too. Don't you realize what it would mean if we told about that? We'd be handing her over to the chair on a platter!"

Ellery gnawed his lower lip. "Dad's convinced, you say, that her story is a fabrication?"

"Yeah. You've got to admit, from his angle, it's a pretty tall yarn."

They were silent.

Finally Ellery said: "Well, clean up this business of the name, anyway. I'm going home to catch up on some sleep, and I'd advise you to do the same, because you're in for a busy day."

"Yeah," mumbled Beau. He stared at the floor as if he saw something of unique interest there.

BEAU faced the new day with a scowl. Times Square at dawn is not a gay place.

The place matched his mood; and yet, as he watched Ellery's nighthawk cab drum off uptown, he felt a certain elation, too. Beau had spawned an idea in the office upstairs, and it was growing with abnormal rapidity. It was such an amazing idea that he had decided to keep it to himself. If Ellery could be mysterious, why couldn't he?

He weighed the idea, turning it over, and the more he weighed it in the cool of early morning, on the deserted sidewalk in Times Square, a cigaret drooping from his lips, the more it staggered him.

If it was so . . . yes, it could wait. He could always pull it out of his hat. Meanwhile, there was a mess to be cleaned. That name business. Kerrie. How could he tell her?

He walked east towards the *Villanoy*, his heels raising echoes on the empty pavement.

The first thing to do was dodge the reporters. They had camped in the *Villanoy* lobby all night. If he knew reporters, they were there still, stretched out on the divans among a litter of cigaret ends and the butts of sandwiches. He entered the hotel by way of the Service Entrance, roused a night-man, a bill exchanged hands, and the man took him up, surreptitiously, to the seventeenth floor.

One of Inspector Queen's men, a detective named Piggott, who had known Beau when he used to visit his father at Headquarters in knee-pants and with barked knees showing, was perched on a chair which leaned against the wall next to the door of 1724. Piggott opened one eye and said, without smiling: "Hello, Mr. *Queen*."

Beau grinned and jammed a cigar into the detective's mouth. He entered 1724 without knocking.

Sergeant Velie was napping in the armchair by the window. He came awake instantly, like a cat.

"Oh, it's you." The Sergeant settled back and closed his eyes again.

Beau opened the bedroom door. The shades were drawn and Kerrie was curled up in a ball on one of the twin beds, under blankets. He could hear her deep, regular breathing. Vi, fully dressed as she lay on the other bed, raised her head with a start. When she saw Beau she slipped off the bed and tiptoed out to join Beau in the sitting room. She closed the door softly behind her.

Her eyes were red-rimmed and her white skin looked pasty, flabby. She said to him: "Calling on your wife for a change?"

"How is she?"

"All right, no thanks to you. The doc gave her a shot of something and after a while she fell asleep."

"That's good. That's good." Beau was nervous; he began walking about.

Vi looked at him. "If you want to go in there, I can't stop you. You're her husband."

"No, no, let her sleep. Good for her. You're aces, Vi. We've got a lot to thank you for."

"Never mind the baloney," said Vi. "You're a first-class rat, do you know that?"

"Hey." Beau turned round slowly. "What is this?"

"You know damn' well." Vi sat down on the edge of a chair and looked him over with a deliberate insolence.

"You let that poor kid take the rap for you, and you didn't have the gumption to stay with her while she was taking it!"

"What goes on here?" Beau flushed deeply.

Vi glanced at the huge figure of Sergeant Velie lying still in the armchair.

"Never mind him! What was that last crack supposed to mean?"

"I don't think you'd want the big boy hearing what I had in mind."

"Don't worry—he's listening! Come on, Velie, can the act." The Sergeant opened his eyes. "Now out with it! What's on your virgin mind now?"

"You asked for it," said Vi calmly, but she went pale. "I say *you* were in that room across the court. I say *you* fired those shots through the window at the Cole woman. I say *you* threw Kerrie's .22 into this room. That's what I say!"

She sat very still suddenly. Beau was glaring down at

152

her with such ferocity that her lower lip began to tremble. She glanced swiftly towards the Sergeant, in a panic.

The Sergeant rose. "Listen, boy—"

"Keep out of this, Velie. You think I bumped off Margo and then framed Kerrie for the job, do you?" Beau spoke very quietly, standing over Vi with his arms dangling.

"Yes!" The cry burst from Vi's lips, defiant through her fear.

"And I suppose you planted that idea in Kerrie's head, too? You did, didn't you?"

"I didn't have to. The idea was already there."

"You—doublecrossing—liar!"

"Ask her," said Vi with a glance of hate; but she shrank. "It was all so pat, your leaving her the way you did. Kerrie had to realize that. She does! She fights against it, but she does. She loves you—God only knows why. She ought to curse the day she ever set eyes on you!"

"Go on," said Beau hoarsely.

"You were in with this Margo. That's the way I figure it . . . Sergeant!" Vi slipped out of the chair and ran from Beau to grab the Sergeant's beefy arm. From behind him she continued defiantly: "You were Margo's sidekick. You'd get Kerrie out of the way, the two of you. You and Margo. When your clever attacks didn't work, you schemed to marry Kerrie and do her out of the money. Then you'd split—"

"I don't want to hear your poisonous version of it," growled Beau. "I want to know what Kerrie thinks!"

"And then Margo lost her head and came here last night and was going to squawk that you and she were partners. You were afraid of that, so you followed her and, just before she could blab, you shot her."

"I said I want to know what Kerrie thinks."

"She thinks what I think. Only she won't admit it to me or to herself. There's one part of her that still believes you're a right guy. And all the time she's taking your rap! Don't you feel proud of yourself?"

Beau drew a deep breath. "Get out of here."

Vi glared back at him.

Beau began to stalk towards her, and she screeched and retreated completely behind the rampart of the Sergeant's body.

"Take it easy, son," rumbled Velie.

"I said scram."

"You can't make me!"

153

"I said scrambo, you forked-tongued copperhead!"

"Kerrie needs me!"

"The way she needs a hole in the head. Are you going to get out of here, or do I have to throw you out?"

He was addressing her over the Sergeant's shoulder now, in a low and clear voice, completely blind to the mountain of flesh between them.

"Leave *you* with her?" shrilled Vi hysterically. "So that you can murder her, too?"

"If you were a man," grunted Beau, "I'd just about break your neck for that."

"Lay off, I said," said Velie, and he grabbed Beau's arm.

They all turned at a clicking sound.

Kerrie was in the bedroom doorway—in her thin nightgown, her hair tumbled about her face, her face as white as the wall.

Beau's neck turned red. He started to say something. But Kerrie stepped back and slammed the bedroom door. Vi cried out and ran after her. The door slammed again.

Beau started after them.

Sergeant Velie was quicker. He set his broad shoulders against the door. "You'd better take a powder yourself, Beau," he said mildly.

"I've *got* to talk to Kerrie! I can't let her think—"

"Isn't she in a tough enough spot without you making it tougher? Go on home and get some shut-eye. You'll feel better in the afternoon."

"But I have to tell her—who I *am*, Velie! I've got to come clean about this name business—I've got to clear that crazy idea of hers up—that I'm trying to frame her for a murder she thinks I pulled off—"

"It's certainly going to convince her," said Sergeant Velie dryly, "when she hears you've been hidin' under an alias ever since she knows you. That under a phony handle you upped and married her—"

At the word "married" Beau swallowed and stepped back, as if the Sergeant had tried to take a poke at him.

He turned and shambled out without another word.

XVII

Mr. Rummell
Becomes Himself Again

WHEN BEAU PLODDED INTO HIS APARTMENT HE PULLED
off all his clothes, set the alarm of his ninety-eight cent
clock, and threw himself onto the bed.

The alarm went off before noon. He opened his eyes
with a groan.

"Sure feels like a hangover," he muttered. "Only worse."

He crawled out of bed, danced under a cold shower,
shaved, dressed, and went out.

On the corner he stopped in at a cigar store for two
packs of cigarets and a nutted chocolate bar. Munching
the chocolate, he headed for the subway.

Kerrie awoke from an exhausted sleep just before
nine. Vi was tossing and snoring on the other bed.

Kerrie crept out of bed and peeped into the sitting
room. Sergeant Velie was gone, but another detective was
reading the morning paper in the armchair. When he saw
her he quickly hid the headlines. She shivered and closed
the door.

When Vi awoke it was noon and Kerrie was fully
dressed, seated at one of the bedroom windows staring
out into the court, her hands in her lap.

Vi said something, but Kerrie did not reply. The blonde
girl yawned, and then made a face, and then joined
Kerrie at the window.

"Kerrie!"

Kerrie looked up, surprised. "Oh, you're up. What?"

"Don't you see those rubbernecks?"

"What?"

The windows facing their side of the court were densely
peopled. Women, men, at least two staring children; and
in one window an enterprising reporter was shouting questions across the court as he leaned perilously out.

"I didn't see them," said Kerrie indifferently.

Vi yanked down the shade; and after a moment, as

if she were just conscious of the reporter's shouts, Kerrie closed the window, too.

It was a curiously peaceful day. Occasionally the door from the sitting room to the corridor opened and slammed as a detective came in. Men were coming in and out all day. There was some activity in 1726, too; Vi peeped from the window and could see men bustling about in there.

But no one entered the bedroom except a detective; and he came in only because Vi, after trying vainly to rouse the telephone operator, complained that they were starving.

"Okay," said the detective. "Why didn't you ask before?"

"Ask!"

"No tickee, no washee." He went out.

"They've cut the line," said Vi in a scared voice.

Kerrie said nothing.

Fifteen minutes later the detective wheeled a table in which was laden with food. He went out immediately.

"Come on, hon. We may as well stoke up."

"Yes," said Kerrie.

She sat down at the table and toyed with a slice of toast. She looked calm enough; only a certain air of abstraction, a deepening of the two lines from her nostrils to the corners of her mouth, pointed to anything unusual inside her.

Vi saw it and said in a small voice: "Kerrie dear, you've simply got to eat. You haven't eaten—"

"I'm not hungry, Vi."

Kerrie went back to the window.

Vi sighed. She finished her breakfast and, after hesitating, Kerrie's, too. She took a bath, borrowed fresh underwear and stockings from Kerrie, dressed, and then the two of them sat still, without conversation, all the long afternoon.

By nine o'clock in the evening Vi was ready to scream. Any noise—a cough, a cry, sobbing—would have been relief. But Kerrie just sat with her hands folded in her lap like some female Buddha carved from stone.

And then there was a commotion outside, the noise of many voices, at least one scuffle. Vi jumped up. Even Kerrie turned her head.

The bedroom door opened and Sergeant Velie, accompanied by several strange men, stood there. The Sergeant was carrying a folded paper.

Kerrie rose, pale.

"I've got a warrant here," said the Sergeant in a flat

156

voice, "for the arrest of Kerrie Shawn. Miss Shawn, will you get ready?"

After that, things became confused, like a motion picture run wild. A cameraman managed to pierce the cordon outside, and bulbs began to flash, and detectives shouted, and reporters wormed through, and there was almost a free-for-all. In the tumult Vi got Kerrie into her hat and a light camel's-hair coat, and Sergeant Velie said Vi couldn't go along, and Vi clung to Kerrie, weeping, until Kerrie said sharply: "Don't act like a baby, Vi!" and kissed her good-bye; and after a while Vi found herself almost alone in 1724, in the midst of bulbs and newspapers and articles of Kerrie's wardrobe, and she sat down on the floor and cried for the benefit of the two female reporters who had remained behind for sinister purposes of their own.

They even helped Vi, when she gathered strength enough to stand up, to get Kerrie's things together in the suitcases, asking questions all the way like two jabbering jays until Vi swore at them and threatened weepily to bang their sleek heads together.

Finally she managed to escape with Kerrie's bag and the aid of a policeman. One of the two newspaper-women said: "Nuts," with disgust, and they followed the course of empire southward, to Centre Street.

Vi reached her hotel with her hat over one ear. When she walked through the lobby she thought two men looked at her in a hard, suspicious way. She locked herself in her room.

Then the telephone began ringing. After a half-hour she told the operator not to ring her at all. So people began knocking at her door. She rang the hotel operator again and threatened to call the police if the pests didn't stop knocking.

The operator said: "Yes, Madam—hold on a minute," and then said: "Sorry, Madam—it *is* the police," and Vi opened the door, and one of the two men who had looked at her hard and suspiciously said not to try any funny stuff but just stay put, sister, see?

"Stay put?" screamed Vi. "You think you're hanging that rap around my neck, too, you wall-eyed flatties?"

"We're not sayin' nothin'," said the other man. "Just take a little friendly advice, see, blondie?"

Vi slammed the door, locked it.

After that, her telephone did not ring and her door was not knocked upon. And she stayed put.

157

BEAU burst into Inspector Queen's office at Police Headquarters, roaring mad.

"What the hell's the idea, Pop! What was I picked up for?" Then he saw Kerrie. He said slowly: "What's this?"

Kerrie looked at him with eyes of liquid pain.

"I wanted to talk to you," said Inspector Queen. He seemed a little shrunken through his spare, wiry body. "As for Miss Shawn, we've decided to hold her for—well, technically as a material witness. But we all know what for."

There were three other men present. Beau recognized them all. One was a stenographer. The other two were assistants of District Attorney Sampson's.

"She's innocent," said Beau. "She told you how it really happened. The real killer was in 1726. He shot Margo through the window across the angle of the court, then tossed in the roscoe. Kerrie picked it up; she was dazed."

"Is that all you've got to say?" asked the Inspector in a queer tone.

"Isn't the truth enough for you?" snarled Beau.

"One moment." Kerrie's voice was calm, low-pitched. "Inspector Queen, you've accused me of murdering my cousin, and I admit the circumstances—"

"Don't admit anything!" yelled Beau. "Let me handle—"

"Please." She looked at him, and he turned away. "I admit the circumstances are against me. But if I shot Margo, I must have had a motive. What was my motive?"

"We know your motive," said the Inspector.

"I couldn't possibly have any! You mean I hated her, I was—jealous of her on account of . . . my husband? But if I were, wouldn't I have shot her *before* I was married? I had nothing to be jealous about, Inspector. We were married. Would I have waited until after my marriage to kill her?"

The Inspector did not reply. The stenographer was quietly recording the conversation, and the two men from the District Attorney's office were listening in a strained silence.

"Or you might say," Kerrie went on, "that I wanted to put Margo out of the way in order to gain financially. But that can't be so, either, you see, because my marriage cut me out of Uncle Cadmus's will. I couldn't possibly inherit Margo's share; in fact, I've even forfeited my own. So don't you see how silly this charge is? There isn't a reason in the world why I should have wanted to kill Margo!"

"But there is," said the Inspector in a flat tone.

"What could it possible be?"

"Something like twenty-five hundred dollars a week for life."

"But I just told you," said Kerrie, bewildered. "Mr. Goossens—Mr. De Carlos will confirm—the will—"

"Yeah," mumbled Beau. "What's the matter with you, Pop?"

"It's true," said the Inspector in a tired voice, "that this girl has no gain-motive if she were married at the time of the murder." He paused, then repeated: "*If she were married.*"

Kerrie sprang to her feet. "What do you mean?"

"It won't do you the least good to put on an act," replied the old man gruffly.

"Ellery!" Kerrie ran to Beau, shook him. "What is your father talking about? Tell me!"

Beau said nothing. But Kerrie saw his eyes, and let go of him with a sudden gesture of revulsion. She stood still where she was, the last drop of color draining from her face.

"I received a wire this afternoon," said the Inspector, "which amounted to an annoymous tip. We weren't able to trace the tipster, because the message had been telephoned into the telegraph office from a midtown pay-station. But the tipster wasn't nearly as important as the tip. We followed that up right away, and it was right. Miss Shawn—"

"Miss Shawn?" whispered Kerrie.

"Miss Shawn, you weren't married last night. The marriage was a fake. It was an attempt to lay a clever smoke-screen down so that it would look as if you had no motive to kill your cousin Margo. You *still* share in your uncle's estate; you still take over Margo's share. What do you say now?"

"Not married last night. . . . Why, that's simply—that's simply not true! We were. In Connecticut. Near Greenwich. By a Justice of the Peace named—named Johnston. Weren't we? *Ellery, weren't we?*"

A frenzy took possession of her. She seized Beau's arm, shaking him, her eyes wild and wide with horror.

"And that isn't all!" shouted the Inspector suddenly,

growing crimson. "This man *isn't* my son—his name's *not* Ellery! It isn't even Queen! His name is Beau Rummell, and he's my son's partner in a confounded private detective agency!"

"Beau—Rummell?" whispered Kerrie. She stumbled back to her chair and sat down, fumbling in her bag for a handkerchief. She remained that way, her eyes on her bag, her fingers fumbling inside aimlessly.

"For God's sake, Pop," said Beau in a small voice.

"It's no use, Beau! There's no record of a marriage license. There's no record or trace of the Justice of the Peace who's suppose to have married you. If there is—let's have it. Produce him! And let's see your license and your marriage certificate! Why, even the address is a phony—it's a house that was just rented for one night! Otherwise it hasn't been occupied for years!"

Scenes flashed across Kerrie's brain . . . The ramshackle building, the weeds, the dust, the odd Mr. Johnston. . . .

Beau said miserably: "All right, it's true! We weren't married. It was an absolute phony. But Kerrie didn't know anything about that, Pop! She thought it was on the level. I rigged the whole thing up myself, I tell you!"

She should have known; if she hadn't been such a blind, trusting fool. . . . The marriage license. She hadn't signed. "Pull," he had said. He hadn't shown it to her. In that house, the "Justice" was going to marry—marry! —them without a second witness. The whole thing, the whole sickening . . .

Kerrie's stomach began to churn. There was a wry twist to her mouth.

"Yes?" said the Inspector flatly.

"You've got to believe me, Pop! This thing is all a mess now. Margo Cole tried three times to kill Kerrie. She hated Kerrie because she—well, she'd taken a shine to me herself. And she was spending more dough than was coming in, and she wanted Kerrie's share of the income. She told me so herself! I'll swear to that on the witness-stand! I played along, figuring that was the best way to protect Kerrie; we didn't have anything on Margo in the way of evidence, so there was no use pulling the law into it. Ellery knows all about this. He'll back me up."

"Don't bring Ellery into it!" thundered the Inspector.

"I've got to, Pop. Even if I didn't, he'd come to bat—"

"Does he know these things of his own knowledge?" demanded the old man quickly.

"No. I told him. But it's true, I tell you! I planned the fake marriage because, with Kerrie apparently married, Margo would temporarily get Kerrie's share, or expect to get it soon, so half her motive against Kerrie would be satisfied. The other half—well," and Beau threw back his shoulders defiantly, "I made a deal with her. I pretended to be her accomplice, saying I was marrying Kerrie to give Margo the extra income, so she and I could split. I told her I loved her, not Kerrie—that the marriage wouldn't mean a thing. She fell for it. Last night, like the she-devil she was, she couldn't resist coming down to crow over Kerrie after the damage, as she thought, was done."

"You expect me to believe this girl here didn't know that marriage was a phony?"

"Do you think she's the kind—" began Beau; then he made a gesture of futility. "I didn't marry her on the level because I didn't want to see her lose that legacy. I didn't tell her the marriage was a fake because, if I had, she wouldn't have gone through with it. You don't know her, I tell you!"

The two Assistant District Attorneys whispered together. Then one of them beckoned the Inspector, and the three of them whispered some more. Finally the Inspector, very pale, said to Beau: "Just where did you go last night, Beau, when you left this girl in that hotel room after you'd checked in?"

Kerrie raised her head at that; her eyes looked hurt, misty, dull.

"For one thing I'm not a skunk!" snarled Beau. "I was in a tough spot. She thought we were married, I knew we weren't. . . . I made some rotten excuse, said I was coming back, and blew. When I got outside I thought of something. There were two people who had to be notified that the marriage wasn't on the up and up—they were the trustees of the Cole estate.

"I went back to my Times Square office and wrote out two letters—one to Goossens, one to De Carlos. They were identical. They said the marriage was a phony, and I was notifying them because the legal question of the passing of Kerrie's share to Margo was a factor; I didn't want Kerrie to lose even a week's income. I said Margo was after Kerrie's scalp, and I wanted them to play ball

161

with me, stall along for a while, until I could pin those murder attempts on Margo. Then I sealed the letters, put special-delivery stamps on them, and mailed them in the lobby slot. The night man in my building let me in and let me out. Then I went back to the *Villanoy*."

"The check-up will be made, of course." The Inspector turned away, stonily.

Beau ran over to Kerrie. "Kerrie, I want you to believe me! I want you to know I love you, and that everything I've done so far was because—damn it, Kerrie, I'd cut off my right arm before I'd pull a dirty trick like that!"

The Inspector and the two lawyers were conferring in whispers again. The attorneys were demanding something, and the Inspector was arguing fiercely against them.

"I think I know who killed Margo," whispered Beau in Kerrie's ear. "It's just come to me—just since last night. I mean since early this morning. All I need is a little time, darling. Kerrie, say something. At least tell me you don't think I'm a murdering heel!"

She turned slowly at that, raising her eyes and fixing them on his. In their hurt, misty way, they were troubled searchlights, probing the darkness.

And suddenly she put her arms about him and pulled him down to her. He closed his eyes gratefully. He felt the straining of her arms, the beating of her heart.

A man tapped her on the shoulder, shoving Beau aside. Beau did not protest.

He watched them lead her away—to the Tombs, as he knew, to go through the whole ghastly and scarifying process of being booked, fingerprinted, locked in a cell. . . . She walked in a dream, seeing nothing.

Beau glanced at the Inspector, who waved his hand.

"Don't leave the city." Inspector Queen's voice was dry; he did not look up from his desk, where he was fussing with some papers.

"Sure, Pop," said Beau gently. "And—thanks."

The Inspector started, then went back to his papers.

Beau left quickly. He knew that he would be followed. He thought it very possible, from the Inspector's peculiar expression and the glances of the two men from the District Attorney's office, that before twenty-four hours had passed he might be lodged, with Kerrie, in the Tombs on an accomplice charge.

In fact, he was sure that only the Inspector's insistence had kept the two attorneys from having him taken into custody on the spot.

Beau walked the streets of downtown New York half the night. He analyzed his case over and over, mercilessly, picking, probing, digging for flaws. And finally, with a grunt of satisfaction, he said to himself: "It's in the groove," and sent Ellery a telegram to meet him at the office at nine o'clock in the morning.

Then Beau went home and to sleep.

At nine they met, and Mr. Queen's haggard appearance said that he knew of Kerrie's arrest, and moreover that he had had no sleep since learning of it.

Beau told him exactly what had happened while Ellery listened in a gloomy silence. "Well," he said at last, "we have some time—these things go slowly, and we need a complete case. Did you check up on De Carlos yesterday?"

"I found some old-timers in the Street who remembered him. They all think De Carlos was a weak sister. Big ideas, but no follow-through. With Cole dominating him from the background, planning the campaigns, De Carlos pulled the big deals in actual practice. By himself, as a planner, De Carlos was useless. As a matter of fact, he's been in the market since Cole's death—did you know that? And he's lost his shirt."

Ellery was thoughtful. "And then, too, he's been spending that million Cole left him like a gob on shore-leave. He must be pretty nearly flat, if they cleaned him in Wall Street."

"He is," said Beau.

"Any trace of his ever having been married?"

"What do you think I am, a Houdini? Far as I could check, no."

"Well, I've been doing some checking myself. For some time. There's always the possibility, but it seems fairly certain, and from the reports I've been receiving, we may assume De Carlos never married. Now, how about Cole's personal belongings?"

"Checked. Lots of duds, odds and ends of jewelry— some pretty valuable stuff, I'd say, watches, rings, studs —and a bunch of personal papers. Nothing to interest us, though."

"Did you find a fountain-pen?"

"No, nor an automatic pencil."

"False teeth?"

"No."

"Eyeglasses, toupee, wig?"

"No."

Miss Penny came in with a telegram. Beau tore it open and began to jig, waving a yellow slip. "I don't know what you've got," he yelled, "but I've got plenty!"

"You can be very annoying at times," said Mr. Queen. "What is that?"

"A wire from our man on the Coast. He's located Captain Angus!"

"What?"

"Absolutely. And he'll be in with him tonight. That clinches it, you sockeroo! That's all I needed to clean up this case!"

"Oh," said Mr. Queen slowly. "You have a theory?"

"Theory? Nuts! I've got the answer!" And Beau began to explain, chattering like a machine-gun. Mr. Queen listened in silence, nodding glumly every once in a while. "What's the matter? You don't look very happy about it!"

"It all points that way, I confess," said Mr. Queen. "I can't disprove your theory—in fact, I can add to it and strengthen it considerably. There's only one point that bothers me, Beau."

"What's that?"

Mr. Queen waved his hand. "It's a small discrepancy —too small at the moment to worry about."

"Then the hell with it! What do you say—do we go to town?"

Mr. Queen sighed. "I suppose we may as well."

They put their heads together, going over Beau's case, checking it, re-examining, working out the details of a plan. Beau's eyes gleamed at certain contributions of Mr. Queen's; his spirits steadily rose, and he looked happy for the first time in months.

And then the telephone rang and Miss Penny said: "It's your father, Mr. Queen."

Beau sat down, losing his grin.

"Well, Dad?" said Ellery.

He listened; and as he listened he stiffened. When finally he set down the instrument he laughed aloud. "What do you know about that?"

"Know about what? Talk, you brass monkey!"

"It's the beginning of the end now, Beau." Mr. Queen rose and shook himself a little, like an athlete before running out to meet his opponent. "Dad just tipped me off.

Margo Cole—hold your chair, now!—was NOT the daughter of Huntley and Nadine Cole. She was NOT Cadmus Cole's niece, or Kerrie's cousin. In fact, she was NOT Margo Cole."

Beau's jaw sagged. "She wasn't— Then who the devil was she?"

"One of the coolest imposters on record!"

And Mr. Queen hustled his speechless partner out of the office and downstairs, bound for a taxicab and Police Headquarters.

XVIII

Enter Miss Bloomer

THEY TOOK A CAB DOWNTOWN.

"How'd Pop ever dig that one up?" demanded Beau, when he had recovered from the shock.

"I didn't like her."

"Talk sense!"

"I am. I got to thinking about the woman who presented herself as Margo Cole, and there was something about her and her story that made me think in terms of flies and honey, if you know what I mean. She seemed too much the woman of the world."

"That's reasoning, all right," grunted Beau. "Lucky guess!"

"Certainly." Ellery laughed. "Except for the little detail of the 'partner' she mentioned to Kerrie just before she was murdered. A partner suggested a plot, and a plot—" He shrugged. "At any rate, I merely suggested to Dad that he have the dead woman's fingerprints taken. He did, and sent photos of them by radio to Scotland Yard and the Sureté. Scotland Yard came through."

"Who was she? I'm still winded!"

"A woman named Ann Bloomer. A London slum product—drunken father, sluttish mother—lived by her wits from adolescence. When she was 19 she was caught by the British police in some blackmailing scheme and sent to the clink for a year. When she was released in 1925 she disappeared from England. 1925, remember, was the year the real Margo Cole's mother died in France."

"But the French police checked this woman!"

"We've all been neatly taken in. Don't you see what happened? When the Bloomer woman appeared in this country, claiming to be Margo Cole, she told a certain story. Well, that story was a consolidation of two stories. That is, *she told the history of the real Margo Cole up to the year 1925; from 1925 on, the story she told was her own history.* That means the real Margo disappeared in 1925—or, at least, there's no record of her existence after that year."

"You mean this business goes back that far?" Beau whistled. "Murder as far back as 1925?"

"Don't know." Mr. Queen gazed somberly out of the taxi window. "Dad's news opens up a new field of speculation and inquiry, however. Anyway, we know Ann Bloomer, who said she had changed her name from Margo Cole to Ann Strange, was actually an English adventuress with no possible relation to the Cole family. Dad checked that, too. And it's that woman who tried to murder Kerrie and was murdered herself for her pains!"

"Say, how'd she get hold of Margo Cole's proofs of identity? Do you suppose—"

"Dad's called Goossens to bring down all those proofs." Beau told the driver to stop at the Tombs.

When Kerrie saw him she gave a little cry and ran into his arms. After a while Mr. Queen coughed.

"You might introduce me to the lady, Beau."

Beau did the honors and, from the safety of his arms, Kerrie eyed Ellery in a puzzled way. "I'm terrible happy to meet the man I *thought* I'd married. So you're Ellery Queen!"

"And you're Kerrie Shawn."

"A little the worse for wear, I'm afraid," sighed Kerrie. "Mr. Queen, haven't we met somewhere?"

"It's one of those annoying probabilities," replied Mr. Queen quickly, "that it's so much better not to bother oneself about. Now that we meet in fact, Miss Shawn, and I've an opportunity of seeing for myself, I don't wonder you've upset Beau's whole self-centered life!"

"I'm not very much to look at these days," said Kerrie with a sad smile. "A little slap-happy from all these flattering attentions from life. . . . Darling." She pressed Beau's hand.

"Look, kid." Beau was embarrassed. "I had to stop in and sort of put my arms around you again. You know. See that you weren't sore at me. But we've got to beat it."

"So soon?" Kerrie cried.

"Some day we'll knock off for a thousand years and go away together and just hold hands the whole damn' time. But right now Ellery and I have work to do."

"All right, Beau." She kissed him. "That's really a nice name. Beau Rummell. Why, do you know—"

"No cracks," said Beau hastily. "Kerrie, you all right? They're treating you okay?"

"Yes, Beau."

"Anything I can get you before I leave?"

"Vi's been here. She brought me a few things she knew I'd need. Beau . . . the police are watching Vi, too."

"Aw, that's just a matter of form," muttered Beau. "They wouldn't earn their play if they didn't look smart."

"Have you—have you hired a lawyer for me yet?"

"What's the matter with me? I'm a lawyer!"

Oh, darling, I know, but—"

Beau kissed her. "We won't need one. Ellery and I'll have this case cracked in one more day."

Kerrie's eyes grew round. "You mean you've found out—"

"Just a little more patience, funny-face. We'd try to spring you, only with that murder rap hanging over your head it's no use trying. They've got to work fast, anyway. Either release you or change the charge—" Beau's face darkened, then he grinned at her. "You'll just have to stay here a little while longer."

"Make it a very little while," Kerrie whispered.

"Miss Shawn, did you know that Margo Cole really wasn't Margo Cole?" asked Mr. Queen suddenly.

"I beg your pardon?" gasped Kerrie.

"Never mind." Mr. Queen smiled in a satisfied way.

"Beau, what does he mean?"

Beau told her. She was bewildered. "But I don't—"

Mr. Queen took her hand. "Don't try. While you're here don't answer too many questions and have a nice rest. Jails are really awfully good places to rest in."

She smiled back faintly. "I'll remember that—the next one I'm in."

"I promise you won't be in this one long!"

"Thanks, Mr. Queen."

"The name is Ellery, Miss Shawn."

"Kerrie, Ellery."

"Charmed! By the way, Beau and I have a lot of explaining to do. Do you think you can wait?"

"Whatever Beau says."

Beau kissed her again, and they left quickly.

"Such faith," observed Mr. Queen, "should be deserved."

Beau did not reply in words. But his eyes and jaw said something that silenced Mr. Queen.

They found Inspector Queen with Lloyd Goossens, elbow-deep in records. Both men seemed worried.

"Well, they're in order," said the Inspector disgustedly. "Every last one of 'em genuine. I don't understand it at all!"

"Nor do I," said Goossens, sucking nervously on his empty pipe. He stared from Beau to Ellery. "Which is which, Inspector?"

"There's the real Ellery Queen," snapped the Inspector, "and this varmint who passed himself off as Queen is Beau Rummell, my son's partner. I wouldn't blame you if you took a poke at both of 'em, Mr. Goossens."

"I'm afraid it's too late for that now," said Goossens sadly, shaking hands with Ellery. "Some day you gentlemen must tell me why you deceived me. At the moment this business about Margo Cole, or rather Ann Bloomer, has me rather floored."

"You're sure the identification papers are in order?"

"Positive. See for yourself. I've brought Miss Shawn's along, too, for comparison."

"How do we know she isn't an imposter, too?" demanded Inspector Queen suddenly.

Beau bridled. "In her case the record's clear! Besides, there's a photo of her when she was a kid of ten or so—"

"I don't like it," growled the old man. "It upsets the whole cart."

"My heart bleeds for you," said Beau with a grin.

The Inspector eyed him peculiarly. "Oh, I don't mean about the case against her. Finding out that the woman who claimed to be Margo Cole was an imposter doesn't really change Kerrie Shawn's motive, if Kerrie Shawn *thought* the woman was Margo Cole. Or even if she knew, the motive still holds. In that case she'd rely on the woman's imposture never coming out. It's not that."

168

"Then what is it?"

The Inspector failed to reply.

"What bothers me," said Goossens, "is my position as executor and trustee in this matter. And being paired with this man De Carlos doesn't—ah—improve matters." He ran his fingers through his thinning hair. "All that money handed over to this Bloomer woman out of Cole's estate—"

"You can't be held responsible for that," said Mr. Queen. "We all made the same mistake. Because the proofs of identity were genuine, we assumed the person presenting them was their owner."

"Oh, I'm safe enough legally," said the lawyer. "It isn't that, Mr. Queen. There will be lots of newspaper talk, a scandal—it won't do my firm's reputation any good, you know; may very well scare away future clients. Well, that's my problem, not yours."

"Talking about legal considerations," remarked Beau, "there's the estate itself, Goossens. The real Margo Cole must be searched for. Kerrie's back in the picture as an heiress—with a charge of murder hanging over her. The Surrogate won't like these little developments—"

Goossens looked unhappy. "Yes, yes, I'm aware of that." He frowned. "By the way, Mr. Queen, you know that technically you disobeyed the testator's instructions in having Mr. Rummell impersonate you. You had no right to give Mr. Rummell a job to do which you were personally hired to accomplish."

"If you mean," said Beau, "that we'll give back the fifteen grand, my friend—take another whiff!"

"No, no," said the lawyer with a nervous smile. "I shan't press the point. But under the circumstances, I think the firm of *Ellery Queen, Inc.,* will have to bow out of the case."

"What do you mean?" demanded Mr. Queen.

"The Surrogate won't like that little business, Mr. Queen. I imagine he'll insist on my engaging a new firm, or doing the job myself."

"You mean of beginning a search for Margo Cole all over again, now that the Bloomer woman has been exposed?"

"Yes."

"We stand," said Mr. Queen firmly, "upon our rights."

Goossens laughed. "I don't believe you have any.

However, it's probably a dead issue. Dead issue—very good!"

Mr. Queen politely laughed, too. "What's that?"

"I mean—Margo Cole is probably dead. She must be. So it's a tempest in a teapot."

"Very possible," admitted Mr. Queen.

"Well . . . I suppose, Inspector, you want to hang on to these records for a while?"

"Yes, leave them here."

The lawyer nodded glumly and left.

"Bad case of cold feet," remarked the Inspector. "Well, I suppose he *is* in a jam." He sat down at his desk and began to finger his little figurine of Bertillon. "As I am. Beau, you and Kerrie are lucky this happened now. It smudges up our case, and the D.A.'s frankly sorry he advised such a quick arrest. And yesterday he wanted to arrest you, too!"

"On what charge?"

"Accessory to the murder." The old man paused, then said quietly: "I talked him out of it. I know you didn't have anything to do with it—not because the facts aren't against it, but because of a lot of things the law won't recognize as evidence."

"But Beau couldn't possibly have committed that murder," protested Mr. Queen with an outraged chuckle.

"I'm not talking about the murder," said his father shortly. "I said accessory."

"Thanks, Pop," said Beau dryly.

"Just the same, my own hands aren't too clean. The Commissioner is thinking of taking me off the case. Now, with this new development . . ." He shook his head.

"It seems to me," observed Mr. Queen, "that we're moving in concentric circles. Let's tackle this thing logically."

The Inspector brightened visibly. "You see daylight?"

"Brilliantly."

"Then you don't believe Kerrie Shawn shot the Bloomer woman?"

"I do not."

The Inspector sank back. "You're prejudiced!"

"Not a bit of it. I have reasons for thinking her innocent."

"Reasons? What reasons? The Lord knows I'm a reasonable man. But if you can explain away the circumstances of this crime—except by some cock-and-bull story

170

like the one Kerrie Shawn tells—I'll eat your hat in Madison Square Garden with catsup and mayonnaise!"

"I may take you up on that," said Mr. Queen; and he rose and began to walk up and down, frowning at the floor. "We must begin from the new fact: that the woman who represented herself as Margo Cole, bearing genuine proofs of Margo-Cole identity, as it were, is a proved imposter named Ann Bloomer.

"Now, with this woman an imposter, the question arises: Where is the real niece of Cadmus Cole, the real daughter of Huntley Cole and Nadine Malloy Cole—the Margo Cole Ann Bloomer pretended to be?

"You'll admit there are two inclusive possibilities: that either the real Margo Cole is alive, today, or she is dead.

"Let's examine the case if she's alive. If she is, why hasn't she come forward to claim her share of her uncle's estate? We'd have to rule out the possibility that she doesn't know anything about her uncle's death and the will he left. This has been the most widely publicized will-case in modern legal history. Cole's death, the odd conditions of his will, have been announced by newspapers, periodical literature, and radio all over the world, not once but many times—in North and South America, Europe, Asia, Australia, even Africa and the South Seas. And this publicity has been going on for several months —first the death, then the publication of the will, then the news of the discovery of the two heiresses, and since then a continuous drumfire of their activities.

"Don't you agree that if the real Margo were alive it's reasonable to assume she'd have heard of Cole's death and her own eligibility as an heiress by this time?"

"Do you mean by that," asked the Inspector, "that because Margo Cole hasn't come forward you think she's dead?"

"Not yet," said Ellery quickly. "I'm merely brushing in the background. I do say that the unusual publicity must have got to her eyes or ears if she's alive. Now, proceeding on this reasonable assumption—that if she's alive she knows—why hasn't she come forward?

"One possible, even probable, answer is that she knows she doesn't qualify under the terms of the will . . . that she is or has been married, for example—a state of affairs which would automatically cut her out of an inheritance."

"I should think," objected Beau, "that, even if she were

or had been married, she'd show up and make a fight for that dough. That's only human."

"But she hasn't; that's a fact. Let's not get involved in counter-theories; let's proceed along the straight line. If she's married, and since she's failed to show up, what then? She would fight, you say. Yes, I agree; she would. But how? By contesting the will? She hasn't done that. Could she fight in another way? Certainly—*if she got hold of a woman like Ann Bloomer and made a deal with her.*"

Both men looked blank.

"A deal like this, for instance: a fifty-fifty split of the income after Ann Bloomer, armed with the proofs of identity furnished her by the real Margo, showed up, was accepted as the legitimate heiress, and began to collect her share. Ann Bloomer's qualifications, from Margo's standpoint, would merely have to be: that she was not and is not married, and that her history could be mortised into Margo's history somewhere along the line—as actually happened, in fact."

"But that means," said the Inspector excitedly, "that this partner Kerrie says the woman mentioned was—the real Margo! Why, if Ann doublecrossed Margo after Ann was accepted as the heiress, if Ann didn't fork over the split, that would be a motive for murder. . . ."

"So it would," chuckled Ellery. "By the way, I thought you didn't believe Kerrie's story!"

"I don't," said the old man, flushing. "I'm just—arguing. For the sake of argument."

Both Beau and Ellery laughed. "At any rate," said Ellery, "I'm not arguing to reach *that* sort of conclusion, even though it might be true. The only conclusion I wish to reach you've already accepted, Dad—that, if the real Margo still lives, she probably hired Ann Bloomer to present herself, furnished Ann with the proofs of identity, and was Ann Bloomer's silent partner in a scheme to get hold of half of Cole's estate, to which she was not entitled. In other words, Ann Bloomer had—had to have—a partner.

"Now, take the other possibility—that the real Margo is dead. Then how did Ann Bloomer get possession of those proofs of identity? From the reports, the Bloomer woman had not the slightest connection with the Cole family, certainly not by a blood tie. Yet the proofs of identity must have been in the possession of some one close to the dead Margo—we're assuming now, remem-

172

ber, that the real Margo is dead. In whose possession? A blood relation? The real Margo's only living relatives by blood were Kerrie Shawn, her cousin, and Cadmus Cole, her paternal uncle. Neither has had the least contact, or could have had from the facts, with the real Margo Cole.

"Then who is left as a possible possessor of those proofs? Such a person as the real Margo Cole's surviving husband, let us say. A good possibility, although it may have been one of a number of differently related persons. In any event, for the Bloomer woman to have got her hands on those proofs of Margo Cole's identity, she must have got them from *some one* who had been close to Margo Cole; and for this person to have turned the proofs over to Ann Bloomer means again a deal, a partnership. So again the vital conclusion arises: *Ann Bloomer had a partner*."

The Inspector stirred. "Couldn't it have been like this? Margo Cole and Ann Bloomer were friends. Ann Bloomer murdered Margo, stole her proofs of identity, and showed up here to pose as Margo Cole. So there's no partner at all!"

"Two things against that theory," replied Ellery, "which, of course, has occurred to me. One is that if Margo and Ann had been friends, why didn't the French police, who checked over every last detail of Margo Cole's movements from her birth until 1925, and of Ann Bloomer's movements from 1925 to date, run across any evidence of such a friendship? They did a careful job, as you know. The answer is: there was no such evidence to run across; there was no such friendship.

"Besides, that theory would indicate that Ann Bloomer was a lone—er—wolverine. Yet she told Kerrie a moment before she was murdered that *she had a partner*."

"We've only Kerrie Shawn's word for that," said the Inspector stubbornly.

"And all sorts of confirmation in what El's just told us," growled Beau. "Don't be pig-headed, Pop!"

The Inspector waved Ellery on.

"Deductively, then," said Ellery, "we've established the existence of a person hitherto unsuspected—Ann Bloomer's partner-in-crime, the person she referred to when she boasted that she *and some one else* had planned the attacks on Kerrie.

"Now Beau told Ann he was marrying Kerrie, that he

was taking Kerrie to the *Villanoy;* he even promised Ann he would leave Kerrie alone for the night, as he did—although for reasons of his own.

"Ann Bloomer must have informed her partner; how else could this partner have known? So the partner went to the *Villanoy* soon after Beau and Kerrie checked in, found out what room they had engaged, and then sent the hotel a wire reserving Room 1726. I've investigated that wire, incidentally, and it was telephoned to Western Union from a pay-station—no doubt from a booth in or near the *Villanoy.* Of course, this covered the trail.

"Room 1726 being reserved, this mysterious partner then let himself in with a passkey of some sort, and awaited developments. The partner heard Ann's arrival, heard the entire conversation through the open windows, heard Ann's injudicious boast about the partnership of the attacks on Kerrie, and shot Ann before she could reveal the identity of her partner—himself. Then he tossed Kerrie's own revolver through the windows into 1724. Ann herself had said she and her partner had planned the attacks on Kerrie, so it's not strange that this partner had possession of Kerrie's stolen .22."

The old man was silent.

"I imagine," continued Ellery gravely, "that this partner had three motives for killing Ann Bloomer.

"Remember Ann's character, her unscrupulousness, her known record for loose living on the Continent, her self-incriminating confession of attempts to murder Kerrie. And think of the situation existing between her and her partner. With the proofs of identity presented by her and accepted by the executor-trustees of the estate and by the Surrogate, she found herself in the driver's seat.

"She no longer needed a partner—any partner; he had served his purpose by giving her the Margo-Cole proofs of identity. She could back down on her bargain with this partner without danger to herself—that is, she could refuse to share the profits with the partner who supplied her with the means of making those profits. And what could this partner do about it?—nothing. To expose the woman as an impostor meant exposing and incriminating himself.

"So the partner lost his share of the loot without a comeback. Natural motive on his part? Revenge.

"Second motive: Fear. Ann Bloomer, a woman with a police record, might be unmasked as an impostor at

174

any time, through the merest mischance. If caught, she would certainly involve her silent and invisible partner. As a matter of fact, when Ann boasted to Kerrie in the hotel room that she and somebody else had planned the murderous attacks, and actually stated: 'I and somebody else. I and—' . . . the partner shot her dead instantly. He couldn't afford to have her reveal his identity. Dead men don't bite. Nor, for that matter, do dead women."

Ellery paused, and Beau said: "You said there were three motives. What's the third?"

"That," replied Mr. Queen, "can wait. Aren't two sufficient?"

"Why couldn't *Kerrie* have been the Bloomer woman's partner?" demanded the Inspector. "Forgetting all this business of Room 1726 and Kerrie's story."

"Come, come, Dad, you're confused. Kerrie's the last person on earth who could have been Ann's partner-in-crime. If Kerrie originally possessed the proofs of Margo Cole's identity—a vast improbability by itself—whether the real Margo Cole were alive or dead, would Kerrie have engineered the imposture and thereby set up a *competing* heiress? For if the real Margo didn't come forward, Kerrie would have had the income from the entire estate, not half. No, Dad, Kerrie didn't need a partner."

Inspector Queen nibbled the end of his mustache. "Where's the proof of all this?"

"We're not ready to submit proof."

"The circumstantial case against the girl is too strong, Ellery. Even if I were convinced, there's Sampson. The D.A. simply can't drop these charges without proof."

Beau winked at Ellery and took him aside. They conferred *sotto voce* for some time.

Ellery looked worried. But he finally nodded and said to his father: "All right. You'll have your proof. I'm going to let Beau run this show, because it's fundamentally his inspiration."

"Let me handle this," said Beau eagerly, "and you'll have your killer in twenty-four hours—yes, and a whole lot more besides!"

"It shouldn't take more than twenty-four hours," agreed Mr. Queen. "Yes, I think we can promise that."

The Inspector hesitated. Then he threw up his hands. "All right. What do you want me to do?"

XIX

The Cadmean Illusion

AT NINE O'CLOCK THAT NIGHT THE MAIN OFFICE OF *Ellery Queen, Inc.* was crowded. The shades had been drawn and all the lights were on. On the desk stood some apparatus. A Headquarters expert sat near the apparatus, looking puzzled.

Kerrie was there in charge of a detective and a matron. She and Violet Day sat in a corner. Vi was nervous. Every few moments Kerrie had to lean over and reassure her. At other times Kerrie kept her eyes on Beau with a faith patient, secret, and maternal.

Inspector Queen was there, looking worried; District Attorney Sampson, looking skeptical; Edmund De Carlos, looking the worse for drink; Goossens, representing the estate and looking unhappy. A stranger with a kit waited in Beau's laboratory-darkroom.

Beau was jumpy. Mr. Queen took him aside. "You're skittering. Look confident, you big ape. You're acting more like an expectant father than anything else of a human nature."

"It's the look in Kerrie's eye," groaned Beau. "You suppose it's going to turn out okay? You're sure you got that message straight?"

"Captain Angus and the Coast operative landed at Newark Airport all right, I tell you," said Ellery impatiently. "They're coming here under police escort and all the trimmings. Get going, will you?"

"I'm all atwitter," said Beau with a feeble grin.

"And you show it! The whole secret of this business is to act Jovian. You're the Messiah, You know it all. A temblor couldn't shake your confidence. Go ahead!"

Beau breathed hard. He stepped forward, and Mr. Queen retired to lean against the door to the reception room.

Beau described in rapid detail the circumstances of Cadmus Cole's visit to that very office three months before, of how the multimillionaire had engaged Ellery's services in an investigation which "turned out to be the search for Cole heirs after he should die." He described Cole—his baldness, his clean-shaven, sunburnt cheeks, his toothless mouth, the way he had bumped into the door-jamb, the way he had squinted: "He seemed, both to Mr. Queen and myself, very nearsighted."

Beau went on to relate how Cole had left his fountain-pen behind—the pen with which he had sat at that very desk and written out a check for fifteen thousand dollars.

"We sent the pen back to his yacht, *Argonaut*," said Beau, "but before doing so, we took microphotographs of some very unusual markings towards the end of the cap." He took an envelope from his pocket and handed it to the Headquarters expert seated by the apparatus at the desk. "Dr. Jolliffe, here are those microphotographs. Will you examine them?"

The expert accepted the envelope. "Of course, I've only your word for it—whatever your purpose is, Mr. Rummell—that these photographs are of that pen."

"We can do better than that," put in Mr. Queen suddenly.

"We certainly can," drawled Beau. "We can produce the pen itself!"

And he stepped before Edmund De Carlos, whipped back the man's coat, plucked a fountain-pen from his vest-pocket—the pen which De Carlos had employed to write out the check for twenty-five thousand dollars and tendered *Ellery Queen, Inc.* as a bribe—and handed the fat black gold-trimmed pen to the expert with an air of triumph.

De Carlos was startled. "I don't see—"

"Dr. Jolliffe," said Beau, "will you please examine this pen under the 'scope and compare its markings with those on the microphotographs?"

The expert went to work. When he looked up he said: "The markings on this pen and the markings on these photographs are identical."

"Then you'd say the microphotographs," demanded Beau, "are of this pen?"

"Unquestionably."

"I'm afraid, Mr. Rummell," remarked the District Attorney, "that I don't get the point."

"You will, Oscar," said Beau grimly. "Just bear in mind that this man De Carlos had in his possession, when

177

he entered this office tonight, a fountain-pen which was in the possession of Cadmus Cole three months ago."

District Attorney Sampson looked bewildered. "I still—"

Beau stood squarely before De Carlos. "What did you say your name was?"

De Carlos stared at him. "Why—Edmund De Carlos, of course. Of all the ridiculous questions—"

"You're a cock-eyed liar," said Beau. *"Your name is Cadmus Cole!"*

The bearded man leaped to his feet. "You're insane!"

He snorted, half-turned away. Beau caught his arm, and the man cried out.

"You're Cadmus Cole," said Beau softly, "—nose for nose, eyes for eyes, mouth for mouth, chin for chin; in fact, feature for feature. And we can prove it!"

"Prove it?" The man licked his lips.

"If you'll be kind enough to remove your beard, your wig, your glasses, and your false teeth, Queen and I will make a formal identification of you as Cadmus Cole."

"Ridiculous! Never heard such nonsense. Inspector, you can't—Mr. District Attorney, I stand on my rights as—"

"One moment," snapped the Inspector. He conferred with District Attorney Sampson inaudibly. Then he came forward and said abruptly to Beau: "You claim this man is really Cole, and that you and Ellery can identify him as such?"

"That's our story," said Beau, "and he's stuck with it."

The Inspector glanced at Ellery, who nodded slowly.

"Then I'm sorry, Mr. De Carlos, or Mr. Cole, or whoever you are," said Inspector Queen in a grim voice, "but you'll have to submit to an identification test."

He reached up himself and pulled at the man's hair, and was obviously flabbergasted when the hair came off the man's head in one piece. Goossens sat open-mouthed, completely and genuinely astonished. Kerrie and Vi were gaping, too.

"Take out your teeth!"

Sullenly, the man complied.

"Now your glasses."

The man did so, and remained blinking and squinting in the harsh glare of the office lights.

"How about this beard?" demanded the Inspector of Beau. "Is that a phony, too?"

"No, it's on the level," replied Beau with a grin. "He

must have grown it between the time he visited us and the time he showed up in New York again after that dramatic little business of his own 'death at sea.' "

"Got a razor?" snapped Inspector Queen.

"Better. A barber." And Beau went into the laboratory. He emerged with the stranger who was carrying the kit. "Okay, Dominic," said Beau, smiling broadly. "Once over—but good! *Kapeesh?*"

The detective who accompanied Kerrie came forward on a sign from the Inspector; but the bearded man sat down voluntarily in his chair and folded his arms, blinking and squinting furiously.

The barber shaved him, and his audience watched the operation with a fascinated expectancy, Beau tense behind the chair, as if he expected the bearded man to leap from the chair and try to escape. But the man sat quietly.

During the shaving of the beard, Mr. Queen went into the reception room, shutting the communicating door carefully. After a moment he returned and took Beau aside.

"They're here," he whispered.

"Who?"

"Captain Angus and the Coast man."

"Oh, baby! Keep 'em out there, El, till I find the psychological moment. Then—socko!"

When the beard was gone and the barber dismissed, Beau and Ellery surveyed that denuded, working face in silence. The sunken cheeks, the squinty eyes, the bald head . . .

"Well?" said Inspector Queen. "Is this the same man who called on you here three months ago?"

"That's Cadmus Cole," said Beau.

"Ellery?"

"The same man," nodded Mr. Queen.

"Frame-up!" mumbled the shaven man, drooling. "It's a frame-up! I'm De Carlos! I'm De Carlos!"

"Why, the bug even talks the same way," grinned Beau, "now that his plate's missing. Doesn't he, Ellery?"

"Identically."

"Of course," said District Attorney Sampson, "again we have only the word of you gentlemen."

"Not at all," retorted Beau. "The day Cole called on us in this office I listened in on the conversation from my office next door. We've developed a system in this agency, Your Worship. We like to keep complete records

179

of our wackier clients. That's why we photographed the pen. That's why," he said, taking a large photograph from his pocket, "I took a candid-camera shot of our friend here through a little convenient arrangement in the wall, and later enlarged it. How's this?"

They crowded around the enlargement, staring from the photograph to the man in the chair.

"No doubt about it," snapped the Inspector. "Except for that fringe of gray on his skull now, it's the same man. I guess your game's up, Cole!"

"I'm *not* Cole!" screamed the man. "I'm Edmund De Carlos! I can furnish a hundred proofs I'm Edmund De Carlos!"

"Yeah?" drawled Beau. He waved at Ellery. "I now retire in favor of my eminent colleague, that noted orator, Mr. Ellery Queen."

Mr. Queen stepped forward. "We've proved you're Cole in three ways," he said to the bald man. "By your possession of Cole's identified fountain-pen, by our personal identification of you as the man who called on us three months ago, and—for legal evidence—by this candid-camera photograph.

"We're in a position to present a fourth proof so damning, Mr. Cole, you may pass judgment on it yourself."

"The name," spat the bald man, "is De Carlos!"

Mr. Queen shrugged and took a photostat from the desk. "This photostat shows the cancelled voucher of a check for fifteen thousand dollars written out by Cadmus Cole in this office the afternoon he engaged our services. It's gone through the Clearing House, as you see.

"Now how can we be sure the signature on this check," he continued, "is genuinely that of Cadmus Cole? There are three ways to authenticate it. First, he wrote it out himself under the eyes of Mr. Rummell and me. Second, and much more conclusive, *Cole's bank authenticated on demand, and later honored, the check exhibiting this signature.* Third, we may compare the signature on this check with the signature on Cadmus Cole's will—the will-signature, incidentally, which was subjected to the most searching scrutiny by the Surrogate, who ultimately probated the will. Mr. Goossens, have you brought the photostat of the Cole will-signature, as I requested?"

The attorney hastily removed a photostat from his brief-case and handed it to Ellery.

"Yes," said Mr. Queen with satisfaction, "the similarity
180

even to a layman's eye is unmistakable. Will you satisfy yourselves?"

The District Attorney and Inspector Queen compared the check-signature and the will-signature.

The Inspector nodded, and Sampson said: "We'd have to have expert opinion, of course, but I admit they look identical."

"And in the face of other evidence, we may take the assumption to be a fact. In other words, the man who wrote out this check in our office three months ago must have been Cadmus Cole. Do you agree?"

They nodded.

Mr. Queen laid down the Cole check-photostat and picked up two other photostats. "These are of a twenty-five thousand dollar check written out the other night, also in this office, also before our eyes, by this gentleman who has been calling himself Edmund De Carlos. I have the original in my possession; it has not been deposited for, at the moment, immaterial reasons." Mr. Queen handed one of the De Carlos-check photostats to the sunburnt man. "Do you deny the signature on this check to be yours?"

"I'm neither denying nor affirming," mumbled the man.

"No matter; Rummell and I will swear to it, and there must be hundreds of specimens of your handwriting extant since you took up residence in the Tarrytown estate of Cadmus Cole.

"Now, ladies and gentlemen," continued Mr. Queen, taking back the photostat, "there exists a strange and exhilarating kinship between the names Cadmus Cole and Edmund De Carlos. Purely a coincidence, of course, but it makes for an attractive little demonstration.

"Note that in the name 'Edmund De Carlos' we have every letter of the alphabet which occurs in the name 'Cadmus Cole' and which would be required in a reconstruction of the name 'Cadmus Cole'! Even, observe, to the capital or initial—C. This makes it possible for us to perform an educational experiment.

"I'm going to take these two photostats of the check written out by Mr. De Carlos, which contains his full signature in his own handwriting, and cut up the De Carlos signature into its components.

"Then I shall rearrange these and paste them down on another sheet of paper, in such an order that they will spell out the name 'Cadmus Cole.' In this way we'll have the name 'Cadmus Cole' written in Edmund De Carlos's handwriting."

With scissors and pastepot Mr. Queen went to work.

When he was finished he observed: "We are now in a position to cap our little climax. Here is Cadmus Cole's authentic signature, taken from the cancelled check-voucher:

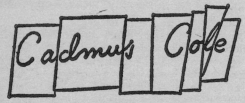

Here is Edmund De Carlos's authentic signature, taken from the original check he wrote out to the order of *Ellery Queen, Inc.*:

And here is a manufactured 'Cadmus Cole' signature—synthesized from two photostats of Edmund De Carlos's signature:

Compare all three, please."

And while they were examining his three exhibits, Mr. Queen added: "As a matter of fact, while this little demonstration piques, in a sense it was unnecessary. You had merely to compare De Carlos' signature on the Cole will—as witness—with Cole's signature—as testator—to see that they were written by the same hand. I've never seen the will before tonight, but I'm surprised you didn't notice the similarity, Mr. Goossens."

"I'm surprised myself," muttered Goossens, staring at the exhibits. "And I imagine the Surrogate will be, too!"

The Inspector straightened up. "That's enough for me.

You're Cole, Mister, and there's no question about *that*."

District Attorney Sampson looked uneasy. "It certainly appears that way."

"Why did you pretend to be dead?" demanded the Inspector of the silent man in the chair. "What happened to the real De Carlos? What's behind this masquerade, Cole? With the murder of Margo Cole's impostor hanging over your head, you've got some mighty tall explaining to do!"

The man in the chair looked about wildly. "But I'm not Cole!" he cried in his mumbly voice. "How many times do I have to tell you that?"

He thrust his false teeth back into his mouth and clapped his glasses on his eyes; and this seemed to give him new strength, for he bounded from the chair and began to dance up and down. "I'm Edmund De Carlos! Why, there's one man that's known me for years and years—he could prove in a second who I am, because he knew Cole well, too!"

"And who might that be?" asked Beau with friendliness.

"Angus, Captain of Cole's yacht *Argonaut!* Just give me a little time, Inspector, a little time to locate Captain Angus! He'll tell you who I am! He'll—"

"What would you say," asked Beau jovially, "if I told you that your Captain Angus is in the next room, waiting to identify you as Cole?"

The sunburnt man's mouth fell open.

"We've been looking for him," continued Beau crisply, "ever since you had yourself reported dead, Cole. One of our operatives finally located him. He'd retired from active service after you docked at Santiago de Cuba and, having no dependents, he decided to take a busman's holiday. He's been on a round-the-world cruise as a passenger. His ship docked in Frisco yesterday, my operative flew him here and—" said Beau as Ellery opened the reception-room door and beckoned—"here he is!"

A tall lean man, wearing a gray suit and carrying a topcoat and a fedora hat, marched in between the San Francisco detective and Sergeant Velie.

Captain Angus was blackened from years of exposure to the ocean sun. His eyes under heavy black brows were a frosty blue-green, the color of icebergs just below the water-line; and he carried himself with an imperious assurance, as if he were accustomed to command and receive obedience.

183

He paused just inside the office and looked about.

"Captain Angus?" said Beau cheerfully, stepping forward. "I'm Rummell; this is Ellery Queen, my partner; and those two worried-looking gentlemen over there are Inspector Queen of the Homicide Squad and District Attorney Sampson of New York County."

The tall man nodded. "Quite a party," he observed dryly, in a resonant bass voice. "Is this all for me, Mr. Rummell?"

"Captain Angus, I want to ask you just one question." Beau stepped aside and pointed at the medium-sized, sunburnt, bald-headed man in the center of the room. "Who is that man?"

Captain Angus looked puzzled. He glanced from the bald man to the others and then back to the bald man. "I don't understand. Who should he be?"

"That's what we're asking *you*, Captain."

The captain grinned and said: "Why, that's Mr. De Carlos. Mr. Edmund De Carlos."

Beau choked, swallowed, spluttered. Then he cried: "De Carlos? Look again! Isn't he Cadmus Cole?"

"Mr. Cole?" Captain Angus threw back his head and guffawed. "I should say not! Mr. Cole is dead."

"Mr. Cole—is—dead?" repeated Mr. Ellery Queen, seeming to find difficulty with the English language.

"Of course! He died aboard the *Argonaut* three months ago. I fixed the shroud around his body with my own hands, sir—old-fashioned canvas, all shipshape, the way we used to do it in sail."

Beau roared: "It's a plant, a frame-up! He's been bribed to say that! You'd better tie the can on him, too, Pop!"

"Just a moment." The tall man lost his geniality, and his tone of voice brought about a sudden silence. "Do I understand you to say I'm mixed up in something crooked, Mister?"

"You heard me," snarled Beau.

"Well, you're a loud-sounding pup," said the Captain softly, "and I'd like nothing better than to thrash you for that, but the fact is I can prove my statement, because I know where at least five members of the crew are, and they'll bear me out to a man. There wasn't anything funnny about Mr. Cole's death—he died just as I reported it by radio to *White Lady*."

"Give it to him properly, Captain," said De Carlos in a vicious tone.

"Besides, this gentleman couldn't be Mr. Cole. Mr. Cole was a little taller than Mr. De Carlos, thinner, and his eyes were of a different color. Mr. De Carlos is near-sighted, has to wear glasses all the time; Mr. Cole had the best eyesight I ever knew a man of his age to have —right down to the end; never wore glasses in his life. He was completely bald; Mr. De Carlos has a fringe. He didn't have teeth, that's true, just as Mr. De Carlos hasn't; but then Mr. Cole never wore a plate—the inside of his mouth was sensitive, he used to say; couldn't stand the feeling of a plate at all. He was a vegetarian, anyway, and didn't need false teeth."

In the corner, forgotten, sat Kerrie; and over her face came an expression of hopelessness.

"And that isn't all," continued the Captain, with a quiet satisfaction at the sight of Beau's consternation. "Mr. Cole had severe arthritis in both hands—*arthritis deformans*, I think it's called. Had it long as I knew him. He once told me he'd got it all of a sudden 'way back in '19 or '20, I don't remember which. Why, his hands were so badly crippled they hardly looked human! All knotted up and discolored. You'd spot 'em in a second. But look at Mr. De Carlos's hands; they're normal in shape and color. Mr. Cole couldn't so much as hold up a pair o' telescopic glasses with either hand. He couldn't even eat by himself, because he couldn't hold a knife or fork. The steward's assistant had to feed him, like a baby."

Beau began to say something in a strangled voice, but the Inspector put up his hand.

"Have you any proof, Captain, that what you say is true?"

Captain Angus smiled. He drew an envelope bulging with snapshots from his breast pocket and threw it on the desk. "I thought these might come in handy," he said. "I'm sort of a camera bug."

The District Attorney seized the envelope and began to look through the photographs. There were dozens of them, large snapshots taken with a sharp, excellent lens.

In many De Carlos appeared beside another man, taller, thinner than De Carlos, completely bald, with twisted and crippled hands. All the photographs had been taken on shipboard, as the backgrounds indicated.

"*That*," said Captain Angus with a sly look at Beau, "was Cadmus Cole."

Ellery grabbed the photographs. Beau took one look

and then, the back of his neck furnace-red, stalked off to a corner . . . the corner opposite the one where Kerrie sat.

"That's enough for me," snapped the Inspector. He made a sign to the detective and matron. Beau looked frightened—the first time Mr. Queen had ever seen such a look on his partner's face. His shoulders sagging, he averted his eyes.

With Vi clinging to her, Kerrie was marched away, and soon only Captain Angus, the San Francisco man De Carlos, Beau, and Ellery were left.

"You'll excuse me, too," said Edmund De Carlos, slapping his wig on his skull. "Captain, you're my guest while in New York—don't forget." He stamped to the door. Then he turned and with a malevolent grin said: "And thank you, gentlemen, for the shave."

But Beau sprang like a cat, forestalling him. "No, you don't," he snarled. "You stay!"

He turned, surprised. Mr. Queen had suddenly begun to laugh. He laughed so hard that he doubled up, clutching his abdomen as he sank into the swivel-chair behind his desk.

Part SIX

XX

Mr. Queen Explains
a Logical Fallacy

"YOU'RE BOTH MAD," EXCLAIMED MR. EDMUND DE Carlos. "Get out of my way."

"What?" said Beau blankly, watching Ellery.

"If you don't let me go, I'll have you arrested!"

Captain Angus scraped his lean jaws, concealing a smile. "This looks like a private fight. So if you gentlemen will excuse me—"

Mr. Queen wiped his streaming eyes. "Please be good enough to remain, Captain," he gasped. He began to laugh again.

"What's so funny about what?" growled Beau. "Anybody would think what happened here tonight's a joke!"

"It is. Oh, it is, Beau. A great joke, and it's on me." Mr. Queen sighed and wiped his eyes once more. "I'd appreciate your remaining too, Mr. De Carlos."

"I don't see why I should!"

"Because I ask you to," said Mr. Queen, smiling. He stared at De Carlos. De Carlos clicked his plate agitatedly. "Sit down, gentlemen, sit down. There's no reason why we shouldn't discuss this fiasco like civilized people. Drink?"

Captain Angus brightened. "Now, that's different."

Ellery produced a fresh bottle of Scotch and several glasses from a desk-drawer. The Captain flung his coat and hat aside, drew up a chair, and accepted a glass companionably.

"You, too, Mr. De Carlos," said Mr. Queen. "Oh, forget it, man! Mistakes will happen in the best-regulated detective agencies."

He smiled so disarmingly, and the bottle gave off such a warmly inviting glow under the lamps, that Mr. De Carlos, although surlily, sat down and accepted a glass, too.

"Beau?"

189

"Don't I look as if I could use one?" Beau asked disgustedly.

"On that basis, you ought to appropriate the bottle. Gentlemen, a toast! To Logic—never sell her short!" Mr. Queen drank and then beamed at them all.

"Where do we go from here?" grunted Beau. "There's Kerrie back in stir, and we're as far from an answer as we ever were."

"Not quite." Mr. Queen leaned back and surveyed them with bright eyes. "Not quite, Beau. This little experience has taught me a lesson: *Always* trust the dictates of pure reason. The little voice warned me, and I was very rude. Ignored him. Completely. Shame on me."

De Carlos suddenly helped himself to another glassful, which he tossed down with a jerk.

"I told you, Beau," continued Mr. Queen, his eyes on De Carlos, "that there was one discrepancy in the array of facts at our disposal which bothered me. But the identification of poor old De Carlos here as Cadmus Cole seemed so indisputable that it made me commit the unforgivable sin . . . the sanctioning of a showdown before the case was complete to the last comma. It embarrassed Mr. De Carlos, it embarrassed me, and as for Inspector Queen, my doting parent," he grimaced, "wait until he gets me alone within the four walls of our loving home. Did you see his expression as he left?"

"I saw it," groaned Beau. "But, Ellery, how in God's name could we have been wrong? I still don't see—"

"We based our conclusion that De Carlos was really Cole on three points: his possession of Cole's fountain-pen; his perfect resemblance to the man who visited us in this office three months ago, once you eliminated the false teeth, wig, glasses, and beard; and the crusher—the incontrovertible fact that the handwriting of both persons was identical."

"Do you really need me?" muttered De Carlos. "I'd prefer—"

"Another drink, Mr. De Carlos?" asked Mr. Queen, glancing at him; and De Carlos reached quickly for the bottle again. "Now the first point, the fountain-pen, was the least decisive of the three . . . a leading, or build-up, point. And yet it was in this point that the discrepancy lay."

"What discrepancy?" howled Beau.

"Why, the fact that those peculiar markings on the

cap of the pen could only have been made by *teeth*. Of course, you saw that, Beau? Those arced patterns of dents? Those deep nicks in the hard rubber composition? It was obvious that the markings were impressed into the cap by some one who was in the habit of *chewing on the end of his fountain-pen*."

"Why, sure," said Beau. "So what?"

"The man who used the pen that day in our office was presumably the owner of the pen, and the owner of the pen was unquestionably in the habit of chewing on it. And yet the man who used the pen that day, the man who called himself Cadmus Cole, didn't have a tooth in his mouth!

"And that was the discrepancy, for I asked myself, not once but dozens of times, and finally wound up by ignoring the question: *How can a toothless man make teeth-marks on the cap of a fountain-pen?*"

Captain Angus poured another drink for himself; but at the sight of De Carlos's face he suddenly offered the glass to the bald man. De Carlos accepted it and drank with a sort of desperation; and the Captain's cold eyes grew colder.

"But De Carlos wears false teeth," protested Beau. "Couldn't those marks have been made by false teeth as well as by real teeth?"

"As a matter of fact," retorted Mr. Queen, "they couldn't have been—not by Mr. De Carlos's false teeth, at any rate."

"Why not?"

"Skip it. Let's examine, or rather re-examine, the second point: our identification of De Carlos as Cole on the basis of exact facial and physical similarity."

"But we were wrong. The Captain has identified De Carlos as De Carlos, not as Cole."

"That's right." nodded the Captain. "He *is* De Carlos."

"I *am* De Carlos," said De Carlos defiantly, glaring about.

"You *are* De Carlos," said Mr. Queen in a soft tone. "Exactly. But there is still no doubt, Mr. De Carlos, that the man who visited us three months ago looked exactly like you. Consequently, I must revise our former conclusion. We said that since Cole came that day, and since you look exactly like Cole, then you must *be* Cole. Now I say that since you are De Carlos, and since the man who visited us three months ago looked exactly like

De Carlos, then the man who visited us three months ago *was* De Carlos!"

"You mean," boomed Captain Angus, "that De Carlos came here three months ago and posed as Mr. Cole?"

"Precisely."

"I'll be damned," gasped Beau.

"Let's rather stick to the point," murmured Mr. Queen. "That's the revised conclusion, gentlemen, and it's the correct conclusion. It also clears up another point that troubled me.

"The man who introduced himself to us as Cadmus Cole came to hire our services. When I asked him, not unreasonably, what we had been hired for, he refused to say.

"Later we discovered that we had been engaged for the simplest possible task—merely to locate a couple of missing heirs. That only deepened the mystery. Why did Cole originally refuse to tell us what he was hiring us for, when it was merely to find two missing heirs?

"But now," grinned Mr. Queen, "you grasp the confirmation of my thesis. Cole made a mystery of why he was hiring us *because he didn't know why himself!* But how could Cole not know? Only in one way: if he wasn't Cole, but some one else!"

De Carlos took still another drink with trembling fingers. His cheeks, where the beard had just been shaven, were deathly pale; his cheekbones and nose, however, were bright red.

"So he was a crook after all," remarked Captain Angus reflectively. "I always suspected it. Sneaky sort. Couldn't look you in the eye." He roared suddenly at De Carlos: "What did you have up your sleeve that time, you black shark?"

"I think I can guess," said Mr. Queen gently. "The secret of his Cole impersonation three months ago lies in his character. He can carry out orders admirably. He can execute a plan concocted by some one else with remarkable efficiency. But, like most men who are trained to unquestioning obedience, he came a cropper when he pushed out on his own. Isn't that so, Mr. De Carlos?

"You knew Cole had made out his will, that he was suffering from heart disease. Cole may even have told you that he felt he had only a short time to live and would probably not return from the last West Indian cruise alive. So he sent you into town to deliver his sealed will to Goossens, with orders to stop in at our office as well and engage Ellery Queen for an *unstated* investigation. That worried you, Mr. De Carlos. What investigation? But you were too discreet to ask Cole. You were worried and you didn't ask Cole for the same reason: you had prepared a little scheme of your own. And that scheme necessitated impersonating your employer, didn't it?"

De Carlos burst out: "You know that, but you don't know why! The Captain could tell you—he knew Cole as well as I did. He was a devil, a—a snake, that man!"

"He had his moments," admitted Captain Angus with a grim nod.

"For years before his death," said De Carlos hoarsely, "he amused himself with me. He'd tell me he knew why I was sticking to him so faithfully—why I kept living that ghastly living death at sea." His face was a uniform mauve now, suffused with passion. "He'd say it was because I expected to come into his fortune when he died. And then he'd laugh and say he was going to leave me a lot of money. And then again he'd seem to change his mind and say he wouldn't leave me a cent. He kept me on a hook like that for years, playing me like a fish!"

Mr. Queen glanced inquiringly at Captain Angus, and the Captain nodded. "It's true. I'll give him that."

"Things got worse between us," cried De Carlos. "The last few months he played only one tune—that he'd leave me nothing. I guess he liked to see me try to act indifferent about it, the old devil! When he made out his will—it was the very first document of his I knew nothing about. He had Angus write it out for him. He wouldn't let me stay in the cabin. So I didn't even know what the will said."

"That's so," said the Captain. "Mr. Cole called me in and dictated his will. I wrote it out in longhand and then, when it was corrected to his satisfaction, he had me type it out. He made me burn the handwritten draft, and he was laughing."

"I was frantic," said De Carlos, clasping and unclasping his hands. "I saw all those years, alone with him, taking his orders, knuckling under to him, enduring his bad temper, having to act a part all the time—wasted, all wasted! Because he didn't have me make out the will and even kept me out of the cabin, I was positive he had cut me off without a cent. He even said to me when he handed me the sealed will to take ashore: 'Don't open it, Edmund.

193

Remember! I've enclosed instructions for the lawyer to examine the seal very carefully—to see if it's been tampered with.' And he laughed that ugly barking laugh of his, as if it were a great joke."

"Of course that wasn't true about the instructions," said Mr. Queen. "He was toying with you, trying to make you squirm."

De Carlos nodded, seizing the bottle. He drank deeply and set the bottle down with a bang. "That was when I made my plan," he said defiantly. "It wasn't very clear. I was half-crazy. . . . Who knew Cole personally? I said to myself. Nobody but Angus and I and the crew had seen him for eighteen years. If Cole died at sea and Angus was willing to throw in with me, why, we could buy off the crew and the two of us could come back and say it was *De Carlos* who died and was buried at sea. Because I'd take over the role of Cole! Nobody would be the wiser, and Angus and I would divide something like fifty million dollars."

He stopped short, frightened by Captain Angus's expression. The seaman seized De Carlos by the collar and said in a low voice: "You dirty rascal. Tell these men this is the first I've ever heard of that thieving plan—tell 'em, or I'll make you wish you'd never been born!"

"No, no, I didn't mean to imply—" began De Carlos hurriedly. "Mr. Queen, Mr. Rummell, I assure you . . . the Captain didn't have the faintest idea of what I had in mind. I hadn't spoken to him about it at all!"

"That's better," scowled the Captain, and he sat down again and helped himself quietly to another drink.

"I see," murmured Mr. Queen. "So that's why you impersonated Cole—shaved the gray fringe off your skull, removed your glasses, your dental plate. Made up that way, you corresponded roughly to Cole. Later, when you expected to return, after Cole died at sea, with the story that *De Carlos* had died, you'd pass yourself off as Cole and there would be three people at least prepared to swear in all sincerity that you *were* Cole—the three people you had visited ashore in the guise of Cole: Goossens, Rummell, and myself. Grandiose in conception, Mr. De Carlos, but a little optimistic, wasn't it?"

"I realized that later," muttered De Carlos with a weak, wry smile. "Anyway, when I got back to the yacht Cole blew up my whole scheme himself without realizing it. He showed me a carbon copy of the will I'd just delivered to Goossens—and I saw that in the will, after all, he'd left me a million dollars. A million! I was so relieved I abandoned my—my plan."

"But you still weren't out of the woods," remarked Mr. Queen. "Because Goossens and Rummell and I had seen you bald, toothless, clean-shaven, and without glasses —really quite denuded, Mr. De Carlos—at the time you passed yourself off as Cole. Obviously, in abandoning your plan, you had to plan to present yourself in our society looking entirely different! You had to get yourself a wig—in Cuba, was it?—put back your plate and glasses, and of course it was immediately after Cole told you he had left you a million that you began to grow a beard."

"Wait a minute." Beau frowned. "There's one thing I don't get—that handwriting business. This worm *did* write out a check, signing Cole's name to it, and the bank *did* pass it. How come? Even the signature on the will—"

"Ah," said Mr. Queen, "that was the beautiful part of it—the part that was so slick and pat that upon it we based a wholly erroneous theory. That handwriting business was the crux of your illusion, wasn't it, De Carlos? It made the whole fantastic project possible. Who would dream that the man who visited us was not Cole when we saw him sign Cole's name before our eyes and the check went through the bank without a hitch?

"But Captain Angus has already given us the answer to that." De Carlos slumped in his seat, drunk and sullen. "Cole's arthritis! *Arthritis deformans* is a crippling disease of the joints for which, once it has fully developed—and it develops very quickly—there's no known cure. It's accompanied by a great deal of pain—"

"Pain?" The Captain made a face. "Mr. Cole used to go near crazy with it. He took from sixty to a hundred and twenty grains of aspirin a day for relief as long as I knew him. I used to tell him he ought to leave the sea, because the damp air only made the pain worse, but I guess he was too sensitive about his crippled hands to go back to a landsman's society."

Ellery nodded. "And the Captain said his hands were so badly misshapen that he had to be fed—couldn't even handle a knife and fork. Obviously, then, he couldn't *write*, either.

"But if he couldn't write, that was the answer to the handwriting problem. Cole was an immensely wealthy man and, even though he had retired, his far-flung holdings must have necessitated an occasional signature on a legal paper. And of course there was the problem of signing checks. He couldn't carry his fortune about with him in cash. Solution? Good Man Friday, who'd been with him for more than twenty-five years.

"Certainly at the time arthritis struck him—which must have been just before he made his post-War killing in Wall Street—De Carlos had been Cole's trusted lieutenant long enough to serve as a useful pair of hands in place of the hands Cole found useless.

"So he had De Carlos begin signing the name 'Cadmus Cole' to everything, including checks. To save tedious explanation, and because he was sensitive about his deformity, as Captain Angus has indicated, he wished to keep his condition a secret. He had you open new accounts in different banks, didn't he, De Carlos? So that from the beginning of his monastic existence, his name in your handwriting wasn't questioned!"

"You mean to say," demanded Captain Angus, "that De Carlos didn't tell you gentlemen that?"

"Overlooked it," said Beau dryly.

"But I don't see— Why, he signed Cole's will for the old gentleman! He had to, because Mr. Cole couldn't even hold a pen, as Mr. Queen says. After I typed out the will, I signed as witness and took the will to the radio operator's cubby, where Sparks signed, too. Then I brought the will back to Mr. Cole's cabin, and he sent for De Carlos, and De Carlos signed Mr. Cole's name, I suppose, after I left. I noticed while I was there," the Captain chuckled, "that Mr. Cole didn't let De Carlos see what was in the will. Having his little joke to the last."

"Just the same," retorted Beau, "it seems to me for a smart hombre Cole was taking one hell of a chance letting this De Carlos potato sign his checks!"

"Not really," said Ellery. "I imagine Cole kept a close watch on you, didn't he, De Carlos? Probably supervised the accounts, and then you were at sea practically all the time, where you couldn't get into mischief even if you wanted to."

"Hold!" said Beau. "Hold. There's another thing. This monkey tried to buy us off. Offered us twenty-five grand to quit poking our noses into the case. Why?"

"Excellent question," agreed Mr. Queen. "Why?" De Carlos squirmed. "Then I'll tell *you*. Because you'd lost most of Cole's legacy by gambling, ill-advised market speculation, night-clubbing, the cutey route, general all-around helling—it didn't take you long to run through what was left of the million after taxes were deducted, did it, De Carlos? And so there you were, almost broke, and the golden goose lying fathoms under. You conceived another brilliant idea."

"You're the devil himself," said De Carlos thickly.

"Please," protested Mr. Queen. "Is that fair to the Old 'Bub? With the woman who posed as Margo Cole dead, and with Kerrie Shawn, the other heiress, arrested and —you fervently hoped—slated for conviction and execution, that left the huge principal of the Cole estate free of heirs and completely in the hands of its trustees. And who were they? Goossens and your worthy self! Does that suggest anything, Mr. De Carlos?"

Beau stared. "Don't tell me Mr. Smart was going to make another deal to milk the estate—with Goossens, this time!"

"The firm of *Ellery Queen, Inc.* being out of the picture," murmured Mr. Queen, "I daresay that was the general idea. And I've no doubt whatever but that Mr. Goossens is as ignorant this moment, De Carlos, of your second plan as the good Captain here was of your first."

De Carlos struggled to his feet. "You've been very clever, Mis—Mis'er Queen—"

"Incidentally," remarked Mis'er Queen, "let me congratulate you on your forbearance. Of course you knew from the very first that Beau Rummell wasn't Ellery Queen, because you met us both three months ago in our proper identities, when *you* were pretending to be Cole. But you couldn't unmask us without revealing how you came to know, so you maintained a discreet silence. Truly a Chestertonian situation!"

"What you go—going to do about it?" demanded Mr. De Carlos, leering. "Huh, Mis'er Queen?"

"For the present, nothing."

"Thought sh—so!" said De Carlos contemptuously. "Jus' a lot o' wind. Farewell, gen'l'men. C'm'up an' see me shome—some time!"

He staggered to the door and disappeared.

"I think," said Captain Angus with a certain grimness, "I'll accept his invitation right now. Help you keep an eye on him. I've nothing better to do, anyway."

"That would be fine, Captain," said Mr. Queen heartily. "We can't have him leaving on a sudden jaunt to Indo-China, can we?"

The Captain chuckled, snatched his coat and hat, and hurried after De Carlos.

"Now that we're back where we started from, what are we going to do?" Beau hurled a paper-knife at the opposite wall. It stuck, quivering.

"Good shot," said Mr. Queen abstractedly. "Oh, we're doing it."

"Doing what?"

"Sitting here engaged in a furious cerebration. At least I am, and I suggest you buckle down, too. We haven't much time. We promised Dad a prisoner in twenty-four hours, and that gives us only until late tomorrow morning."

"Quit clowning," growled Beau. He flung himself at the leather sofa and scowled at the ceiling. "Poor Kerrie."

"I'm *not* clowning."

Beau swung his legs to the floor. "You mean you really think there's a chance to crack this hazel-nut?"

"I do."

"But it's more of a mess now than before!"

"Darkest before the dawn, every cloud has a silver lining, and so on," murmured Mr. Queen. "There are heaps of new facts. Heaps. Selection is what we need, Beau—selection, arrangement, and synthesis. Everything's here. I feel it. Don't you?"

"No, I don't," said Mr. Rummell rudely. "The only thing I feel is sore. If there were only some one I could punch in the nose! And with Kerrie back in the can, eating her heart out . . ." He seized the bottle of Scotch and said with a glower: "Well, what are you waiting for? Go ahead and think!"

XXI

The Fruits
of Cerebration

MR. QUEEN MADE CERTAIN PREPARATIONS FOR HIS EN-gagement with ratiocination.

He opened a fresh package of cigarets and lined the twenty white tubules up on the desk before him, so that they resembled the rails of a picket fence. He filled a water goblet with what was left of the Scotch and set it conveniently at his elbow. Mr. Rummell, sizing up the situation, vanished. He returned ten minutes later bearing another quart of Scotch and a tall carton of coffee.

Mr. Queen barely acknowledged this thoughtfulness. He removed his jacket, laid it neatly on a chair, loosened his necktie, and rolled up his shirt-sleeves.

Then, with the goblet in one hand and a cigaret in the other, he seated himself in the swivel-chair, set his feet upon the desk, and began.

Beau lay down on the sofa and thought desperately.

At one-thirty a.m. the silence was riven by a peculiar series of noises. Mr. Queen started out of deep thought. But it was only Mr. Rummell, on the sofa, snoring.

"Beau."

The snores persisted. Mr. Queen rose, filled a glass with coffee, went to the sofa, and nudged Mr. Rummell.

"Huh? What? Well, I was listening—" began Mr. Rummell contentiously, his eyes struggling to open.

"Strange," croaked Mr. Queen. "I wasn't saying anything. Here, drink this coffee."

Beau rumpled his hair, yawning. "Ought to be ashamed of myself. I *am* ashamed of myself. How's it coming?" He drank.

"There are one or two points," observed Mr. Queen, "that still elude me. Otherwise, *on marche*. I beg your pardon. I always break out in a foreign language at this time of the night. Do you think you can keep awake long enough to answer a few questions?"

"Shoot."

"It's an odd situation," said Mr. Queen, beginning a circumambient patrol of the office. "First time in my experience I've had to rely completely on the senses of another person. Complicates matters. You were in this from the beginning, and I was on the outside trying to look in. I've the feeling that the master-key to this case is hidden in an out-of-the-way place—a chance remark, some innocuous event . . ."

"I'll help all I can," said Beau dispiritedly. "I fell asleep when my limited brain couldn't hold any more. I've shot my bolt, kid. It's up to you now."

Mr. Queen sighed. "I'm duly impressed by the responsibility. Now I'm going over the case from the start. At every point where I omit something that actually happened, or where something occurred which you forgot to mention, sing out. Supply the missing link. I don't care how trivial it is. In fact, the more trivial the better."

"Go ahead."

The inquisition began. Mr. Queen kept it up mercilessly, until Beau's lids drooped again and he had to fight with himself to keep awake.

Suddenly Mr. Queen displayed a ferocious exultancy. He waved Beau back to the sofa and began to race up and down, mumbling to himself excitedly.

"That's it. That's it!" He scurried around the desk and sat down. Seizing a pencil, he began to scribble feverishly, setting down facts in order, like a mathematician working out a problem in calculus. Beau lay, exhausted, on the sofa.

"Beau!"

"Well?" Beau sat up.

"I've got it." And Mr. Queen, having delivered this epic intelligence with the utmost calm, the stranger for its having been preceded by such fury, set the pencil down and began to tear up his notes. He tore them into tiny fragments, heaped them in an ashtray, and set fire to the heap. He did not speak again until the scraps were ashes.

Beau searched his partner's face anxiously. What he saw there seemed to satisfy him, for he jumped off the sofa and exclaimed: "Damned if I don't think you have! When do I go to work?"

"Instantly." Mr. Queen sat back beaming. "We have a chance, Beau, and excellent chance. You've got to work fast, though. And cautiously."

"What do you want me to do?"

"I know who killed the Bloomer woman. Logically it can be only one person. I've ironed out all the discrepancies, and there can't be the least doubt of the guilt of the person I have in mind."

"Who is it?" asked Beau grimly.

"Wait, wait; don't begrudge me my brief hour of triumph." And Mr. Queen said in a dreamful voice: "Our friend made two mistakes, one of which, I'm afraid, will prove fatal. We can capitalize on those mistakes if we jump right in. Any way I look at it—and I've looked at it every way—there are three pieces of

200

evidence which we should be able to produce to make the guilt of Ann Bloomer's murderer stand up in court."

"Three pieces of evidence?" Beau shook his head. "Either I'm a moron and you're a genius, or I'm normally intelligent and you're talking through your hat."

Mr. Queen chuckled. "Two of them are waiting for us—all we have to do is extend our hands at the proper time and they're ours. The third . . ." He rose abruptly. "The third is tough. It's the vital proof, and the hardest to find."

"What's it look like and where is it?"

"I know what it looks like—roughly," said Mr. Queen with a faint smile. "As for where it is, however, I haven't the foggiest notion."

"Then how did you figure out its existence in the first place?" demanded Beau, exasperated.

"Very simply. It *must* exist. Every consideration of logic cries out its existence. Every fact in the case demands that it exist. It's your job to locate it, and you have until noon tomorrow to do it!"

"I don't know what the devil you're jawing about," said Beau with impatience, "but tell me what it is, and I'm off."

Mr. Queen told him. And as he spoke, Mr. Rummell's black eyes glittered with wonder.

"Holy smoke!" he breathed. "Holy smoke."

Mr. Queen basked in this eloquent atmosphere of admiration.

"Though how in the world you figured it out—"

"Nothing up my sleeve," said Mr. Queen airily. "The little gray cells, as M. Poirot is wont to remark. At any rate, there's no time for explanations now. You've got to burn up the wires, rouse people from their beds—what time is it? three o'clock!—cut through several miles of red tape, grease a number of dry and itching palms, gather a crew of assistants . . . in short, get that evidence by noon!"

Beau grabbed the telephone.

As for Mr. Queen, he stretched out on the sofa with a grunt of pure sensuality and was fast asleep before Beau had finished dialing the first number.

MR. QUEEN awoke to find the sun poking at his eyelids and, to judge from its taste, a piece of old flannel mouldering in his mouth.

He groaned and sat up, rubbing the sleep from his eyes. The office was empty; the litter of glasses and ashes had been cleaned away; and by his wrist-watch it was nine o'clock, so he made the elementary deduction that Miss Hecuba Penny had reported for the day.

He staggered to the door and peered into the reception room. Miss Penny, as deduced, sat primly at her desk knitting the one hundred and fifteenth hexagon of wool which was to go into her third afghan since becoming an employee of *Ellery Queen, Inc.*

"Morning," croaked Mr. Queen. "See anything of Mr. Rummell?"

"No, but I found this note for you, Mr. Queen. Can I get you your breakfast?"

"The only thing I crave at the moment is a bath, 'Cuba, and I fear I'll have to attend to that myself."

The note, in Beau's powerful scrawl, said: "Do you snore! I'm hot on the track. I'll make the noon deadline or bust. How's the bank account? It's taking an awful shellacking, because this thing is costing a pile of jack! Beau. P.S.—What bank account? B."

Mr. Queen grinned and retired to the laboratory for a wash. With his face freshly scrubbed, he felt better. He also experienced a gentle thrill of anticipation as he sat down to the telephone.

"Inspector Richard Queen? This is an old friend."

"Oh, it's you," said the Inspector's grumpy voice. "Where were you all night?"

"Carousing with the Muses," replied Mr. Queen grandiloquently. "Just an intellectual lecher. . . . Disappointed, eh? Well, I wasn't giving you a chance to crow."

"I'm laughing with tears in my eyes! Sampson and I have been talking the case over all night and— Never mind." The Inspector paused. "What's on your celebrated mind?"

"I sense authoritarian confusion," murmured Mr. Queen, still in the lush vein. "Despite all the fireworks last night—those cerebral Roman candles—you and Sampson can't be so positive now that Kerrie Shawn lied to you. Poor Authority! Well, that's life. How would you like to attend a lecture this morning, Dad?"

"What, another? I've no time for lectures!"

"I believe," said his son, "you'll find time for this one. The speaker gave a poor performance last night, I'm told, but he guarantees to lay 'em in the aisles today."

"Oh." And the Inspector was silent again. Then he demanded suspiciously: "What have you got this time? Another resurrection from the dead?"

"If you're referring to the late Cadmus Cole, the answer is no. But I should appreciate your cooperation in a reinvestigation of Ann Bloomer's murder on the scene."

"You mean in the *Villanoy*? In 1724?" The Inspector was puzzled. "More phony melodrama?"

"I said the scene," said Ellery gently. "That includes Room 1726, Father. Don't ever forget that."

"All right, including 1726! But both the suite and the single room were gone over with a finecomb. You can't make me believe there's still something there we've overlooked!"

Mr. Queen laughed. "Now look, Dad, don't be obstreperous. Are you going to play ball with *Ellery Queen, Inc.*, or do I have to appeal directly to the Commissioner?"

"You'd do that to your own father, you scoundrel?" chuckled the Inspector suddenly. "Well, all right. But I warn you. If you fizzle this time, Sampson's going to go through with an indictment of Kerrie Shawn."

"If *I* fizzle it!" said Mr. Queen, plainly astonished. "I like that. Who's supposed to be solving this case—the Homicide Squad or a picayune, one-horse outfit? But I feel magnanimous today. The agency to the rescue!"

"Disrespectful, ungrateful—"

"Shall we say eleven-thirty at the *Villanoy?*"

XXII

Mr. Queen and
the Dragon's Teeth

"THE OLD MAN'S GOT HIS SOUR PUSS ON," WHISPERED Sergeant Velie to Mr. Queen as they stood in the sitting room of 1726 a little before noon watching the silent procession of Mr. Queen's audience.

"You're telling me?" murmured Mr. Queen. "I have to live with that sour puss. . . Ah, Kerrie. How are you feeling this exceptional morning?"

"Terrible, thank you." There were bluish circles under her eyes; her skin was a little gray and taut. "Where's Beau? He hasn't even—"

"Beau," replied Mr. Queen, "is on an assignment, but he should be here any moment now. He's losing a lot of sleep on your account, Kerrie."

"Not as much as I've lost on his, I'll bet," retorted Kerrie. "Is this something—important?"

"To you—all-important," said Ellery cheerfully. "One demonstration, and the nightmare's over for good. Now sit down there, Kerrie, like a good girl, and do nothing at all but listen."

"I—think I'll sit next to Vi. Poor Vi! You'd think, to look at her, that she's the one who's charged with . . . that nasty word."

"That's what friends are for. Ah, Sampson. Worried, as usual. How's the ailing throat?"

"Never mind the state of my health," said the District Attorney testily. "You'd be better thinking of your own! Is this on the level? Have you really got something this time?"

"Why not wait to see? Come in, Captain Angus! None the worse for your last night's experience, apparently, which is more than I can say, Mr. De Carlos, about *you*. How are you feeling this morning? Yes, yes, I know—merrily we roll along and, suddenly, there's the hangover. . . . Mr. Goossens! Sorry to trouble you again, but I can assure you this is the last of it. And Inspector Queen. Good morning!"

The Inspector said just one word. "Well?"

"You'll see."

Mr. Queen glanced at his wrist-watch casually. Where the devil was Beau with the evidence? He smiled, cleared his throat, and advanced to the center of the room.

"Yesterday," he began, "Beau Rummell made a certain promise which I seconded. We promised that within twenty-four hours we should turn over to the authorities the murderer of Ann Bloomer, alias Margo Cole. We're ready to keep that promise. The murderer of Ann Bloomer is in this room."

Inspector Queen and District Attorney Sampson stared squarely at Kerrie Shawn. She flushed and looked down at her fingers. Then, defiantly, she stared back at them.

"That person," continued Mr. Queen, "can save a lot of wear and tear on your servant's larynx by surrendering now. I can assure you," he said, glancing pointedly over their heads, "that the ball is over. Will you unmask voluntarily, or shall I have to do it for you?"

Where was Beau?

The Inspector and the District Attorney made an unconscious survey. The objects of their attention were painfully conscious, however. They held their breath until they could hold it no longer; then they expelled it in concert—the innocent with the guilty.

And Inspector Queen and District Attorney Sampson looked troubled, and Mr. Queen went on with a shrug. "Hope," he remarked, "but I assure you—no charity. Very well, you force me to elucidate. And because your crime was a completely mercenary one, and because you insist upon being discovered, as the antique phrase goes, in the 'full panoply' of your guilt, I promise you there will be no mercy, either."

But again there was only silence.

Where was Beau?

"The case," said Mr. Queen abruptly, "or, rather, the solution of the case, hinges upon three facts. Three facts, and three pieces of evidence.

"The facts first. They are the three characteristics of the killer of Ann Bloomer which I've been able to piece together from an exhaustive analysis of the data at my disposal.

"The first characteristic is really a point of identification. As explained to you last night, Mr. Edmund De Carlos—" here De Carlos choked, and Mr. Queen paused until he had swallowed the obstruction in his throat— "Mr. De Carlos by an oversight left behind him, when he called upon us disguised as Cadmus Cole three months ago, a fountain-pen. This pen was unique in possessing certain identifying marks which distinguished it from all other pens of similar design and manufacture . . . despite the fact that such pens were, and are, sold by the hundreds of thousands the world over.

"Let me explain that statement. The scratches and dents—the entire series of little arced patterns on the cap of the pen—could only have been made by human teeth. Now human teeth are, in their modest way, an eloquent symbol of man: they are invariably imperfect. I'm not referring to dental caries or any other pathological manifestation. I'm referring simply to structure and design. No two sets of teeth, no matter how healthy, are identical.

The shape of the arch, the size of the individual teeth, the way they lie in the arch in relation to one another, and so on—these all vary with individuals. Two sets of teeth might appear identical to the layman, but any dentist could show you dozens of points of difference after the most casual examination.

"It's scarcely necessary to belabor the point. In the old days any one could spot a set of false teeth in a stranger's mouth—the teeth were too *regular*. Unnaturally so. These days dentists hold a mirror up to Nature. They turn out dental plates which fool most laymen. And why are we fooled? Because modern dental plates exhibit teeth not only natural in color but irregularly aligned and imperfectly shaped as well.

"Criminological science has long recognized the value of teeth-marks as clues to identity. Where clear impressions of teeth can be found, they are as incontrovertible evidence as fingerprints. True, the teethmarks on the cap of the fountain-pen in question are not the impression of a full set of teeth, or even the substantial number of a full set. The marks of, at most, two or three upper teeth and two or three lowers. But even that is sufficient for the careful observer."

They were tightly, watchfully quiet, as if each had a deep personal stake in the least word being uttered by Mr. Queen. He glanced at his watch again.

"I must now confess," he went on with a faint smile, "to having engineered an unquestionably illegal suppression of important evidence. How important I leave you to judge. But I did suppress it when Mr. Rummell and I found it beneath the radiator of Room 1726 only a short time after the murderer of Ann Bloomer fled from it. In short, it was a companion-piece of the fountain-pen—an automatic pencil of the same hard black rubber composition, with similar gold trimming."

Inspector Queen glared at District Attorney Sampson, who glared back, then both glared at Mr. Queen.

The Inspector rose and roared: "You found what?"

"I'll take my punishment later, please," said Mr. Queen. "Meanwhile, may I continue? The facts were these: The room had been prepared for occupancy only a short time before, and was spotless. The pencil had fallen between the radiator and the window and had rolled under the radiator. Since the murderer stood at the window before and during the firing of the murder-weapon, it was obvious that the pencil had been dropped by that worthy accidentally during or directly preceding the commission of the crime. Incidentally, Dad, the ashes, burnt matchstick, and cigaret butt were mine. I left them for you—I had to leave something in lieu of the pencil, didn't I?"

Inspector Queen sank back, purple.

Mr. Queen continued in haste: "Examination of the pencil indicated that it was part of the writing set to which the pen belonged, that the same person had owned both implements, *for the bite-marks on the pencil were identical with the bite-marks on the pen.*

"Now that," said Mr. Queen in a sharper tone, "is a scientific fact. I've verified that fact by applying for expert opinion since—a concession to legal considerations, for I was satisfied even before consulting authority that the teeth-marks were identical. The person who had the deplorable habit of chewing on his pen and pencil possesses a very long canine in a certain characteristic relation to the tooth below it and the teeth to either side. I could give you the technical picture as it was given to me, but I'm sure it would bore you.

"Just bear in mind that the dent bored by the point of that canine, and the impression of the teeth adjacent to that canine, make identification positive. The identical picture is presented by both pen and pencil. They must have been scarred by the same teeth.

"Now, who dropped that pencil in the room from which the shots were fired which killed Ann Bloomer? The person who occupied the room during the commission of the crime; in other words, the murderer. Or, in still other words—if we can establish the ownership of the pen-and-pencil set, we arrive at once at the identity of the murderer."

De Carlos was struggling to express himself.

"Yes, Mr. De Carlos?"

"It's not—it's not mine," he gasped. "Not mine!"

"No?" asked Mr. Queen softly. "Then perhaps we can eliminate a deal of gabble right now, Mr. De Carlos. If the pen and pencil aren't yours, to whom do they belong?"

De Carlos looked about in a sort of bafflement. Then his chin sank, and his eyes, and he muttered: "I'm not talking. I'm not saying a word."

"Perhaps the moment will come," murmured Mr.

Queen, "when you will feel more disposed to conversation, Mr. De Carlos.

"Second characteristic of the murderer: a very curious point that I almost overlooked. Unfortunately for our bashful marksman, I am a methodical creature. I went back over the ground and saw it—really for the first time—in its proper perspective and proportions.

"The police on the day following Miss Shawn's and Mr. Rummell's supposed marriage, received an anonymous tip by telegraph. The obliging tipster indicated that the marriage had been no marriage at all. This information, followed by immediate corroboration when investigation proved the marriage, as advertised, to have been a hoax, supplied the authorities with a perfect motive in the case they were building against Miss Shawn.

"Now who would be interested in copper-riveting the case against Miss Shawn? Obviously the person who had stolen her revolver, who had used it to kill Ann Bloomer, and who had then tossed it into this room across the angle of the court from 1726—in other words, the thoughtful individual who was trying to frame Miss Shawn for the murder . . . the murderer in person. If any further corroboration of this deduction were needed, I should merely like to point out that the means employed in tipping off the police—telegraph message given to the telegraph office by telephoning from a pay-station—was exactly the means employed in reserving Room 1726 at the *Villanoy* on the night of the murder."

Inspector Queen nodded guiltily, as if this indeed had occurred to him, and the District Attorney reddened, as if it had not.

"Which brings us," continued Mr. Queen in dulcet tones, "to characteristic number three. On another and less memorable occasion I pointed out, through a strictly logical exercise, that the woman who posed as Margo Cole—that is, Ann Bloomer—must have had a partner . . . a silent, invisible partner who provided the notorious Miss Bloomer with the various proofs of identity which established her as one of the missing Cole heiresses.

"This silent partner had three motives for killing Ann Bloomer: revenge, if Miss Bloomer after being accepted as Margo Cole refused to split the loot—in the light of Miss Bloomer's known character, a distinct possibility; fear that she might expose her partner, either deliberately if she should accidentally be discovered to be an impostor, or

208

—as actually occurred—through a slip of the tongue in an unguarded moment; and a third motive which I must again," Mr. Queen said with an apologetic smile, "hold back as a special tidbit for your future delectation.

"At any rate, discover the identity of Miss Bloomer's partner, the mysterious shadow behind her false claim, and you obviously discover her murderer.

"What do we find then, in recapitulation? That the person we seek is: A—the owner of the pen-and-pencil set; B—the person who tipped off the police to the fact that the supposed marriage between Miss Shawn and Mr. Rummell was a hoax; and C—Ann Bloomer's silent partner.

"Or, to put it another way, we must find the one and only person who had criminal opportunity—the pencil places that person in the room from which the fatal shots were fired; who had criminal motive—as Ann Bloomer's vengeful partner seeking also to seal her lips forever as to his identity; and who wished to frame Miss Shawn —and did so by tipping off the police about the fake marriage.

"That's a fairly complete picture," murmured Mr. Queen. "Need I continue? Won't our friend the silent partner step forward and end this excruciating suspense?"

And in the ensuing silence Mr. Queen thought furiously: "Damn Beau! Why isn't he here?"

And, also in the silence, as if in response to Mr. Queen's unexpressed question, the telephone rang.

They started, nervously. But Mr. Queen smiled as he leaped for the telephone. "A call I've been expecting. You'll excuse me?"

A voice said in his ear—a tired but jubilant voice: "Beau Rummell. Who is this?"

"You're speaking to the proper party," said Mr. Queen sharply. "Well?"

"I've got the goods, my fran'."

"Well, well." Mr. Queen expelled a long, ecstatic breath. "How soon can you be here with the—er—merchandise?"

"I'm downtown. Say fifteen minutes. How's it going?"

"So far, so good."

"Save the last poke for me. Kerrie all right?"

"Bearing up like a Spartan. Hurry, will you?"

Mr. Queen hung up and turned again to his audience. There was a rustle among them—the strangest little sound. Not of impatience. Nor of fatigue. Nor yet of relief from the unnatural silence. Rather it was the rendition of a tension, a physical expression to relieve an intolerable strain.

And one face there was ghastly.

Mr. Queen chose to ignore its damning pallor. He remarked cheerfully: "Let's examine Point B more closely. Who tipped off the police that the marriage was a hoax, thereby driving the last nail into the frame-up of Miss Shawn?

"There were four persons who knew the marriage was a hoax before the tip was sent. And only four.

"One was my partner, Beau Rummell, the 'bridegroom.' Well, how about Mr. Rummell as a possibility? No, no, he is eliminated on numerous counts. I need mention only one. At the instant the shots were fired Mr. Rummell was stepping out of the elevator on the seventeenth floor of the *Villanoy*. The elevator operator has testified to this. Since a body cannot occupy two different sections of space at the same time, Mr. Rummell obviously couldn't also have been in Room 1726 at that instant. And so he cannot be the person we are looking for."

Mr. Queen lit a cigaret. "The second person who knew the marriage was a hoax was—myself. I could make out some excellent arguments against the theory that I was Ann Bloomer's accomplice and subsequent murderer, of course—"

"Keep going," growled District Attorney Sampson.

"Thank you, Mr. Sampson," murmured Mr. Queen. "A magnificent compliment. By the way, Miss Day—I believe you're Miss Day, although I've never been formally presented—why are you looking so completely miserable?"

Vi jumped visibly, going pale at having every one's attention so abruptly focussed upon her. "I—accused Beau Rummell of . . . Never mind. Of course, I didn't know—"

"I see." Mr. Queen smiled. "Mr. Rummell's told me all about that. Very amusing. I hope you'll apologize, Miss Day."

Kerrie smiled and pressed Vi's hand, and Vi sank back on the verge of tears.

"I don't want to interrupt," murmured Kerrie, "but I —thought pretty much the same thing once."

"Yes, Beau is a secretive individual. Seems tough. Not

210

really, though. I hope *you'll* apologize, too!" Kerrie flushed and lowered her gaze. "I'm sure you will, to Mr. Rummell's complete satisfaction. Now where was I?

"Oh, yes! That makes two of our four possibilities. The remaining pair are Messrs. Goossens and De Carlos, the trustees of the Cole estate. The evening Mr. Rummell and Miss Shawn registered at the *Villanoy* as man and wife, the evening of the murder, Mr. Rummell deserted his 'wife' almost as soon as they had checked in. Quit her cold, the softie. A gentleman beneath it all, you see. Wouldn't take advantage of an innocent girl—"

"Get on, get on," snapped the Inspector.

"Your wish is my command. At any rate, driven to the outer world by his conscience, Mr. Rummell thought of how he might occupy his time. He decided to occupy it usefully. He went up to our office and wrote two letters identical in content—one addressed to Mr. Goossens, one addressed to Mr. De Carlos.

"The letters informed these gentlemen, as co-trustees, that the marriage was a hoax, and begged the recipients to keep this intelligence confidential. Beau wrote only because, had he not informed the trustees of the true state of affairs, they would have had to take immediate steps to cut her out of her uncle's will. Being in fact unmarried, Miss Shawn was still entitled to her inheritance.

"My partner sent these two letters by special delivery. It was late at night, so of course the letters must have been delivered early the following morning. By the morning after the crime, then, two people more knew that the marriage had been a hoax—the aforesaid Messrs. Goossens and De Carlos. Theoretically, then, either of you two gentlemen," and Mr. Queen addressed himself with a smile to the two trustees, "could have sent the anonymous tip to the police."

"I didn't!" cried De Carlos.

"Nor I," said Goossens.

"Wait a minute," barked the Inspector. "You've mentioned four, Ellery. There are really five. You're forgetting this phony Justice of the Peace who performed the fake marriage ceremony. He certainly knew!"

"Now, Dad," said Mr. Queen sadly. "Must you steal my thunder?"

"Five!"

"Four." Mr. Queen shook his head. "I said four, and I still say four. Acrobatic mathematics, really."

"Rummell, Goossens, De Carlos, you, and the phony Justice—that makes five!"

"This pains me," murmured Mr. Queen. "I *must* dissent: four. Because, you see, *I* was the phony Justice."

He grinned at Kerrie, who stared back with parted lips. The Inspector could only wave his fragile hand feebly.

"Go on," said Lloyd Goossens, lighting his pipe. "It seems Mr. De Carlos and I are to be eliminated by some logical process. I'm curious to hear how you do it."

"I don't want to hear!" yelled De Carlos. "I'm getting out of here! I've had enough of this—"

"Not quite enough, Mr. De Carlos." Ellery eyed him and De Carlos collapsed in his chair in a sort of agony. "And since you're so reluctant to hear, you shall. We must pay special attention to you, Mr. De Carlos. You've caused more trouble in this case, I'm sure, than you're worth! You've been a confuser of issues, a brilliantly red herring, from the very first. And yet, oddly enough, for all the sleepless nights you've given me, I must confess this case would never have been solved had you not been a factor in it."

"I must say," began De Carlos helplessly, "I must say—"

"I'll say it for you, shall I?" Mr. Queen smiled. "You see, you're the man who, in the guise of Cole, brought that blessed, significant, colossal fountain-pen into my life. Did that pen belong to you? Did it?"

"I told you it didn't!" cried De Carlos. "It didn't!"

"Oh, I know it didn't. Not because you say so, however. It can't be your pen because of your teeth, you see."

"Certainly, certainly," said De Carlos with eagerness. "As you know—I have false teeth—"

"Nonsense. A man with a plate in his mouth might have made those identifying marks on the pen. But not a man with *your* plate, Mr. De Carlos. You should send your dentist an extra fee; he's really a very bad dentist, for which you should show your gratitude. Because when I examined your plate—remember the incident, Mr. De Carlos? when Mr. Rummell converted you into a human cocktail-shaker and your plate flew out of your mouth?— when I examined it, as I say, I saw that it was a genuine

212

old-timer . . . one of those hideous plates with in-humanly regular teeth, so regular, so perfectly aligned, that they simply could not have made those deep dents in the pen.

"No, those dents could have been made only by a canine out of line, and longer and more pointed than normal. So I knew the pen wasn't yours."

De Carlos wiped his face with a handkerchief.

"Now, then, I asked myself, how did Mr. De Carlos get hold of that pen? Well, the reasonably assumptive source would have been Cole, the man De Carlos was impersonating at the time I first saw the pen in his pos-session. *Was* the pen Cole's?

"It might have been at that time, for all I knew; but Captain Angus scotched that theory last night, and the photographs he produced supported his story: Cadmus Cole didn't have a tooth in his mouth, and moreover never wore a plate.

"So the pen wasn't Cole's. If it wasn't Cole's, and it wasn't yours, Mr. De Carlos, then you must have got hold of it by accident or taken it by mistake, believing it to be yours. A mental leap in the dark—but the gap could be supported by a solid confirmation.

"I knew you were badly myopic. In impersonating Cole three months ago, you had been forced to put aside your spectacles, since Cole didn't wear any. As a result you were badly handicapped: your vision was blurred, you bumped into the door-jamb twice, you squinted and strained—in fine, exhibited every evidence of acute near-sightedness.

"Now a man who could mistake a door-jamb for empty space might easily mistake one fountain-pen for another. So, I reasoned, if you had visited some one just before coming to our office that day, you might have picked up the wrong pen there. *Did* you visit some one else before you appeared in our office that day? Oh, yes, indeed. You told us so yourself. You even told us whom you had visited. You had visited Mr. Goossens, for the purpose of delivering into his hands Cadmus Cole's sealed will.

"Just a moment," said Mr. Queen swiftly, at the gasp and lightning movement before him, "I'm not finished. Was it Goossens's pen De Carlos left behind in our office? Let's see. If De Carlos took Goossens's pen by mistake, then he probably left his own pen behind in Goossens's office."

He darted forward and flipped back the attorney's coat. Goossens was so astonished his pipe almost fell out of his mouth. Mr. Queen snatched an ordinary black fountain-pen out of the man's vest-pocket and held it up. There were a few scratches and dents on the cap.

"Still up to your old biting tricks, eh, Goossens?" said Mr. Queen. He turned and held the pen up before De Carlos's nose. "Mr. De Carlos, is this your property?"

De Carlos pointed with a shaking finger at the tiny initials, E D C, on the body of the pen.

"Then I think it high time, Mr. Lloyd Goossens," said Mr. Queen in a curt voice, whirling about, "that you stopped play-acting and confessed to the murder of Ann Bloomer!"

XXIII

St. Ellery Slays
the Dragon

INSPECTOR QUEEN AND DISTRICT ATTORNEY SAMPSON jumped up, and Sergeant Velie moved quickly towards them from the door. But Mr. Queen waved them back.

Goossens stared up at him. Then he shook his head, as if in bewilderment. Finally, he took his pipe out of his mouth and chuckled. "Very amusing, Mr. Queen. A little grisly in its humor, but I'm one man who appreciates a joke."

But when he saw how those about him were, in a rising horror, pushing their chairs imperceptibly away from his vicinity, he lost his smile and shouted: "You're mad! Do you think you can get away with this?"

"To the bitter end," said Mr. Queen reflectively. Then he sighed. "Very well, we'll go on." The Inspector, the Sergeant, and Sampson remained standing, however, their eyes on the attorney.

"Mr. De Carlos! You'll swear, if necessary, that this pen I just removed from Goossens's pocket belongs to you?"

"Yes, yes," said De Carlos excitedly. "I'll tell you just how it happened. While I was in Goossens's private office delivering Cole's will, I took out my own pen to write a list of ports we expected to stop at during the coming West Indian cruise. I laid the pen down on his desk. When I left, I must have picked up Goossens's pen by mistake, because I recall when I came in that he was writing. Neither of us noticed what I did. When your messenger delivered the other pen to the yacht, I received it; I knew it wasn't mine, and saw what must have happened. But we were sailing and it was too late to do anything about returning it. Later, I forgot the whole incident."

"And so, I fancy, did Mr. Goossens," remarked Mr. Queen dryly, leaning against a table and folding his arms on his chest. "Your first mistake, Goossens: not getting rid of De Carlos's pen. A trivial mistake, but then you didn't realize the significance of those teeth-marks on your own pen, or that they tied up with the marks on the pencil of your set which you dropped in Room 1726. And since then, falling into your old nervous habit of chewing on the caps of pens, you've been maltreating De Carlos's pen in the same way. . . . Let me see your pipe, please."

He said it so casually, and walked towards Goossens so idly, and took the pipe from the man's mouth so very swiftly, that the lawyer was caught unprepared. When he realized the significance of Ellery's action, he sprang to his feet.

But it was too late. Mr. Queen was examining the stem of the pipe intently, and Goossens's arms were pinned immovably back by the iron hands of Sergeant Velie.

"Proof number two," observed Mr. Queen, nodding with satisfaction. "If you'll compare the end of this pipestem with the caps of the fountain-pen and pencil, Dad, you'll find all three bear the identical impressions of his teeth. Beau told me that he never saw Goossens without a pipe, and on the few occasions of my own meetings with him, I remarked the same thing. The habitual pipe-smoker is so accustomed to gripping a pipestem with his teeth that even when he isn't smoking his pipe he'll unconsciously try to compensate for the lack by biting on something else. A laboratory examination will prove that Goossens made the same marks on the stem of his pipe as appear on the pen and pencil. Well, Goossens, have you anything to say for publication now?"

And Goossens said quietly: "It's really all right, Sergeant. You don't have to keep holding on to me as if I were a . . . criminal." He laughed at the absurdity of the notion.

Sergeant Velie glanced at Inspector Queen, who nodded. The Sergeant held on to Goossens's wrists with one hand and with the other swiftly searched him. When he was satisfied his prisoner was unarmed, he stepped back.

Goossens shook himself. "Do you believe this nonsense, Inspector Queen? Or you, Mr. Sampson? I hope you both realize what a beautiful suit for slander you're setting up!"

"Not to mention," drawled Mr. Queen, "one for false arrest. Oh, quite beautiful—"

There was an altercation in the corridor. Sergeant Velie hurried to the door and opened it.

"Oh, there you are!" said Beau Rummell cheerfully. "Velie, tell this floogie I'm one of the best people."

"Come in, Beau, come in!" called Mr. Queen. "You couldn't have timed your entrance more dramatically."

Beau ran in and stopped short when he saw Goossens, on his feet and pale with anger, in the center of the room. "Oh," he said. "The third act, hey? Well, here's curtains!"

And, with a yearning glance towards Kerrie, Beau drew Ellery aside, handing him a large manila envelope. Ellery quickly extracted from the envelope what looked like a photostat, while Beau whispered in his ear for some time. And as Mr. Queen both looked and listened, an expression of beatitude overspread his lean countenance.

He advanced towards Goossens, waving the photostat.

Goossens frowned. "It's all very dramatic, as you say, but is it legal?" He laughed shortly. "Don't forget, Mr. Queen, I'm a lawyer. If you're foolish enough to take this before a court, I'll make you wish you'd never been born—any of you! Your so-called evidence can be blown to bits—teeth-marks. Pen and pencil. An old pipe. . . . Why, no jury in the world would swallow that sort of stuff!"

"Possibly not," murmured Mr. Queen, "but we're now in possession of a third item of evidence that a jury *will* swallow.

"So far I've shown that you own the pencil found on the scene of the crime—proving opportunity; and that you could have tipped off the police about the faked marriage—your second error, by the way. Now I'll prove *you had motive*—that you, and you alone, fulfill the third requirement of Ann Bloomer's murderer!

"This third proof will implicate you directly, Mr. Goossens. It will indicate that you were Ann Bloomer's silent partner. It will indicate that the plot, from the beginning, was your brain-child—the plot to palm off an impostor as Margo Cole. In fact, I think I know *when* you conceived and executed that part of the plot, Mr. Goossens!"

"Indeed?" sneered the lawyer.

"You got your first flash of inspiration when De Carlos, pretending to be Cole, delivered Cole's sealed will. You opened that will, Goossens, and you had a reason for opening it—a reason that will be clear to these people when I reveal the nature of my last proof.

"You opened the will, digested its conditions, and saw your opportunity. You left very suddenly on what purported to be a 'business trip'—and where did you go? To Europe, Goossens! Your own secretary gave me that information when I telephoned your office a few days after De Carlos's visit as Cole . . . in fact, I remember it especially well because just as I set down the telephone my appendix burst. A pathological commemoration of an important event, Goossens! The only trouble was that I didn't appreciate its significance at the time.

"And why did you go to Europe suddenly? Because you knew that Margo Cole had lived in France. Because you knew so much about Margo Cole's history that it was evident to your quick, clever, and harried intelligence that an impostor would have to come from France, too. Somehow during that business trip you ran across Ann Bloomer, exactly the type of woman your plan required. And she agreed to go in with you."

Goossens bit his lip. His cheeks were chalky now.

"You had the proofs of Margo Cole's identity in your possession. You didn't give them to the Bloomer woman in France. You probably coached her in Margo Cole's history then, but you held back the proofs until the last moment—fearing, very justly, a possible double-cross. You handed Ann Bloomer those proofs as she was leaving the *Normandie* in Quarantine! For it was you, and you alone, brief-case in hand, who boarded the *Normandie* ostensibly to greet 'Margo Cole' and escort

217

her to the cutter in which the rest of us were waiting. Those proofs of Margo Cole's identity were in YOUR brief-case when you boarded the *Normandie*. But they were in Ann Bloomer's bag when you escorted her to the cutter a few minutes later.

But Ann Bloomer doublecrossed you after all. Entrenched here as Margo Cole, she backed out of her bargain with you. Also, she had probably investigated you undercover, in her canny way, and discovered that you were in a stew of trouble, Mr. Goossens—oh, a veritable salmagundi! You've been quite a rounder in your time—you live with your azure-blooded wife for polite reasons only; your real life is replete with women, champagne, gambling parlors, and the like. Your father left you a respectable practice in the administration of estates, but you went through his money quickly . . . and then you began to race through the moneys entrusted to your stewardship as trustee of estates.

"And so now you had started a vicious circle—constantly stealing from one estate to cover a shortage in another, and you had reached a point where you could conceal your peculations no longer without fresh sources of funds. You were desperate, and that was your motive for leaping at the chance to make a fortune quickly when fate dropped the Cole estate into your lap.

"Somehow Ann Bloomer, I believe, found all this out, and knew she had a powerful weapon against you. One word from her to arouse suspicion that you were fraudulently administering the estate in your trusteeship, and you were ruined. That was the weapon she held over you as she wriggled out of her pact to split the Margo Cole income with you.

"You were probably clever enough not to show your rage. You saw another way: to remove the menace you yourself, a modern Frankenstein, had created—this female monster—and at the same time—your third and last and most important motive—*to gain absolute control over the Cole millions!*

"Because it was in line with your new goal, you even fell in with Ann's pleasant little scheme to murder Kerrie. She may have forced you to become her accomplice, using her threat of exposure as a lever; I don't know; it would be the logical thing for her to do, because as an accomplice you wouldn't be able to expose her as a murderess.

218

"At any rate, when the attacks failed, and Ann visited this hotel-room to taunt Kerrie, you shot the woman dead. By doing this you accomplished at one swoop a number of purposes: to revenge yourself on her, to prevent her from revealing your identity as her partner, to be rid of her permanently, to frame Kerrie Shawn for the murder and be rid of *her;* and the ultimate goal of all—to be free then to administer the Cole estate for charity, since the will provided that if the heirs died, you were still to administer the estate for charitable purposes! In that capacity, you would have a peculative field-day lasting years. And you reasoned—accurately, I think—that you could easily persuade Mr. Edmund De Carlos, your co-trustee, to swing in with you.

"While I may be slightly off in some of the details, I fancy I've roughly covered the subject, Goossens?

Goossens stammered: "You—you talked about a proof of motive." Then he got a grip on his nerves and deliberately smiled. "And I've listened and heard nothing but the ravings of a fantastic imagination. Where's this wonderful proof of yours?"

"Admirable, Goossens, admirable," applauded Mr. Queen. "You could have been a great trial lawyer; quite the dramatic flair. Do you deny," he snapped, "that you put Ann Bloomer up to posing as Margo Cole?"

"I certainly do deny it," replied the lawyer hoarsely. "I never saw the woman before she showed up on the *Normandie.* I was taken in just as the rest of you were. You can't make me the goat, Queen! I thought she was really Margo Cole!"

"Ah," said Mr. Queen; and his quiet sigh was so fat with satisfaction that Goossens stiffened and grew still. "You really thought she was Margo Cole." Mr. Queen turned swiftly. "You heard that statement, Sampson? That's the killer-diller. That's a demonstrable lie!"

"What do you mean?" whispered Goossens.

"In this manila envelope," replied Mr. Queen, handing it to the District Attorney, "is the plain evidence of your lie. It's the third and completely incriminating article of evidence I promised to produce against you.

"It explains how you knew all about Margo Cole even before the Cole will was delivered to you. It explains how you happened to have in your possession all the proofs of Margo Cole's identity. Shall I explain how that was?

219

"In 1925, when Margo Cole's mother died in France, Margo left that country and came to the United States. She was penniless and probably too angry with Cadmus Cole to look him up. She drifted out to California— Mr. Rummell, who has been exceedingly busy in the past eight hours, and being instructed what to search for, has found the evidence and uncovered a good deal of the story. Margo Cole became a waitress in a Los Angeles restaurant.

"And that's where you met her, Goossens—while you were attending college in Los Angeles in 1926. You were twenty-five years old and already gorging wild oats. You got drunk one night and *married Margo Cole!* You kept that marriage secret even from your father. Your wife, the true Margo, died in Los Angeles shortly after, and you had her buried quickly and quietly, no doubt heaving a great sigh of relief at her having considerably got you out of a bad hole.

"In this manila envelope," cried Mr. Queen, "are the photostats of two documents: Margo Cole's death-certificate, in which she is recorded as Margo Cole *Goossens*, and your 1926 marriage license—wired East by radio at the behest of our invaluable Mr. Rummell, who must be pretty tired by this time.

"Of course, since I knew that Ann Bloomer's partner must have furnished her with the proofs of Margo Cole's identity, it was an alluring possibility that he possessed those proofs through the most plausible means in the world —marriage to Margo Cole. And it was this conjecture of mine that sent Mr. Rummell on his successful all-night, transcontinental telephone, telegraph, and radio-photographic mission. Satisfied, Goossens?"

But Goossens only sank into his chair, as if the weight of his body were suddenly insupportable, and he covered his face with his trembling hands.

AND thus it came to pass that on a certain improbably glorious day in late September Mr. Beau Rummell said to Miss Kerrie Shawn: "Well, funny-face, where do we go from here?"

"First," said Miss Shawn, "we clean up our affairs—I mean mine. You know, the estate, and all that poky business. Who's running it now, darling? Of course, Mr. De Carlos and Mr. Goossens—"

"The Surrogate will probably appoint some bank to act as trustee for the estate."

"It doesn't make much difference." Kerrie sighed. "As soon as that's settled, and the—the trial is over, we'll find ourselves forgotten, ignored, and poor as church-mice."

"Poor? You're barmy!"

"Oh, didn't I tell you? We're going to be married. And then we'll live unhappily ever after. Beau Rummell, you need a shave!"

"Are we back on that marriage theme again?" growled Beau. "After all the trouble I went to to save that beautiful boodle of dough for you, Kerrie, I simply won't—"

And so, after Lloyd Goossens's trail and conviction, Mr. Rummell and Miss Shawn were married, and they began to live unhappily ever after. It was an authentic marriage this time, complete with accredited parson, verified license, the proper number of witnesses, and half the reporters in the world, who were curious to see a young woman in this crass age so out of tune with the spirit of man that she would give up "a fortune," as they unanimously expressed it, "for love."

Of course, there were gifts. Inspector Queen, who felt he owed Kerrie *something*, sent a set of handsome Swedish silver cutlery. Violet Day sent—silently—a beautiful Lalique flower-bowl. It took her last cent. The gifts from Hollywood were modest but legion.

Strangely, Mr. Ellery Queen sent nothing. Mr. Rummell was hurt.

"It's not the idea of the gift, y'understand," he complained to Kerrie, "but after all—"

"Perhaps he's sick, Beau."

"Say, I never thought of that!" Beau became alarmed. "I haven't seen him for days—"

They took a cab to the Queen apartment. Mr. Queen was out. Mr. Queen was at the office of *Ellery Queen, Inc.*

"Office?" exclaimed Beau. "He *must* be sick!"

But they found Mr. Queen ensconced in his swivel-chair the veritable mirror of health and spirits.

"Ah, the newlyweds," said Mr. Queen, hastening to bestow a partner's kiss on the bride. "How's married life?"

"Never mind that," snapped Beau. "Where you been keeping yourself? You ducked out after the wedding—"

"I've been sitting here in this lonely tomb," murmured

221

Mr. Queen, "reflecting. On life's little ironies. By the way, why aren't you two in a nice, expensive place for your honeymoon?"

"Because we can't afford it," said Kerrie, "And Atlantic City was *so* lovely."

"Yeah, I'm still getting that taffy out of my teeth," said Beau. "I'd have been around sooner, El, only you know how it is. Just married, have to scout around for a flat—"

"Atlantic City—flat!" Mr. Queen looked horrified. "What are you thinking of?"

"The old budget," said Beau. He wore the faintly hang-dog look of the hopelessly married man. "I can't afford to kid around, Ellery. As soon as we get settled, I'll come back to the office and start peddling the old personality again. You know. Confidential Matters Handled Confidentially? Give Us a Try—We Never Fail. The old grind—"

"Not a bit of it," said Mr. Queen firmly. "I'm scouting around myself. For a new partner."

"What?" yelled Beau. "Hey, what is this? What's the matter with *me?*"

"My good man, you're through—*fini.*"

Beau looked stricken. "But, Ellery . . . for the love of Mike . . . I've got to make a living, don't I?"

"Not at all."

"And besides," said Beau angrily, "what d'ye mean I'm through! Whose dough is it, anyway, in this dump? You're one hell of a guy. I never thought you'd—"

Kerrie patted her husband's swelling biceps gently. "Can't you see the gentleman has something up his sleeve? Be quiet and listen, Beau!"

"You see," said Mr. Queen dreamily, while Beau gawped at him, "I sat here after your wedding in a perfect dither of thought, and the main thought ran: What can I give those two idiots for a wedding present?"

Kerrie laughed. Beau blushed.

"Shall it be," continued Mr. Queen, "a First Folio, or the 1856 British Guiana number thirteen, or one of the crown jewels of some illustrious potentate, or a ten-room house completely furnished, with interior murals by Rivera? No, I said to myself, too common, too mundane. My gift to Mr. and Mrs. Rummell must be of the essence, gargantuan, *crème de la crème,* epical. And, do you know, I've hit it?"

Kerrie clapped her hands. "What is it? I know I'll just love it!"

"I believe," murmured Mr. Queen, "you will."

"Come on, give, you exasperating stand-in for Madam Chairman!" roared Beau.

"I have decided," said Mr. Queen, beaming, "to present you with a gift worthy of myself. I have decided to give you," said Mr. Queen, and then he darted off into one of those conversational bypaths he was so fond of treading, "—I haven't ascertained the exact figure, of course; you'll have to be patient with me, chickadees, but I should say it will come to—oh, let's be conservative. Let's say almost fourteen million dollars."

"Fourteen—" Kerrie blinked.

Beau said hoarsely: "Come again?"

"Don't hold me to that figure," said Mr. Queen hastily. "It may come to no more than a paltry thirteen millions."

"Oh, he's joking," groaned Kerrie.

"Listen, you ape!" bellowed Beau. "What is this?"

Mr. Queen chuckled. "My talents have been chiefly engaged, since your nuptials, in trying to dope out a way to break old man Cole's will. You two *would* be married, and that meant, under the will, that Kerrie lost a very helpful five thousand a week for life . . . now that Margo Cole's death has been established."

"You mean you've—broken it?" asked Beau in an awed voice.

"We're getting there, getting there. It revolves about a delicate point, but the best legal authority seems to be on our side. You're a lawyer, or you were. What is the law's purpose in requiring that a testator's signature to a will be attested by witnesses?"

"Why," said Beau, scratching his newly-shaven cheeks, "to make sure there's no fraud, I suppose. To have proof that the signature of the testator was his legal signature, and was set down on a specific will at a specific date. Same idea as lies behind the notarization of contracts—proof of signature."

"Well, the legal technicality on which the will is probably going to be broken involves the attestation of the witnesses.

"According to Captain Angus's story he and the radio operator signed in attestation of the testator's signature *before* the testator's signature was put down on the will.

223

As a matter of fact, the radio operator, in not signing in Cole's presence, not only attested a signature which still did not exist, but he can't even say truthfully that what he signed was a will; or if it was a will, the specific will the testator intended. And then even Captain Angus left the cabin before De Carlos wrote down Cole's name, so he can't testify honestly when that signature was written.

"There are other points, but I fancy those will suffice. The Surrogate will probably be only too happy to grasp at the legal technicality and declare the will invalid— it's an awfully screwy and unfair testament. At any rate, with the will broken, Cole will be considered, as you know, to have died intestate. And since Margo Cole died leaving no issue, and Miss Kerrie Shawn, now Mrs. Beau Rummell, is the only living heiress of the testator —well, you can imagine!

"What do you think of my modest little wedding present, Mrs. Rummell?"

But Mrs. Rummell only began to sniffle, and Beau stood there alternately scowling and grinning like a lunatic. . . .

IN the course of time Mr. Queen received letters from Paris, Monte Carlo, Cairo, Bali—very obese letters they were, written on the lush stationary of disgustingly wealthy people, and designed to bring a beam to the sourest countenance. There were even letters from a certain Miss Violet Day who, it appeared, had been re-engaged by Mrs. Rummell to act as secretary-companion and spent most of her time beating the pants off Mr. Rummell at ping-pong, a fact which kept Mr. Rummell in a state of constant rage.

But Mr. Queen only smiled vaguely and proceeded about his business, which was to worry himself to a shadow over another case.

Which case?

Well, that's another story.

CALAMITY
TOWN

PART ONE

1. *Mr Queen Discovers America*

ELLERY QUEEN stood knee-deep in luggage on the Wrightsville station platform and thought: 'This makes me an admiral. Admiral Columbus.' The station was a squatty affair of black-red brick. On a rusty hand truck under the eaves two small boys in torn blue overalls swung their dirty legs and chewed gum in unison, staring at him without expression. The gravel about the station was peppered with horse droppings. Cramped two-story frame houses and little stoop-shouldered shops with a cracker-barrel look huddled to one side of the tracks—the city side, for up a steep street paved with square cobbles Mr Queen could see taller structures beyond and the fat behind of a retreating bus. To the other side of the station there were merely a garage, an ex-trolley labeled PHIL'S DINER, and a smithy with a neon sign. The rest was verdure and delight.

'Country looks good, by jake,' murmurs Mr Queen enthusiastically. 'Green and yellow. Straw colors. And sky of blue, and clouds of white'—bluer blue and whiter white than he recalled ever having seen before. City—country; and here they met, where Wrightsville station flings the twentieth century into the astonished face of the land.

'Yes, sir, my boy. You've found it. *Porter!*'

The Hollis Hotel, Upham House, and the Kelton among them could not offer the stranger at their desks one pitiful room. It seemed boom times had hit Wrightsville two

7

jumps ahead of Mr Queen. The last room at the Hollis was filched from under his nose by a portly man with 'defence industry' written all over him. Undiscouraged, Mr Queen checked his bags at the Hollis, ate a leisurely lunch in the Coffee Shoppe, and read a copy of the *Wrightsville Record*—Frank Lloyd, Publisher and Editor. He memorized as many of the names mentioned in the *Record* as seemed to have local prominence, bought two packs of Pall Malls and a Wrightsville street map from Mark Doodle's son Grover at the lobby cigar stand, then struck out across the red-cobbled Square under the hot sun.

At the horse trough in the center of the Square, Mr Queen paused to admire Founder Wright. Founder Wright had once been a bronze, but he now looked mossy, and the stone trough on which he stood had obviously been unused for years. There were crusty bird droppings on the Founder's Yankee nose. Words on a plaque said that Jezreel Wright had founded Wrightsville when it was an abandoned Indian site, in the Year of Our Lord 1701, had tilled the land, started a farm, and prospered. The chaste windows of the Wrightsville National Bank, *John F. Wright, Pres.*, smiled at Mr Queen from across the Square, and Mr Queen smiled back: O Pioneers!

Then he circumnavigated the Square (which was round); peered into Sol Gowdy's Men's Shop, the Bon Ton Department Store, Dunc MacLean—Fine Liquors, and William Ketcham—Insurance; examined the three gilded balls above the shop of J. P. Simpson, the jardinieres of green and red liquid in the window of the High Village Pharmacy, *Myron Garback, Prop.*, and turned to survey the thoroughfares which radiated like spokes from the hub of the Square. One spoke was a broad avenue: the red-brick Town Hall, the Carnegie Library, a glimpse of park, tall praying trees, and beyond, a cluster of white new WPA-looking buildings. Another spoke was a street lined with stores and full of women in house dresses and men in work clothes. Consulting his street map, Mr Queen ascertained that this avenue of commerce was Lower Main; so he made for it. Here he found the *Record* office; he peered in and saw the big press being shined up by old Phinny Baker after the morning's run. He sauntered up Lower Main, poking his nose into the crowded five-and-dime, past the new Post Office building, past the Bijou Theater, past J. C. Pettigrew's real estate office; and he went into Al Brown's Ice Cream Parlor and had a New York College Ice and listened to the chatter of tanned

8

boys and red-cheeked girls of high-school age. He heard Saturday night 'dates' being arranged right and left—for Danceland, in the Grove, which he gathered was at Wrightsville Junction three miles down the line, admission one dollar per person, 'and for pete's sake Marge keep your mother away from the parking lot, will you? I don't wanna get caught like two weeks ago and have you start bawling!'

Mr. Queen strolled about the town, approving and breathing deeply of wet leaves and honeysuckle. He liked the stuffed eagle in the Carnegie Library vestibule; he even liked Miss Aikin, the elderly Chief Librarian, who gave him a very sharp look, as if to say: 'Don't you try to sneak a book out of *here!*' He liked the twisting narrow streets of Low Village, and he went into Sidney Gotch's General Store and purchased a package of Old Mariner Chewing Tobacco just as an excuse to smell the coffee and rubber boots and vinegar, the cheeses and kerosene. He liked the Wrightsville Machine Shop, which had just reopened, and the old cottonmill factory, diagonally across from the Low Village World War Memorial. Sidney Gotch told him about the cotton mill. It had been a cotton mill, then an empty building, then a shoeshop, then an empty building again; he could see for himself the splintery holes in the windows where the Low Village boys threw rocks in summer and snowballs in winter on their way to that vine-covered building up Lower Dade Street there—St John's Parochial School. But now 'specials' prowled around the mill with long fat holsters strapped to their thighs and eyes in their heads that would not smile; the boys, said Sidney Gotch, just yelled 'Yahhhh!' and took it out on Mueller's Feed Store three doors up the block, near the corner of Whistling Avenue. And the woollen mill had taken on extra help—army orders. 'Boom times, brother! No wonder you couldn't get a room. I've got an uncle from St. Paul and a cousin from Pittsburgh doublin' up with me and Betsy right now!' In fact, Mr Queen liked everything. He glanced up at the big clock on the Town Hall steeple. Two-thirty. No room, eh? Walking rapidly, he made his way back to Lower Main and neither paused nor pried until he reached the shop marked J. C. PETTIGREW, REAL ESTATE.

2. *Calamity House*

HIS NUMBER twelves up on his desk, J.C. was napping
when Mr Queen came in. He had just come from the
weekly Chamber of Commerce lunch at Upham House,
and he was full of Ma Upham's fried chicken. Mr Queen
woke him up. 'My name,' said Mr Queen, 'is Smith, I've
just landed in Wrightsville, and I'm looking for a small
furnished house to rent on a month-to-month basis.'

'Glad to know you, Mr Smith,' said J.C., struggling into
his gabardine 'office' jacket. 'My, it's warm! Furnished
house, hey? I can see you're a stranger. No furnished
houses in Wrightsville, Mr Smith.'

'Then perhaps a furnished apartment—'

'Same thing.' J.C. yawned. 'Excuse *me!* Certainly is
hotting up, isn't it?'

'It certainly is,' said Ellery.

Mr Pettigrew leaned back in his swivel chair and picked
a strand of chicken out of his teeth with an ivory pick,
after which he examined it intently. 'Housing's a problem.
Yes, sir. People pouring into town like grain in a hopper.
To work in the Machine Shop especially. Wait a minute!'
Mr Queen waited. 'Course!' J.C. flicked the shred of
chicken off his pick delicately. 'Mr Smith, you superstitious?'

Mr Queen looked alarmed. 'I can't say I am.'

'In that case,' said J.C. brightening; then he stopped.
'What business you in? Not that it makes any difference,
but—'

Ellery hesitated. 'I'm a writer.'

The real estate man gaped. 'You write *stories?*'

'That's it, Mr Pettigrew. Books and such.'

'Well, well,' beamed J.C. 'I'm real honored to meet you,
Mr Smith. Smith ... Now that's funny,' said J.C. 'I'm a
reading man myself, but I just don't seem to recollect an
author named—what did you say your first name was, Mr
Smith?'

'I didn't say, but it's Ellery. Ellery Smith.'

10

'Ellery Smith,' said J.C., concentrating.

Mr Queen smiled. 'I write under a pen name.'

'Ah! Name of . . . ?' But when Mr Pettigrew saw that Mr 'Smith' simply kept smiling, he rubbed his jaw and said: 'Course you'd give references?'

'Would three months' rent in advance give me a good character in Wrightsville, Mr Pettigrew?'

'Well, I should smile!' grinned J.C. 'You come with me, Mr Smith. I've got exactly the house you're looking for.'

'What did you mean by asking me if I'm superstitious?' asked Ellery as they climbed into J.C.'s pea-green coupé and drove off. 'Is the house haunted?'

'Uh . . . no,' said J.C. 'Though there *is* a sort of a queer yarn connected with that house—might give you an idea for one of your, now, books, hey?' Mr 'Smith' agreed; it might. 'This house, it's next door to John F.'s own place on the Hill. John F. Wright, that is. He's president of the Wrightsville National. Oldest family in town. Well, sir, three years ago one of John F.'s three daughters—the middle one, Nora—Nora got herself engaged to this Jim Haight. Jim was head cashier at John F.'s bank. Wasn't a local boy—he'd come to Wrightsville from New York a couple of years before that with fine recommendations. Started out as an assistant teller, and he was making good. Steady boy, Jim; stayed away from the bad element, went to the library a lot, didn't have much fun, I s'pose—a movie at Louie Cahan's Bijou, or standing around Band Concert Nights with the rest of the boys, watching the girls parade up and down eating popcorn, and joshing 'em. Worked hard—plenty of up-and-go, Jim had, and independent? Say, I never saw a lad stand on his two feet like Jim did. We all liked him a heap.' Mr Pettigrew sighed, and Ellery wondered why such a glowing subject should depress him.

'I take it Miss Nora Wright liked him more than anyone,' said Ellery, to grease the wheels of the story.

'That's a fact,' muttered J.C. 'Wild about the boy. Nora'd been the quiet kind before Jim came along—has to wear specs, and I guess it made her think she wasn't attractive to boys, 'cause she used to sit in the house while Lola and Patty went out with fellows—reading or sewing or helping her ma with organization work. Well, sir, Jim changed all that. Jim wasn't the kind to be stopped by a pair of eye-glasses. Nora's a pretty girl, and Jim started to rush her, and she changed . . . my, she changed!' J.C. frowned. 'S'pose I'm blabbing too much. Anyway, you get

11

the idea. When Jim and Nora got engaged, the town said it was a fine match, especially after what had happened to John's oldest daughter, Lola.'

Ellery said quickly: 'And what was that, Mr Pettigrew?'

J.C. swung the coupé into a broad country road. They were well away from town now, and Ellery feasted his eyes on the succulent greens of the countryside.

'Did I say something about Lola?' asked the real estate man feebly. 'Why ... Lola, she'd run away from home. Eloped with an actor from a visiting stock company. After, a while she came back home to Wrightsville. Divorced.' J.C. set his lips stubbornly, and Mr Queen realized he wasn't going to hear any more about Miss Lola Wright. 'Well, anyway,' continued J.C., 'John and Hermione Wright decided to give Jim and their Nora a furnished house for a wedding present. John cut off part of his property near his own house and built. Right next door, 'cause Hermy wanted Nora as close by as possible, seeing she'd ... lost one of her girls already.'

'Lola,' nodded Mr Queen. 'Divorced, you said? Came back home afterwards. Then Lola Wright doesn't live with her father and mother any more?'

'No,' said J.C. shortly. 'So John built Jim and Nora a sweet little six-roomer next door. Hermione was putting in rugs and furniture and drapes and linen and silver—the works—when all of a sudden it happened.'

'What happened?' asked Mr Queen.

'To tell the truth, Mr Smith, nobody knows,' said the real estate man sheepishly. 'Nobody 'cepting Nora Wright and Jim Haight. It was the day before the wedding and everything looked fine as corn silk, when Jim Haight ups and leaves town! Fact. Ran away. That was three years ago, and he's not been back since.' They were on a winding, rising road. Ellery saw wide old houses on voluptuous lawns, and elms and maples and cypress and weeping willows taller than the houses. Mr Pettigrew scowled at the Hill road. 'The next morning John F. found a note of resignation on his desk at the bank, but not a word as to why Jim'd skipped town. And Nora wouldn't say a blessed word. Just shut herself up in her bedroom and wouldn't come out for her father or mother or sister Patricia or even old Ludie, the hired girl who's practically brought the three Wright girls up. Nora just kept bawling in her room. My daughter Carmel and Patty Wright are thick as molasses, and Pat told Carmel the whole thing.

12

Pat did a heap of crying herself that day. I guess they all did.'

'And the house?' murmured Mr Queen.

J.C. drove his car to the side of the road and shut off the motor. 'Wedding was called off. We all thought Jim'd turn up, thinking it was just a lovers' spat; but he didn't. Whatever broke those two up must have been awful important!' The real estate man shook his head. 'Well, there was the new house, all ready to be lived in, and no one to live in it. Terrible blow to Hermione. Hermy let out that Nora'd jilted Jim. But people did keep jawing about it, and after a while . . . ' Mr Pettigrew paused.

'Yes?' prompted Ellery.

'After a while people began saying Nora'd gone . . . crazy and that that little six-roomer was jinxed.'

'Jinxed!'

J.C. smiled a sickly smile. 'Funny how some folks are, isn't it? Thinking the house had anything to do with Jim and Nora's breaking up! And of course ain't nothing wrong with Nora. I mean, she's not crazy. Crazy!' J.C. snorted. 'That wasn't the whole of it. When it looked like Jim wasn't coming back, John F. decided to sell that house he'd built for his daughter. Pretty soon along came a buyer—relative of Judge Martin's wife Clarice, man named Hunter of the Boston branch of the family. I was handling the deal.'

J.C. lowered his voice. 'Mr Smith, I give you my word I'd taken this Mr Hunter over to the house for a last inspection before signing the papers, and we were looking around the living room and Mr Hunter was saying, "I don't like the sofa just there," when he gets kind of a scared look all of a sudden and grabs his heart and falls down right in front of me! Died on the spot! I didn't sleep for a week.' He swabbed his forehead. 'Doc Willoughby said it was heart failure. But that's not what the town said. The town said it was the house. First Jim ran away, then a buyer dropped dead. And to make it worse, some smart-aleck of a cub reporter on Frank Lloyd's *Record* wrote up Hunter's death and he called the house "Calamity House" in his yarn. Frank fired him. Frank's friendly with the Wrights.'

'Of all the nonsense!' chuckled Mr Queen.

'Just the same, nobody'd buy,' muttered J.C. 'John offered to rent. Nobody'd rent. Too unlucky, people said. Still want to rent, Mr Smith?'

'Yes, indeed,' said Mr Queen cheerfully. So J.C. started

his car again. 'Family seems ill-fated,' observed Ellery. 'One daughter running off and another's life blasted by a love affair. Is the youngest daughter normal?'

'Patricia?' J.C. beamed. 'Prettiest, smartest filly in town next to my Carmel! Pat's going steady with Carter Bradford. Cart's our new County Prosecutor . . . Here we are!'

The real estate man steered his coupé into the driveway of a Colonial-style house sunk into the hillside far off the road. It was the largest house, and the trees on its lawns were the tallest trees, that Ellery had seen on the Hill. There was a small white frame house close by the large one, its windows shuttered.

Mr Queen kept looking at the blind and empty little house he intended to rent all the way up to the wide Wright porch. Then J.C. rang the bell and old Ludie in one of her famous starched aprons opened the front door and asked them what in tarnation.

3. *'Famed Author to Live in Wrightsville'*

'I'LL TELL Mr John you're callin',' sniffed Ludie, and she stalked out, her apron standing to each side of her like a Dutch cap.

'Guess Ludie knows we're here to rent Calamity House,' grinned Mr Pettigrew.

'Why should that make her look at me as if I were a Nazi *Gauleiter?*' asked Mr Queen.

'I expect Ludie doesn't think it proper for folks like the John F. Wrights to be renting out houses. Sometimes I don't know who's got more pride in the family name, Ludie or Hermy!'

Mr Queen took inventory. Lived in. There were a few aged mahogany pieces of distinction, and a beautiful fireplace of Italian marble. And at least two of the oil paintings had merit. J.C. noticed his interest. 'Hermione picked out all the pictures herself. Knows a lot about art, Hermy does—Here she is now. And John.'

Ellery rose. He had expected to meet a robust, severe-faced female; instead, he saw Hermy. Hermy always fooled strangers that way; she's so tiny and motherly and sweet-looking. John Fowler Wright was a delicate little man with a brown country-club face. Ellery liked him at sight. He was carrying a stamp album with practised care. 'John, this is Mr Ellery Smith. He's looking to rent a furnished house,' said J.C. nervously. 'Mr Wright, Mrs Wright, Mr Smith. A-hrmm!'

John F. said in his reedy voice that he was mighty proud to meet Mr Smith, and Hermy held out her hand at arm's length with a sweet 'How do you do, Mr Smith,' but Mr 'Smith' saw the iced gleam in Hermy's pretty blue eyes and decided that in this instance, too, the female was deadlier than the male. So he was most gallant with her. Hermy unbent a little at that and poked her slender lady's fingers in her sleek gray hair, the way she always did when she was pleased, or fussed, or both.

'Of course,' said J.C. respectfully, 'I thought right off of that beautiful little six-roomer you built next door, John—'

'I don't at all like the idea,' said Hermione in her coolest voice, 'of renting, John. I can't imagine, Mr Petti-grew—'

'Maybe if you knew who Mr Smith *is*,' said J.C. quickly.

Hermy looked startled. John F. hitched forward in his wing chair near the fireplace. 'Well?' demanded Hermy. 'Who is he?'

'Mr Smith,' said J.C., throwing it away, 'is Ellery Smith, the famous author.'

'Famous *author!*' gasped Hermy. 'But I'm so bowled *over!* Here on the coffee table, Ludie!' Ludie clanked down a tray bearing a musical pitcher filled with ice and grape-juice-and-lemonade punch, and four handsome crystal goblets. 'I'm *sure* you'll like our house, Mr Smith,' Hermy went on swiftly. 'It's a little dream house. I decorated it with my own hands. Do you ever lecture? Our Women's Club—'

'Good golfing hereabouts, too,' said John F. 'How long would you want to rent for, Mr Smith?'

'I'm sure Mr Smith is going to like Wrightsville so well he'll stay on and *on*,' interrupted Hermy. 'Do have some of Ludie's punch, Mr Smith—'

'Thing is,' said John F., frowning, 'the way Wrights-

15

ville's shooting up, I'll probably be able to sell pretty soon—'

'That's easy, John!' said J.C. 'We can write in the lease that in case a buyer comes along Mr Smith is to vacate pending reasonable notice—'

'Business, business!' said Hermy gaily. 'What Mr Smith wants is to *see* the house. Mr Pettigrew, you stay here and keep John and his poky old stamps company. Mr Smith?' Hermy held on to Ellery's arm all the way from the big house to the little house, as if she were afraid he'd fly away if she let go. 'Of course, the furniture's protected by dust covers now, but it's really lovely. Early American bird's-eye maple, and brand-new. Just look, Mr Smith. Isn't it *darling?*'

Hermy dragged Ellery upstairs and downstairs, from cellar to peaked attic, exhibited the chintzy master bedroom, extolled the beauties of the living room with its maple pieces and art-filled niches and hooked rug and half-empty bookshelves . . . 'Yes, yes,' said Ellery feebly. 'Very nice, Mrs Wright.'

'Of course, I'll see you get a housekeeper,' said Hermy happily. 'Oh, dear! Where will you do your work? We could fix over the second bedroom upstairs into a study. You *must* have a study for your Work, Mr Smith.' Mr 'Smith' said he was sure he'd manage handsomely. 'Then you do like our little house? I'm so glad!' Hermione lowered her voice. 'You're in Wrightsville incognito, of course?'

'Such an impressive word, Mrs Wright . . .'

'Then except for a few of our *closest* friends I'll make sure nobody knows who you are,' beamed Hermy. 'What kind of Work are you planning, Mr Smith?'

'A novel,' said Ellery faintly. 'A novel of a particular sort, laid in a typical small city, Mrs Wright.'

'Then you're here to get Colour! How *apt!* You chose our own dear Wrightsville! You must meet my daughter Patricia immediately, Mr Smith. She's the cleverest child. I'm sure Pat would be a great help to you in getting to know Wrightsville . . .'

Two hours later Mr Ellery Queen was signing the name 'Ellery Smith' to a lease whereunder he agreed to rent Number 460 Hill Drive, furnished, for a period of six months beginning August 6, 1940, three months' rental paid in advance, one month's vacating notice to be given by lessor in event of a sale, at the rental of $75 per month.

'The truth is, Mr Smith,' confided J.C. as they left the

16

Wright house, 'I kind of held my breath in there for a minute.'

'When was that?'

'When you took that pen of John F.'s and signed the lease.'

'You held your breath?' Ellery frowned. 'Why?'

J.C. guffawed. 'I remembered the case of poor old Hunter and now he dropped dead in that very house. Calamity House! That's a hot one! Here you are, still fit as a fiddle!'

And he got into his coupé still overcome by mirth, bound for town to pick up Ellery's luggage at the Hollis Hotel ... and leaving Ellery in the Wright driveway feeling irritated.

When Ellery returned to his new residence, there was a tingle in his spine. There *was* something about the house, now that he was out of Mrs Wright's clutches, something— well, *blank,* unfinished, like Outer Space. Ellery almost said to himself the word 'inhuman', but when he got to that point he took himself in hand, sternly. Calamity House! As sensible as calling Wrightsville Calamity Town! He removed his coat, rolled up his shirt sleeves, and sailed into things.

'Mr Smith,' cried a horrified voice, 'what are you *doing?*' Ellery guiltily dropped a dust cover as Hermione Wright rushed in, her cheeks flushed and her gray hair no longer sleek. 'Don't you dare touch a thing! Alberta, come in. Mr Smith won't bite you.' A bashful Amazon shuffled in. 'Mr Smith, this is Alberta Manaskas. I'm sure you'll find her most satisfactory. Alberta, don't stand there. Start the upstairs!' Alberta fled. Ellery murmured his gratitude and sank into a chintz-cloaked chair as Mrs Wright attacked the room about him with terrifying energy.

'We'll have this in apple-pie order in a jiffy! By the way, I trust you don't mind. On my trip into town to fetch Alberta, I *happened* to drop into the *Record* office— whoo! this dust!—and had a confidential chat with Frank Lloyd. The editor and published, you know.' Ellery's heart scuttled itself.

'By the way, I also took the liberty of giving Logan's a grocery and meat order for you. Although of course you'll dine with *us* tonight. Oh, dear, did I forget . . . ? Electricity . . . gas . . . water . . . no, I attended to everything. Oh, the telephone! I'll do that first thing tomorrow. Well, as I was saying, I knew that no matter *how* hard we tried,

17

sooner or later everyone would know you're in Wrights-ville, Mr Smith, and of course as a newspaper man Frank would *have* to do a story on you, so I thought I'd better ask Frank as a personal favour not to mention in his write-up that you're the famous author—Patty baby! Carter! Oh, my darlings, I have *such* a surprise for you!' Mr Queen rose, fumbling for his jacket. His only coherent thought was that she had eyes the colour of brook water bubbling in the sun.

'So you're the famous author,' said Patricia Wright, looking at him with her head cocked. 'When Pop told Carter and me just now what Mother had snagged, I thought I'd meet a baggy-pantsed poet with a hangdog look, melancholy eyes, and a pot. I'm *pleased*.' Mr Queen tried to look suave, and mumbled something.

'Isn't it wonderful, dearest?' cried Hermy. 'You must forgive me, Mr Smith. I know you think I'm terribly provincial. But I really *am* overwhelmed. Pat dear—introduce Carter.'

'Carter! Darling, I'm so sorry. Mr Smith, Mr Bradford.' Shaking hands with a tall young man, intelligent-looking but worried, Ellery wondered if he were worried about how to hold on to Miss Patricia Wright. He felt an instant sympathy.

'I suppose,' said Carter Bradford politely, 'We must all seem provincial to you, Mr Smith. Fiction or nonfiction?'

'Fiction,' said Ellery. So it was war.

'I'm *pleased*,' said Pat again, looking Ellery over. Carter frowned; Mr Queen beamed. 'I'll do this room, Muth ... You won't be hurting *my* feelings, Mr Smith, if after we've stopped interfering in your life you change things around again. But for now—'

As he watched Pat Wright setting his house in order under Carter Bradford's suspicious eye, Ellery thought: 'May the saints grant me calamities like this each blessed day. Carter my boy, I'm sorry, but I'm cultivating your Patty!'

His good humor was not dispelled even when J.C. Pettigrew hurried back from town with his luggage and flourished the last edition of the *Wrightsville Record*. Frank Lloyd, publisher and editor, had kept his word to Hermione Wright only technically. He had said nothing about Mr Smith in the body of the news item except that he was 'Mr Ellery Smith of New York.' But the headline on the story ran:—FAMED AUTHOR TO LIVE IN WRIGHTSVILLE!

4. *The Three Sisters*

MR ELLERY 'SMITH' was a sensation with the *haut monde* on the Hill and the local intelligentsia: Miss Aikin, the Librarian, who had studied Greek; Mrs Holmes, who taught Comparative Lit at Wrightsville High; and, of course, Emmeline DuPré, known to the irreverent as the 'town crier', who was nevertheless envied by young and old for having the miraculous good fortune to be *his neighbor*. Emmy DuPré's house was on Ellery's other side. Automobile traffic suddenly increased on the Hill. Interest became so hydra-headed that Ellery would have been unmoved if the Wrightsville Omnibus Company had started running a sightseeing bus to his door. Then there were invitations. To tea, to dinner, to luncheon; and one—from Emmeline DuPré—asking him to breakfast, 'so that we may discuss the Arts in the coolth of a Soft Morning, before the Dew vanishes from the Sward.' Ben Danzig, High Village Rental Library and Sundries, said he had never had such a rush on Fine Stationery.

So Mr Queen began to look forward to escaping with Pat in the mornings, when she would call for him dressed in slacks and a pullover sweater and take him exploring through the County in her little convertible. She knew everybody in Wrightsville and Slocum Township, and introduced him to people named variously O'Halleran, Zimbruski, Johnson, Dowling, Goldberger, Venuti, Jacquard, Wladislaus, and Broadbeck—journeymen machinists, toolers, assembly-line men, farmers, retailers, hired hands, white and black and brown, with children of unduplicated sizes and degrees of cleanliness. In a short time, through the curiously wide acquaintanceship of Miss Wright, Mr Queen's notebook was rich with funny lingos, dinner-pair details, Saturday-night brawls down on Route 16, square dances and hepcat contests, noon whistles whistling, lots of smoke and laughing and pushing, and the color of America, Wrightsville edition.

'I don't know what I'd do without you,' Ellery said one

morning as they returned from Low Village. 'You seem so much more the country-club, church-social, Younger-Set type of female. How come, Pat?'

'I'm that, too,' grinned Pat. 'But I'm a Sociology Major, or I was—got my degree in June; and I guess I just can't help practising on the helpless population. If this war keeps up—'

'Milk Fund?' asked Ellery vaguely. 'That sort of thing?'

'Barbarian! Milk Funds are Muth's department. My dear man, sociology is concerned with more than calcium for growing bones. It's the science of civilization. Now take the Zimbruskis—'

'Spare me,' moaned Mr Queen, having met the Zimbruskis. 'By the way, what does Mr Bradford, your local Prosecutor, think of all this, Patty?'

'Of me and sociology?'

'Of me and you.'

'Oh.' Pat tossed her hair to the wind, looking pleased. 'Cart's jealous.'

'Hmmm. Look here, my little one—'

'Now don't start being noble,' said Pat. 'Trouble with Cart, he's taken me for granted too long. We've practically grown up together. Do him good to be jealous.'

'I don't know,' smiled Ellery, 'that I entirely relish the role of love-irritant.'

'Oh, please!' Pat was shocked. 'I *like* you. And this is more fun.' Suddenly, with one of her quick sidelong glances: 'You know what people are saying, incidentally—or don't you?'

'What now?'

'You told Mr Pettigrew that you're a famous writer—'

'Mr Pettigrew supplied the adjective "famous" all by himself.'

'You've also said you don't write under the name Ellery Smith, that you use a pseudonym ... but you didn't tell anyone *which* pseudonym.'

'Lord, no!'

'So people are saying that maybe you aren't a famous author after all,' murmured Pat. 'Nice town, huh?'

'Which people?'

'People.'

'Do *you* think I'm a fraud?'

'Never mind what I think,' retorted Pat. 'But you should know there's been a run on the Authors' Photograph File at the Carnegie Library, and Miss Aikin reports you're simply not there.'

20

'Pish,' said Ellery. 'And a couple of tushes. I'm just not famous enough.'

'That's what I told her. Mother was furious at the very thought, but I said: "Muth, how do we *know*?" and do you know—poor Mother didn't sleep a wink all night?'

They laughed together. Then Ellery said: 'Which reminds me. Why haven't I met your sister Nora? Isn't she well?'

He was appalled by the way Pat stopped laughing at mention of her sister's name. 'Nora?' repeated Pat in a perfectly flat voice, a voice that told nothing at all. 'Why, Nora's all right. Let's call it a morning, Mr Smith.'

That night Hermione officially unveiled her new treasure. The list was *intime*. Just Judge and Clarice Martin, Doc Willoughby, Carter Bradford, Tabitha Wright, John F.'s only living sister—Tabitha was the 'stiff-necked' Wright who had never quite 'acceped' Hermione Bluefield—and editor-publisher Frank Lloyd of the *Record*. Lloyd was talking politics with Carter Bradford; but both men merely pretended to be interested in each other. Carter was hurling poisonous looks at Pat and Ellery in the 'love seat' by the Italian fireplace; while Lloyd, a brown bear of a man, kept glancing restlessly at the staircase in the foyer.

'Frank had a crush on Nora before Jim . . . He's still crazy about her,' explained Pat. 'When Jim Haight came along and Nora fell for him, Frank took the whole thing pretty badly.' Ellery inspected the mountainous newspaper editor from across the room and inwardly agreed that Frank Lloyd would make a dangerous adversary. There was iron in those deep-sunk green eyes. 'And when Jim walked out on Nora, Frank said that—'

'Yes?'

'Never mind what Frank said,' Pat jumped up. 'I'm talking too much.' And she rustled towards Mr Bradford to break another little piece off his heart. Pat was wearing a blue taffeta dinner gown that swished faintly as she moved.

'Milo, this is *the* Ellery Smith,' said Hermy proudly, coming over with big, lumbering Doc Willoughby in tow.

'Don't know whether you're a good influence or not, Mr Smith,' chuckled Doc. 'I just came from another confinement at the Jacquards'. Those Canucks! Triplets this time. Only difference between me and Dr Dafoe is that no lady in Wright County's been considerate enough to bear more than four at one time. Like our town?'

'I've fallen in love with it, Dr Willoughby.'

'It's a good town. Hermy, where's my drink?'

'If you're broad-minded,' snorted Judge Martin, strolling up with Clarice hanging—heavily—on his arm. Judge Martin was a gaunt little man with sleepy eyes and a dry manner. He reminded Ellery of Arthur Train's Mr Tutt.

'Eli Martin!' cried Clarice. 'Mr Smith, you just ignore this husband of mine. He's miserable about having to wear his dinner jacket and he'll take it out on you because you're the cause. Hermy, everything's just *perfect.*'

'It's nothing at all,' murmured Hermione, pleased. 'Just a little intimate dinner, Clarice.'

'I don't like these doodads,' growled the Judge, fingering his bow tie. 'Well, Tabitha, and what are *you* sniffing about?'

'Comedian!' said John F.'s sister, glaring at the old jurist. 'I can't imagine what Mr Smith must be thinking of us, Eli!'

Judge Martin observed dryly that if Mr Smith thought less of him for being uncomfortable in doodads, then *he* thought less of Mr Smith. A crisis was averted by the appearance of Henry Clay Jackson announcing dinner. Henry Clay was the only trained butler in Wrightsville, and the ladies of the upper crust, by an enforced Communism, shared him and his rusty 'buttlin' suit'. It was an unwritten law among them that Henry Clay was to be employed on ultra-special occasions only.

'Dinnuh,' announced Henry Clay Jackson, 'is heaby suhved!'

Nora Wright appeared suddenly between the roast lamb-wreathed-in-mint-jelly-flowers and the pineapple mousse. For an instant the room was singing-still. Then Hermione quavered: 'Why, *Nora* darling,' and John F. said gladly: 'Nora baby,' through a mouthful of salted nuts, and Clarice Martin gasped: 'Nora, how *nice!*' and the spell was broken.

Ellery was the first man on his feet. Frank Lloyd was the last; the thick neck under his shaggy hair was the color of brick. Pat saved the day. 'I must say this is a fine time to come down to dinner, Nora!' she said briskly. 'Why, we've finished Ludie's best lamb. Mr Smith, Nora.'

Nora offered him her hand. It felt as fragile and cold as a piece of porcelain. 'Mother's told me all about you,' said Nora in a voice that sounded unused.

'And you're disappointed. Naturally,' smiled Ellery. He held out a chair.

'Oh, no! Hello, Judge, Mrs Martin. Aunt Tabitha ... Doctor ... Carter ...'

Frank Lloyd said, 'Hullo, Nora,' in gruff tones; he took the chair from Ellery's hands neither rudely nor politely; he simply took it and held it back for Nora. She turned pink and sat down. Just then Henry Clay marched in with the magnificent mousse, molded in the shape of a book, and everybody began to talk.

Nora Wright sat with her hands folded, palms up, as if exhausted; her colorless lips were twisted into a smile. Apparently she had dressed with great care, for her candy-striped dinner gown was fresh and perfectly draped, her nails impeccable, and her coiffure without a single stray wine-brown hair. Ellery glimpsed a sudden, rather appalling, vision of this slight bespectacled girl in her bedroom upstairs, fussing with her nails, fussing with her hair, fussing with her attractive gown ... fussing, fussing, so that everything might be just so ... fussing so long and so needlessly that she had been an hour late to dinner.

And now that she had achieved perfection, now that she had made the supreme effort of coming downstairs, she seemed emptied, as if the effort had been too much and not entirely worth-while. She listened to Ellery's casual talk with a fixed smile, white face slightly lowered, not touching her mousse or demitasse, murmuring a monosyl-lable occasionally ... but not as if she were bored, only as if she were weary beyond sensation.

And then, as suddenly as she had come in, she said: 'Excuse me, please,' and rose. All conversation stopped again. Frank Lloyd jumped up and drew her chair back. He devoured her with a huge and clumsy hunger; she smiled at him, and at the others, and floated out ... her step quickening as she approached the archway from the dining room to the foyer. Then she disappeared; and everyone began to talk at once and ask for more coffee.

Mr Queen was mentally sifting the evening's grist as he strolled back to his house in the warm darkness. The leaves of the big elms were talking; there was an oversize cameo moon; and his nose was filled with the scents of Hermione Wright's flowers. But when he saw the small roadster parked by the curb before his house, dark and empty, the sweetness fled. It was simply night; and something was about to happen. A gun-metal cloud slipped across the moon, and Mr Queen made his way along the edge of his lawn on the muffling grass toward the little house. A point of fire took shape on his porch. It was swaying back and forth about waist-high to a standing man.

'Mr Smith, I presume?' A woman's contralto. Slightly fuzzed with husk. It had a mocking quality.

'Hullo!' he called, mounting the porch steps. 'Mind if I turn on the porch light? It's so beastly dark—'

'Please do. I'm as curious to see you as you are to see me.'

Ellery touched the light switch. She was curled up in a corner of the slide-swing blinking at him from behind the streaming veil of her cigarette. The dove suède of her slacks was tight over her thighs; a cashmere sweater molded her breasts boldly. Ellery gathered a full-armed impression of earthiness, overripe, and growing bitter. She laughed, a little nervously he thought, and flipped her cigarette over the porch rail into the darkness.

'You may turn off the light now, Mr Smith. I'm a fright, and besides I shouldn't want to embarrass my family by making them aware I'm in their immediate neighborhood.'

Ellery obediently switched off the porch light. 'Then you're Lola Wright.' The one who had eloped, and come back divorced. The daughter the Wrights never mentioned.

'As if you didn't know!' Lola Wright laughed again, and it turned into a hiccup. 'Excuse *me*. Seventh hiccup of a seventh Scotch. I'm famous too, you know. The *drinking* Wright girl.'

Ellery chuckled. 'I've heard the vile slanders.'

'I was all prepared to hate your guts, from the kowtowing that's been going on, but you're all right. Shake!' The swing creaked, and steps shuffled to the tune of an unsteady laugh, and then the moist heat of her hand warmed his neck as she groped. He gripped her arms to save her from falling.

'Here,' he said, 'You should have stopped at number six.'

She placed her palms against his starched shirt and pushed strongly. 'Whoa, Geronimo! The man'll think li'l Lola's stinko.' He heard her totter back to the swing, and its creak. 'Well, Mr Famous Author Smith, and what do you think of us all? Pygmies and giants, sweet and sour, snaggled-toothed and slick-magazine ads—good material for a book, eh?'

24

'Elegant.'

'You've come to the right place.' Lola Wright lit another cigarette: the flame trembled. 'Wrightsville! Gossipy, malicious, intolerant ... the great American slob. More dirty linen to the square inch of backyard than New York or Marseilles.'

'Oh, I don't know,' argued Mr Queen. 'I've spent a lot of loose time prowling, and it seems a pretty nice place to me.'

'Nice!' She laughed. 'Don't get me started. I was born here. It's wormy and damp—a breeding place of nastiness.'

'Then why,' murmured Mr Queen, 'did you come back to it?'

The red tip of her cigarette waxed three times in rapid succession. 'None of your business. Like my family?'

'Immensely. You resemble your sister Patricia. Same physical glow, too.'

'Only Patty's young, and my light's going out.' Lola Wright mused for a moment. 'I suppose you'd have to be polite to an old bag named Wright. Look, Brother Smith. I don't know why you came to Wrightsville, but if you're going to be palsy with my kind, you'll hear a lot about little Lola eventually, and ... well ... I don't give a damn what Wrightsville thinks of me, but an alien ... that's different. Good grief! I still have vanity!'

'I haven't heard anything about you from your family.'

'No?' He heard her laugh again. 'I feel like baring my bosom tonight. You'll hear I drink. True. I learned it from—I learned it. You'll hear I'm seen in all the awful places in town, and what's worse, *alone*. Imagine! I'm supposed to be "fast". The truth is I do what I damned please, and all these vultures of women on the Hill, they've been tearing at me with their claws!'

She stopped. 'How about a drink?' asked Ellery.

'Not now. I don't blame my mother. She's narrow, like the rest of them; her social position is her whole life. But if I'd play according to her rules, she'd still take me back—she's got spunk, I'll give her that. Well, I won't play. It's my life, and to hell with rules! Understand?' She laughed once more. 'Say you understand. Go on. Say it.'

'I understand,' Ellery said.

She was quiet. Then she said: 'I'm boring you. Goodnight.'

'I want to see you again.'

'No. Goodbye.'

Her shoes scraped the invisible porch floor. Ellery turned on the light again. She put up her arm to hide her eyes.

'Well, then, I'll see you home, Miss Wright.'

'Thanks no. I'm—' She stopped.

Patricia Wright's gay voice called from the darkness below: 'Ellery? May I come up and have a goodnight cigarette with you? Carter's gone home and I saw your porch light—' Pat stopped, too. The two sisters stared at each other.

'Hello, Lola!' cried Pat. She vaulted up the steps and kissed Lola vigorously. 'Why didn't you tell me you were coming?'

Mr Queen put the light out again very quickly. But he had time to see how Lola clung—briefly—to her taller, younger sister.

'Lay off, Snuffles,' he heard Lola say in a muffled voice. 'You're mussing my hair-do.'

'And that's a fact,' said Pat cheerfully. 'You know, Ellery, this sister of mine is the most attractive girl ever to come out of Wrightsville. And she insists on hiding her light under frumpy old slacks!'

'You're a darling, Pats,' said Lola, 'but don't try so hard. It's no dice, and you know it.'

Pat said miserably: 'Lo dear ... why don't you come back?'

'I think,' remarked Mr Queen, 'I'll walk down to that hydrangea bush and see how it's making out.'

'Don't,' said Lola. 'I'm going now. I really am.'

'Lola!' Pat's voice was damp.

'You see, Mr Smith? Snuffles. She was always snuffling as a brat. Pat, now stop it. This is old hat for us two.'

'I'm all right.' Pat blew her nose in the darkness. 'I'll drive home with you.'

'No, Patsy. Night, Mr Smith.'

'Goodnight.'

'And I've changed my mind. Come over and have a drink with me any time you like. Night, Snuffy!' And Lola was gone.

When the last rattle of Lola's 1932 coupé died, Pat said in a murmur: 'Lo lives in a two-room hole down in Low Village, near the Machine Shop. She wouldn't take alimony from her husband, who was a rat till the day he died, and she won't accept money from Pop. Those clothes she wears—six years old. Part of her trousseau.

26

She supports herself by giving piano lessons to Low Village hopefuls at fifty cents a throw.'

'Pat, why does she stay in Wrightsville? What brought her back after her divorce?'

'Don't salmon or elephants or something come back to their birthplace ... to die? Sometimes I think it's almost as if Lola's ... hiding.' Pat's silk taffeta rustled suddenly. 'You make me talk and talk. Good night, Ellery.'

'Night, Pat.'

Mr Queen stared into the dark for a long time. Yes, it was taking shape. He'd been lucky. The makings were here, rich and bloody. But the crime—the crime. Where was it? *Or had it already occurred?*

Ellery went to bed in Calamity House with a sense of events past, present, and future.

On the afternoon of Sunday, August twenty-fifth, nearly three weeks from the day of Ellery's arrival in Wrightsville, he was smoking a postprandial cigarette on his porch and enjoying the improbable sunset when Ed Hotchkiss's taxicab charged up the Hill and squealed to a stop before the Wright house next door. A hatless young man jumped out of the cab. Mr Queen felt a sudden agitation and rose for a better view.

The young man shouted something to Ed Hotchkiss, bounded up the steps, and jabbed at the Wright doorbell. Old Ludie opened the door. Ellery saw her fat arm rise as if to ward off a blow. Then Ludie scuttled back out of sight, and the young man dashed after her. The door banged. Five minutes later it was yanked open; the young man rushed out, stumbled into the waiting cab, and yelled to be driven away.

Ellery sat down slowly. It might be. He would soon know. Pat would come flying across the lawn ... There she was ... 'Ellery! You'll never guess!'

'Jim Haight's come back,' said Ellery.

Pat stared. 'You're wonderful. Imagine—after three years! After the way Jim ran out on Nora! I can't believe it yet. He looks so much *older* ... He had to see Nora, he yelled. Where was she? Why didn't she come down? Yes, he knew what Muth and Pop thought of him, but that could wait—where was Nora? And all the time he kept shaking his fist in poor Pop's face and hopping up and down on one foot like a maniac!'

'What happened then?'

'I ran upstairs to tell Nora. She went deathly pale and

27

plopped down on her bed. She said: *"Jim?"* and started to bawl. Said she'd rather be dead, and why hadn't he stayed away, and she wouldn't see him if he came crawling to her on his hands and knees—the usual feminine tripe. Poor Nora!'

Pat was in tears herself.

'I knew it was no good arguing with her—Nora's awfully stubborn when she wants to be. So I told Jim, and he got even more excited and wanted to run upstairs, and Pop got mad and waved his best mashie at the foot of the stairs, like Horatius at the bridge, and ordered Jim out of the house, and—well, Jim would have had to knock Pop down to get by him, so he ran out of the house screaming that he'd see Nora if he had to throw bombs to get in. And all of this time I was trying to revive Muth, who conveniently fainted as a sort of strategic diversion ... I've got to get back!' Pat ran off. Then she stopped and turned around. 'Why in heaven's name,' she asked slowly, 'do I come running to you with the most intimate details of my family's affairs, Mr Ellery Smith?'

'Maybe,' smiled Ellery, 'because I have a kind face.'

'Don't be foul. Do you suppose I'm f—' Pat bit her lip, a faint blush staining her tan. Then she loped away.

Mr Queen lit another cigarette with fingers not quite steady. Despite the heat, he felt chilled suddenly. He threw the unsmoked butt into the grass and went into the house to haul out his typewriter.

5. *Lover Come Back*

GABBY WARRUM, the one-toothed agent at the railroad station, saw Jim Haight get off the train. Gabby told Emmeline DuPré. By the time Ed Hotchkiss dropped Jim off at Upham House, where Ma for old times' sake managed to wangle a bed for him, Emmy DuPré had phoned nearly everyone in town who wasn't picnicking in Pine Grove or swimming in Slocum Lake.

Opinion, as Mr Queen ascertained by prowling around town Monday and keeping his steel-trap ears open, was divided. J. C. Pettigrew, Donald Mackenzie, and the rest of the Rotary bunch, who were half Country Club and half tradespeople, generally opined that Jim Haight ought to be run out on a rail. The ladies were stoutly against this: Jim was a nice young man; whatever'd happened between him and Nora Wright three years ago wasn't *his* fault, you can bet your last year's bonnet!

Frank Lloyd disappeared. Phinny Baker said his boss had gones off on a hunting trip up in the Mahoganies. Emmeline DuPré sniffed. 'It's funny Frank Lloyd should go hunting *the very next morning* after James Haight gets back to Wrightsville. Ran away, of course. That big wind-bag!' Emmy was disappointed that Frank hadn't taken one of his deer rifles and gone stalking through the streets of Wrightsville for Jim, like Owen Wister's Virginian (starring, however, Gary Cooper).

Old Soak Anderson, the town problem, discovered by Mr Queen Monday noon lying on the stone pedestal of the Low Village World War Memorial, rubbed his salt-and-pepper stubble and declaimed: ' "O most lame and impotent conclusion!" '

'Are you feeling well this morning, Mr Anderson?' asked Ellery, concerned.

'Never better, sir. But my point is one with the Proverb, the twenty-sixth, I believe, which states: "Whoso diggeth a pit shall fall therein." I refer, of course, to the reappearance in this accursed community of Jim Haight. Sow the wind, sir; sow the wind!'

The yeast in all this ferment acted strangely. Having returned to Wrightsville, Jim Haight shut himself up in his room at Upham House; he even had his meals served there, according to Ma Upham. Whereas Nora Wright, the prisoner, began to show herself! Not in public, of course. But on Monday afternoon she watched Pat and Ellery play three sets of tennis on the grass court behind the Wright house, lying in a deck chair in the sun, her eyes protected by dark glasses hooked over her spectacles; and she kept smiling faintly. On Monday evening she strolled over with Pat and a hostile Carter Bradford 'to see how you're coming along with your book, Mr Smith.' Ellery had Alberta Manaskas serve tea and oatmeal cookies; he treated Nora quite as if she were in the habit of dropping in. And then on Tuesday night . . .

Tuesday night was bridge night at the Wrights'. Carter Bradford usually came to dinner, and Carter and Pat paired against Hermione and John F. Hermy thought it

29

might be 'nice' to have Mr Smith in on Tuesday, August twenty-seventh to make a fifth; and Ellery accepted with alacrity.

'I'd much rather watch tonight,' said Pat. 'Carter dear— you and Pop against Ellery and Mother. I'll heckle.'

'Come on, come on, we're losing time,' said John F. 'Stakes, Smith? It's your option.'

'Makes no difference to me,' said Ellery. 'Suppose I toss the honour over to Bradford.'

'In that case,' said Hermy quickly, 'let's play for a tenth. Carter, *why* don't they pay Prosecutors more?' Then she brightened. 'When you're Governor . . .'

'Penny a point,' said Carter; his lean face was crimson.

'But Cart, I didn't mean—' wailed Hermione.

'If Cart wants to play for a cent, by all means *play* for a cent,' said Pat firmly. 'I'm sure he'll win!'

'Hello,' said Nora. She had not come down to dinner— Hermy had said something about a 'headache'. Now Nora was smiling at them from the foyer. She came in with a basket of knitting and sat down in the big chair under a piano lamp. 'I'm really winning the war for Britain.' she smiled, 'all by myself. This is my tenth sweater!'

Mr and Mrs Wright exchanged startled glances, and Pat absently began to ruffle Ellery's hair. 'Play cards,' said Carter in a smothered voice.

The game began under what seemed to Ellery promising circumstances, considering the warm vital hand in his hair and Carter's outthrust lower lip. And, in fact, after two rubbers Cart slammed his cards down on the table.

'Why, Cart!' gasped Pat.

'Carter Bradford,' said Hermy, 'I never *heard*—'

'What on earth?' said John F., staring at him.

'If you'd stop *jumping around,* Pat,' cried Carter, 'I'd be able to concentrate on this ding-busted game!'

'Jumping *around?*' said Pat indignantly. 'Cart Bradford, I've been sitting here on the arm of Ellery's chair all evening not saying a word!'

'If you want to play with his beautiful hair,' roared Cart, 'why don't you take him outside under the moon?'

Pat turned the machine-gun of her eyes on him. Then she said contritely to Ellery: 'I'm sure you'll forgive Cart's bad manners. He's really had a decent bringing-up, but associating with hardened criminals so much—'

Nora yelped. Jim Haight stood in the archway. His Palm Beach suit hung tired and defeated; his shirt was dark with perspiration. He looked like a man who has been running at top speed in a blazing heat without purpose or plan—just running. And Nora's face was a cloud-torn sky.

'Nora.' The pink in Nora's cheeks spread and deepened until her face seemed a mirror to flames. Nobody moved. Nobody said a word.

Nora sprang toward him. For an instant Ellery thought she meant to attack him in a spasm of fury. But then Ellery saw that Nora was not angry; she was in a panic. It was the fright of a woman who had long since surrendered hope of life to live in a suspension of life, a kind of breathing death; it was the fear of joyous rebirth.

Nora darted by Jim and skimmed up the stairs. Jim Haight looked exultant. Then he ran after her. And silence. Living Statues, thought Ellery. He ran his finger between his neck and his collar; it came away dripping. John F. and Hermy Wright were saying secretive things to each other with their eyes, as a man and woman learn to do who have lived together for thirty years. Pat kept glaring at the empty foyer, her chest rising and falling visibly; and Carter kept glaring at Pat, as if the thing that was happening between Jim and Nora had somehow become confused in his mind with what was happening between him and Pat.

Later . . . later there were overhead sounds: the opening of a bedroom door, a slither of feet, steps on stairs. Nora and Jim appeared in the foyer. 'We're going to be married,' said Nora. It was as if she were a cold lamp and Jim had touched the button. She glowed from within and gave off a sort of heat.

'Right off,' said Jim. He had a deep defiant voice; it was harsher than he meant, rasped by emery strain. 'Right off!' Jim said. 'Understand?' He was scarlet from the roots of his sandy hair to the chicken skin below his formidable Adam's apple. But he kept blinking at John F. and Hermy with a dogged, nervous bellicosity

'Oh, Nora!' cried Pat, and she pounced and kissed Nora's mouth and began to cry and laugh. Hermy was smiling the stiff smile of a corpse. John F. mumbled, 'I'll be dinged,' and heaved out of his chair and went to his daughter and took her hand, and he took Jim's hand, just standing there helplessly. Carter said: 'It's high time, you two lunatics!' and slipped his arm about Pat's waist. Nora did not cry. She kept looking at her mother. And then Hermy's petrification broke into little pieces and she ran to Nora, pushing Pat and John F. and Carter aside. She kissed Nora and kissed Jim and said something in a hysterical tone that made no sense but seemed the right thing to say just the same.

Mr Queen slipped out, feeling a little lonely.

6. 'Wright-Haight Nuptials Today'

HERMY PLANNED the wedding like a general in his field tent surrounded by maps of the terrain and figures representing the accurate strength of the enemy's forces. While Nora and Pat were in New York shopping for Nora's trousseau, Hermione held technical discussions with old Mr Thomas, sexton of the First Methodist Church; horticultural conferences with Andy Birobatyan, the one-eyed Armenian florist in High Village; historic conversations with the Reverend Dr Doolittle *in re* rehearsals and choir-boy arrangements; talks with Mrs Jones the caterer, with Mr Graycee of the travel agency, and with John F. at the bank on intrafamiliar banking business.

But these were Quartermaster's chores. The General Staff conversations were with the ladies of Wrightsville. 'It's just like a movie, dear!' Hermy gushed over the telephone. 'It was nothing more than a lover's quarrel to begin with—Oh, yes, darling, *I* know what people are saying!' said Hermy coldly. 'But my Nora doesn't have to grab anybody. I don't suppose you recall last year how that handsome young Social Registrite from Bar Harbor ... Of course not! Why should we have a *quiet* wedding? My dear, they'll be married in church and ... *Naturally* as a bride ... Yes, to South America for six weeks ... Oh, John is taking Jim back into the bank ... Oh, no, dear, an *officer's* position ... Of course, darling! Do you think I'd marry my Nora off and not have *you* at the wedding?'

On Saturday, August thirty-first, one week after Jim's return to Wrightsville, Jim and Nora were married by Dr Doolittle in the First Methodist Church. John F. gave the

32

bride away, and Carter Bradford was Jim's best man. After the ceremony, there was a lawn reception on the Wright grounds. Twenty Negro waiters in mess jackets served; the rum punch was prepared from the recipe John F. had brought back with him from Bermuda in 1928. Emmeline DuPré, full-blown in an organdie creation and crowned with a real rosebud tiara, skittered from group to group remarking how 'well' Hermione Wright had carried off a 'delicate' situation, and didn't Jim look interesting with those purple welts under his eyes? Do you suppose he's been drinking these three years? How romantic! Clarice Martin said rather loudly that *some* people were born troublemakers.

During the lawn reception Jim and Nora escaped by the service door. Ed Hotchkiss drove the bride and groom over to Slocum Township in time to catch the express. Jim and Nora were to stay overnight in New York and sail on Tuesday for Rio. Mr Queen, who was prowling, spied the fleeing couple as they hurried into Ed's cab. Wet diamonds in her eyes, Nora clung to her husband's hand. Jim looked solemn and proud; he handed his wife into the cab gingerly, as if she might bruise under less careful manipulation.

Mr Queen also saw Frank Lloyd. Lloyd, returning from his 'hunting trip' the day before the wedding, had sent a note to Hermy 'regretting' that he couldn't attend the ceremony or reception as he had to go upstate that very evening to attend a newspaper publishers' convention in the Capital. Gladys Hemmingworth, his Society reporter, would cover the wedding for the *Record*. 'Please extend to Nora my very best wishes for her happiness. Yours, F. Lloyd.'

But F. Lloyd, who should have been two hundred miles away, was skulking behind a weeping willow near the grass court behind the Wright house. Mr Queen experienced trepidation. What had Patty once said? 'Frank took the whole thing pretty badly.' And Frank Lloyd was a dangerous man ... Ellery, behind a maple, actually picked up a rock as Jim and Nora ran out of the kitchen to get into the cab. But the weeping willow wept quietly, and as soon as the taxi disappeared F. Lloyd left his hiding place and stamped off into the woods behind the house.

Pat Wright trudged up onto Ellery's porch the Tuesday night after the wedding and said with artificial cheeriness: 'Well, Jim and Nora are somewhere on the Atlantic.'

'Holding hands under the moon.'

33

Pat sighed. Ellery sat down beside her on the swing. They rocked together, shoulders touching. 'What happened to your bridge game tonight?' Ellery finally asked.

'Oh, Mother called it off. She's exhausted—been in bed practically since Sunday. And poor old Pop's pottering around with his stamp albums, looking lost. I didn't realize—quite—what it means to lose a daughter.'

'I noticed your sister Lola—'

'Lola wouldn't come. Mother drove down to Low Village to ask her. Let's not talk about . . . Lola.'

'Then whom shall we talk about?'

Patty mumbled: 'You.'

'Me?' Ellery was astonished. Then he chuckled. 'The answer is yes.'

'What?' cried Pat. 'Ellery, you're ribbing me!'

'Not at all. Your dad has a problem. Nora's just married. This house, under lease to me, was originally designed for her. He's thinking—'

'Oh, El, you're such a darling! Pop hasn't known *what* to do, the coward! So he asked me to talk to you. Jim and Nora do want to live in their . . . well, I mean who'd have thought it would turn out this way? As soon as they get back from their honeymoon. But it's not fair to you—'

'All's fair,' said Ellery. 'I'll vacate at once.'

'Oh, no!' said Pat. 'You've a six-month lease, you're writing your novel, we've really no right, Pop feels just awful—'

'Nonsense,' smiled Ellery. 'That hair of yours drives me quite mad. It isn't human. I mean it's like raw silk with lightning bugs in it.'

Pat grew very still. And then she wiggled into the corner of the swing and pulled her skirt down over her knees.

'Yes?' said Pat in a queer voice.

Mr Queen fumbled for a match. 'That's all. It's just—extraordinary.'

'I see. My hair isn't human, it's just extraordinary,' Pat mocked him. 'Well, in that case I must dash. Cart's waiting.'

Mr Queen abruptly rose. 'Mustn't offend Carter! Will Saturday be time enough? I imagine your mother will want to renovate the house, and I'll be leaving Wrightsville, considering the housing shortage—'

'How stupid of me,' said Pat. 'I almost forgot the most important thing.' She got off the swing and stretched

34

lazily. 'Pop and Mother are inviting you to be our house guest for as long as you like. Goodniiiiiight!'

And she was gone, leaving Mr Queen on the porch of Calamity House in a remarkably better humor.

7. *Hallowe'en: The Mask*

JIM AND NORA returned from their honeymoon cruise in the middle of October, just when the slopes of Bald Mountain looked as if they had been set on fire and everywhere you went in town you breathed the cider smoke of leaves burning. The State Fair was roaring full blast in Slocum: Jess Watkins's black-and-white milker, *Fanny IX*, took first prize in the Fancy Milch class, making Wrightsville proud. Kids were sporting red-rubber hands from going without gloves, the stars were frostbitten, and the nights had a twang to them. Out in the country you could see the pumpkins squatting in mysterious rows, like little orange men from Mars. Town Clerk Amos Bluefield, a distant cousin of Hermione's, obligingly died of thrombosis on October eleventh, so there was even the usual 'important' fall funeral. Nora and Jim stepped off the train the color of Hawaiians. Jim grinned at his father-in-law. 'What! Such a small reception committee?'

'Town's thinking about other things these days, Jim,' said John F. 'Draft registration tomorrow.'

'Holy smoke!' said Jim. 'Nora, I clean forgot!'

'Oh, lordy,' breathed Nora. 'Now I've got something else to worry about!' And she clung to Jim's arm all the way up the hill.

'The town's just agog,' declared Hermy. 'Nora baby, you look *wonderful!*'

Nora did. 'I've put on ten pounds,' she laughed.

'How's married life?' demanded Carter Bradford.

'Why not get married and find out for yourelf, Cart?' asked Nora. 'Pat dear, you're ravishing!'

'What chance has a man got,' growled Carter, 'with that smooth-talking hack writer in the house—'

'Unfair competition,' grinned Jim.

35

'In the *house*,' exclaimed Nora. 'Mother, you never wrote me!'

'It was the least we could do, Nora,' said Hermy, 'seeing how sweet he was about giving up his lease.'

'Nice fella,' said John F. 'Bring back any stamps?'

But Pat said impatiently: 'Nora, shake off these men and let's you and I go somewhere and . . . talk.'

'Wait till you see what Jim and I brought—' Nora's eyes grew big as the family limousine stopped in the Wright driveway. 'Jim, *look!*'

'Surprise!' The little house by the big one glistened in the October sunshine. It had been repainted: the fresh white of the clapboard walls, the turkey-red of the shutters and 'trim', the Christmas green of the newly landscaped grounds made it look like a delectable gift package.

'It certainly looks fine,' said Jim. Nora smiled at him and squeezed his hand.

'And just wait, children,' beamed Hermy, 'till you see the *inside*.'

'Absolutely spick and utterly span,' said Pat. 'Ready to receive the lovebirds. Nora, you're blubbing!'

'It's so beautiful,' wept Nora, hugging her father and mother. And she dragged her husband off to explore the interior of the house that had lain empty, except for Mr Queen's short tenure, for three frightened years.

Mr Queen had packed an overnight bag the day before the newlyweds' return and had taken the noon train. It was a delicate disappearance, under the circumstances, and Pat said it showed he had 'a fine character'. Whatever his reason, Mr Queen returned on October seventeenth, the day after national registration, to find bustle and laughter in the little house next door, and no sign whatever that it had recently been known as Calamity House. 'We do want to thank you for giving up the house, Mr Smith,' said Nora. There was a housewifely smudge on her pert nose.

'That hundred-watt look is my reward.'

'Flatterer!' retorted Nora, and tugged at her starchy little apron. 'I look a sight—'

'For ailing eyes. Where's the happy bridegroom?'

'Jim's down at the railroad station picking his things up. Before he came back from his apartment in New York he'd packed his books and clothes and things and shipped them to Wrightsville care of General Delivery, and they've been held in the baggage room ever since. Here he is! Jim, did you get everything?'

Jim waved from Ed Hotchkiss's cab, which was heaped with suitcases and nailed boxes and a wardrobe trunk. Ed and Jim carried them into the house. Ellery remarked how fit Jim looked, and Jim with a friendly handclasp thanked him for 'being so decent about moving out,' and Nora wanted Mr 'Smith' to stay for lunch. But Mr 'Smith' laughed and said he'd take advantage of that invitation when Nora and Jim weren't so busy getting settled; and he left as Nora said: 'Such a mess of boxes, Jimmy!' and Jim grunted: 'You never know how many books you've got till you start packing 'em. Ed, lug these boxes down the cellar meanwhile, huh?'

The last thing Ellery saw was Jim and Nora in each other's arms. Mr Queen grinned. If the bride's house hid a calamity within its walls, the calamity was hidden superlatively well.

Ellery attacked his novel with energy. Except for mealtimes he remained within the sanctuary of his quarters on the top floor, the whole of which Hermy had placed at his disposal. Hermy and Pat and Ludie could hear his portable clacking away until immoral hours. He saw little of Jim and Nora, although at dinner he kept his ears alert for dissonances in the family talk. But Jim and Nora seemed happy. At the bank Jim had found waiting for him a private office with a new oak desk and a bronze plaque saying MR HAIGHT V.-PRES. Old customers dropped in to wish him luck and ask about Nora, not without a certain vulturous hope.

The little house was popular, too. The ladies of the Hill called and called, and Nora gave them tea and smiles. Sharp eyes probed corners, looking for dust and despair; but they were disappointed, and Nora giggled over their frustrated curiosity. Hermy was very proud of her married daughter.

So Mr Queen decided he had been an imaginative fool and that Calamity House was buried beyond resurrection. He began to make plans to invent a crime in his novel, since life was so uncooperative. And, because he liked all the characters, he was very glad.

The twenty-ninth of October came and went, and with it the published figures of the Federal draft lottery in Washington. Jim and Carter Bradford drew high order-numbers; Mr Queen was observed to drop in at the Hollis Hotel early on the morning of the thirtieth for a New York newspaper, upon reading which he was seen by Mark Doodle's son Grover to shrug and toss the paper away.

The thirty-first was mad. People on the Hill answered mysterious doorbells all day. Menacing signs in colored chalk appeared on pavements. As evening came on, costumed gnomes began to flit about town, their faces painted and their arms flapping. Big sisters complained bitterly about the disappearance of various compacts and lipsticks, and many a gnome went to bed with a tingling bottom. It was all gay and nostalgic, and Mr Queen strolled about the neighborhood before dinner wishing he were young again, so that he, too, might enjoy the wicked pleasures of Hallowe'en. On his way back to the Wright house, he noticed that the Haight place next door was lit up; and on impulse he went up the walk and rang his ex-doorbell.

But it was Pat, not Nora, who answered the door. 'Thought you'd run out on me,' said Pat. 'We *never* see you any more.' Ellery fed his eyes for a moment. 'Now what?' demanded Pat, blushing. 'If you aren't the wackiest man! Nora? It's the famous author.'

'Come in!' called Nora from the living room. He found her struggling with an armful of books, trying to pick up more from disorderly stacks on the floor.

'Here, let me help you,' said Ellery.

'Oh, dear, no,' said Nora. 'You just watch us.' And Nora plodded up the stairs.

'Nora's turning the second bedroom upstairs into a study for Jim,' explained Pat.

Pat was stacking books from the floor in her arms and Ellery was idly examining titles on the half-filled bookshelves when Nora came downstairs for more books. 'Where's Jim, Nora?' asked Ellery.

'At the bank,' said Nora, stooping. 'An awfully important director's meeting.' And just then a book slid off the top of the fresh pile in her arms, and another, and another, while Nora crouched there horrified at the cascade. Half the books were on the floor again.

Pat said: 'Oh, look, Nor! Letters!'

'Letters? Where? Of all—They are!' One of the volumes which had fallen from Nora's arms was over-sized and fat, bound in tan cloth. From among the leaves some envelopes had tumbled. Nora picked them up curiously. They were not sealed.

38

'Oh, three poky old envelopes,' said Pat. 'Let's get going with these books or we'll never be through, Nora.'

But Nora frowned 'There's something inside each one, Pat. These are Jim's books. I wonder if . . .' She removed a single sheet of folded notepaper from one of the envelopes and spread it smooth, reading slowly to herself.

'Nora,' said Mr Queen. 'What's the matter?'

Nora said faintly: 'I don't understand—' and returned the sheet to its envelope. She took a similar sheet from the second envelope, read it, returned it to its envelope, the third, read it . . . And as she thrust it back into the third envelope, her cheeks were the color of wet sand. Pat and Ellery glanced at each other, puzzled.

'*Boo!*'

Nora whirled, shrieking. In the doorway crouched a man wearing a papier-mâché mask, his fingers were curled before his fantastic face, opening and closing hungrily. Nora's eyes turned up until they were all whites. And then she crumpled, still clutching the three envelopes.

'Nora!' Jim ripped off the ludicrous Hallowe'en mask. 'Nora, I didn't mean—'

'Jim, you fool,' panted Pat, flinging herself to her knees by Nora's still body. 'That's a smart joke! Nora dear—Nora!'

'Look out, Pat,' said Jim hoarsely; he seized Nora's limp figure, scooped her up, half-ran up the stairs with her.

'It's only a faint,' said Ellery, as Pat dashed into the kitchen. 'She'll be all right, Patty!' Pat came stumbling back with a glass of water, which slopped over with each step. 'Here, wench.' Ellery took it from her and sped up the stairs with the glass, Pat treading on his heels.

They found Nora on her bed, in hysterics, while Jim chafed her hands and groaned self-abasements. 'Excuse me,' said Ellery. He shouldered Jim aside and put the glass to Nora's blue lips. She tried to push his hand away. He slapped her, and she cried out; but she drank the water, choking. Then she sank back on the pillow, covering her face with her palms. 'Go away,' she sobbed.

'Nora, you all right now?' asked Pat anxiously.

'Yes. Please. Leave me alone. Please!'

'Go on, now,' said Jim. 'Leave us alone.'

Nora let her hands fall. Her face was swollen and puffed. 'You, too, Jim.'

Jim gaped at her. Pat steered him out. Ellery shut the bedroom door, frowning, and they went downstairs. Jim made for the liquor cabinet, poured himself a stiff Scotch, and tossed it down with one desperate motion. 'You know how nervous Nora is,' said Pat disapprovingly. 'If you hadn't had too much to drink tonight—'

Jim was angry, sullen. 'Who's tight? Don't you go telling Nora I've been drinking! Understand?'

'Yes, Jim,' said Pat quietly. They waited. Pat kept going to the foot of the stairs and looking up. Jim shuffled around. Ellery whistled a noiseless tune. Suddenly Nora appeared.

'Nora! Feeling better?' cried Pat.

'Worlds.' Nora came downstairs smiling. 'Please forgive me, Mr Smith. It was just being scared all of a sudden.'

Jim seized her in his arms. 'Oh, Nora—'

'Forget it dear,' laughed Nora.

There was no sign of the three envelopes.

8. *Hallowe'en:*
The Scarlet Letters

WHEN JIM AND NORA came up on the porch after dinner, Nora was quite gay.

'Pat told me about that silly mask, Jim Haight,' said Hermy. 'Nora dearest, you're sure you're all right?'

'Of course, Mother. All this fuss over a scare!'

John F. was studying his son-in-law in a puzzled, secretive way. Jim seemed a little sheepish; he grinned vaguely.

'Where's Carter, Pat?' demanded Hermy. 'Wasn't he supposed to go with us to Town Hall tonight?'

'I've a headache, Muth. I phoned Cart to say I was going to bed. Night!' Pat went quickly into the house.

'Come along, Smith,' said John F. 'There's a good speaker—one of those war correspondents.'

'Thanks, Mr Wright, but I've some work on my novel. Have a nice time!'

When Jim's new car rolled off down the Hill, Mr Ellery Queen stepped off the Wright porch and, by the light of the pumpkin moon, noiselessly crossed the lawn. He circled Nora's house once, inspecting the windows. All dark.

Then Alberta had already left—Thursday night was her night off. Ellery opened the kitchen door with a skeleton key, locked it behind him and, using his flashlight sparingly, made his way through the hall to the living room. He climbed the stairs making no sound. At the landing, he paused, frowning. There was a luminous line under Nora's bedroom door! He listened intently. Inside, drawers were being pulled open and pushed shut. A thief? Another Hallowe'en prank? Gripping the flashlight like a club, Ellery kicked the door open. Miss Patricia Wright screamed as she sprang from her stooped position over the lowest drawer of Nora's vanity. 'Hello,' said Mr Queen affably.

'Worm!' gasped Pat. 'I thought I'd *die*.' Then she blushed under his amused glance. 'At least *I* have an excuse! I'm her sister. But you ... you're just a plain snoop, *Mr Ellery Queen!*'

Ellery's jaw waggled. 'You little demon,' he said admiringly. 'You've know me all along.'

'Of course,' retorted Pat. 'I heard you lecture once on *The Place of the Detective Story in Contemporary Civilization*. Very pompous it was, too.'

'Wellesley?'

'Sarah Lawrence. I thought at the time you were very handsome. *Sic transit gloria*. Don't look so concerned. I shan't give your precious incognito away.' Mr Queen kissed her. 'Mmm,' said Pat. 'Not bad. But inopportune ... No, please, Ellery. Some other time. Ellery, those letters—you're the only one I can confide in. Muth and Pop would worry themselves sick—'

'And Carter Bradford?' suggested Mr Queen dryly.

'Cart,' said Miss Wright, flushing, 'is ... well, I just wouldn't want Cart to know anything's wrong. If it is,' she added quickly. 'I'm not sure anything is.'

Ellery said: 'Yes, you are. Delicious lipstick.'

'Wipe it off. Yes,' said Pat damply, 'I am ... Why didn't Nora say what was in those letters?' she burst out. 'Why did she come back to the living room tonight without them? *Why did she chase us all out of her bedroom?* Ellery, I'm ... scared.'

Ellery squeezed her cold hands. 'Let's look for them.'

He found them in one of Nora's hatboxes. The hatbox lay on the shelf of Nora's closet, and the three envelopes had been tucked between the tissue paper and the floor of the box beneath a little flowered hat with a saucy mauve veil.

'Very clumsy technique,' mourned Mr Queen.

'Poor Nor,' said Pat. Her lips were pale. 'Let me see!' Ellery handed her the three letters. In the upper right-hand corner of each envelope, where a stamp should have been, appeared a date written in red crayon. Pat frowned. Ellery took the envelopes from her and arranged them in chronological order, according to the crayoned dates. The dates were 11/28, 12/25, and 1/1. 'And all three,' mused Pat, 'are addressed to "Miss Rosemary Haight." She's Jim's only sister. We've never met her. But it's queer there's no street or city address . . .'

'Not necessarily,' said Ellery, his brows together. 'The queerness lies in the use of the crayon.'

'Oh, Jim's always used a thin red crayon instead of a pencil—it's a habit of his.'

'Then his sister's name on these envelopes is in Jim's handwriting?'

'Yes. I'd recognize this scrawl of Jim's anywhere. For pete's sake, Ellery, what's *in* them?'

Ellery removed the contents of the first envelope, crumpled a bit from Nora's clutch when she had fainted. The note was in Jim's handwriting, too, Pat said, and written in the same red crayon:—

Nov. 28

DEAR SIS: I know it's been a long time, but you can imagine I've been rushed. Haven't time to drop you more than a line, because my wife got sick today. Doesn't seem like much, but I don't know. If you ask me, the doctor doesn't know what it is, either. Let's hope it's nothing. Of course, I'll keep you posted. Write me soon.

Love, Jim

'I can't understand it,' said Pat slowly. 'Nora's never felt better. Muth and I were just remarking about it the other day. Ellery—'

'Has Nora seen Dr Willoughby recently?'

'No. Unless . . . But I'm sure she hasn't.'

'I see,' said Ellery in a voice that told nothing.

'Besides, that date—November twenty-eigth. That's a month away, Ellery! How could Jim know . . . ?' Pat stopped. Then she said hoarsely: 'Open the second one!'

The second note was shorter than the first, but it was written in the same red crayon in the same scrawl.

December 25th

SIS: I don't want to worry you. But I've got to tell you.

42

It's much worse. My wife is terribly ill. We're doing everything we can.   In haste, JIM

'In haste, Jim,' repeated Pat. 'In haste—and dated December twenty-fifth!' Ellery's eyes were clouded over now,
hiding. 'But how could Jim know Nora's illness is worse
when Nora isn't even sick?' cried Pat. 'And two months in
advance!'

'I think,' said Mr Queen, 'We'd better read the third
note.' And he took the sheet of paper from the last
envelope.

'Ellery, what . . . ?'

He handed it to her and began to walk up and down
Nora's bedroom, smoking a cigarette with short, nervous
puffs.

Pat read the note wide-eyed. Like the others, it was in
Jim's hand, a red-crayon scrawl. It said:—

Jan. 1

DEAREST SIS: She's dead. She passed away today.
My wife, gone. As if she'd never been. Her last moments
were—I can't write any more. Come to me if you can.

JIM

Ellery said: 'Not now, honey child,' and threw his arm
about Pat's waist.

'What does it mean?' she sobbed.

'Stop blubbering.' Pat turned away, hiding her face.

Ellery replaced the messages in their envelopes and
returned the envelopes to their hiding place exactly as he
had found them. He set the hatbox back on the shelf of
the closet, closed the vanity drawer in which Pat had been
rummaging, straightened Nora's hand mirror. Another
look around, and he led Pat from the room, switching off
the ceiling light by the door. 'Find the door open?' he
asked Pat.

'Closed,' she replied in a strangled voice.

He closed it. 'Wait. Where's that fat tan book—the one
the envelopes fell out of this evening?'

'In Jim's study.' Pat seemed to have difficulty pronounc-
ing her brother-in-law's name.

They found the book on one of the newly installed
shelves in the bedroom Nora had converted into a study
for her husband. Ellery had switched on the mica-shaded
desk lamp, and it threw long shadows on the walls. Pat
clung to his arm, throwing glances over her shoulder.

43

'Pretty fresh condition,' said Ellery in a mutter, plucking the book from the shelf. 'Cloth hasn't even begun to fade, and the edges of the pages are clean.'

'What is it?' whispered Pat.

'Edgcomb's *Toxicology*.'

'Toxicology!' Pat stared at it in horror.

Ellery sharply scrutinized the binding. Then he let the book fall open in his hands. It broke obediently to a dog-eared page—the only dog-eared page he could find. The book's spine showed a deep crack which ran parallel with the place in the book where it had broken open to reveal the dog-eared page. The three envelopes, then, had been lying between these two pages, thought Ellery. He began to read—to himself.

'What,' said Pat feverishly, 'What would Jim Haight be doing with a book on toxicology?'

Ellery looked at her. 'These two facing pages deal with various arsenious compounds—formulae, morbific effects, detection in organs and tissues, antidotes, fatal dosages, treatment of diseases arising from arsenious poisoning—'

'*Poisoning!*'

Ellery laid the book down within the brightest focus of the lamp. His finger pointed to the words in bold type: *Arsenious Oxid* (As_2O_3). His finger moved down to a paragraph which described arsenious oxid as 'white, tasteless, poisonous,' and gave the fatal dosage. This paragraph had been underlined in light red crayon.

In a quite clear voice that emerged from between wry, unwilling lips, Pat said: '*Jim is planning to murder Nora.*'

44

PART TWO

9. *Burnt Offering*

'JIM IS planning to murder Nora.'

Ellery set the book upon the shelf. With his back to Pat, he said: 'Nonsense.'

'You saw the letters yourself! You read them!'

Mr Queen sighed. They went downstairs in the dark, his arm about her waist. Outside, there was the old moon, and a stencil of cold stars. Pat shivered against him, and his clasp tightened. They drifted across the silver lawn and came to rest beneath the tallest elm. 'Look at the sky,' said Ellery, 'and tell me that again.'

'Don't feed me philosophy! Or poetry. This is the good old USA in the Year of Our Madness nineteen-forty. Jim is insane. He must be!' She began to cry.

'The human mind—' began Mr Queen; and he stopped. He had been about to say that the human mind was a curious and wonderful instrument. But it occurred to him in time that this was a two-way phrase, a Delphic hedge. The fact was . . . it looked bad. Very bad.

'Nora's in danger,' sobbed Pat. 'Ellery, what am I going to do?'

'Time may spade up some bones of truth, Patty.'

'But I can't take this alone! Nora—you saw how Nora took it. Ellery, she was scared green. And then . . . just as if nothing had happened. She's decided already, don't you see? *She's decided not to believe it.* If you waved those letters under her nose, Nora wouldn't admit anything now! Her mind opened for just a second; now it's shut down tight, and she'd lie to God.'

'Yes,' said Ellery, and his arms comforted her.

45

'He was so much in love with her! You saw it all happen. You saw the look on his face that night when they came downstairs to say they were going to be married. Jim was *happy*. When they got back from their honeymoon he seemed even happier.' Pat whispered: 'Maybe he *has* gone mad. Maybe that's been the whole thing all along. A dangerous maniac!' Ellery said nothing. 'How can I tell Mother? Or my father? It would kill them, and it wouldn't do any good. And yet—I've got to!'

A car throbbed up the Hill in the darkness.

'You're letting your emotions get in the way of your thinking, Pat,' said Ellery. 'A situation like this calls for observation and caution. And a disciplined tongue.'

'I don't understand . . .'

'One false accusation, and you might wreck the lives not only of Jim and Nora, but of your father and mother too.'

'Yes . . . And Nora waited so long—'

'I said there's time. There is. We'll watch, and we'll see, and meanwhile it will be a secret between us . . . Did I say "we"?' Ellery sounded rueful. 'It seems I've declared myself in.'

Pat gasped. 'You wouldn't back out *now?* I took it for granted. I mean, I've counted on you from that first awful moment. Ellery, you've *got* to help Nora! You're trained to this sort of thing. Please don't go away!' Pat shook him.

'I just said "we", didn't I?' said Ellery, almost irritably. There was something wrong. A sound had gone wrong somewhere. A sound that had stopped. A car? Had that been a car before? It hadn't passed . . . 'Cry it out now, but when it's over it's over, do you understand?' And now he shook her.

'Yes,' wept Pat. 'I'm a snuffling fool. I'm sorry.'

'You're not a fool, but you must be a heroine. No word, no look, no *attitude*. As far as the rest of Wrightsville is concerned, those letters don't exist. Jim is your brother-in-law, and you like him, and you're happy about him and Nora.' She nodded against his shoulder. 'We mustn't tell your father or mother or Frank Lloyd or—'

Pat raised her head. 'Or whom?'

'No,' said Ellery with a frown. 'I can't make *that* decision for you, too.'

'You mean Cart,' said Pat steadily.

'I mean the Prosecutor of Wright County.'

Pat was silent. Ellery was silent. The moon was lower now, its bosom ruffled with slate flounces of cloud. 'I couldn't tell Carter,' murmured Pat. 'It never even occurred to me. I can't tell you why. Maybe it's because he's connected with the police. Maybe it's because he's not in the family—'

'I'm not in the family, either,' said Mr Queen.

'You're different!'

Despite himself, Mr Queen experienced a chill of pleasure. But his voice was impersonal. 'At any rate, you've got to be my eyes and ears, Pat. Stay with Nora as much as possible without arousing her suspicions. Watch Jim without seeming to. Report everything that happens. And whenever possible you must work me into your family gatherings. Is all that clear?'

Pat actually smiled up at him. 'I *was* being silly. Now it doesn't seem half so bad, with you under this tree, and the moonlight touching that flat plane of your right cheek ... you're very handsome, you know, Ellery—'

'Then why in hell,' growled a male voice from the darkness, 'don't you kiss him?'

'Cart!' Pat snuggled against the black chest of the elm.

They could hear Bradford breathing somewhere near—breathing short deep ones. Too absurd, thought Mr Queen. A man of logic should evade such encirclements by chance. But at least it cleared up the minor irritation of the sound-that-had-stopped. It had been Carter Bradford's car.

'Well, he *is* handsome,' said Pat's voice from the tree trunk. Ellery grinned to himself.

'You lied to me,' cried Carter. He materialized: no hat, and his chestnut hair angry. 'Don't hide in a bush, Pat!'

'I'm not hiding,' said Pat peevishly, 'and it isn't a bush, it's a tree.' She came out of the darkness, too; and they faced each other with punctilio. Mr Queen watched with silent enjoyment.

'You told me over the phone that you had a headache!'

'Yes.'

'You said you were going to bed!'

'I am.'

'Don't quibble!'

'Why not? You raise such unimportant points, Mr Bradford.'

Carter's arms flapped under the unfriendly stars. 'You lied to get rid of me. You didn't want me around. You had a date with this scribbler! Don't deny it!'

'I do deny it.' Pat's voice softened. 'I did lie to you, Cart, but I didn't have a date with Ellery.'

'That,' remarked Mr Queen from his observation post, 'happens to be the truth.'

'Stick your two cents out, Smith!' shouted Carter. 'I'm trying to keep my temper or I'd drape you over the lawn!'

Mr 'Smith' grinned and held his peace.

'All right, so I'm jealous,' muttered Cart. 'But you don't have to be a sneak, Pat! If you don't want me, say so.'

'This has nothing to do with my wanting you or not wanting you,' said Pat in a timid-turtle voice.

'Well, do you or don't you?'

Pat's eyes fell. 'You've no right to ask me that—here—now.' Her eyes flashed up. 'You wouldn't want a sneak, anyway, would you?'

'All right! Have it your way!'

'Cart ... !'

His voice came back in a bellow of defiance. 'I'm through!'

Pat ran off toward the big white house.

Thought Mr Queen as he watched her slim figure race across the lawn: In a way it's better ... much better. You don't know what you're in for. And Mr Carter Bradford, when you meet him next, may very well be an enemy.

When Ellery returned from his pre-breakfast walk the next morning, he found Nora and her mother whispering on the Wright porch. 'Good morning!' he said cheerfully. 'Enjoy the lecture last night?'

'It was very interesting.' Nora looked distressed, and Hermione preoccupied, so Ellery began to go into the house.

'Mr Smith,' said Hermy. 'Oh, dear, I don't know how to say it! Nora dear—'

'Ellery, what happened here last night?' asked Nora.

'Happened?' Ellery looked blank.

'I mean with Pat and Carter. You were home—'

'Is anything wrong with Pat?' asked Ellery quickly.

'Of course there is. She won't come down to breakfast. She won't answer any questions. And when Pat sulks—'

'It's Carter's fault,' Hermy burst out. 'I *thought* there was something queer about her "headache" last night! Please, Mr Smith, if you know anything about it—if something happened after we went to Town Hall last night which her mother ought to know—'

'Has Pat broken off with Cart?' asked Nora anxiously. 'No, you don't have to answer, Ellery. I can see it in your

48

face. Mother, you'll simply have to give Patty a talking-to. She can't keep doing this sort of thing to Cart.'

Ellery walked Nora back to the little house. As soon as they were out of earshot of Mrs Wright, Nora said: 'Of course you had something to do with it.'

'I?' asked Mr Queen.

'Well . . . don't you agree Pat's in love with Carter? I'm sure you could help by not making Carter jealous—'

'Mr Bradford,' said Mr Queen, 'would be jealous of a postage stamp Patty licked.'

'I know. He's so hotheaded, too! Oh, dear.' Nora sighed. 'I'm making a mess of it. Will you forgive me? And come in to breakfast?'

'Yes to both questions.' And as he helped Nora up the porch steps, he wondered just how guilty she really was.

Jim was full of political talk, and Nora . . . Nora was wonderful. No other word for it, thought Ellery. Watching and listening, he could detect no least tinkle of falsity. They seemed so much like two young people luxuriating in the blessedness of early marriage that it was a temptation to dismiss the incidents of the previous evening as fantasy.

Pat arrived, with Alberta and eggs, in a rush. 'Nora! How nice,' she said, as if nothing at all had happened. 'Can you spare a starving gal an egg or two? Morning, Jim! Ellery! Not that Ludie didn't have breakfast for me. She *did*. But I just felt that nosy impulse to look in on the lovebirds . . .'

'Alberta, another setting,' said Nora, and she smiled at Pat. 'You *do* talk in the morning! Ellery, sit down. The honeymoon being over, *my* husband doesn't rise for my family any more.'

Jim stared. 'Who—Patso?' He grinned. 'Say, you *are* grown-up! Let me look. Yep. A real glamour girl. Smith, I envy you. If I were a bachelor—'

Ellery saw the swift cloud darken Nora's face. She pressed more coffee on her husband. Pat kept chattering. She wasn't a very good actress—couldn't look Jim in the eye. Heroic, though. Remembering instructions in the midst of her own troubles . . . But Nora was superb. Yes, Pat had been right. Nora had decided not to *think* about the letters or their horrible implication. And she was using the minor crisis of Pat and Cart to help her not to think.

'I'll fix your eggs myself, darling,' said Nora to Pat. 'Alberta's a jewel, but how could she know you like four-minute coddling, to the second? Excuse me.' Nora left the dining room to join Alberta in the kitchen.

'That Nora,' chuckled Jim. 'She's a real hen. Say! What time is it? I'll be late at the bank. Patty, you been crying? You're talking sort of funny, too. Nora!' he shouted. 'Didn't the mail come yet?'

'Not yet!' Nora called from the kitchen.

'Who, me?' said Pat feebly. 'Don't—don't be a goop, Jim.'

'*All* right, *all* right,' said Jim, laughing. 'So it's none of my damn business. Ah! There's Bailey now. 'Scuse!' Jim hurried out to the foyer to answer the postman's ring. They heard him open the front door; they heard old Mr Bailey's cracked 'Mornin', Mr Haight,' Jim's joshing response, the little slam of the door, and Jim's slow returning footsteps, as if he were shuffling through the mail as he came back. Then he walked into the field of their vision and stopped, and they saw him staring at one of the several envelopes the postman had just delivered. His face was liverish. And then he vaulted upstairs. They heard his feet pound on the carpeting and a moment later a door bang.

Pat was gaping at the spot Jim had just vacated. 'Eat your cereal,' said Ellery.

Pat flushed and bent quickly over her plate. Ellery got up and walked without noise to the foot of the staircase. After a moment he returned to the breakfast table. 'He's in his study, I think. Heard him *lock the door* . . . No! Not now. Here's Nora.'

Pat choked over her Crackle-Crunch. 'Where's Jim?' asked Nora as she set the eggs before her sister.

'Upstairs,' said Ellery, reaching for the toast.

'Jim?'

'Yes, Nora.' Jim reappeared on the stairs; he was still pale, but rigidly controlled. He had his coat on, and carried several unopened letters of assorted sizes.

'Jim! Is anything wrong?'

'Wrong?' Jim laughed. 'I never saw such a suspicious woman! What the devil should be wrong?'

'I don't know. But you look so pale—'

Jim kissed her. 'You ought to've been a nurse! Well, got to be going. Oh, by the way. Here's the mail. The usual junk. Bye, Patty! Smith! See you soon.' Jim raced out.

After breakfast, Ellery said something about 'strolling in the woods' behind the house and excused himself. A half hour later Pat joined him. She came hurrying through the underbrush with a Javanese scarf tied around her head, looking back over her shoulder as if someone were chasing her. 'I thought I'd never get away from Nora,' Pat panted. She dropped to a stump. 'Whoo!'

Ellery blew smoke thoughtfully. 'Pat, we've got to read that letter Jim just received.'

'Ellery . . . where's this all going to end?'

'It stirred Jim up tremendously. Can't be coincidence. Somehow this morning's letter ties in with the rest of this puzzle. Can you lure Nora out of the house?'

'She's going to High Village this morning with Alberta to do some shopping. There's the station wagon! I'd recognize that putt-putt in Detroit.'

Mr Queen ground out his cigarette carefully. 'All right, then,' he said.

Pat kicked a twig. Her hands were trembling. Then she sprang off the stump. 'I feel like a skunk,' she moaned. 'But what else can we do?'

'I doubt if we'll find anything,' said Ellery as Pat let him into Nora's house with her duplicate key. 'Jim locked the door when he ran upstairs. He didn't want to be caught doing . . . whatever it was he did.'

'You think he destroyed the letter?'

'Afraid so. But we'll have a look, anyway.'

In Jim's study, Pat set her back against the door. She looked ill. Ellery sniffed. And went directly to the fireplace. It was clean except for a small mound of ash. 'He burned it!' said Pat.

'But not thoroughly enough.'

'Ellery, you've found something!'

'A scrap that wasn't consumed by the fire.'

Pat flew across the room. Ellery was examining a scrap of charred paper very carefully. 'Part of the envelope?'

'The flap. Return address. But the address has been burned off. Only thing left is the sender's name.'

Pat read: ' "Rosemary Haight." Jim's sister.' Her eyes widened. 'Jim's sister Rosemary! Ellery, the one he wrote those three letters to about Nora!'

'It's possible that—' Ellery did not finish.

'You were going to say it's possible there was a first letter we didn't find, because he'd already sent it! And that this is the remains of his sister's answer.'

'Yes.' Ellery tucked the burnt scrap away in his wallet. 'But on second thought I'm not so sure. Why should his sister's reply bother him so much, if that's what it is? No, Patty, this is something different, something new.'

'But what?'

'That,' said Mr Queen, 'is what we've got to find out.'
He took her arm, looking about. 'Let's get out of here.'

That night they were all sitting on the Wright porch
watching the wind blow the leaves across the lawn. John
F. and Jim were debating the presidential campaign with
some heat, while Hermy anxiously appeased and Nora and
Pat listened like mice. Ellery sat by himself in a corner,
smoking.

'John, you know I don't like these political arguments!'
said Hermy. 'Goodness, you men get so hot under the
collar—'

John F. grunted. 'Jim, there's dictatorship coming in
this country, you mark my words—'

Jim grinned. 'And you'll eat 'em ... *All* right, Mother!'
Then he said casually: 'Oh, by the way, darling, I got a
letter from my sister Rosemary this morning. Forgot to
tell you.'

'Yes?' Nora's tone was bright. 'How nice. What does
she write, dear?'

Pat drifted toward Ellery and in the darkness sat down
at his feet. He put his hand on her neck; it was clammy.
'The usual stuff. She does say she'd like to meet you—all
of you.'

'Well, I should think so!' said Hermy. 'I'm very anxious
to meet your sister, Jim. Is she coming out for a visit?'

'Well ... I *was* thinking of asking her, but—'

'Now, Jim,' said Nora. 'You know I've asked you dozens of times to invite Rosemary to Wrightsville.'

'Then it's all right with you, Nor?' asked Jim quickly.

'All right!' Nora laughed. 'What's the matter with you?
Give me her address and I'll drop her a note tonight.'

'Don't bother, darling. I'll write her myself.'

When they were alone, a half hour later, Pat said to
Ellery: 'Nora was scared.'

'Yes. It's a poser.' Ellery circled his knees with his
arms. 'Of course, the letter that stirred Jim up this morning was the same letter he just said he got from his sister.'

'Ellery, Jim's holding something back.'

'No question about it.'

'If his sister Rosemary just wrote about wanting to
come out for a visit, or anything as trivial as that ... *why
did Jim burn her letter?*'

Mr Queen kept the silence for a long time. Finally he
mumbled: 'Go to bed, Patty. I want to think.'

On November the eighth, four days after Franklin Delano Roosevelt had been elected to the Presidency of the United States for a third term, Jim Haight's sister came to Wrightsville.

10. *Jim and the Fleshpot*

'MISS ROSEMARY HAIGHT,' wrote Gladys Hemmingworth in the Society column of the *Wrightsville Record*, 'was strikingly accoutered in a *naturel* French suède travelling suit with sleeveless jerkin to match, a dashing jacket of platinum-fox fur topped with the jauntiest fox-trimmed archery hat of forest green, and green suède wedgies and bag ...'

Mr Ellery Queen happened to be taking a walk that morning ... to the Wrightsville station. So he saw Rosemary Haight get off the train at the head of a safari bearing luggage and pose for a moment, in the sun, like a movie actress. He saw her trip over to Jim and kiss him, and turn to Nora with animation and embrace her, presenting a spruce cheek; and Mr Queen also saw the two women laugh and chatter as Jim and the safari picked up the visitor's impedimenta and made for Jim's car. And Mr Queen's weather eye clouded over.

That night, at Nora's, he had an opportunity to test his first barometric impression. And he decided that Rosemary Haight was no bucolic maiden on an exciting journey; that she was pure metropolis, insolent and bored and trying to conceal both. Also, she was menacingly attractive. Hermy, Pat, and Nora disliked her instantly; Ellery could tell that from the extreme politeness with which they treated her. As for John F., he was charmed, spryly gallant. Hermy reproached him in the silent language of the eye. And Ellery spent a troubled night trying to put Miss Rosemary Haight together in the larger puzzle, and not succeeding.

Jim was busy at the bank these days and, rather with relief, Ellery thought, left the problem of entertaining his sister to Nora. Dutifully Nora drove Rosemary about the countryside, showing her the 'sights'. It was a little difficult for Nora to sustain the charming-hostess illusion. Pat confided in Ellery, since Rosemary had a supercilious attitude towards everything and wondered 'how in heaven's name you can be *happy* in such a dull place, Mrs. H!'

Then there was the gauntlet of the town's ladies to run ... teas for the guest, very correct with hats on in the house and white gloves, an ambitious mah-jongg party, a wiener roast on the lawn one moonlit night, a church social ... The ladies were cold. Emmeline DuPré said Rosemary Haight had a streak of 'commerce' whatever that was, Clarice Martin thought her clothes too 'you-know', and Mrs Mackenzie at the Country Club said she was a born bitch and look at those silly men drooling at her! The Wright women found themselves constrained to defend her, which was hard, considering that secretly they agreed to the truth of all the charges.

'I wish she'd leave,' said Pat to Ellery a few days after Rosemary's arrival. 'Isn't that a horrid thing to say? But I do. And now she's sent for her trunks!'

'But I thought she didn't like it here.'

'That's what I can't understand, either. Nora says it was supposed to be a "flying" visit, but Rosemary acts as if she means to dig in for the winter. And Nora can't very well discourage her.'

'What's Jim say?'

'Nothing to Nora but—' Pat lowered her voice and looked around—'apparently he's said something to Rosemary, because I happened in just this morning and there was Nora trapped in the serving pantry while Jim and Rosemary, who evidently thought Nora was upstairs, were having an argument in the dining room. That woman has a temper!'

'What was the argument about?' asked Ellery eagerly.

'I came in at the tail end and didn't hear anything important, but Nora says it was ... well, frightening. Nora wouldn't tell me what she'd heard, but she was terribly upset—she looked the same way as when she read those three letters that tumbled out of the toxicology book.'

Ellery muttered: 'I wish I'd heard that argument. Why can't I put my finger on *something*? Pat, you're a rotten assistant detective!'

'Yes, sir,' said Pat miserably.

Rosemary Haight's trunk arrived on the fourteenth.

Steve Polaris, who ran the local express agency, delivered the trunk himself—an overgrown affair that looked as if it might be packed with imported evening gowns. Steve lugged it up Nora's walk on his broad back and Mr Queen, who was watching from the Wright porch, saw him carry it into Nora's house and come out a few minutes later accompanied by Rosemary, who was wearing a candid red, white, and blue negligee. She looked like an enlistment poster. Ellery saw Rosemary sign Steve Polaris's receipt book and go back into the house. Steve slouched down the walk grinning—Steve had the most wolfish eye, Pat said, in all of Low Village.

'Pat,' said Ellery urgently, 'do you know this truckman well?'

'Steve? That's the only way you *can* know Steve.'

Steve tossed his receipt book on the driver's seat of his truck and began to climb in. 'Then distract him. Kiss him, vamp him, do a striptease—anything, but get him out of sight of that truck for two minutes!'

Pat instantly called: 'Oh, Ste-e-e-eve!' and tripped down the porch steps. Ellery followed in a saunter. No one was in sight anywhere on the Hill.

Pat was slipping her arm through Steve's and giving him one of her quick little-girl smiles, saying something about her piano, and there wasn't a man she knew strong enough to move it from where it was to where she wanted it, and of course when she saw Steve ... Steve went with Pat into the Wright house, visibly swollen. Ellery was at the truck in two bounds. He snatched the receipt book from the front seat. Then he took a piece of charred paper from his wallet and began riffling the pages of the book ... When Pat reappeared with Steve, Mr Queen was at Hermione's zinnia bed surveying the dead and dying blossoms with the sadness of a poet. Steve gave him a scornful look and passed on.

'Now you'll have to move the piano back,' said Pat. 'I *am* sorry—I could have thought of something not quite so bulky ... Bye, Stevie!' The truck rolled off with a flirt of its exhaust.

'I was wrong,' mumbled Ellery.

'About what?'

'About Rosemary.'

'Stop being cryptic! And why did you send me to lure Steve away from his truck? The two are connected, Mr Queen!'

'I had a flash from on high. It said to me: ' "This woman

55

Rosemary doesn't seem cut from the same cloth as Jim Haight. They don't seem like brother and sister at all—" '

'Ellery!'

'Oh, it was possible. But my flash was wrong. She *is* his sister.'

'And you proved that through Steve Polaris's truck? Wonderful man!'

'Through his receipt book, in which this woman had just signed her name. I *have* the real Rosemary Haight's signature, you'll recall, my dear Watson.'

'On that charred flap of envelope we found in Jim's study—the remains of his sister's letter that he'd burned!'

'Precisely, my dear Watson. And the signature "Rosemary Haight" on the flap of the letter and the signature "Rosemary Haight" in Steve's receipt book are the work of the same hand.'

'Leaving us,' remarked Pat dryly, 'exactly where we were.'

'No,' said Mr Queen with a faint smile. 'Before we only *believed* this woman was Jim's sister. Now we *know* it. Even your primitive mind can detect the distinction, my dear Watson?'

The longer Rosemary Haight stayed at Nora's, the more inexplicable the woman became. Jim was busier and busier at the bank; sometimes he did not even come home to dinner. Yet Rosemary did not seem to mind her brother's neglect half so much as her sister-in-law's attentions. The female Haight tongue was forked; more than once its venom reduced Nora to tears ... shed, it was reported to Mr Queen by his favourite spy, in her own room, alone. Towards Pat and Hermione, Rosemary was less obvious. She rattled on about her 'travels'—Panama, Rio, Honolulu, Bali, Banff, surf riding and skiing and mountain climbing and 'exciting' men—much talk about exciting men—until the ladies of the Wright family began to look harried and grim, and retaliated.

And yet Rosemary stayed on.

Why? Mr Queen was pondering this poser as he sat one morning in the window seat of his workroom. Rosemary Haight had just come out of her brother's house, a cigarette at a disgusted angle to her red lips, clad in jodhpurs and red Russian boots and a Lana Turner sweater. She stood on the porch for a moment, slapping a crop against her boots with impatience, at odds with Wrightsville. Then she strode off into the woods behind the Wright grounds.

56

Later, Pat took Ellery driving; and Ellery told her about seeing the Haight woman enter the woods in a riding habit.

Pat turned into the broad concrete of Route 16, driving slowly. 'Bored,' she said. 'Bored blue. She got Jake Bushmill the blacksmith to dig her up a saddle horse from somewhere—yesterday was her first day out, and Carmel Pettigrew saw her tearing along the dirt road toward Twin Hill like—I quote—one of the Valkyries. Carmel—silly dope!—thinks Rosemary's just too-too.'

'And you?' queried Mr Queen.

'That panther laziness of hers is an act—underneath, she's the restless type, and hard as teak. A cheap wench. Or don't you think?' Pat glanced at him sidewise.

'She's terribly attractive,' said Ellery evasively.

'So's a man-eating orchid,' retorted Pat; and she drove in silence for eight-tenths of a mile. Then she said: 'What do you make of the whole thing, Ellery—Jim's conduct, Rosemary, the three letters, the visit, Rosemary's staying on when she hates it . . . ?'

'Nothing,' said Ellery. But he added: 'Yet.'

'Ellery—look!' They were approaching a gaudy bump on the landscape, a one-story white stucco building on whose walls oversized red lady-devils danced and from whose roof brittle cut-out flames of wood shattered the sky. The tubing of the unlit neon sign spelled out VIC CARLATTI'S *Hot Spot*. The parking lot to the side was empty except for one small car.

'Look at what?' demanded Ellery, puzzled. 'I don't see anything except no customers, since the sun is shining and Carlatti's patrons don't creep out of their walls until nightfall.'

Judging from that car on the plot,' said Pat, a little pale, 'there's *one* customer.'

Ellery frowned. 'It does look like the same car.'

'It is.' Pat drove up to the entrance, and they jumped out.

'It might be business, Pat,' said Ellery, not with conviction.

Pat glanced at him scornfully and opened the front door. There was no one in the chrome-and-scarlet leather interior but a bartender and a man mopping the postage-stamp dance floor. Both employees looked at them curiously. 'I don't see him,' whispered Pat.

'He may be in one of those booths . . . No.'

'The back room . . .'

'Let's sit down.'

They sat down at the nearest table and the bartender came over, yawning. 'What'll it be, folks?'

'Cuba Libre,' said Pat, nervously looking around.

'Scotch.'

'Uh-huh.' The bartender strolled back to his bar.

'Wait here,' said Ellery. He got up and made for the rear, like a man looking for something.

'It's over that way,' said the man with the mop, pointing to a door marked HE. But Ellery pushed against a partly open red-and-gold door with a heavy brass lock. It swung noiselessly.

The room beyond was a gambling room. In a chair at the empty roulette table sprawled Jim Haight, his head on one arm of the table. A burly man with a cold cigar stub in his teeth stood half turned away from Ellery at a telephone on the far wall. 'Yeah. I said Mrs Haight, stoopid.' The man had luxuriant black brows which almost met and a gray flabby face. 'Tell her Vic Carlatti.'

'Stoopid' would be Alberta. Ellery stood still against the red-and-gold door. 'Mrs Haight? This is Mr Carlatti of the Hot Spot,' said the proprietor in a genial bass. 'Yeah . . . No, I ain't making no mistake, Mrs Haight. It's about Mr Haight . . . Now wait a minute. He's settin' in my back room right now, cockeyed . . . I mean drunk . . . Now don't get bothered, Mrs Haight. Your old man's okay. Just had a couple of shots too many and passed out. What'll I do with the body?'

'Just a moment,' said Ellery pleasantly.

Carlatti slewed his big head around. He looked Ellery up and down. 'Hold on a second, Mrs Haight . . . Yeah? What can I do for you?'

'You can let me talk to Mrs Haight,' said Ellery, crossing over and taking the phone from the man's furry hands. 'Nora? This is Ellery Smith.'

'Ellery!' Nora was frantic. 'What's the matter with Jim? How is he? How did you happen to—'

'Don't get excited, Nora. Pat and I were driving past Carlatti's place and we noticed Jim's car parked outside. We're in here now and Jim's all right. Just had a little too much to drink.'

'I'll drive right down—the station wagon—'

'You'll do nothing of the kind. Pat and I will have him home in half an hour. Don't worry, do you hear?'

'Thank you,' whispered Nora, and hung up.

Ellery turned from the telephone to find Pat bending over Jim, shaking him. 'Jim. Jim!'

'It's no use, girl friend,' growled Carlatti. 'He's carrying a real load.'

'You ought to be ashamed of yourself, getting him tight!'

'Now don't get tough, babe. He came in here under his own steam. I got a licence to sell liquor. He wants to buy, he can buy. Get him outa here.'

'How did you know who he was? How did you know whom to call?' Pat was fizzing with indignation.

'He's been here before, and besides I frisked him. And don't gimme that fishy eye. Come on, pig. Blow!'

Pat gasped. 'Excuse me,' said Ellery. He walked past Carlatti as if the big man were not there, and then suddenly he turned and stepped hard on Carlatti's bulldog toe. The man bellowed with pain and reached swiftly for his back pocket. Ellery set the heel of his right hand against Carlatti's chin and pushed. Carlatti's head snapped back; and as he staggered Ellery punched him in the belly with the other hand. Carlatti groaned and sank to the floor, clutching his middle with both hands and staring up, surprised. 'Miss Pig to you,' said Ellery. He yanked Jim out of his chair and got him in a fireman's grip. Pat picked up Jim's crushed hat and ran to hold the door open.

Ellery took the wheel going back. In the open car, with the wind striking his face and Pat shaking him, Jim began to revive. He goggled glassily at them.

'Jim, whatever made you do a silly thing like this?'

'Huh?' gurgled Jim, closing his eyes again.

'In mid-afternoon, when you should be at the bank!'

Jim sank lower in the seat, muttering. 'Stupefied,' said Ellery. There was a deep cleft between brows. His rearvision mirror told him a car was overtaking them rapidly—Carter Bradford's car. Pat noticed, and turned. And turned back, very quickly. Ellery slowed down to let Bradford pass. But Bradford did not pass. He slowed down alongside and honked his horn. A lean gray Yankee with a red face and jellyfish eyes sat beside him. Obediently, Ellery pulled up at the side of the road; and Bradford stopped his car, too.

Pat said: 'Why, hel*lo*, Cart,' in a surprised voice. 'And Mr Dakin! Ellery, this is Chief Dakin of the Wrightsville police. Mr Ellery Smith.'

Chief Dakin said: 'How do, Mr Smith,' in a polite voice, and Ellery nodded.

'Anything wrong?' asked Carter Bradford, a little awkwardly. 'I noticed Jim here was—'

'Well, that's extremely efficient, Cart,' said Pat warmly. 'Practically Scotland Yardish, or at the very least F.B.I. Isn't it, Ellery? The Public Prosecutor and the Chief of Police—'

'There's nothing wrong, Bradford,' said Ellery.

'Nothing that a bicarbonate of soda and a good night's sleep won't fix,' said Chief Dakin dryly. 'Carlatti's?'

'Something like that,' said Ellery. 'Now if you don't mind, gentlemen, Mr Haight needs his bed—badly.'

'Anything I can do, Pat . . .' Cart was flushed. 'Matter of fact, I was thinking of calling you up—'

'You were thinking of calling me up.'

'I mean—'

Jim stirred between Pat and Ellery, mumbling. Pat said severely: 'Jim. How do you feel?' He opened his eyes again. They were still glassy, but something behind the glaze made Pat look at Ellery with a swift fear. 'Say, he's in a bad way, at that,' said Dakin.

'Relax, now, Jim,' soothed Ellery. 'Go to sleep.'

Jim looked from Pat to Ellery to the men in the other car, but he did not recognize any of them. The mumble became intelligible: 'Wife my wife damn her oh damn wife . . .'

'Jim!' cried Pat. 'Ellery, get him home!'

Ellery released his hand brake quickly. But Jim was not to be repressed. He pulled himself up and his cheeks, pale from sickness, grew scarlet. 'Rid of her!' he shouted. 'Wait'n' see! I'll get rid of the bas'ard! I'll kill 'a bas'ard!'

Chief Dakin blinked, and Carter Bradford looked immensely surprised and opened his mouth to say something. But Pat pulled Jim down savagely and Ellery shot the convertible forward, leaving Bradford's car behind. Jim began to sob, and in the middle of a sob he suddenly fell asleep again. Pat shrank as far from him as she could. 'Did you hear what he *said*, Ellery? Did you?'

'He's crazy blind.' Ellery stepped hard on the gas pedal.

'It's true, then,' moaned Pat. 'The letters—Rosemary . . . Ellery, I tell you Rosemary and Jim have been putting on an act! They're in cahoots to—to— And Cart and Chief Dakin heard him!'

'Pat.' Ellery kept his eyes on the road. 'I haven't wanted

60

to ask you this before, but ... Has Nora any considerable sum of money, or property, in her own right?'

Pat moistened her lips very slowly. 'Oh ... no. It couldn't be ... that.'

'Then she has.'

'Yes,' Pat whispered. 'By my grandfather's will. Pop's father. Nora automatically inherited a lot of money when she married, held in trust for her if and when. Grandfather Wright died soon after Lola eloped with that actor—he'd cut Lola off because of that, and divided his estate between Nora and me. I get half when I marry, too—'

'How much did Nora get?' asked Ellery. He glanced at Jim. But Jim was stertorously asleep.

'I don't know. But Pop once told me it's more than Nora and I could ever spend. Oh Lord—Nora!'

'If you start to cry,' said Ellery grimly. 'I'll dump you overboard. Is this inheritance to you and Nora a secret?'

'Try to keep a secret in Wrightsville,' said Pat. 'Nora's money . . .' She began to laugh. 'It's like a bad movie. Ellery—what are we going to *do?*' She laughed and laughed.

Ellery turned Pat's car into the Hill drive. 'Put Jim to bed,' he muttered.

11. *Thanksgiving: The First Warning*

THE NEXT morning Mr Queen was knocking at Nora's door before eight. Nora's eyes were swollen. 'Thanks for—yesterday. Putting Jim to bed while I was being so silly—'

'Rubbish,' said Ellery cheerfully. 'There hasn't been a bride since Eve who didn't think the world was going under when hubby staggered home under his first load. Where's the erring husband?'

'Upstairs shaving.' Nora's hand trembled as she fussed with the gleaming toaster on the breakfast table.

'May I go up? I shouldn't want to embarrass your

61

sister-in-law by prowling around the bedroom floor at this hour—'

'Oh, Rosemary doesn't get up till ten,' said Nora. 'These wonderful November mornings! Please do—and tell Jim what you think of him!'

Ellery laughed and went upstairs. He knocked on the master-bedroom door, which was half-open, and Jim called from the bathroom: 'Nora? Gosh, darling, I knew you'd be my sweet baby and forgive—' His voice blurred when he spied Ellery. Jim's face was half shaved; the shaved half was pasty, and his eyes puffed. 'Morning, Smith. Come in.'

'I just dropped by for a minute to ask you how you were feeling, Jim.' Ellery draped himself against the bathroom jamb.

Jim turned, surprised. 'How did *you* know?'

'How did *I* know! Don't tell me you don't remember. Why, Pat and I brought you home.'

'Gosh,' groaned Jim, 'I wondered about that. Nora won't talk to me. Can't say I blame her. Say, I'm awfully grateful, Smith. Where'd you find me?'

'Carlatti's place on Route 16. The *Hot Spot*.'

'That dive?' Jim shook his head. 'No wonder Nora's sore.' He grinned sheepishly. 'Was I sick during the night! Nora fixed me up, but she wouldn't say a word to me. What a dumb stunt!'

'You did some pretty dumb talking on the ride home, too, Jim.'

'Talking? What did I say?'

'Oh ... something about "getting rid of" some bastard or other,' said Ellery lightly.

Jim blinked. He turned back to the mirror again. 'Out of my head, I guess. Or else I was thinking of Hitler.' Ellery nodded, his eyes fixed on the razor. It was shaking. 'I don't remember a damn thing,' said Jim. 'Not a damn thing.'

'I'd lay off the booze if I were you, Jim,' said Ellery amiably. 'Not that it's any of my business, but ... well, if you keep saying things like that, people might misunderstand.'

'Yeah,' said Jim, fingering his shaved cheek. 'I guess they would at that. Ow, my head! Never again.'

'Tell that to Nora,' laughed Ellery. 'Well, morning, Jim.'

'Morning. And thanks again.'

Ellery left, smiling. But the smile vanished on the landing. It seemed to him that the door to the guest room was open a handsbreadth wider than when he had gone in to talk to Jim.

Mr Queen found it harder and harder to work on his novel. For one thing, there was the weather. The countryside was splashy with reds and oranges and yellowing greens; the days were frost-touched now as well as the nights, hinting at early snows; nights came on swiftly, with a crackle. It was a temptation to roam back-country roads and crunch the crisp dry corpses of the leaves underfoot. Especially after sunset, when the sky dropped its curtains, lights sparkled in isolated farmhouses, and an occasional whinny or howl came from some black barn. Wilcy Gallimard came into town with five truckloads of turkeys and got rid of them in no time. 'Yes, sir,' said Mr Queen to himself. 'Thanksgiving's in the air—everywhere except at 460 Hill Drive.'

Then there was Pat, whose recent habit of peering over her own shoulder had become chronic. She clung to Ellery so openly that Hermione Wright began to make secret plans in her head and even John F., who never noticed anything but flaws in mortgages and rare postage stamps, looked thoughtful . . . It made work very difficult.

But most of all it was watching Jim and Nora without seeming to that occupied Ellery's time. Things were growing worse in the Haight household. For Jim and Nora no longer 'got along'. There were quarrels so bitter that their impassioned voices flew through the November air all the way across the driveway to the Wright house through closed windows. Sometimes it was about Rosemary; sometimes it was about Jim's drinking; sometimes it was about money. Jim and Nora continued to put up a brave show before Nora's family, but everyone knew what was going on.

'Jim's got a new one,' reported Pat to Ellery one evening. 'He's gambling!'

'Is he?' said Mr Queen.

'Nora was talking to him about it this morning,' Pat was so distressed she could not sit still. 'And he admitted it—*shouted* it at her. And in the next breath asked her for money. Nora pleaded with him to tell her what was wrong, but the more Nora pleads the angrier and harder Jim gets. Ellery, I think he's touched. I really do!'

'That's not the answer,' said Ellery stubbornly. 'There's a pattern here. His conduct doesn't *fit*, Patty. If only he'd talk. But he won't. Ed Hotchkiss brought him home in the cab last night. I was waiting on the porch—Nora'd gone to bed. Jim was pretty well illuminated. But when I began to pump him—' Ellery shrugged. 'He swung at me ... Pat.'

Pat jerked. 'What?'

'He's pawning jewelry.'

'Pawning jewelry! Whose?'

'I followed him at lunch today, when he left the bank. He ducked into Simpson's, on the Square, and pawned what looked to me like a cameo brooch set with rubies.'

'That's Nora's! Aunt Tabitha gave it to her as a high-school graduation present!'

Ellery took her hands. 'Jim has no money of his own, has he?'

'None except what he earns.' Pat's lips tightened. 'My father spoke to him the other day. About his work. Jim's neglecting it. You know Pop. Gentle as a lamb. It must have embarrassed him dreadfully. But Jim snapped at him, and poor Pop just blinked and walked away. And have you noticed how my mother's been looking?'

'Dazed.'

'Muth won't admit anything's wrong—even to me. Nobody will, nobody. And Nora's worse than any of them! And the town—Emmy DuPré's busier than Goebbels! They're all whispering ... I hate them! I hate the town, I hate Jim ...'

Ellery had to put his arms around her.

Nora planned Thanksgiving with a sort of desperation—a woman trying to hold on to her world as it growled and heaved about her. There were two of Wilcy Gallimard's fanciest toms, and chestnuts to be grated in absurd quantities, and cranberries from Bald Mountain to be mashed, and turnips and pumpkins and goodies galore ... all requiring preparation, fuss, work, with and without Alberta Manaskas's help ... all requiring *concentration*. And while her house filled with savory odors, Nora would brook no assistance from anyone but Alberta—not Pat, not Hermione, not even old Ludie, who went about muttering for days about 'these snippy young know-it-all brides.'

Hermy dabbed at her eyes. 'It's the first Thanksgiving since we were married, John, that I haven't made the family dinner. Nora baby—your table's so beautiful!'

64

'Maybe this time,' chuckled John F., 'I won't have indigestion. Bring on that turkey and stuffing!'

But Nora shooed them all into the living room—things weren't quite ready. Jim, a little drawn, but sober, wanted to stay and help. Nora smiled pallidly at him and sent him after the others.

Mr Queen strolled out to the Haight porch, so he was the first to greet Lola Wright as she came up the walk.

'Hello,' said Lola. 'You bum.'

'Hello yourself.'

Lola was wearing the same pair of slacks, the same tight-fitting sweater, the same ribbon in her hair. And from her wry mouth came the same fumes of Scotch. 'Don't look at me that way, stranger! I'm invited. Fact. Nora. Family reunion an' stuff. Kiss and make up. I'm broadminded. But you're a bum just the same. How come no see little Lola?'

'Novel.'

'Your eye,' laughed Lola, steadying herself against his arm. 'No writer works more than a few hours a day, if that. It's my Snuffy. You're making love to Pat. 'Sall right. You could do worse. She's even got a brain on that swell chassis.'

'I could do worse, but I'm not doing anything, Lola.'

'Ah, noble, too. Well, give 'em hell, brother. Excuse me. I've got to go jab my family's sensibilities.' And Lola walked, carefully, into her sister's house. Mr Queen waited on the porch a decent interval, and then followed. He came upon a scene of purest gaiety. It took keen eyes to detect the emotional confusion behind Hermy's sweet smile, and the quivering of John F.'s hand as he accepted a Martini from Jim. Pat forced one on Ellery; so Ellery proposed a toast to 'a wonderful family', at which they all drank grimly.

Then Nora, all flushed from the kitchen, hustled them into the dining room; and they dutifully exclaimed over the magazine-illustration table ... Rosemary Haight holding on to John F.'s arm.

It happened just as Jim was dishing out second helpings of turkey. Nora was passing her mother's plate when she gasped, and the full platter fell into her lap. The plate—Nora's precious Spode—crashed on the floor. Jim gripped the arms of his chair. Nora was on her feet, palms pressed against the cloth, her mouth writhing in a horrid spasm.

'Nora!'

Ellery reached Nora in one leap. She pushed at him

feebly, licking her lips, white as the new cloth. Then with a cry she ran, snatching herself from Ellery's grip with surprising strength. They heard her stumble upstairs, the click of a door.

'She's sick. Nora's sick!'

'Nora—where are you?'

'Call Doc Willoughby, somebody!'

Ellery and Jim reached the upper floor together, Jim looking around like a wild man. But Ellery was already pounding on the bathroom door. 'Nora!' Jim shouted. 'Open the door! What's the matter with you?'

Then Pat got there, and the others. 'Dr Willoughby will be right over,' said Lola. 'Where is she? Get out of here, you men!'

'Has she gone crazy?' gasped Rosemary.

'Break the door down!' commanded Pat. 'Ellery, break it down! Jim—Pop—help him!'

'Out of the way, Jim,' said Ellery. 'You're a bloody nuisance!'

But at the first impact, Nora screamed. 'If anyone comes in here I'll—I'll . . . *Don't come in!*'

Hermy was making mewing sounds, like a sick cat, and John F. kept saying: 'Now Hermy. Now Hermy. Now Hermy.'

At the third assault the door gave. Ellery catapulted into the bathroom, and pounced. Nora was leaning over the basin, trembling, weak, greenish, swallowing huge spoonfuls of milk of magnesia. She turned a queerly triumphant look on him as she slumped, fainting, into his arms.

But later, when she came to in her bed, there was a scene. 'I feel like a—like an animal in a zoo! Please, Mother—get everybody out of here!' They all left except Mrs Wright and Jim. Ellery heard Nora from the upper-hall landing. Her tone was stridulant; the words piled on one another. 'No, no, no! I *won't* have him! I don't *want* to see him!'

'But dearest,' wailed Hermy, 'Dr Willoughby—surely the doctor who brought you into the world—'

'If that old—old goat comes near me,' screamed Nora, 'I'll do something desperate! I'll commit suicide! I'll jump out the window!'

'Nora,' groaned Jim.

'Get out of here! Mother, you too!'

Pat and Lola went to the bedroom door and called their mother urgently. 'Mother, she's hysterical. Let her alone—

she'll calm down.' Hermy crept out, followed by Jim, who was red about the eyes and seemed bewildered.

They heard Nora gagging inside. And crying.

When Dr Willoughby arrived, breathless, John F. said it was a mistake, and sent him away.

Ellery softly closed his door. But he knew before he turned on the light that someone was in the room. He pressed the switch and said: 'Pat?'

Pat lay on his bed in a cramped curl. There was a damp spot on the pillow, near her face. 'I've been waiting up for you.' Pat blinked in the light. 'What time is it?'

'Past midnight.' Ellery switched the light off and sat down beside her. 'How is Nora?'

'She says she's fine. I guess she'll be all right.' Pat was silent for a moment. 'Where did *you* disappear to?'

'Ed Hotchkiss drove me over to Connhaven.'

'Connhaven! That's seventy-five miles.' Pat sat up abruptly. 'Ellery, what did you do?'

'I took the contents of Nora's plate over to a research laboratory. Connhaven has a good one, I discovered. And . . .' He paused. 'As you say, it's seventy-five miles—from Wrightsville.'

'Did you—did they—?'

'They found nothing.'

'Then maybe—'

Ellery got off the bed and began to walk up and down in the dark room. 'Maybe anything. The cocktails. The soup. The hors d'oeuvres. It was a long shot; I knew it wouldn't work out. Wherever she got it, though, it was in her food or drink. Arsenic. All the symptoms. Lucky she remembered to swallow milk of magnesia—it's an emergency antidote for arsenic poisoning.'

'And today is . . . Thanksgiving Day,' said Pat stiffly. 'Jim's letter to Rosemary—dated November twenty-eighth . . . today. "My wife is sick." *My wife is sick,* Ellery!'

'Whoa, Patty. You've been doing fine . . . It could be a coincidence.'

'You think so?'

'It may have been a sudden attack of indigestion. Nora's in a dither. She's read the letters, she's seen that passage about arsenic in the toxicology book—it may all be psychological.'

'Yes . . .'

'Our imaginations may be running away with us. At any

67

rate, there's time. If a pattern exists, this is just the beginning.'

'Yes . . .'

'Pat, I promise you: *Nora won't die.*'

'Oh, Ellery.' She came to him in the darkness and buried her face in his coat. 'I'm so glad you're here . . .'

'Get out of my bedroom,' said Mr Queen tenderly, 'before you pa comes at me with a shotgun.'

12. *Christmas:*
The Second Warning

THE FIRST snows fell. Breaths steamed in the valleys. Hermy was busy planning her Christmas baskets for the Poor Farm. Up in the hills skis were flashing and boys watched restlessly for the ponds to freeze. But Nora . . . Nora and Jim were enigmas. Nora recovered from her Thanksgiving Day 'indisposition', a little paler, a little thinner, a little more nervous, but self-possessed. But occasionally she seemed frightened, and she would not talk. To anyone. Her mother tried. 'Nora, what's wrong? You can tell me—'

'Nothing. What's the matter with everybody?'

'But Jim's drinking, dear. It's all over town,' groaned Hermy. 'It's getting to be a—a national disgrace! And you and Jim *are* quarreling—that *is* a fact . . .'

Nora set her small mouth. 'Mother, you'll simply have to let me run my own life.'

'Your father's worried—'

'I'm sorry, Mother. It's my life.'

'Is it Rosemary who's causing all these arguments? She's always taking Jim off and whispering to him. How long is she going to stay with you? Nora darling, I'm your mother. You can confide in your mother—' But Nora ran away, crying.

Pat was ageing visibly. 'Ellery, the three letters . . . they're still in Nora's hatbox in her closet. I looked last night. I couldn't help it.'

'I know,' sighed Ellery.

'You've been keeping tabs, too?'

'Yes. Patty, she's been rereading them. They show signs of being handled—'

'But why won't Nor face the truth?' cried Pat. 'She knows that November twenty-eighth marked the first attack—that first letter told her so! Yet she won't have the doctor, she won't take any steps to defend herself, she refuses help . . . I can't understand her!'

'Maybe,' said Ellery carefully, 'Nora's afraid to face the scandal.' Pat's eyes opened wide. 'You told me how she retreated from the world when Jim left her on their scheduled wedding day several years ago. There's a deep streak of small-town pride in your sister Nora, Pat. She can't abide being talked about. If this ever came out—'

'That's it,' said Pat in a wondering voice. 'I was stupid not to have seen it before. She's ignoring it, like a child. Close your eyes and you won't see the bogeyman. You're right, Ellery. *It's the town she's afraid of!*'

The Monday evening before Christmas Mr Queen was sitting on a stump just beyond the edge of the woods, watching 460 Hill Drive. There was no moon; but it was a still night and sounds carried crisply and far. Jim and Nora were at it again. Mr Queen chafed his cold hands. It was about money. Nora was shrill. Where was he spending his money? What had happened to her cameo brooch? 'Jim, you've got to tell me. This can't go on. It can't!'

Jim's voice was a mutter at first, but then it began to rise, like lava. 'Don't put me through a third degree!'

Mr Queen listened intently for something new, a clue to conduct. He heard nothing he had not already learned. Two young people screaming at each other on a winter's night, while he sat like a fool in the cold and eavesdropped. He rose from the stump and, skirting the fringe of woods, made for the Wright house and warmth. But then he stopped. The front door of Calamity House—how much apter the phrase seemed these days!—had slammed. Ellery sprinted through the snow, keeping in the shadows of the big house. Jim Haight was plowing down the walk unevenly. He jumped into his car. Ellery ran to the Wright garage. He had an arrangement with Pat Wright: she always left the keys of her convertible in the ignition lock for his use in an emergency. Jim's car sloshed down the Hill at a dangerous pace, and Ellery followed. He did not turn on

69

Pat's headlights; he could see well enough by the lights of Jim's car. Route 16 . . . Vic Carlatti's . . .

It was almost ten o'clock when Jim staggered out of the *Hot Spot* and got into his car again. By the weave and lurch of the car Ellery knew Jim was very drunk. Was he going home? No. The turn-off to town. Going into town! Where?

Jim skidded to a stop before a poor wooden tenement in the heart of Low Village. He reeled into the dark hallway. A 25-watt bulb burned drearily in the hall; by its light Ellery saw Jim creep up the stairs, knock at a door with a split, paint-blistered panel. 'Jim!' Lola Wright's exclamation. The door closed.

Ellery slipped up the stairs, feeling each step for its creaky spot before putting his full weight on it. At the landing he did not hesitate; he went swiftly to Lola's door and pressed his ear to the thin panel. 'But you got to,' he heard Jim cry. 'Lola, don' turn me down. 'M a desp'r't man. 'M desp'r't . . .'

'But I've told you, Jim, I haven't any money,' said Lola's cool voice. 'Here, sit down. You're filthy drunk.'

'So I'm drunk.' Jim laughed.

'What are you desperate about?' Lola was cooing now. 'There—isn't that more comfortable? Come on, Jim, tell little Lola all about it . . .' Haight began to weep. His weeping became muffled, and Ellery knew that his face was pressed to Lola's breast. Lola's maternal murmur was indistinct. But then she gasped, as if in pain, and Ellery almost crashed through the door. 'Jim! You pushed me!'

'All 'a same! Goo-goo. Tell Lola. Oh, yeah? Take your han's off me! I'm not tellin' you anything!'

'Jim, you'd better go home now.'

'Gonna gimme dough or you gonna not gimme dough?'

'But Jim, I told you . . .'

'Nobody'll gimme dough! Get in trouble, his own wife won' shell out. Know what I oughta do? Know what? I oughta—'

'What, Jim?'

'Nothin'. Nothin' . . . ' His voice trailed. There was a long interval. Apparently Jim had dropped off. Curious, Ellery waited. And then he heard Lola's faint cry and Jim's awakening snort. 'I said take your han's off me!'

'Jim, I wasn't—you fell asleep—'

'You were s-searchin' me! What you lookin' for? *Huh?*'

'Jim. Don't ... do that. You're hurting me.' Lola's voice was beautifully controlled.

'I'll hurt you plen'y! I'll show you—'

Mr Queen opened the door. Lola and Jim were dancing on a worn patch of carpet in the middle of a poor, neat room. His arms were around her and he was trying drunkenly to bend her backward. She had the heel of her hand under his chin. His head was far back, his eyes glaring. 'The United States Marines,' sighed Mr Queen, and he plucked Jim from Lola and sat him down on a sagging sofa. Jim covered his face with his hands. 'Any damage, Lola?'

'No,' panted Lola. 'You *are* a one! How much did you hear?' She straightened her blouse, fussed with her hair, turned a bit away. She took a bottle of gin from the table and, as if it didn't matter, put it in a cupboard.

'Just a scuffling,' said Ellery mildly. 'I was coming up to pay you that long-overdue visit. What's the matter with Jim?'

'Plastered.' Lola gave him her full face now. Composed. 'Poor Nora! I can't imagine why he came *here*. Do you suppose the idiot's fallen in love with me?'

'You ought to be able to answer that yourself,' grinned Ellery. 'Well, Mr Haight, I think you'd best say nighty-night to your attractive sister-in-law and let your old pal take you home.'

Jim sat there rocking. And then he stopped rocking and his head flopped. He was asleep doubled up, like a big rag doll with sandy hair. 'Lola,' said Ellery quickly. 'What do you know about this business?'

'What business?' Her eyes met his, but they told nothing.

After a moment Ellery smiled. 'No hits, no runs, one error. Some day I'll fight my way out of this unmerciful fog! Night.'

He slung Jim across his shoulders; Lola held the door open.

'Two cars?'

'His and mine—or rather Pat's.'

'I'll drive Jim's back in the morning. Just leave it parked outside,' said Lola. 'And Mr Smith—'

'Miss Wright?'

'Call again.'

'Perhaps.'

'Only next time,' Lola smiled, 'knock.'

With unexpected firmness, John F. took command for the family. 'No fuss, Hermy,' he said, waggling his thin forefinger at her. 'This Christmas somebody else does the work.'

'John Fowler Wright, what on earth—?'

'We're all going up to the mountains for Christmas dinner. We'll spend the night at the Lodge, and roast chestnuts around Bill York's fire, and we'll have *fun*.'

'John, that's a *silly* idea! Nora took my Thanksgiving away from me, now you want my Christmas. I won't hear of it.'

But after looking into her husband's eyes, Hermy decided his command was not a whim, and she stopped arguing.

So Ed Hotchkiss was hired to drive the Christmas gifts up to Bill York's Lodge on top of Bald Mountain, with a note to Bill from John F. concerning dinner, and lodgings, and 'special preparations'—old John was mighty mysterious about the whole thing, chortling like a boy.

They were to drive up to Bald Mountain in two cars directly after dinner Christmas Eve. Everything was ready—the snow chains were on the rear tires, old Ludie had already left, released for the holiday, and they were stamping about outside the Wright house waiting for Jim and Nora to join them ... when the door of Nora's house opened and out came Rosemary Haight, alone. 'Where are Jim and Nora, for goodness' sake?' called Hermy. 'We'll never get to the Lodge!'

Rosemary shrugged. 'Nora's not going.'

'What!'

'She says she doesn't feel well.'

They found Nora in bed, still weak and greenish, and Jim prowling aimlessly about the room. 'Nora baby!' cried Hermy.

'Sick again?' exclaimed John F.

'It's nothing,' said Nora; but it was an effort for her to talk. 'Just my stomach. You all go on ahead to the Lodge.'

'Well do no such thing,' said Pat indignantly. 'Jim, haven't you called Dr Willoughby?'

'She won't let me.' Jim said it in a lifeless voice.

'Won't *let* you! What are you—a man or a worm—? What's she got to say about it? I'm going downstairs this minute—'

'Pat,' faltered Nora. Pat stopped. 'Don't.'

'Now Nora—'

72

Nora opened her eyes. They burned. 'I won't have it,' said Nora through her teeth. 'I'm saying this for the last time. I won't have interference. Do you understand? I'm all right. I'm—all—right.' Nora bit her lip, then with an effort continued: 'Now please. Go on. If I feel better in the morning, Jim and I will join you at the Lodge—'

'Nora,' said John F., clearing his throat, 'it's time you and I had an old-fashioned father-and-daughter talk . . .'

'*Let me alone!*' Nora screamed.

They did so.

On Christmas Day Ellery and Pat drove up to Bald Mountain, retrieved the gifts from Bill York at the Lodge, and drove back to Wrightsville with them. They were distributed in a distinctly unhallowed atmosphere.

Hermy spent the day in her room. Pat fixed a Christmas 'dinner' of left-over lamb and a jar of mint jelly, but Hermy would not come down, and John F. swallowed two mouthfuls and dropped his fork, saying he wasn't hungry. So Pat and Ellery ate alone. Later, they walked over to see Nora. They found Nora asleep, Jim out, and Rosemary Haight curled up in the living room with a copy of *Look* and a box of chocolates. She shrugged at Pat's question about Jim. Had another fight with Nora and ran out. Nora was fine . . . weak, but getting along all right. What does one do for excitement in this one-horse town? Wrightsville! Christmas! And, petulantly, Rosemary went back to her magazine.

Pat ran upstairs to satisfy herself about Nora. When she came back she winked urgently, and Ellery took her outside again. 'I tried to talk to her—she wasn't asleep at all. I . . . almost told her I knew about those letters! Ellery, Nora's got me frightened. She threw something at me!' Ellery shook his head. 'She won't talk. She got hysterical again. And she's sick as a cat! I tell you,' Pat whispered, 'the schedule's working out. Ellery, *she was poisoned again yesterday!*'

'You're getting to be as bad as Nora,' said Ellery. 'Go up and take a nap, Pat. Can't a woman be sick occasionally?'

'I'm going back to Nora. I'm *not* going to leave her alone!'

When Pat had run back, Ellery took a long walk down the Hill, feeling unhappy. The day before, while the others had been upstairs with Nora, he had quietly gone to the dining room. The table had not yet been cleared of the dinner dishes. He had sampled the remains of Nora's corned-beef hash. It had been a minute sample, but the effects were not long in making themselves known. He felt extreme stomachic pain, and nausea. Very quickly, then, he had swallowed some of the contents of a bottle he had taken to carrying about with him—ferric hydroxid, with magnesia, the official arsenic antidote. No possible doubt. Someone had mixed an arsenic compound into Nora's corned-beef hash. And only Nora's. He had tasted the hash on the other two plates. The pattern was working out. First Thanksgiving, then Christmas. So death was scheduled for New Year's Day.

Ellery recalled his promise to Pat: to save her sister's life.

He plodded through the drifts. His mind was swirly with thoughts that seemed to take recognizable shapes, but did not.

13. *New Year's:*
The Last Supper

NORA SPENT four days after Christmas Eve in bed. But on the twenty-ninth of December she appeared fresh, gay ... too gay, and announced that she was through being sick, like some old lady; that she'd spoiled the family's Christmas, but she was going to make up for it, so everybody was invited to a New Year's Eve party! Even Jim brightened at that and clumsily kissed her. Pat, witnessing the embrace, choked up and turned away. But Nora kissed Jim back, and for the first time in weeks they looked at each other in the old, secret way of lovers.

Hermy and John F. were overjoyed by this sudden return of Nora's spirits. 'A dandy idea, Nora!' said Hermy. 'Now you plan the whole thing yourself. I shan't lift a *finger*. Unless, of course, you'd like me to . . .'

'No, indeed!' smiled Nora. 'It's my party, and I'm going to boss it. Oh, darling,' and Nora threw her arms about Pat, 'you've been such an angel this week, and I was so

74

mean to you ... throwing things! Can you ever forgive me?'

'You mug,' said Pat grimly, 'I'd forgive you anything if you'd only keep acting this way!'

'It's a good mood for Nora to be in,' Ellery said to Pat when she told him. 'Who's Nora inviting?'

'The family, and the Judge Martins, and Doc Willoughby, and Nora's even going to ask Frank Lloyd!'

'Hmm. Get her to invite Carter Bradford, too.'

Pat blanched. 'Cart?'

'Now, now. Bury the hatchet. It's a new year—'

'But why Cart? The pig didn't even send me a Christmas card!'

'I want Bradford here New Year's Eve. And you've got to get him here if it takes crawling to do it.'

Pat looked him in the eye. 'If you insist—'

'I insist.'

'He'll be here.'

Cart told Pat over the phone that he would 'try' to come—nice of her to ask him—quite a surprise, in fact—but of course he had numerous other 'invitations'—he wouldn't want to disappoint Carmel Pettigrew—but—well—he'd 'manage' to drop in. Yes—yes, count on it. I'll drop in ...

'Oh, Cart,' said Pat, despite herself, 'why can't people be friends?' But Cart had already hung up.

Editor-Publisher Frank Lloyd came early. He showed up in a vast and sulky unconviviality, greeting people in monosyllables or not at all, and at the first opportunity made for the 'bar', which was a makeshift affair off the kitchen, in Nora's pantry.

One would have said Mr Queen's interest in matters culinary that evening was unnatural. He haunted the kitchen, watching Alberta, watching Nora, watching the stove and the ice box and who came in and went out and what they did in the vicinity of anything edible or potable. And he did it all with such a self-effacement and eagerness that when Alberta left for her own New Year's Eve party at the home of some Lithuanian friends in Low Village, Nora exclaimed: 'My goodness, Ellery, you *are* a homebody, aren't you? Here, stuff some olives.' And so Mr Queen stuffed some olives, while Jim was busy in the adjacent pantry fixing drinks. From where Mr Queen stuffed the olives he had a perfect view of his host.

Nora served a sumptuous buffet supper, preceded by canapés and pigs-in-blankets and stuffed celery-stalks and relishes and cocktails; and before long Judge Eli Martin was saying to Aunt Tabitha, who glared about her disapprovingly: 'Come, come, Tabby, take a drink and oil that soul of yours. It creaks to high heaven. Here—a Manhattan—good for you!'

But John F.'s sister snarled: 'Reprobate!' and read Clarice Martin a lecture on the dangers of old fools drinking. Clarice, who was drifting about like the Lady of the Lake, misty-eyed, said of course Tabitha was *perfectly* right, and went on sipping her cocktail.

Lola was not there. Nora had invited her, but Lola had said over the phone: 'Sorry, sis. I have my own celebration planned. Happy New Year!'

Rosemary Haight held court in a corner, getting the men to fetch and carry for her—not out of interest in them, surely, for she seemed bored, but more as if she felt it necessary to keep in practice ... until Pat, watching good old Doc Willoughby trotting off to replenish Rosemary's glass, said: 'Why can't men see through a woman like that?'

'Maybe,' said Mr Queen dryly, 'because they're stopped by the too, too, solid flesh.' And he strolled off to the kitchen again—in Jim's wake, Patty's troubled eyes noticed. For the dozenth time.

Gala evenings in the 'nice' homes of Wrightsville were not noted for their hilarity; but Rosemary Haight, the outlander, exercised an irresistible influence for the worst. She became quite merry on numerous Manhattans, to the pointed disgust of Aunt Tabitha. Her spirits infected the men especially, so that talk became loud and laughter a little unsteady, and twice Jim had to visit the pantry to concoct new delights with rye and vermouth, and Pat had to open another bottle of maraschino cherries. And both times, Mr Queen appeared smiling at Jim's elbow, offering to help.

There was no sign of Carter Bradford. Pat kept listening for the doorbell. Someone turned on the radio, and Nora said to Jim: 'We haven't danced since our honeymoon, darling. Come on!' Jim looked unbelieving; then a grin spread over his face and, seizing her, he danced her madly off. Ellery went into the kitchen abruptly to mix himself a drink—his first of the evening.

It was fifteen minutes to midnight when Rosemary waved a dramatic arm and commanded: 'Jim! 'Nother drink!'

Jim said pleasantly: 'Don't you think you've had enough, Rosemary?' Surprisingly, Jim had drunk very little himself.

Rosemary scowled. 'Get me one, killjoy!' Jim shrugged and made for the kitchen, followed by the Judge's admonition to 'mix up a mess of 'em, boy!' and Clarice Martin's giggle.

There was a door from the hall to the kitchen, and an archway from the kitchen to the butler's pantry; there was a dining-room door to the butler's pantry, too. Mr Ellery Queen stopped at the hall door to light a cigarette. It was half-open; he could see into the kitchen, and into the butler's pantry. Jim moved about the pantry, whistling softly as he got busy with the rye and vermouth. He had just finished filling a fresh batch of glasses with Manhattans and was reaching for the bottle of maraschino cherries when someone knocked on the back door of the kitchen. Ellery became tense; but he resisted the temptation to take his eyes off Jim's hands.

Jim left the cocktails and went to the door. 'Lola! I thought Nora said—'

'Jim.' Lola sounded in a hurry. 'I had to see you—'

'Me?' Jim seemed puzzled. 'But Lo—'

Lola pitched her voice low; Ellery was unable to make out the words. Jim's body blocked Lola out; whatever was happening, it took only a few moments, for suddenly Lola was gone and Jim had closed the back door, crossing the kitchen a little abstractedly to return to the pantry. He plopped a cherry into each glass.

Ellery said: 'More fixin's, Jim?' as Jim came through to the hall carrying the tray of full glasses carefully. Jim grinned, and they went into the living room together to be greeted by jubilant shouts.

'It's almost midnight,' said Jim cheerfully. 'Here's a drink for everyone to toast the New Year in.' And he went about the room with the tray, everyone taking a glass.

'Come on, Nora,' said Jim. 'One won't hurt you, and New Year's Eve doesn't come every night!'

'But Jim, do you really think—'

'Take this one.' He handed her one of the glasses.

'I don't know, Jim—' began Nora doubtfully. Then she took it from him, laughing.

'Now you be careful, Nora,' warned Hermy. 'You know you haven't been well. Ooh! I'm *dizzy*.'

'Souse,' said John F. gallantly, kissing Hermy's hand. She slapped him playfully.

'Oh, one sip won't hurt me, Mother,' protested Nora.

'Hold it!' yelled Judge Martin. 'Here's the ol' New Year rolling in right now. Yip-ee!' And the old jurist's shout was drowned in a flood of horns and bells and noise makers coming out of the radio.

'To the New Year!' roared John F., and they all drank, even Aunt Tabitha, Nora dutifully taking a sip and making a face, at which Jim howled with laughter and kissed her.

That was the signal for everybody to kiss everybody else, and Mr Queen, struggling to keep everything in view, found himself seized from behind by a pair of warm arms. 'Happy New Year,' whispered Pat; and she turned him around and kissed him on the lips. For an instant the room, dim with candlelight, swam; then Mr Queen grinned and stooped for another; but Pat was snatched from his arms by Doc Willoughby, who growled: 'How about me?' and Ellery found himself foolishly pecking the air.

'More!' shrieked Rosemary. ' '*Nother drink!* Let's all get stinking—what the hell!' And she waved her empty glass coyly at Judge Martin. The Judge gave her a queer glance and put his arm around Clarice. Frank Lloyd drank two cocktails quickly. Jim said he had to go down to the cellar for another bottle of rye—he was all 'out' upstairs here.

'Where's my drink?' insisted Rosemary. 'What kinda joint is this? New Year's an' no drinks!' She was angry. 'Who's got a drink?' Nora was passing her, on her way to the radio. 'Hey! Nora! *You* got a drink . . . !'

'But Rosemary, I've drunk from it—'

'I wanna drink!'

Nora made a face and gave her unfinished cocktail to Rosemary, who tossed it down like a veteran and staggered over to the sofa, where she collapsed with a silly laugh. A moment later she was fast asleep.

'She *snores*,' said Frank Lloyd gravely. 'The beaushous lady snores,' and he and John F. covered Rosemary with newspapers, all but her face; and then John F. recited 'Horatius at the Bridge' with no audience whatever, until Tabitha, who was a little flushed herself, called him another old fool; whereupon John F. seized his sister and waltzed her strenuously about the room to the uncoöper-

ative strains of a rumba. Everybody agreed that everybody was a little tight, and wasn't the new year *wonderful?* All but Mr Ellery Queen, who was again lingering at
the hall door to the kitchen watching Jim Haight make
cocktails.

At thirty-five minutes past midnight there was one
strange cry from the living room and then an even
stranger silence. Jim was coming out of the kitchen with a
tray and Ellery said to him: 'That's a banshee, at least.
What are they up to now?' And the two men hurried to
the living room. Dr Willoughby was stooped over Rosemary Haight, who was still lying on the sofa half covered
with newspapers. There was a tiny, sharp prickle in Mr
Queen's heart.

Doc Willoughby straightened up. He was ashen. 'John.'
The old doctor wet his lips with his tongue.

John F. said stupidly: 'Milo, for jiminy sake. The girl's
passed out. She's been . . . sick, like other drunks. You
don't have to act and look as if—'

Dr Willoughby said: 'She's dead, John.' Pat, who had
been the banshee, sank into a chair as if all the strength
had suddenly gone out of her. And for the space of
several heartbeats the memory of the sound of the word
'dead' in Dr Willoughby's cracked bass darted about the
room, in and out of corners and through still minds, and it
made no sense.

'Dead?' said Ellery hoarsely. 'A . . . heart attack, Doctor?'

'I think,' said the doctor stiffly, 'arsenic.'

Nora screamed and fell over in a faint, striking her
head on the floor with a thud. As Carter Bradford came
briskly in. Saying: 'Tried to get here earlier—where's
Pat?— Happy New Year, everybody . . . *What the devil!*'

'Did you give it to her?' asked Ellery Queen, outside the
door of Nora's bedroom. He looked a little shrunken; and
his nose was pinched and pointy, like a thorn.

'No doubt about it,' croaked Dr Willoughby. 'Yes,
Smith. I gave it to her . . . Nora was poisoned, too.' He
blinked at Ellery. 'How did you happen to have ferric
hydroxid on you? It's the accepted antidote for arsenic
poisoning.'

Ellery said curtly: 'I'm a magician. Haven't you heard?'
and went downstairs. The face was covered with newspapers now. Frank Lloyd was looking down at the papers.

Carter Bradford and Judge Martin were conferring in hoarse low tones. Jim Haight sat in a chair shaking his head in an annoyed way, as if he wanted to clear it but could not. The others were upstairs with Nora. 'How is she?' said Jim. 'Nora?'

'Sick.' Ellery paused just inside the living room. Bradford and the Judge stopped talking. Frank Lloyd, however, continued to read the newspapers covering the body. 'But luckily,' said Ellery, 'Nora took only a sip or two of that last cocktail. She's pretty sick, but Dr Willoughby thinks she'll pull through all right.' He sat down in the chair nearest the foyer and lit a cigarette.

'Then it was the cocktail?' said Carter Bradford in an unbelieving voice. 'But of course. Both women drank of the same glass—both were poisoned by the same poison.' His voice rose. 'But that cocktail was Nora's! *It was meant for Nora!*'

Frank Lloyd said, still without turning: 'Carter, stop making speeches. You irk the hell out of me.'

'Don't be hasty, Carter,' said Judge Martin in a very old voice.

But Carter said stridently: 'That poisoned cocktail was meant to kill Nora. And *who mixed it? Who brought it in?*'

'Cock Robin,' said the newspaper publisher. 'Go way, Sherlock Holmes.'

'I did,' said Jim. 'I did, I guess.' He looked around at them. 'That's a queer one, isn't it?'

'Queer one!' Young Bradford's face was livid. He went over and yanked Jim out of the chair by his collar. 'You damn murderer! You tried to poison your own wife and by pure accident got your sister instead!'

Jim gaped at him. 'Carter,' said Judge Martin feebly.

Carter let go, and Jim fell back, still gaping. 'What can I do?' asked the Wright County Prosecutor in a strangled voice. He went to the phone in the foyer, stumbling past Mr Queen's frozen knees, and asked for Chief Dakin at Police Headquarters.

PART THREE

14. *Hangover*

THE HILL was still celebrating when Chief Dakin hopped out of his rattletrap to run up the wet flags of the Haight walk under the stars of 1941. Emmeline DuPré's house was dark, and old Amos Bluefield's—the Bluefield house bore the marks of mourning in the black smudges of its window shades. But all the others—the Livingstons', the F. Henry Minikins', the Dr Emil Poffenbergers', the Granjons', and the rest—were alive with lights and the faint cries of merriment.

Chief Dakin nodded: it was just as well. Nobody would notice that anything was wrong. Dakin was a thin, flapping countryman with light dead eyes bisected by a Yankee nose. He looked like an old terrapin until you saw that his mouth was the mouth of a poet. Nobody ever noticed that in Wrightsville except Patricia Wright and, possibly, Mrs Dakin, to whom the Chief combined the best features of Abraham Lincoln and God. Dakin's passionate baritone led Mr Bishop's choir at the First Congregational Church on West Livesey Street in High Village each Sunday. Being a temperance man, and having his woman, the Chief would chuckle, what was there left in life but song? And, in fact, Dakin was interrupted by Prosecutor Bradford's telephone call in the midst of an 'at-home' New Year's Eve carol fest.

'Poison,' said Dakin soberly to Carter Bradford over the body of Rosemary Haight. 'Now I wonder if folks don't overdo this New Year celebrating. What kind of poison, Doc?'

Dr Willoughby said: 'Arsenic. Some compound. I can't tell you which.'

'Rat-killer, hey?' Then the Chief said slowly. 'I figure this kind of puts our Prosecutor in a spot—hey, Cart?'

'Awkward as hell! These people are my friends.' Bradford was shaking. 'Dakin—take charge, for God's sake.'

'Sure, Cart,' said Chief Dakin, blinking his light eyes at Frank Lloyd. 'Hi, Mr Lloyd.'

'Hi yourself,' said Lloyd. 'Now can I go peddle my papers?'

'Frank, I told you—' began Carter peevishly.

'If you'll be so kind as not to,' said Dakin to the newspaper publisher with an apologetic smile. 'Thank you. Now how come this sister of Jim Haight's swallowed rat-killer?'

Carter Bradford and Dr Willoughby told him. Mr Queen, seated in his corner like a spectator at a play, watched and listened and pondered how much like a certain New York policeman Chief Dakin of Wrightsville seemed. That ingrown air of authority ... Dakin listened to the agitated voices of his townsfellows respectfully; only his light eyes moved—they moved over Mr 'Smith's' person three times, and Mr 'Smith' sat very still. And noted that, after the first quick glance on entering the room, Chief Dakin quite ignored Haight who was a lump on a chair.

'I see,' said Dakin, nodding. 'Yes, sir,' said Dakin. 'Hmm,' and he shambled off with his loose gait to the kitchen.

'I can't believe it,' groaned Jim Haight suddenly. 'It's an accident. How d⁻ know how the stuff got into it? Maybe some kid. A window. A joke. Why, this is *murder*.'

No one answered him. Jim cracked his knuckles and stared owlishly at the filled-out newspapers on the sofa.

Red-faced Patrolman Brady came in from outdoors, a little out of breath and trying not to look embarrassed. 'Got the call,' he said to no one in particular. 'Gosh.' He tugged at his uniform and trod softly into the kitchen after his chief.

When the two officers reappeared, Brady was armed with numerous bottles, glasses, and odds and ends from the kitchen 'bar'. He disappeared; after a few moments he came back, empty-armed. In silence Dakin indicated the various empty and half-empty cocktail glasses in the living room. Brady gathered them one by one, using his patrolman's cap as a container, picking them up in his scarlet fingers delicately, at the rim, and storing them in the hat as if they had been fresh-laid pigon eggs. The Chief nodded and Brady tiptoed out. 'For fingerprints,' said Chief Dakin to the fireplace. 'You never can tell. And a chemical analysis, too.'

'What!' exclaimed Mr Queen involuntarily.

The Dakin glance X-rayed Mr Queen's person for the fourth time: 'How do, Mr Smith,' said Chief Dakin, smiling. 'Seems like we're forever meeting in jams. Well, twice, anyway.'

'I beg pardon?' said Mr 'Smith', looking blank.

'That day on Route 16,' sighed the Chief. 'I was driving with Cart here. The day Jim Haight was so liquored up?' Jim rose; he sat down. Dakin did not look at him. 'You're a writer, Mr Smith, ain't you?'

'Yes.'

'Heard tell all over town. You said "What"?'

Ellery smiled. 'Sorry. Wrightsville—fingerprints ... It was stupid of me.'

'And chem lab work? Oh, sure,' said Dakin. 'This ain't New York or Chicago, but the new County Courthouse building, she's got what you might call unexpected corners.'

'I'm interested in unexpected corners, Chief.'

'Mighty proud to know a real live writer,' said Dakin. 'Course, we got Frank Lloyd here, but he's more what you'd call a hick Horace Greeley.' Lloyd laughed and looked around, as if for a drink. Then he stopped laughing and scowled. 'Know anything about this, Mr Smith?' asked Dakin, glancing at Lloyd's great back.

'A woman named Rosemary Haight died here tonight.' Ellery shrugged. The only *fact* I can supply. Not much help, I'm afraid, considering that the body's lying right here.'

'Poisoned, Doc Willoughby says,' said Dakin politely. 'That's another fact.'

'Oh, yes,' said Ellery with humility. And tried to become invisible as Dr Willoughby sent him a thick-browed question. Watch yourself. Doc Willoughby is remembering that little bottle of ferric hydroxid you whipped out when Nora Haight required an antidote against arsenic poisoning and even minutes were precious ... Will the good doctor tell the good policeman the strange fact that a stranger to the house and the people and the case carried so strange a preparation as ferric hydroxid about with him when, strangely, one woman died and another was made

83

seriously ill by the poison for which it was the official antidote? Dr Willoughby turned away. He suspects I know something involving the Wright family, thought Ellery. He's an old friend. He brought the three girls into the world ... He's uneasy. Shall I make him still uneasier by confiding that I purchased the drug because I promised Patty Wright her sister Nora wouldn't die? Mr Queen sighed. It was getting complicated.

'The family,' said Chief Dakin. 'Where they at?'

'Upstairs,' said Bradford. 'Mrs Wright insists that Nora— Mrs Haight—be moved over to the Wright house.'

'This is no place for her, Dakin,' said Dr Willoughby. 'Nora's pretty sick. She'll need plenty of care.'

'It's all right with me,' said the Chief. 'If it's all right with the Prosecutor.'

Bradford nodded hastily and bit his lip. 'Don't you want to question them?'

'Well, now,' said the Chief slowly, 'I can't see the sense of making the Wrights feel worse'n they feel already. At least right now. So if you've got no objection, Cart, let's call it a night.'

Carter said stiffly: 'None at all.'

'Then we'll have a get-together right here in this room in the mornin',' said Dakin. 'You tell the Wrights, Cart. Sort of keep it unofficial.'

'Are you remaining here?'

'For a spell,' drawled Dakin. 'Got to call in somebody to haul this *corpus* out of here. Figure I'll phone old man Duncan's parlors.'

'No *morgue?*' asked Mr Queen, despite himself.

The Dakin eyes made another inspection. 'Well, no, Mr Smith ... Okay for you, Mr Lloyd. Go easy on these folks in your paper, hey? This'll raise plenty of hallelujah as it is, I guess ... No, sir, Mr Smith. Got to use a reg'lar undertaking parlor. You see,' and the Chief sighed, 'ain't never had a homicide in Wrightsville before, and I been Chief here for pretty near twenty years. Doc, would you be so kind? Coronor Salemson's up in Piny Woods on a New Year vacation.'

'I'll do the autopsy,' said Dr Willoughby shortly. He went out without saying goodnight.

Mr Queen rose. Carter Bradford walked across the room, stopped, looked back. Jim Haight was still sitting in the chair. Bradford said in an angry voice: 'What are you sitting here for, Haight?'

Jim looked up slowly. 'What?'

84

'You can't sit here all night! Aren't you even going up to your wife?'

'They won't let me,' said Jim. He laughed, and took out a handkerchief to wipe his eyes. 'They won't let me.' He leaped from the chair and dashed upstairs. They heard the slam of a door—he had gone into his study.

'See you in the morning, gents,' said Chief Dakin, blinking at Ellery.

They left the Chief in the untidy living room, alone with Rosemary Haight's body. Mr Queen would like to have stayed, but there was something in Chief Dakin's eyes that discouraged company.

Ellery did not see Patricia Wright until they all gathered in the same untidy room at ten o'clock on the morning of New Year's Day ... all except Nora, who was in her old bed in the other house, guarded by Ludie behind the closed vanes of the Venetian blinds. Dr Willoughby had already seen her this morning, and he forbade her leaving the room or even setting foot out of bed. 'You're a sick biddy, Nora,' he had said to her sternly. 'Ludie, remember.'

'She'll have to fight me,' said old Ludie.

'But where's Mother? Where's Jim?' moaned Nora, tossing on the bed.

'We've got to ... go out for a few minutes, Nora,' said Pat. 'Jim's all right—'

'Something's happened to Jim, too!'

'Don't be a worry-wart,' said Pat crossly, fleeing.

Ellery waylaid her on Nora's porch. 'Before we go in,' he said quickly, 'I want to explain—'

'I don't blame you, Ellery.' Pat was almost as sick-looking as Nora. 'It might have been worse. It might have been ... Nora. It almost was.' She shivered.

'I'm sorry about Rosemary,' said Ellery.

Pat looked at him blankly. Then she went inside. Ellery lingered on the porch. It was a gray day, like Rosemary Haight's face: a gray day and a cold day, a day for corpses ... Someone was missing—Frank Lloyd. Emmy DuPré chittered by, stopped, studied Chief Dakin's car at the curb, frowned ... walked on slowly, craning at the two houses. A car drove up. Frank Lloyd jumped out. Then Lola Wright. They ran up the walk together. 'Nora! Is she all right?' gasped Lola. Ellery nodded. Lola dashed inside.

'I picked Lola up,' said Lloyd. He was breathing heavily, too. 'She was walking up the Hill.'

'They're waiting for you, Lloyd.'

'I thought,' said the publisher, 'you might think it funny.' There was a damp copy of the *Wrightsville Record* in his overcoat pocket.

'I think nothing funny on mornings like this. Did Lola know?' They walked into the house.

'No. She was just taking a walk, she said. Nobody knows yet.'

'They will,' said Ellery dryly, 'when your paper hits the streets.'

'You're a damn snoop,' growled Lloyd, 'but I like you. Take my advice and hop the first train out.'

'I like it here,' smiled Ellery. 'Why?'

'Because this is a dangerous town.'

'How so?'

'You'll see when the news gets around. Everybody who was at the party last night will be smeared.'

'There's always,' remarked Mr Queen, 'the cleansing property of a clear conscience.'

'That makes you apple pie.' Lloyd shook his heavy shoulders. 'I don't figure you.'

'Why bother? For that matter, you're not a simple sum in arithmetic yourself.'

'You'll hear plenty about me.'

'I already have.'

'I don't know,' said the newspaper publisher savagely, 'why I stand here in the foyer gassing with a nitwit!' He shook the floor striding into the living room.

'The poison,' said Dr Willoughby, 'is arsenic trioxid, or arsenious oxid, as you prefer. "White" arsenic.'

They were sitting in a rough circle, like unbelievers at a séance. Chief Dakin stood at the fireplace, tapping his false teeth with a rolled paper. 'Go ahead, Doc,' said Dakin. 'What else did you find? That part's right. We checked in our own lab during the night.'

'It's used in medicine mostly as an alternative or tonic,' said the doctor tonelessly. 'We never prescribe a bigger therapeutic dose than a tenth of a grain. There's no way of telling from the dregs of the cocktail, of course—at least with accuracy—but judging from the speed with which the poison acted, I'd estimate there were three or four grams in that glass.'

'Prescribe any of that stuff recently for ... anyone you know, Doc?' muttered Carter Bradford.

'No.'

'We've established a bit more,' said Chief Dakin soberly, looking around. 'Most probably it was plain ordinary rat poison. And moreover, no trace of the poison was found anywheres except in that one cocktail which Mrs Haight and her sister-in-law drank—not in the mixing glass, nor the rye whisky, nor the vermouth, nor the bottle of cherries, nor any of the other glassware.'

Mr Queen surrendered. 'Whose fingerprints did you find on the poisoned-cocktail glass, Chief Dakin?'

'Mrs Haight's. Rosemary Haight's. Jim Haight's. No others.' Ellery could see them translate silently. Nora's . . . Rosemary's . . . Jim's . . . no others. His own thoughts were admiring. Chief Dakin had not remained idle after they left him last night. He had taken the fingerprints of the corpse. He had found some object unmistakably Nora Haight's, probably in her bedroom, and had taken *her* fingerprints. Jim Haight had been in the house all night, but Ellery was willing to make a large bet that Jim had not been disturbed, either. There were plenty of *his* things in the house, too . . . Very pretty. Very considerate. It disturbed Mr Queen powerfully—the prettiness and considerateness of Chief Dakin's methods. He glanced over at Pat. She was watching Dakin as if the Chief had hypnotized her. 'And what did your autopsy show, Doc?' asked Dakin deferentially.

'Miss Haight died of arsenic trioxid poisoning.'

'Yes, sir. Now let's get this organized,' said Dakin. 'If you folks don't mind?'

'Go ahead, Dakin,' said John F. impatiently.

'Yes, Mr Wright. So we know the two ladies were poisoned by that one cocktail. Now, who mixed it?' No one said anything. 'Well, I already know. It was you, Mr Haight. You mixed that cocktail.'

Jim Haight had not shaved. There were muddy ruts under his eyes. 'Did I?' There was a frog in his throat; he cleared it several times. 'If you say so—I mixed so many—'

'And who came in from the kitchen and handed out the tray of drinks?' asked Chief Dakin. 'Including the one that was poisoned? You did, Mr Haight. Am I wrong? Because that's my information,' he said apologetically.

'If you're trying to insinuate—' began Hermione in an imperious voice.

'All right, Mrs Wright,' said the Chief. 'Now maybe I'm wrong. But you mixed that cocktail, Mr Haight, you handed it out, so it looks like you're the only one could

87

have dosed it up good with rat-killer. But it only *looks* that way. *Were* you the only one? Did you leave those cocktails you were making even for a few seconds any time up to the time you brought the tray into this room last night?'

'Look,' said Jim. 'Maybe I'm crazy. Maybe the things that happened last night knocked my brains for a loop. What *is* this? Am I suspected of having tried to poison my wife?'

As if this had been a fresh wind in a stale room, the air became breathable again. John F.'s hand dropped from his eyes, Hermy's color came back, and even Pat looked at Jim.

'This *is* nonsense, Chief Dakin!' said Hermy coldly.

'Did you, Mr Haight?' asked Dakin.

'Of course I brought that tray in here!' Jim got up and began to walk up and down before the Chief, like an orator. 'I'd just mixed the Manhattans—that last batch—and was going to put the maraschino cherries in, but then I had to leave the pantry for a few minutes. That's it!'

'Well, now,' said Dakin heartily, '*Now* we're getting places, Mr Haight. Could someone have slipped in from the living room and poisoned one of them cocktails without you knowing or seeing? While you were gone, I mean?'

The fresh wind died, and they were in choking miasma once more. *Could someone have slipped in from the living room—*

'I didn't poison that cocktail,' said Jim, 'so somebody *must* have slipped in.'

Dakin turned swiftly. 'Who left the living room while Mr Haight was mixing that last mess of drinks in the kitchen? This is very important, please. Think hard on it!' Ellery lit a cigarette. Someone must have noticed that he had been missing simultaneously with Jim. It was inevitable ... But then they all began to chatter at once, and Ellery blew smoke in great clouds. 'We'll never get anywheres this way,' said the Chief. 'So much drinking and dancing going on, and the room dark on account of only candles being lit ... Not,' added Dakin suddenly 'that it makes much difference.'

'What do you mean?' asked Pat quickly.

'I mean that ain't the important point Miss Wright.' And this time Dakin's voice was quite, quite chill. Its chill deepened the chill in the room. 'The important point is: Who had control of the *distribution* of the drinks? Answer me that! Because the one who handed that cocktail out—that's *got* to be the one who poisoned it!'

Bravo, bumpkin, thought Mr Queen. You're wasting your smartness on the desert air . . . You don't know what I know, but you've hit the essential point just the same. You ought to capitalize your talents . . .

'*You* handed 'em out, James Haight,' said Chief Dakin. 'No poisoner'd have dropped rat-killer in one of those drinks and left it to Almighty God to decide who'd pick up that poisoned one! No, sir. It don't make sense. *Your wife got that poisoned cocktail, and you was the one handed it to her. Wasn't you?*'

And now they were all breathing heavily like swimmers in a surf, and Jim's eyes were red liquid holes. 'Yes, I did hand it to her!' he yelled. 'Does that satisfy your damn snooping disposition?'

'A-plenty,' said the Chief mildly. 'Only thing is, Mr Haight, you didn't know one thing. You went out of the living room to make more drinks, or fetch another bottle, or something. You didn't know your sister Rosemary was going to yell for another drink, and you didn't know that your wife, who you figured would drink the whole glassful, would just take a couple of sips and then your sister would pull the glass out of her hand and guzzle the rest down. So instead of killing your wife, you killed your sister!'

Jim said hoarsely: 'Of course you can't believe I planned or did anything like that, Dakin.'

Dakin shrugged. 'Mr Haight, I only know what my good horse sense tells me. The facts say you, and only you, had the—what do they call it?—the opportunity. So maybe you won't have what they call motive—*I* dunno. Do you?'

It was a disarming question—man to man. Mr Queen was quite bathed in admiration. This was finesse exquisite.

Jim muttered: 'You want to know why I should try to murder my wife four months after our marriage. Go to hell.'

'That's no answer. Mr Wright, can you help us out? Do you know of any reason?'

John F. gripped the arms of his chair, glancing at Hermy. But there was no help there; only horror.

'My daughter Nora,' mumbled John F., 'inherited a hundred thousand dollars—her grandfather's legacy—when she married Jim. If Nora died . . . Jim would get it.'

Jim sat down, slowly, looking around, around. Chief

Dakin beckoned to Prosecutor Bradford. They left the room. Five minutes later they returned, Carter paler than pale, staring straight before him, avoiding their eyes. 'Mr Haight,' said Chief Dakin gravely, 'I'll have to ask you not to try to leave Wrightsville.'

Bradford's work, thought Ellery. But not from compassion. From duty. There was no legal case yet. Damning circumstances, yes; but no case. There would be a case, though. Glancing over the whole lean, shambling countryman that was Chief of Police Dakin, Mr Queen knew there would be a case and that, pending the proverbial miracle, James Haight was not long for the free streets of Wrightsville.

15. *Nora Talks*

AT FIRST all Wrightsville could talk about was the fact itself. The delicious fact. A body. A corpse. At the Wrights'. *At the Wrights'!* The snooty, stuck-up, we're better-than-you-are First Family! *Poison!* Just *imagine*. Who'd have thought? And so soon after, too. Remember that wedding?

The woman. Who was she? Jim Haight's sister. Rosalie—Rose-Marie? No, Rosemary. Well, it doesn't make any difference. She's dead. I saw her once. Tricked up. You *felt* something about her. Not nice. My dear, I was telling my husband only the other day ...

So it's murder. Rosemary Haight, that woman from heaven knows where, she got a mess of poison in a Manhattan cocktail, and it was really meant for Nora Haight. There it is right in Frank Lloyd's paper ... Frank was *there*. Drinking. Wild party. Fell down dead. Foaming at the mouth. Shh, the children! ... Cinch Frank Lloyd hasn't told the *whole* story ... Of course not. After *all*. The *Record*'s a family newspaper!

Four-sixty Hill Drive. Calamity House. Don't you remember? That story in the *Record* years ago? First Jim Haight ran away from his own wedding, leaving Nora Wright looking silly—and the house all built and furnished

90

and everything! Then that Mr Whozis from Where? Anyway, *he* dropped dead just as he was going to buy it from John F. Wright. And now—*murder* in it! Say, I wouldn't set foot in that jinxed house for all the money in John F.'s vaults!

Bess, did *you* hear? *They say* ... For some days Wrightsville could talk about nothing but the fact.

Siege was laid, and Mr Ellery 'Smith' Queen found himself inadvertently a soldier of the defending force. People streamed up and down the Hill like trekking ants, pausing outside the Wright and Haight houses to pick up some luscious leaf-crumb and bear it triumphantly down into the town. Emmeline DuPré was never so popular. Right next door! Emmy, what do you *know*? Emmy told them. Emmy's porch became a hiring hall for the masses. If a face showed at a window of either house, there was a rush, and a gasp.

'What's happening to us?' moaned Hermione. 'No. I *won't* answer the phone!'

Lola said grimly: 'We're a Chamber of Horrors. Some Madame Tussaud'll start charging admission soon!' Since the morning of New Year's Day, Lola had not left. She shared Pat's room. At night she silently washed her underwear and stockings in Pat's bathroom. She would accept nothing from her family. Her meals she took with Jim in the 'unlucky' house. Lola was the only member of the family to show herself out of doors the first few days of January. On January second she said something to Emmy DuPré which turned Emmy pale and sent her scuttling back to her porch like an elderly crab in a panic. 'We're waxworks,' said Lola. 'Jack-the-Ripper multiplied by seven. Look at the damn body-snatchers!'

Alberta Manaskas had vanished in a Lithuanian dither, so Lola cooked Jim's meals. Jim said nothing. He went to the bank as usual. John F. said nothing. *He* went to the bank. In the bank father-in-law and son-in-law said nothing to each other. Hermy haunted her room, putting handkerchiefs to her little nose. Nora was in a tossing fever most of the time, wailing to see Jim, being horridly sick, keeping her pillow blue with tears. Carter Bradford shut himself up in his office at the County Courthouse. Large plain men came and went, and at certain times of the day he conferred in pointed secrecy with Chief of Police Dakin.

Through all this Mr Queen moved silently, keeping out of everyone's way. Frank Lloyd had been right. There was

91

talk about 'that man Smith—who *is* he?' There were other remarks, more dangerous. He noted them all in his notebook, labeled: 'The Mysterious Stranger—a Suspect'. He was never far from Nora's room. On the third day after the crime, he caught Patty as she came out and beckoned her upstairs to his room. He latched the door. 'Pat, I've been thinking.'

'I hope it's done you good.' Pat was listless.

'When Dr Willoughby was here this morning, I heard him talk to Dakin on the phone. Your County Coroner, Salemson, has cut his vacation short and he's come back to town on the double. Tomorrow there will be an inquest.'

'Inquest!'

'It's the law, darling.'

'You mean we'll have to . . . leave the *house?*'

'Yes. And testify, I'm afraid.'

'Not Nora!'

'No, Willoughby refuses to let her leave her bed. I heard him say so to Dakin.'

'Ellery . . . what are they going to *do?*'

'Establish the facts for the record. Try to get at the truth.'

Pat said: 'The truth?' and looked terrified.

'Pat,' said Ellery gravely, 'you and I are at the crossroads in this labyrinth—'

'Meaning?' But she knew what he meant.

'This is no longer a potential crime. It's a crime that's happened. A woman has died—the fact that she died by accident makes no difference, since a murder was planned and a murder was executed. So the law comes into it . . .' Ellery said grimly . . . 'a most efficient law, I must say . . . and from now on it's snoop, sniff, and hunt until *all* the truth is known.'

'What you're trying to say, and are saying so badly,' said Pat steadily, 'is that we've got to go to the police with what *we* know . . . and *they* don't.'

'It's within our power to send Jim Haight to the electric chair.'

Patty sprang to her feet. Ellery pressed her hand. 'It can't be that clear! You're not convinced yourself! Even *I'm* not, and I'm her sister . . .'

'We're talking now about facts and conclusions from facts,' said Ellery irritably. 'Feelings don't enter into it— they certainly won't with Dakin, although they might with Bradford. Don't you realize you and I are in possession of

92

four pieces of information not known to the police—four facts that convict Jim of having plotted and all but carried out the murder of Nora?'

'Four?' faltered Pat. 'As many as that?'

Ellery sat her down again. She looked up at him with her forehead all tight and wrinkled. 'Fact one: the three letters written by Jim and now at the bottom of Nora's hatbox next door—the three letters establishing his *anticipation of her death* at a time when she wasn't even ill! Clearly premeditation.' Pat moistened her lips. 'Fact two: Jim's desperate need for money. This fact, which *we* know because he's been pawning Nora's jewelry and demanding money of her, plus the fact *Dakin* knows—that on Nora's death Jim would come into a large inheritance—combined would fix a powerful motive.'

'Yes. Yes . . .'

'Fact three: the toxicology book belonging to Jim, with its underlined section in Jim's characteristic red crayon . . . a section dealing with arsenious trioxid, the very poison with which subsequently Nora's cocktail was spiked and from which Nora nearly died. And fourth,' Ellery shook his head, 'something I alone can establish, because I had Jim under observation every moment New Year's Eve: the fact that no one but Jim *could* have put poison into that fatal cocktail, *or did*. So I'm in a position to establish that Jim not only had the *best* opportunity to poison that drink, but the *only* opportunity.'

'And that doesn't even include his threat against Nora that afternoon when we brought him away from the *Hot Spot* blind drunk—when he said he was going to get rid of her. Dakin heard it, Cart heard it . . .'

'Or,' added Ellery gently, 'the two previous occasions on which Nora's been poisoned by arsenic—Thanksgiving and Christmas, coinciding with the dates of Jim's first two letters . . . Pretty conclusive, put together, Patty. How could anyone disbelieve, knowing all this, that Jim planned Nora's death?'

'Yet you don't believe it,' said Pat.

'I didn't say that,' said Ellery slowly. 'I said . . .' He shrugged 'The point is: We've got to decide now. Do we talk at the inquest tomorrow, or don't we?'

Pat bit a fingernail. 'But suppose Jim *is* innocent? How can I—how can you—set up as judge and jury and condemn somebody to death? Somebody you *know*? Ellery, I couldn't.' Pat made faces, a distressed young woman. 'Besides,' she said eagerly, 'he won't try it again, Ellery!

Not now. Not after he killed his sister by mistake. Not after the whole thing's out and the police—I mean, *if* he did . . .'

Ellery rubbed his hands together as if they itched, walking up and down before her, frowning, scowling. 'I'll tell you what we'll do,' he said at last. 'We'll put it up to Nora.' Pat stared. 'She's the victim, Jim's her husband. Yes, let Nora make the decision. What do you say?'

Pat sat still for a moment. Then she got up and went to the door. 'Mother's asleep, Pop's at the bank, Ludie's downstairs in the kitchen, Lola's next door . . .'

'So Nora's alone now.'

'And Ellery.' Ellery unlatched his door. 'Thanks for being such a swell clam—' He opened the door. 'Taking such a personal risk—being involved—' He gave her a little push towards the stairs.

Nora lay in a knot under the blue comforter, staring at the ceiling. Scared through and through, thought Ellery.

'Nora.' Pat went quickly to the bed, took Nora's thin hand between both her brown ones. 'Do you feel strong enough to talk?'

Nora's eyes flew from her sister to Ellery, and then darted into hiding like timid birds. 'What is it? What's the matter?' Her voice was tight with pain 'Is Jim—did they—?'

'Nothing's happened, Nora,' said Ellery.

'It's just that Ellery feels—I feel—it's time the three of us understood one another,' said Pat. Then she cried: 'Nora, please! Don't shut yourself up! Listen to us!' Nora braced herself and pushed against the bed until she was sitting up. Pat leaned over her and, for an instant, she looked like Hermy. She drew the edges of Nora's bed jacket together. Nora stared at them.

'Don't be frightened,' said Ellery. Pat propped the pillow against Nora's shoulders and sat down on the edge of the bed and took Nora's hand again. And then in a quiet voice Ellery told Nora what he and Pat had learned—from the beginning. Nora's eyes grew larger and larger.

'I tried to talk to you,' cried Pat, 'but you wouldn't listen! Nora, *why?*'

Nora whispered: 'Because it isn't true. Maybe at first I thought . . . But it's not. Not Jim. You don't know Jim. He's scared of people, so he acts cocky. But inside he's like a little boy. When you're alone with him. And he's weak. Much too weak to—to do what you think he did. Oh, please!' Nora began to cry in her hands. 'I love him,'
94

she sobbed. 'I've always loved Jim! I'll never believe he'd want to kill me. Never. Never!'

'But the facts, Nora—' said Ellery wearily.

'Oh, the facts!' She took her hands away; her wet eyes were blazing. 'What do I care about the facts? A woman *knows*. There's something so horribly wrong you can't make sense out of it. I don't know who tried to poison me three times, but I do know it wasn't Jim!'

'And the three letters, Nora? The letters in Jim's hand-writing announcing your illness, your . . . death?'

'He didn't write them!'

'But Nora darling,' said Pat, 'Jim's handwriting—'

'Forged.' Nora was panting now. 'Haven't you ever heard of forgery? They were forged!'

'And the threat against you we heard him make, that day I told you about, when he was drunk?' asked Ellery.

'He wasn't responsible!'

No tears now. She was fighting. Ellery went over the whole damning case with her; she fought back. Not with counterfacts. With faith. With an adamant, frightening faith. And at the end Ellery was arguing with two women, and he had no ally. 'But you don't reason—' he exploded, throwing up his hands. Then he smiled. 'What do you want me to do? I'm softheaded, but I'll do it.'

'Don't say anything about these things to the police!'

'All right, I won't.'

Nora sank back, closing her eyes. Pat kissed her and then signalled to Ellery. But Ellery shook his head. 'I know you're pretty well pooped, Nora,' he said kindly, 'but as long as I'm becoming an accessory, I'm entitled to your full confidence.'

'Anything,' said Nora tiredly.

'Why did Jim run out on you that first time? Three years ago, just before you were to be married, when Jim left Wrightsville?'

Pat looked at her sister anxiously. 'That.' Nora was surprised. 'That wasn't anything. It couldn't have anything to do—'

'Nevertheless, I'd like to know.'

'You'd have to know Jim. When we met and fell in love and all, I didn't realize just how independent Jim was. I didn't see anything wrong in—well, accepting help from Father until Jim got on his feet. We'd argue about it for hours. Jim kept saying he wanted me to live on his cashier's salary.'

'I remember those battles,' murmured Pat, 'but I didn't dream they were so—'

'I didn't take them seriously enough, either. When Mother told me Father was putting up the little house and furnishing it for us as a wedding gift, I thought I'd keep it a surprise for Jim. So I didn't tell him until the day before the wedding. He got furious.'

'I see.'

'He said he'd already rented a cottage on the other side of town for fifty dollars a month—it was all we'd be able to afford, he said, we'd just have to learn to live on what he earned.' Nora sighed. 'I suppose I lost my temper, too. We ... had a fight. A bad one. And then Jim ran away. That's all.' She looked up. 'That's really all. I never told Father or Mother or anyone about it. Having Jim run out on me just because of a thing like that—'

'Jim never wrote to you?'

'Not once. And I ... thought I'd die. The whole town was talking ... Then Jim came back, and we both admitted what fools we'd been, and here we are.'

So from the very first it had been the house, thought Ellery. Queer! Wherever he turned in this case, the house was there. Calamity House ... Ellery began to feel that the reporter who had invented the phrase was gifted with second sight. 'And these quarrels you and Jim have been having since your marriage?'

Nora winced. 'Money. He's been asking for money. And my cameo, and other things ... But that's just temporary,' she said quickly. 'He's been gambling at that roadhouse on Route 16—I suppose every man goes through a phase like that—'

'Nora, what can you tell me about Rosemary Haight?'

'Not a thing. I know she's dead, and it sounds an awful thing to say, but ... I didn't like her. At all.'

'Amen,' said Patty grimly.

'Can't say I was smitten myself,' murmured Ellery. 'But I mean—do you know anything about her that might tie her in with ... well, the letters, Jim's conduct, the whole puzzle?'

Nora said tightly: 'Jim wouldn't talk about her. But I know what I felt. She was *no good*, Ellery. I don't see how she ever came to be Jim's sister.'

'Well, she was,' said Ellery briskly, 'and you're tired, Nora. Thanks. You'd have been wholly justified in telling me to mind my own business about all this.' Nora

squeezed his hand, and he left as Pat went into the
bathroom to wet a towel for her sister's head. Nothing.
Utter nothing. And tomorrow the inquest!

16. *The Aramean*

CORONER SALEMSON was nervous about the whole thing.
Any audience more numerous than three paralyzed his
vocal cords; and it is a matter of public record that the
only time the coroner opened his mouth at Town Meeting
except for breathing purposes—he had asthma—was one
year when J. C. Pettigrew reared up and demanded to
know why the office of Coroner shouldn't be voted out of
existence—Chic Salemson hadn't had a corpus to justify
his salary in his nine years' tenure. And then all the
Coroner could stammer was: 'But suppose!' And so now,
at last, there was a corpus.

But a corpus meant an inquest, and that meant the
Coroner had to sit up there in Judge Martin's court
(borrowed from the County for the occasion) and pre-
side; and that meant talk, and lots of it, before hundreds of
glittering Wrightsville eyes—not to mention the eyes of
Chief Dakin and Prosecutor Bradford and County Sheriff
Gilfant and Lord knows who. To make matters worse,
there was John F. Wright. To think of the exalted Name
linked nastily with a murder weakened the Coroner's
knees; John F. was his household god.

So as Coroner Salemson rapped feebly for order in the
jammed courtroom he was a nervous, miserable, and desperate man. And all through the selection of the Coroner's
Jury he became more nervous, and more miserable, and
more desperate, until finally his nervousness and misery
were swallowed by his desperation, and he saw what he
must do to cut his ordeal short and save—if saving was
possible—the honor of the Wright name.

To say that the old Coroner sabotaged the testimony
deliberately would be unjust to the best horseshoe pitcher
in Wright County. No, it was just that from the first the
Coroner was convinced no one named Wright, or connect-

ed with anyone named Wright, could possibly have had the least pink or brownish stain on his conscience. So obviously it was either all a monstrous mistake, or the poor woman committed suicide or something, and strike this out, and that's just *supposing* . . . and the result was that, to the disgust of Dakin, the relief of the Wrights, the sad amusement of Mr Ellery Queen and—above all—the disappointment of Wrightsville, the confused Coroner's Jury brought in a harmless verdict of 'death at the hands of person or persons unknown' after several days of altercation, heat, and gavel breaking.

Chief Dakin and Prosecutor Bradford immediately retired to Bradford's office for another conference, the Wrights sped home thankfully, and Coroner Salemson fled to his twelve-room ancestral home in the Junction, where he locked himself in with trembling hands and got drunk on an old bottle of gooseberry wine left over from his orphaned niece Eppie's wedding to old man Simpson's son Zachariah in 1934.

Gently, gently, into one neat six-foot hole in the ground. What's her name? Rosalie? Rose-Marie? They say she was a glamour girl. The one they're burying—the one Jim Haight poisoned by mistake—his sister . . . Who says Jim Haight . . . ? Why, it was right there in the *Record* only yesterday! Didn't you read it? Frank Lloyd didn't *say* so, just like that; but you know if you read between the lines . . . Sure, Frank's sore. Sweet on Nora Wright, Frank was, and Jim Haight cut him out. Never did like Haight. Kind of cold proposition—couldn't look you in the eye, 'pears to me . . . So he was the one, huh? Why don't they arrest him? That's what I'd like to know!

Ashes to ashes . . . Think there's dirty work going on? Wouldn't be bowled over! Cart Bradford and that Patricia Wright started necking years ago. That's Haight's sister-in-law. Aaah, the rich always get away with murder. Nobody's getting away with murder in Wrightsville. Not if we have to take the law—

Gently, gently . . . Rosemary Haight was buried in East Twin Hill Cemetery, not (people were quick to remark) in West Twin Hill Cemetery, where the Wrights had interred their dead for two hundred-odd years. The transaction was negotiated by John Fowler Wright, acting for his son-in-law James Haight, and Peter Callendar, sales manager of the Twin Hill Eternity Estates, Inc., selling

98

price sixty dollars. John F. handed Jim the deed to the grave in silence as they drove back from the funeral.

The next morning Mr Queen, rising early for purposes of his own, saw the words WIFE KILLER printed in red school chalk on the sidewalk before Calamity House. He erased them.

'Morning,' said Myron Garback of the High Village Pharmacy.

'Morning, Mr Garback,' said Mr Queen, frowning. 'I've got a problem. I've rented a house and there's a small greenhouse in the garden—found vegetables growing there, by George! In January!'

'Yes?' said Myron blankly.

'Well, now, I'm mighty fond of home-grown tomatoes and there's a fine tomato plant or two in my greenhouse, only the plant's overrun with some kind of round little bug—'

'Mmmm. Yellowish?'

'That's right. With black stripes on their wings. At least,' said Mr Queen helplessly. 'I think they're black.'

'Eating the leaves, are they?'

'That's just what the pests are doing, Mr Garback!'

Myron smiled indulgently. '*Doryphora decemlineata*. Pardon me. I like to show off my Latin. Sometimes known as the potato beetle, more commonly called a potato bug.'

'So that's all they are,' said Mr Queen with disappointment. 'Potato bugs! *Dory*—what?'

Myron waved his hand. 'It doesn't matter. I suppose you'll want something to discourage them, eh?'

'Permanently,' said Mr Queen with a murderous scowl.

Myron bustled off and returned with a small tin carton, which he began to wrap in the High Village Pharmacy's distinctive pink-striped wrapping paper. 'This'll do the trick!'

'What's in it that discourages them?' asked Mr Queen.

'Arsenic—arsenious oxid. About fifty per cent. Technically . . .' Myron paused. 'I mean, strictly speaking, it's copper aceto-arsenite in this preparation, but it's the arsenic that slaughters 'em.' He tied the package and Mr Queen handed him a five-dollar bill. Myron turned to the cash register. 'Want to be careful with that stuff, of course. It's poisonous.'

'I certainly hope so!' exclaimed Mr Queen.

'*And* five,' said Myron. 'Thank you. Call again.'

'Arsenic, arsenic,' said Mr Queen loquaciously. 'Say isn't

that the stuff I was reading about in the *Record?* I mean that murder case? Some woman swallowed it in a cocktail at a New Year's Eve party?'

'Yes,' said the pharmacist. He gave Ellery a sharp look and turned away, presenting his graying nape and heavy shoulders to his customer.

'Wonder where they got it,' said Mr Queen nosily, leaning on the counter again. 'You'd need a prescription wouldn't you, from a doctor?'

'Not necessarily.' It seemed to Ellery that Pharmacist Garback's voice took on an edge. 'You didn't need one just now! There's arsenic in a lot of commercial preparations.' He fussed with some cartons on the shaving-preparations shelf.

'But if a druggist did sell a person arsenic without a prescription—'

Myron Garback turned about hotly. 'They won't find anything wrong with *my* records! That's what I told Dakin, and the only way Mr Haight could have got it would have been when he bought—'

'Yes?' asked Ellery, breathing not at all.

Myron bit his lip. 'Excuse me, sir,' he said. 'I really mustn't talk about it.' Then he looked startled. 'Wait a minute!' he exclaimed. 'Aren't you the man who—?'

'No, indeed,' said Mr Queen hastily. 'Good morning!' And he hurried out. So it had been Garback's pharmacy. A something. A trail. And Dakin had picked it up. Quietly. They were working on Jim Haight—quietly.

Ellery struck out across the slippery cobbles of the Square towards the bus stop near the Hollis Hotel. An iced wind was whistling, and he put up his overcoat collar and half-turned to protect his face. As he turned, he noticed a car pull into a parking space on the other side of the Square. The tall figure of Jim Haight got out and strode quickly towards the Wrightsville National Bank. Five small boys with strapped books swinging over their shoulders spied Jim and began to troop after him. Ellery stopped, fascinated. They were evidently jeering Jim, because Jim stopped, turned, and said something to them with an angry gesture. The boys backed off, and Jim turned away.

Ellery shouted. One of the boys had picked up a stone. He threw it, hard. Jim went down on his face.

Ellery began to run across the Square. But others had seen the attack, and, by the time he reached the other side of the Square, Jim was surrounded by a crowd. The boys had vanished. 'Let me through, please!' Jim was dazed. His hat had fallen off. Blood oozed from a dark stain on his sandy hair.

'Poisoner!' said a fat woman. 'That's him—that's the poisoner! . . .' 'Wife killer! . . .' 'Why don't they arrest him? . . .' 'What kind of law have we got in this town, anyway? . . .' 'He ought to be strung up! . . .' A small dark man kicked Jim's hat. A woman with doughy cheeks jumped at Jim, screaming.

'Stop that!' growled Ellery. He cuffed the small man aside, stepped between the woman and Jim, and said hastily: 'Out of this, Jim. Come on!'

'What hit me?' asked Jim. His eyes were glassy. 'My head—'

'*Lynch the dirty bastard!*'

'Who's the other one?'

'Get him, too!'

Ellery found himself, absurdly, fighting for his life with a group of blood-maddened savages who were dressed like ordinary people. As he struck back, he was thinking: This is what comes of meddling. Get out of this town. It's no good. Using his elbows, his feet, the heels of his hands, and occasionally a fist, he maneuvered the screeching crowd with him towards the bank building. 'Hit back, Jim!' he shouted. 'Defend yourself!'

But Jim's hands remained at his sides. One sleeve of his overcoat had disappeared. A rivulet of blood coursed down a cheek. He let himself be pushed, poked, punched, scratched, kicked. Then a one-woman Panzer division struck the crowd from the direction of the curb. Ellery grinned painfully over a swollen lip. Hatless, white-mittened, fighting mad. 'You cannibals! Let 'em alone!' Pat screamed.

'Ouch!'

'Serves you right, Hosy Malloy! And you—Mrs Landsman! Aren't you ashamed? And you drunken old witch, you—yes, I mean you, Julie Asturio! Stop it! *Stop it, I say.*'

'Attaboy, Patsy!' shouted a man from the edge of the crowd. 'Break it up, folks—come on, that's no way to carry on!'

Pat burst through to the struggling men. At the same moment Buzz Congress, the bank 'special', ran out and hit the crowd with himself. Since Buzz weighed two hundred and fifteen pounds, it was a considerable blow; people squawked and scattered, and between them Ellery and Pat got Jim into the bank. Old John F. ran by them and breasted the crowd, his gray hair whipping in the wind. 'Go home, you lunatics!' roared John F. 'Or I'll sail into you myself!'

Someone laughed, someone groaned, and then, with a sort of outgoing-tidal shame, the mob ebbed away. Ellery, helping Pat with Jim, saw through the glass doors, at the curb, the big silent figure of Frank Lloyd. There was a bitter twist to the newspaper publisher's mouth. When he saw Ellery watching him, he grinned without mirth, as if to say: 'Remember what I told you about this town?' and lumbered off across the Square.

Pat and Ellery drove Jim back to the little house on the Hill. They found Dr Willoughby waiting for them—John F. had phoned him from the bank. 'Some nasty scratches,' said Dr Willoughby, 'a few ugly bruises, and that's a deep scalp wound, but he'll be all right.'

'How about Mr Smith, Uncle Milo?' asked Pat anxiously. 'He looks like a fugitive from a meat grinder, too!'

'Now, now, I'm perfectly fine,' protested Ellery.

But Dr Willoughby fixed up Ellery, too.

When the doctor had gone, Ellery undressed Jim, and Pat helped get him into bed. He immediately turned over on his side resting his bandaged head on a limp hand, and closed his eyes. They watched him for a moment and then tiptoed from the room. 'He didn't say a word,' moaned Pat, 'Not one word. All through the whole thing . . . He's like that man out of the Bible!'

'Job,' said Ellery soberly. 'The silent, suffering Aramean. Well, your Aramean had better stay away from town from now on!' After that day, Jim stopped going to the bank.

17. *America Discovers Wrightsville*

THE ACTIVITIES of Mr Ellery Queen during the trying month between January and February were circumambient. For, no matter in how straight a line he started, he invariably finished by finding himself back in the same place ... and, moreover, with the realization that Chief Dakin and Prosecutor Bradford had been there before him. Quietly, quietly. Ellery did not tell Pat what a web was being woven in those secret investigations of the law. There was no point in making her feel worse than she felt already.

Then there was the Press. Apparently one of Frank Lloyd's vitriolic editorials had splashed heavily enough to deposit a drop in Chicago; for early in January, and shortly after Rosemary Haight's funeral, a smartly dressed woman with a thirty-eight waistline, silver-sprayed hair, and tired eyes got off the afternoon express and had Ed Hotchkiss drive her directly to 460 Hill Drive. The next day the readers of two hundred and fifty-nine large newspapers in the United States learned that good old Roberta was in there once again battling for love.

The leading paragraph of *Roberta's Column*, by Roberta Roberts, said:—

> Today in a small American city named Wrightsville there is being enacted a fantastic romantic tragedy, with a Man and a Woman the tragic protagonists and a whole community playing the role of villain.

That was enough for the others. Roberta had her nose in something yum-yummy. Editors began to call for back numbers of the *Wrightsville Record*. By the end of January a dozen first-line reporters had arrived in town to see what Bobby Roberts had dug up. Frank Lloyd was cooperative, and the first stories that trickled back over the wires put the name of Jim Haight on the front page of every newspaper in America.

The out-of-town newspaper men and women swarmed over the town, interviewing and writing and drinking straight bourbon at Vic Carlatti's *Hot Spot* and Gus Olesen's *Roadside Tavern* and making Dunc MacLean, next door to the Hollis Hotel, put in a hurry call to the liquor wholesaler. During the day they lolled about the County Courthouse spitting on Janitor Hernaberry's spotless lobby tiles, trailing Chief Dakin and Prosecutor Bradford for stories and photographs, and generally showing no decent respect for the opinions of mankind (although they wired same faithfully to their editors). Most of them stayed at the Hollis, commandeering cots when they could find no legitimate accommodations. Manager Brooks complained that they were turning his lobby into a 'slophouse'.

Later, during sessions of the trial, they spent their nights either on Route 16 or at the Bijou Theater on Lower Main, where they ganged up on young Louie Cahan, the manager, cracking Indian nuts all over the theatre and catcalling whenever the hero made love to the heroine. On Grab Bag Night one of the reporters won a set of dishes (donated by A. A. Gilboon, House Furnishings, Long-Term Payments) and 'accidentally on purpose', as everyone said indignantly, dropped all sixty pieces on the stage while the rest of them whistled, howled, and stamped their feet. Louie was good and sore, but what could he do?

Bitter speeches about 'those newspaper tramps' and 'self-constituted privileged characters' were delivered to good effect at a special meeting of the Country Club Board by Donald Mackenzie, President of the Wrightsville Personal Finance Corporation (PFC Solves Your Unpaid-Bills Problem!), and Dr Emil Poffenberger, Dental Surgeon, 132 Upham Block, High Village. Yet there was something infectious in their cynical high spirits, and Mr Ellery Queen was saddened to observe how Wrightsville gradually took on an air of County Fair. New and shiny stock began to appear in the shop windows; prices for food and lodging went up; farmers who had never before come into town on week nights began to parade the Square and Lower Main with their square-toed, staring families; and it became impossible to find parking space within a radius of six blocks of the Square. Chief Dakin had to swear in five new policemen to help direct traffic and keep the peace. The unwilling author of all this prosperity barricaded himself at 460 Hill Drive and refused to see anyone but the Wrights, Ellery, and later Roberta Roberts. To the remainder of the Press Jim was adamant. 'I'm still a taxpayer!' he cried to Dakin over the phone. 'I've got a right to some privacy! Put a cop at my door!'

'Yes, Mr Haight,' said Chief Dakin politely; and that afternoon Patrolman Dick Gobbin, who had been an invisible watcher in plain clothes for some time, on orders put on a uniform and became visible. And Jim went back to his cellaret.

'It's getting worse,' reported Pat to Ellery. 'He's drinking himself stupid. Even Lola can't do anything with him. Ellery, is it just that he's scared?'

'He's not scared at all. Goes deeper than funk, Patty. Hasn't he seen Nora yet?'

'He's ashamed to go near her. Nora's threatening to get out of bed and go over there herself, only Dr Willoughby said if she did he'd send her to the hospital. I slept with her last night. She cried all night.'

Ellery glumly surveyed his glass of Scotch, filched from John F.'s modest, little-used bar. 'Nora still thinks he's an innocent babe?'

'Of course. She wants him to fight back. She says if he'd only come over to see her she knows she could persuade him to stand up and defend himself from these attacks. Did you see what those damn reporters are writing about Jim *now?*'

'Yes,' sighed Ellery, emptying his glass.

'It's all Frank Lloyd's fault! That grump! Turning on his best friends! Pop's so furious he says he'll never speak to Frank again.'

'It's better to keep out of Lloyd's way,' said Ellery with a frown. 'He's a large animal, and he's thoroughly aroused. An angry beast with a hysterical typewriter. I'll tell your father myself.'

'Never mind. I don't think he wants to talk to ... anybody,' said Pat in a low voice. Then she burst out: 'How can people be such vermin? Mom's friends—they don't call her any more, they're whispering the vilest things behind her back, she's being impeached by two of her organizations—even Clarice Martin's stopped calling!'

'The Judge's wife,' murmured Ellery. 'Which suggests another interesting problem . . . Never mind. Have you seen Carter Bradford lately?'

'No,' said Pat shortly.

'Patty. What do you know about this woman Roberta Roberts?'

'The only decent reporter in town!'

'Strange what different conclusions she draws from the same facts. Did you see this?' Ellery showed Pat a Chicago newspaper, flipped back to *Roberta's Column*. A paragraph had been ringed, and Pat read it quickly:—

The longer I investigate this case, the surer I feel that James Haight is a misunderstood, hounded man, a martyr to what is at best a circumstantial case and the victim of Wrightville's mobbism. Only the woman he is alleged by Wrightville gossips to have tried to poison is standing by her husband four-square, with never a doubt or a backward look. More power to you, Nora Wright Haight! If faith and love still mean anything in this wretched world, your husband's name will be cleared and you will triumph over the pack.

'That's a *wonderful* tribute!' cried Pat.

'A little emotional, even for a famous *entrepreneuse* of love,' said Mr Queen dryly. 'I think I'll explore this female Cupid.'

But exploration only confirmed the evidence of his eyes. Roberta Roberts was heart and soul behind the struggle to get Jim a just hearing. One talk with Nora, and they became fighters in a common cause. 'If you could only get Jim to come up here for a talk,' said Nora urgently. 'Won't you try, Miss Roberts?'

'He'd listen to you,' Pat interposed. 'He said only this morning'—Pat neglected to mention his condition when he said it—'that you were the only friend he had in the world.'

'Jim's a queer love,' said Roberta thoughtfully. 'I've had two talks with him and I admit I haven't got anything but his confidence. Let me take another crack at the poor dope.'

But Jim refused to stir from the house.

'Why Jim?' asked the newspaper woman patiently. Ellery was present, and Lola Wright—a more silent Lola these days.

'Lemme alone.' Jim had not shaved; under the stubble his skin was gray; and he had drunk a lot of whisky.

'You can't just lie around the house like a yellow dog and let these people spit on you, Jim! See Nora. She'll give you strength, Jim. She's ill—don't you know that? Don't you care?'

Jim turned a tortured face to the wall. 'Nora's in good hands. Her family's taking care of her. And I've done her enough harm already. Lemme alone!'

'But Nora believes in you, honey.'

'I'm not gonna see Nora till this is all over,' he muttered. 'Till I'm Jim Haight again in this town, not some lousy hyena.' And he raised himself and fumbled for his glass, and drank, and sank back, and not all of Roberta's urging and prodding could rouse him again.

When Roberta had gone, and Jim was asleep, Ellery said to Lola Wright: 'And what's *your* angle, my dear Sphinx?'

'No angle. Somebody has to take care of Jim. I feed

him and put him to bed and see that he has a fresh bottle of pain-killer every once in a while.' Lola smiled.

'Unconventional,' said Mr Queen, smiling back. 'The two of you, alone, in this house.'

'That's me,' said Lola. 'Unconventional Lola.'

'You haven't expressed any opinion, Lola—'

'There's been too much expression of opinion,' she retorted. 'But if you want to know, I'm a professional underdog-lover. My heart bleeds for the Chinese and the Czechs and the Poles and the Jews and the Negroes—it's leaking practically all the time, and every time one of my underdogs is kicked, it leaks a little more. I see this poor slob suffering, and that's enough for me.'

'Apparently it's enough for Roberta Roberts, too,' mumbled Ellery.

'Miss Love-Conquers-All?' Lola shrugged. 'If you ask me, that dame's on Jim's side so she can get in where the other reporters can't!'

18. *St Valentine's Day: Love Conquers Nothing*

CONSIDERING that Nora was bedridden as a result of arsenic poisoning, that John F. was finding his cronies shying away from him and transferring their business to Hallam Luck's Public Trust Co., that Hermione was having the lady-finger put on her, that Pat was sticking close to Nora's bedside, and even Lola had been jolted out of her isolation—considering all this, it was wonderful how the Wrights kept bravely pretending even among themselves, that nothing out of the ordinary had happened. No one referred to Nora's condition except as an 'illness', as if she were suffering from laryngitis or some mysterious but legal 'woman's complaint'. John F. talked business at his desk in his old dry way—if he attended far fewer board meetings it was because he was 'tied up' ... obviously; and the fact that he quite disappeared from the weekly luncheons of the Chamber of Commerce at Ma Upham's

107

was gravely excused on grounds of dyspepsia. As for Jim—he was not mentioned at all.

But Hermy, after the first emotional storms, did some calking and sail patching. No one was going to run *her* out of town. And grimly she began to employ her telephone again. When impeachment proceedings began at her Women's Club, Madame President astounded everyone by making a personal appearance, in her smartest winter suit, and acting as if nothing had happened whatsoever. She was impeached notwithstanding; but only after various abalone ears burned and the ladies grew scarlet under the lash of Hermy's scorn. And at home she took charge as of old. Ludie, who might have been expected to snarl back, instead went about with a relieved expression. And by the beginning of February things took on such an air of normality that Lola actually returned to her nun's flat in Low Village and, Nora being better, Pat assumed the task of cooking Jim's meals and straightening Nora's house.

On Thursday, February thirteenth, Dr Willoughby said that Nora could get out of bed. There was much joy in the household. Ludie baked a gargantuan lemon-meringue pie, Nora's favorite; John F. came home early from the bank with a double armful of American Beauty roses (and where he got them, in Wrightsville, in February, he refused to say!); Pat stretched as if she were cramped and then washed her hair and did her nails, murmuring things like: 'My God! How I've let myself go!' Hermy turned the radio on for the first time in weeks to hear the war news ... It was like coming out of a restless sleep to find yourself safely awake. Nora wanted to see Jim instantly; but Hermione refused to let her out of the house—'The first day, dear! Are you insane?'—and so Nora phoned next door. After a while she hung up, helplessly; there was no answer. 'Maybe he's gone out for a walk or something,' said Pat.

'I'm sure that's what it is, Nora,' said Hermy, fussing over Nora's hair. Hermy did not say that Jim was in the house that very moment—she had just glimpsed his gray face pressed against the Venetian blinds of the master bedroom.

'I know!' said Nora, with a little excitement; and she telephoned Ben Danzig. 'Mr Danzig, send me the biggest, most expensive Valentine you've got. Right away!'

'Yes, ma'am,' said Ben; and in a half hour it was all

over town that Nora Haight was all right again. Sending Valentines! *Is there another man, do you suppose?*

It was a gorgeous thing, quilted in pink satin and bordered with real lace, framing numerous fat Cupids and sweet with St Valentine sentiment—Ben Danzig's most exclusive number, 99A. Nora addressed the envelope herself, and licked the stamp and affixed it, and sent Ellery out to mail it. She was almost gay. Mr Queen, playing Hermes to Eros, dropped the Valentine in the box at the bottom of the Hill with the uncomfortable feeling of a man who watches a battered pugilist getting to his knees after the fourth knockdown.

In the mail Friday morning there was no Valentine for Nora. 'I'm going over there,' she said firmly. 'This is silly. Jim's sulking. He thinks the whole world's against him. I'm going—'

Ludie came in, very stiff and scared, and said: 'It's that Chief Dakin and Mr Bradford, Miss Hermy.'

'Dakin!' The color left Hermy's girlish cheeks. 'For ... me, Ludie?'

'Says he wants to be seeing Miss Nora.'

Nora said: 'Me?' in a quivery voice.

John F. rose from the breakfast table. 'I'll handle this!' They went into the living room.

Mr Queen left his eggs and ran upstairs. Pat yawned 'Whozit?' when he rapped on her door.

'Come downstairs!'

'Whaffor?' He heard her yawn again. 'Come in, come in.' Ellery merely opened the door. Pat was bunched under the bedclothes, looking rosy and mussed and young again.

'Dakin and Bradford. To see Nora. I think this is it.'

'Oh!' Panic. But only for a moment. 'Throw me my robe, like a darling. It's arctic in here.' Ellery handed it to her, turned to walk out. 'Wait for me in the hall, Ellery. I mean—I want to go downstairs with you.'

Pat joined him in three minutes. She held onto his arm all the way downstairs. As they came in, Chief Dakin was saying: 'Course, Mrs Haight, you understand I've got to cover the whole ground. I'd told Doc Willoughby to let me know when you'd be up and about—'

'So kind of you,' said Nora. She was frightened almost out of her wits. You could see it. Her figure had a wooden stillness, and she looked from Dakin to Bradford and back again like a puppet being jerked by invisible hands.

109

'Hello,' said Pat grimly. 'Isn't it early for a social call, Mr Dakin?'

Dakin shrugged. Bradford regarded her with a furious misery. He seemed thinner, almost emaciated. 'Sit down and be quiet, baby,' said Hermione faintly.

'I don't know what you can expect Nora to tell you,' said John F. frigidly. 'Patricia, sit down!'

'Patricia?' said Pat. She sat down. 'Patricia' was a bad sign. John F. hadn't called her Patricia in such a formal voice since the last time he'd used his old-fashioned razor strop on her bottom, and that had been many many years ago. Pat contrived to grasp Nora's hand. She did not look at Bradford once; and after the first unhappy glance, Bradford did not look at her.

Dakin nodded pleasantly to Ellery. 'Glad to see you, Mr Smith. Now if we're all set—Cart, did you want to say somethin'?'

'Yes!' exploded Cart. 'I wanted to say that I'm in an impossible position. I wanted to say—' He made a helpless gesture and stared out of the window at the snow-covered lawn.

'Now, Mrs Haight,' said Dakin, blinking at Nora, 'would you mind telling us just what happened New Year's Eve as you saw it? I've got everybody else's story—'

'Mind? Why should I mind?' It came out froggy, and Nora cleared her throat. And began to talk shrilly and rapidly, making rapid little meaningless signs with her free hand. 'But I can't really tell you anything. I mean, all that I saw—'

'When your husband came around to you with the tray of cocktails, didn't he sort of pick out one special glass for you? I mean, didn't you want to take one glass and he fixed it so you took another?'

'How can I remember a thing like that?' asked Nora indignantly. 'And that's a—a nasty implication!'

'Mrs Haight.' The Chief's voice was suddenly chilly. 'Did your husband ever try to poison you before New Year's Eve?'

Nora snatched her hand from Pat's and jumped up. 'No!'

'Nora dear,' began Pat, 'you mustn't get excited—'

'You're sure, Mrs Haight?' insisted Dakin.

'Of course, I'm sure!'

'There's nothing you can tell us about the fights you and Mr Haight been having?'

'Fights!' Nora was livid now. 'I suppose it's that horrible

110

DuPré creature—*or*—' The 'or' was so odd even Carter Bradford turned from the window. Nora had uttered the word with a sudden sickish emphasis and glared directly at Ellery. Dakin and Bradford glanced quickly at him, and Pat looked terrified. Mr and Mrs Wright were hopelessly lost.

'Or what, Mrs Haight?' asked Dakin.

'Nothing. Nothing! Why don't you let Jim alone?' Nora was crying hysterically now. 'All of you!'

Dr Willoughby came in with his big man's light step; Ludie's face, white and anxious, peered over his shoulder, then vanished. 'Nora,' he said with concern. 'Crying again? Dakin, I warned you—'

'Can't help it, Doc,' said the Chief with dignity. 'I got my job to do, and I'm doing it. Mrs Haight, if there's nothing you can tell us that helps your husband—'

'He didn't do it, I tell you!'

'Nora,' said Dr. Willoughby insistently.

'Then I'm afraid we got to do it, Mrs Haight.'

'Do what, for heaven's sake?'

'Arrest your husband.'

'Arrest—Jim?' Nora began to laugh, her hands in her hair. Dr Willoughby tried to take her hands in his, but she pushed him away. Behind the glasses her pupils were dilated. 'But you can't arrest Jim! He didn't do anything! You haven't a thing on him—!'

'We've got plenty on him,' said Chief Dakin.

'I'm sorry, Nora,' mumbled Carter Bradford. 'It's true.'

'Plenty on him,' whispered Nora. Then she screamed at Pat: 'I knew too many people knew about it! That's what comes of taking strangers into the house!'

'Nora!' gasped Pat. 'Darling . . .'

'Wait a moment, Nora,' began Ellery.

'Don't *you* talk to me!' Nora shrieked. 'You're against him because of those three letters! They wouldn't arrest Jim if you hadn't told them about the letters—!' Something in Ellery's gaze seemed to penetrate her hysteria, and Nora broke off with a gasp, swaying against Dr Willoughby, an enormous new fear leaping into her eyes. She looked quickly at Dakin, at Bradford, saw the astonishment, then the flash of exultation. And she backed up against the broad chest of the doctor and froze there, her hand to her mouth, sick with realization.

'What letters?' demanded Dakin.

'Nora, what letters?' cried Bradford.

'No! I didn't mean—'

Carter ran over to her and seized her hand. 'Nora! *What letters?*' he asked fiercely.

'No,' groaned Nora.

'You've got to tell me! If there are letters, you're concealing evidence—'

'Mr Smith! What do you know about this?' demanded Chief Dakin.

'Letters?' Ellery looked astonished, and shook his head.

Pat rose and pushed Bradford. He staggered back. 'You let Nora alone,' said Pat in a passionate voice. 'You Judas!'

Her violence kindled an answering violence. 'You're not going to presume upon my friendship! Dakin, search this house, and the house next door!'

'Should have done it long ago, Cart,' said the Chief mildly. 'If you hadn't been so blamed set—' He disappeared.

'Carter,' said John F. in very low tones, 'you're never to come here again. Do you understand?'

Bradford looked as if he were going to cry. And Nora collapsed in Dr Willoughby's arms with a moan like a sick cat.

With Bradford's frigid permission Nora was taken upstairs to her bedroom by Dr Willoughby. Hermy and Pat hurried along with them, helpless and harried.

'Smith.' Bradford did not turn.

'Save your breath,' advised Mr Queen politely.

'I know it's no use, but I've got to warn you—if you're contributing to the suppression of evidence . . .'

'Evidence?' echoed Mr Queen, as if he had never heard the word before.

'Those letters!'

'What *are* these letters you people are talking about?'

Cart spun around, his mouth working. 'You've been in my way ever since you came here,' he said hoarsely. 'You've wormed your way into this house, alienated Pat from me—'

'Here, here,' said Ellery kindly. 'Mind your verbs.'

Cart stopped, his hands two fists. Ellery went to the window. Chief Dakin was deep in conversation with little Dick Gobbin, the patrolman, on the Haight porch . . . The two policemen went into the house. Fifteen minutes later Messrs Queen and Bradford were still standing in the same positions. Pat came in with a noise. Her face shocked them. She went directly to Ellery. 'The most awful thing's happened.' And she burst into tears.

'Pat! For heaven's sake!'

'Nora—Nora is—' Pat's voice blurred and shook.

Dr Willoughby said from the doorway: 'Bradford?'

'What's happened?' asked Bradford tensely.

And then Chief Dakin came in, unknowing, and his face was like a mask. He was carrying Nora's hatbox and the fat tan book with the neat gilt title, Edgcomb's *Toxicology*. Dakin stopped. 'Happened?' he asked quickly. 'What's this?'

Dr Willoughby said 'Nora Haight is going to have a baby. In about five months.' And then there was no sound at all but Pat's exhausted sobs against Ellery's chest.

'No . . .' said Bradford in a wincing voice. 'That's . . . too much.' And with a queer gesture toward Chief of Police Dakin he stumbled out. They heard the front door slam.

'I won't be responsible for Mrs Haight's life,' said Dr Willoughby harshly, 'if she's put through any more scenes like the one just now. You can call in Wright County's whole medical fraternity to confirm what I just said. She's pregnant, in an extremely nervous condition, she has a naturally delicate constitution to begin with—'

'Look, Doc,' said Dakin, 'it ain't my fault if—'

'Oh, go to hell,' said Dr Willoughby. They heard him climbing furiously back up the stairs.

Dakin stood in the middle of the room, Nora's hatbox in one hand and Jim's book on poisons in the other. Then he sighed and said: 'But it *ain't* my fault. And now these three letters in Mrs Haight's hatbox, and this medical book with the arsenic part all marked up—'

'All right, Dakin,' said Ellery. His arms tightened about Pat.

'These three letters,' said Dakin doggedly. 'They practically make our case. And finding 'em in Mrs Haight's closet . . . Looks mighty odd to me. I don't get this—'

Pat cried: 'Doesn't that convince you? Would Nora have kept those letters if she thought Jim was trying to poison her? Are you all so stupid—'

'So you did know about the letters,' said the Chief, blinking. 'I see. And you're in on this, too, Mr Smith. Not that I blame you. I got a family, too, and it's good to be loyal to friends. I got nothing against Jim Haight, or you Wrights . . . But I got to find the facts. If Jim Haight's innocent he'll be acquitted never you worry . . .'

'Go away, please,' said Ellery.

113

Dakin shrugged and left the house, taking his evidence with him. He looked angry and bitter.

At eleven o'clock that morning, February fourteenth, the day of St Valentine, when all Wrightsville was giggling over comic cards and chewing candy out of heart-shaped boxes, Chief of Police Dakin returned to 460 Hill Drive with Patrolman Charles Brady, nodded to Patrolman Dick Gobbin, and Patrolman Dick Gobbin knocked on the front door. When there was no answer, they went in. They found Jim Haight snoring on the living-room sofa in a mess of cigarette butts, dirty glasses, and half-empty whisky bottles. Dakin shook Jim, not ungently, and finally Jim snorted. His eyes were all red and glassy. 'Hunh?'

'James Haight,' said Dakin, holding out a blue-backed paper, 'I hereby arrest you on the charge of the attempted murder of Nora Wright Haight and the murder of Rosemary Haight.'

Jim screwed up his eyes, as if he could not see well. Then he reddened all over his face. He shouted: 'No!'

'Better come without a fuss,' said Dakin; and he walked out with a quick, relieved step.

Charles Brady said later to the reporters at the Courthouse: 'Seemed like Haight just caved in. Never saw anything like it. You could just see the fella sort of fold up, in pieces, like a contraption. I says to Dick Gobbin: "Better take that side of him, Dick, he's gonna collapse," but Jim Haight, he just made a kind of shoving motion at Dick and I'll be doggone if he don't start to laugh—all folded up! An' he says, so you could hardly hear him through the laughin' —an' let me tell you fellas the stink of booze was enough to send you higher'n a kite—he says: "Don't tell my wife." And he comes along nice and quiet. Now wasn't that a crazy thing for a fella to say who's just been arrested for murder? "Don't tell my wife." Facin' a murder rap an' thinkin' of sparin' his wife's feelin's! How could anybody keep it from her, anyway? Don't tell my wife! I tell you the fella's a nut.'

All Patrolman Gobbin said was: 'G-o-b-b-i-n. That's right, fellas. Hey, this'll give my kids a real kick!'

PART FOUR

19. *War of the Worlds*

Mr Boris Connell *Feb. 17, 1941*
News & Features Syndicate
Press Ass'n Bldg.
Chicago, Ill.

DEAR BORIS:

Double Mickeys to you for that hot wire, but perhaps your celebrated news nose has been misled by the tons of garbage my fellow 'journalists' have been slinging back from Wrightsville.

I believe Jim Haight is innocent, and I'm going to say so in my column till I have no column. In my naïve way I still believe a man is innocent until he's proved guilty. Jim Haight has been condemned to death by all the smart lads and lassies sent here by their editors to dish out a Roman holiday for the great American mob. Somebody has to have principles. So I'm elected—plurality, one vote. And Wrightsville's in an ugly mood. People here talk about nothing else. Their talk is pure Fascism. It's going to be 'fun' watching them pick an 'unbiased' jury.

To appreciate what's happening, you've got to realize that only two months ago John F. and Hermione Wright were the lares and penates of this community. Today, they and their three swell daughters are untouchables—and everybody's scrambling to pick up the first stone. A slew of former Wright 'admirers' and 'friends' have been looking for a soft spot to jab the knife in; and are they jabbing! It's enough to make even me sick, and you know I've seen pretty nearly everything in the way of human meanness, malice, and downright cussedness.

It's a war of two worlds. The decent little world is hopelessly outclassed in armament, numbers, and about everything but guts and morale. The Wrights have a few real friends who are sticking by—Judge Eli Martin, Dr Milo

115

Willoughby, a visiting writer named Ellery Smith (ever hear of him? *I* haven't!). Together they're putting up a propaganda battle. The Wrights are magnificent—in the face of everything, they're bunched solidly behind Jim Haight. Even this girl Lola Wright, who's been on the outs with her family for years, has moved back home; or at least she's there constantly. They're all fighting not only for Nora's husband but for her unborn child as well. Despite the tripe I dish out for my 'public' every day, I still believe in some fundamental decencies, and that little tyke can use a powerful voice!

Let me tell you something. I was in Jim's cell today in the County Courthouse, and I said to him: 'Jim, did you know your wife is going to have a baby?' He just sat down on his cell bunk and started to bawl, as if I'd hit him where a lady shouldn't.

I haven't been able to see Nora yet, though I may get Dr Willoughby's permission in a day or so. (I mean, since Jim's arrest.) Nora's collapsed, and she can't see anyone but her family. How would you like to be in her shoes? And if *she's* behind Jim—the man who's supposed to have plotted her death—then there's really something to fight for.

I know this is wasted time and paper, Boris, since your blood is composed of nine parts bourbon and one part club soda; so this is positively my last 'explanation'. From now on, if you want to know what's really happening in Wrightsville on the Haight murder case, read my column. And if you get nasty and break my contract before it runs out, I'll sue the N & F Syn and I'll keep suing it till I take away everything but that expensive bridgework behind your ruby lips.   As ever, ROBERTA ROBERTS

Roberta Roberts did not quite know the facts. Two days after Jim's arrest, Hermione Wright called a council of war. She closed the upstairs drawing-room doors with a grim bang. It was Sunday, and the family had just returned from church—Hermy had insisted that they attend services. They all looked weary from the ordeal. 'The question,' began Hermy, 'is what to do.'

'What can we do, Muth?' asked Pat tiredly.

'Milo.' Hermy took Doc Willoughby's big puffy hand. 'I want you to tell us the truth. How is Nora?'

'She's a sick girl, Hermy, a very sick girl.'

'That's not enough, Milo! How sick?'

Dr Willoughby's eyes shifted. 'Hard to say. She's dangerously nervous, excited, unstrung. Naturally her pregnancy isn't helping. Jim's arrest, thinking about the trial—

116

she's got to be kept calmed down. Medicine alone won't do it. But if her nerves can be brought back to normal—'

Hermy patted his big hand absently. 'Then there's no question of what we've got to do.'

'When I see how worn-out Nora is—' said John F. in despair. 'She's begun to look the way she used to. How are we going—'

'There's one way, John,' said Hermy tightly. 'It's for all of us to get behind Jim and fight for him!'

'When he's ruined Nora's life?' cried John F. 'He's been bad luck from the day he came to Wrightsville!'

'John.' Hermy's voice was steel-lined. 'Nora wants it that way and, more important, for her health's sake she's got to *have* it what way. So it's going to be that way.'

'All *right*,' John F. almost shouted.

'John!' He subsided, muttering. 'And another thing. Nora mustn't know.'

'Mustn't know what?' demanded Pat.

'That we don't mean it.' Hermy's eyes began to redden up. 'Oh, that man! If Nora weren't his wife—'

Doc Willoughby said: 'So you think the boy's guilty. Hermione?'

'Think! If I'd known before about those three horrible letters, that medical book . . . Of course I think he's guilty!'

'The dirty dog,' muttered John F. 'He ought to be shot down, like a dirty dog.'

'I don't know,' moaned Pat. 'I just don't.'

Lola was smoking a cigarette. She flipped it into the fireplace viciously. 'Maybe I'm crazy,' she snapped. 'But I find myself feeling sorry for the twerp, and I don't usually spare any sympathy for murderers.'

'Eli, what's your opinion?' asked Hermy.

Judge Martin's sleepy face was grave. 'I don't know what young Bradford's got in the way of evidence. It's a highly circumstantial case. But on the other hand there's not a single fact I know of to cast doubt on the circumstances. I'd say Jim is in for a rough time.'

'Took generations to build up the Wright name,' mumbled John F., 'and one day to tear it down!'

'There's been enough damage done already,' sighed Pat. "When your own family runs out on you—'

'What's this?' demanded Lola.

'Aunt Tabitha, Lo. I thought you knew. She's closed up her house and gone to Los Angeles for a 'visit' to Cousin Sophy's.'

'That Zombie still around?'

'Tabitha makes me sick!' said Hermione.

'You can't blame her so much, Hermy,' said John F. feebly. 'You know how she hates scandal—'

'I know I shan't run away, John! Nobody in this town's going to see me with *my* head hanging.'

'That's what I told Clarice,' chuckled Judge Martin. Then he rubbed his dry cheeks, like a cricket. 'Clarice would have come, Hermione, only—'

'I understand,' said Hermy quietly. 'Bless you for standing by us, Eli—you, and Milo, and you, Mr Smith. You more than anyone. After all, Judge Martin and Dr Willoughby are lifelong friends. But you're practically a stranger to us, and Patricia's told me how loyal you've been . . .'

'I've wanted to thank you, Smith,' said John F. awkwardly, 'but I think you know how hard it is—'

Ellery looked uncomfortable. 'Please. Don't think about me at all. I'll help all I can.'

Hermy said in a low voice: 'Bless you . . . Now that things have come out in the open, we'll completely understand, though, if you decide to leave Wrightsville—'

'I'm afraid I couldn't even if I wanted to,' smiled Ellery. 'The Judge will tell you I'm practically an accessory to the crime.'

'Suppressing evidence,' grinned Judge Eli. 'Dakin will have the hounds after you if you try to run away, Smith.'

'So you see? I'm stuck,' said Mr Queen. 'Let's say no more about it.' Pat's hand stole into Ellery's and squeezed hard.

'Then if we all understand one another,' declared Hermione in a firm tone, 'we're going to hire the best lawyer in the state to defend Jim. We're going to show Wrightsville a united front!'

'And if Jim's found guilty, Muth?' asked Pat quietly.

'We'll have done our best, dear. In the long run, such a verdict, hard as it seems, would be the best solution to our problem—'

'What a vile thing to say,' snapped Lola. 'Mother, that's not right or fair. You say that because you're convinced Jim's guilty. You're as bad as the rest of this town. Best solution—!'

'Lola, do you realize that if it were not for the intervention of providence,' Hermy cried, 'your sister would be a corpse this very minute?'

118

'Let's not quarrel,' said Pat wearily. Lola lit another cigarette, looking angry.

'And if Jim's acquitted,' said Hermy stiffishly, 'I'm going to insist that Nora divorce him.'

'Mother!' Now Pat was shocked. 'Even if a jury finds Jim *innocent*, you'll still believe he's guilty?'

'Now Hermy, that's not right,' said Judge Martin.

'I mean he's not the right man for my Nora,' said Hermy. 'He's brought her nothing but grief. Nora will divorce than man if *I've* got anything to say about it!'

'You won't,' said Doc Willoughby dryly.

Lola kissed her mother on the cheek. Ellery heard Pat gasp, and guessed that history had just been made. 'You old Trojan,' laughed Lola. 'When you get there you'll insist on running Heaven. Imagine—*you* urging a divorce!' And she added grimly: 'Why didn't you feel that way about *my* divorce from Claude?'

'This isn't . . . the same,' said Hermy, embarrassed. And suddenly Mr Queen saw a bright, bright light. There was an old antagonism between Hermione Wright and her daughter Lola that cut deep into their personalities. Pat was too young to have been a cause of irritation. But Nora—Nora had always been the preferred. Nora had always stood between Hermione and Lola emotionally, an innocent rope in a psychological tug-of-war. Hermy was saying to Judge Martin: 'We'll need an extra-fine lawyer for Jim, Eli. Whom can you suggest?'

'Will I do?' asked Judge Martin.

John F. was startled. 'Eli! You?'

'But Uncle Eli,' protested Pat, 'I thought—it's your court—I thought you'd have to sit—'

'In the first place,' said the old jurist dryly, 'that's not possible. I'm involved. I was present on the scene of the crime. I am known to have strong ties with the Wright family. Legally and ethically, I can't sit on this case.' He shook his head. 'Jim will be tried before Judge Newbold. Newbold's a complete outsider.'

'But you haven't pleaded a case in fifteen years, Eli,' said John F. suspiciously.

'Of course, if you're afraid I won't do—' He smiled at their protestations. 'I forgot to mention that I'm retiring from the Bench, so . . .'

'You old fraud,' growled Dr Willoughby. 'John, Eli's quitting the Bench just to defend this case!'

'Now Eli, we can't let you do that,' said John F.

'Nonsense,' said the Judge gruffly. 'Don't go getting any

119

sentimental ideas. Was going to retire anyway. Old Has-
been Martin. Itching to get to work again, instead of
dozing my life away in a robe. If you want a has-been in
your corner, we won't say any more about it.'

Hermy burst into tears and ran from the room.

20. *No Time for Pride*

THE NEXT morning Pat rapped on Ellery's door and he
opened it to find her dressed for the street. 'Nora wants to
see you.' She looked around the room curiously. Ludie
had already done the room, but it was briskly littered
again, as if Ellery had been hard at work for some time.

'Right with you.' Ellery looked fatigued. He fussed with
some pencil-scrawled papers on the desk; the typewriter
carriage held a sheet. He slipped the cover over the
portable and, putting the papers in a desk drawer, locked
it. The key he dropped casually into his pocket, and put
on his jacket.

'Working?' asked Pat.

'Well . . . yes. This way out, Miss Wright.' Mr Queen
walked her out of his room and locked the door.

'Your novel?'

'In a way.' They went down to the second floor.

'What does "in a way" mean?'

'Yes and no. I've been . . . you might call it reconnoiter-
ing.' Ellery looked her over. 'Going out? You look cute.'

'I've a special reason for looking cute this morning,'
murmured Pat. 'In fact, I'll have to look irresistible.'

'You do. But where are you going?'

'Can't a girl have any secrets from you, Mr Queen?' Pat
stopped him outside Nora's room and looked him in the
eye. 'Ellery, you've been going over your notes on the
case, haven't you?'

'Yes.'

'Find anything?' she asked eagerly.

'No.'

'Damn!'

'It's a queer thing,' grumbled Ellery, putting his arm
120

around her. 'Something's been annoying me for weeks. Flying around in my skull. Can't catch it . . . I thought it might be a fact—something trivial—that I'd overlooked. You know, I . . . well, I based my novel on you people—the facts, the events, the interrelationships. So everything's in my notes that's happened.' He shook his head. 'But I can't put my finger on it.'

'Maybe,' frowned Pat, 'it's a fact you don't *know*.'

Ellery held her off at arm's length. 'That,' he said slowly, 'is very likely. Do *you* know anything that—'

'You know if I did, I'd tell you, Ellery.'

'I wonder.' Then he shrugged and said: 'Well! Let's go in and see Nora.'

Nora was sitting up in bed, reading the *Wrightsville Record*. She was thinner, unhealthy-looking. Ellery was shocked to see how transparent the skin of her hands had grown. 'I always say,' grinned Mr Queen, 'that the test of a woman's attractiveness is—how does she look in bed of a winter's morning.'

Nora smiled wanly and patted the bed. 'Do I pass?'

'*Summa cum laude,*' said Ellery, sitting down beside her.

Nora looked pleased. 'Most of it's powder, lipstick—yes, and a dab of rouge on each cheek—and of course this ribbon in my hair is a help. Charming liar! Patty darling, sit down.'

'I really have to be going, Nora. You two can talk—'

'But Pats, I want you to hear this, too.' Pat glanced at Ellery; he blinked, and she sat down in the chintz-covered chair on the other side of the bed. She seemed nervous, and Ellery kept watching her as Nora talked. 'First,' said Nora, 'I owe you an apology.'

'Who, me,' said Ellery, astonished. 'For what, Nora?'

'For having accused you of telling the police about those three letters and the toxicology book. Last week. When Chief Dakin said he was going to arrest Jim and I lost my head.'

'You see? I'd forgotten it. You do the same.'

Nora took his hand. 'It was a malicious thought. But for the moment I couldn't imagine who'd told them but you. You see, I thought they knew—'

'You weren't responsible, Nora,' said Pat. 'Ellery understands that.'

'But there's something else,' cried Nora. 'I can apologize for a nasty thought, but I can't wipe out what I did to

Jim.' Her lower lip quivered. 'If not for me, they'd never have found out about those letters!'

'Nor dear,' said Pat, leaning over her, 'you know you mustn't. If you keep crying, I'll tell Uncle Milo and he won't let you have *any* company.'

Nora sniffled with her handkerchief to her nose. 'I don't know why I didn't burn them. Such a stupid thing—to keep them in that hatbox in my closet! But I had some idea I'd be able to find out who really wrote them—I was sure Jim hadn't—'

'Nora,' said Ellery gently. 'Forget it.'

'But I practically handed Jim over to the police!'

'That isn't true. Don't forget Dakin came here last week *prepared* to arrest Jim. Questioning you beforehand was just a formality.'

'Then you think those letters and the book don't make any essential difference?' asked Nora eagerly.

Ellery got up from the bed and looked out of the window at the winter sky. 'Well . . . not too much.'

'You're lying to me!'

'Mrs Haight,' said Pat firmly, 'you've had enough company for one morning. Ellery, scram.'

Ellery turned around. 'This sister of yours, Pat, will suffer more from doubt than from knowledge. Nora, I'll tell you exactly what the situation is.' Nora gripped her comforter with both hands. 'If Dakin was prepared to arrest Jim *before* he knew about the letters and the toxicology book, then obviously he and Carter Bradford thought they had a good case.' Nora made a tiny sound. '*With* the letters and the book, therefore, they just as obviously have a better case. Now that's the truth, you've got to face it, you've got to stop accusing yourself, you've got to be sensible and get well again, you've got to stand by Jim and give him courage.' He leaned over her and took her hand. 'Jim needs your strength, Nora. You have a strength he lacks. He can't face you, but if he knows you're behind him, never wavering, having faith—'

'Yes,' breathed Nora, her eyes shining. 'I have. Tell him I have.' Pat came around the bed and kissed Ellery on the cheek.

'Going my way?' asked Ellery as they left the house.

'Which way is that?'

'Courthouse. I want to see Jim.'

'Oh. I'll drive you down.'

'Don't go out of your way—'

122

'I'm going to the Courthouse, too.'

'To see Jim?'

'Don't ask me questions!' cried Pat a little hysterically.

They drove down the Hill in silence. There was ice on the road, and the chains sang cheerfully. Wrightsville looked nicely wintry, all whites and reds and blacks, no shading; it had the country look, the rich and simple cleanliness, of a Grant Wood painting. But in town there were people, and sloppy slush, and a meanness in the air; the shops looked pinched and stale; everybody was hurrying through the cold; no one smiled. In the Square they had to stop for traffic; a shopgirl recognized Pat and pointer her out with a lacquered fingernail to a pimpled youth in a leather storm-breaker. They whispered excitedly as Pat kicked the gas pedal. On the Courthouse steps Ellery said: 'Not *that* way, Miss Wright,' and steered Pat around to the side entrance.

'What's the idea?' demanded Pat.

'The press,' said Mr Queen. 'Infesting the lobby. I assume we'd rather not answer questions.'

They took the side elevator. 'You've been here before,' said Pat slowly.

'Yes.'

Pat said: 'I think I'll pay Jim a visit myself.'

The County Jail occupied the two topmost floors of the Courthouse. As they stepped out of the elevator into the waiting room, an odor of steam and Lysol rushed into their noses, and Pat swallowed hard. But she managed a smile for the benefit of Wally Planetsky, the officer on duty.

'If it ain't Miss Pat,' said the officer awkwardly.

'Hullo, Wally. How's the old badge?'

'Fine, fine, Miss Pat.'

'Wally used to let me breath on his badge and shine it up when I was in grade school,' Pat exclaimed. 'Wally, don't stand there shifting from one foot to the other. You know what I'm here for.'

'I guess,' muttered Wally Planetsky.

'Where's his cell?'

'Judge Martin's with him, Miss Pat. Rules say only one visitor at a time—'

'Who cares about the rules? Take us to my brother-in-law's cell, Wally!'

'This gentleman a reporter? Mr Haight, he won't see any reporters excepting that Miss Roberts.'

'No, he's a friend of mine and Jim's.'

'I guess,' muttered Planetsky again; and they began a

long march, interrupted by unlocking of iron doors, locking of iron doors, steps on concrete, unlocking and locking and steps through corridors lined with man-sized bird cages; and at each step the odor of steam and Lysol grew stronger, and Pat grew greener, and toward the last she clung tightly to Ellery's arm. But she kept her chin up.

'That's it,' murmured Ellery; and she swallowed several times in succession.

Jim sprang to his feet when he spied them, a quick flush coming to his sallow cheeks; but then he sat down again, the blood draining away, and said hoarsely: "Hello there, I didn't know you were coming.'

'Hello, Jim!' said Pat cheerily. 'How are you?'

Jim looked around his cell. 'All right,' he said with a vague smile.

'It's clean, anyway,' grunted Judge Martin, 'which is more than you could say about the *old* County Jail. Well, Jim, I'll be on my way. I'll drop in tomorrow for another talk.'

'Thanks, Judge.' Jim smiled the same vague smile up at the Judge.

'Nora's fine,' said Pat with an effort, as if Jim had asked.

'That's swell,' said Jim. 'Fine, uh?'

'Yes,' said Pat in a shrill voice.

'That's swell,' said Jim again.

Mercifully, Ellery said: 'Pat, didn't you say you had an errand somewhere? There's something I'd like to say to Jim in private.'

'Not that it will do you the least good,' said Judge Martin in an angry tone. It seemed to Ellery that the old jurist's anger was assumed for the occasion. 'This boy hasn't the sense he was born with! Come along, Patricia.'

Pat turned her pale face to Ellery, mumbled something, smiled weakly at Jim, and fled with the Judge. Keeper Planetsky relocked the cell door after them, shaking his head.

Ellery looked down at Jim; Jim was studying the bare floor of his cell. 'He wants me to talk,' mumbled Jim suddenly.

'Well, why not, Jim?'

'What could I say?'

Ellery offered him a cigarette. Jim took it, but when Ellery held a lighted match up he shook his head and slowly tore the cigarette to shreds. 'You could say,' murmured Ellery between puffs, 'you could say that you didn't

124

write those three letters, or underline that paragraph on arsenic.'

For an instant Jim's fingers stopped tormenting the cigarette; then they resumed their work of destruction. His colorless lips flattened against his face in something that was almost a snarl.

'Jim.' Jim glanced at him, and then away. 'Did you really plan to poison Nora?' Jim did not even indicate that he had heard the question. 'You know, Jim, often when a man is guilty of a crime he's much better off telling the truth to his lawyer and friends than keeping quiet. And when he's not guilty, it's actually criminal to keep quiet. It's a crime against himself.' Jim said nothing. 'How do you expect your family and friends to help you when you won't help yourself?' Jim's lips moved 'What did you say, Jim?'

'Nothing.'

'As a matter of fact, in this case,' said Ellery briskly, 'your crime of silence isn't directed half so much against yourself as it is against your wife and the child that's coming. How can you be so far gone in stupidity or listlessness that you'd drag them down with you, too?'

'Don't say that!' said Jim hoarsely. 'Get out of here! I didn't ask you to come! I didn't ask Judge Martin to defend me! I didn't ask for anything! I just want to be let alone!'

'Is that,' asked Ellery, 'what you want me to tell Nora?'

There was such misery in Jim's eyes as he sat, panting, on the edge of his cell bunk that Ellery went to the door and called Planetsky. All the signs. Cowardice. Shame. Self-pity . . . But that other thing, the stubbornness, *the refusal to talk about anything,* as if in the mere act of self-expression there were *danger* . . .

As Ellery followed the guard down the eye-studded corridor a cell exploded in his brain with a great and disproportionate burst of light. He actually stopped walking, causing old Planetsky to turn and look at him in surprise. But then he shook his head and strode on again. He'd almost had it that time—by sheer divination. Maybe the next time . . .

Pat drew a deep breath outside the frosted-glass door on the second floor of the County Courthouse, tried to see her reflection, poked nervously at her mink hat, tried out a smile or two, not too successfully, and then went in.

125

Miss Billcox looked as if she were seeing a ghost. 'Is the Prosecutor in, Billy?' murmured Pat.

'I'll . . . see, Miss Wright,' said Miss Billcox, and fled.

Carter Bradford came out to her himself, in a hurry, 'Come in, Pat.' He looked tired, and astonished. He stood aside to let her pass, and as she passed she heard his uneven breathing. O Lord, she thought. Maybe. Maybe it isn't too late.

'Working?' His desk was covered with legal papers.

'Yes, Pat.' He went around his desk to stand behind it. One sheaf of bound papers lay open—he closed it surreptitiously and kept his hand on it as he nodded toward a leather chair. Pat sat down and crossed her knees.

'Well,' said Pat, looking around. 'The old office—I mean the new office—doesn't seem to have changed, Cart.'

'About the only thing that hasn't.'

'You needn't be so careful about that legal paper,' smiled Pat. 'I haven't got X-ray eyes.' He flushed and removed his hand. 'There isn't a shred of Mata Hari in my makeup.'

'I'm *not*—' Cart began angrily. Then he pushed his fingers through his hair in the old, old gesture. 'Here we are, scrapping again. Pat, you look simply delicious.'

'It's nice of you to say so,' sighed Pat, 'when I really am beginning to look my age.'

'Look your age! Why, you're—' Cart swallowed hard. Then he said, as angrily as before: 'I've missed you like hell.'

Pat said rigidly. 'I suppose I've missed you, too.' Oh, dear! That wasn't what she had meant to say at all. But it was hard, facing him this way, alone in a room together for the first time in so long—hard to keep from feeling . . . feelings.

'I dream about you,' said Cart with a self-conscious laugh. 'Isn't that silly?'

'Now, Cart, you know perfectly well you're just saying that to be polite. People don't dream about people. I mean in the way *you* mean. They dream about animals with long noses.'

'Maybe it's just before I drop off.' He shook his head. 'Dreaming or not dreaming, it's always the same. Your face. I don't know why. It's not such a wonderful face. The nose is wrong, and your mouth's wider than Carmel's, and you've got that ridiculous way of looking at people sidewise, like a parrot—' And she was in his arms, and it was just like a spy drama, except that she hadn't planned

126

the script exactly this way. *This* was to come after—as a reward to Cart for being a sweet, obliging, self-sacrificing boy. She hadn't thought of herself at all, assuming regal stardom. Certainly this pounding of her heart wasn't in the plot—not with Jim caged in a cell six stories above her head and Nora lying in bed across town trying to hold on to something. His lips were on hers and he was pressing, pressing.

'Cart. No. Not yet.' She pushed. 'Darling. Please—'

'You called me darling! Damn it, Pat, how could you play around with me all these months, shoving that Smith fellow in my face—'

'Cart,' moaned Pat. 'I want to talk to you . . . first.'

'I'm sick of talk! Pat, I want you so blamed much—' He kissed her mouth; he kissed the tip of her nose.

'I want to talk to you about Jim, Cart!' cried Pat desperately.

She felt him go cold in one spasm. He let her go and walked to the wall with the windows that overlooked the Courthouse plaza, to stare out without seeing anything, cars or people or trees or Wrightsville's gray-wash sky.

'What about Jim?' he asked in a flat voice.

'Cart. Look at me!' Pat begged.

He turned around. 'I can't do it.'

'Can't look at me? You are!'

'Can't withdraw from the case. That's why you came here today, isn't it—to ask me?'

Pat sat down again, fumbling for her lipstick. Her lips. Blobbed. Kiss. Her hands were shaking, so she snapped the bag shut. 'Yes,' she said, very low. 'More than that. I wanted you to resign the Prosecutor's office and come over to Jim's defense. Like Judge Eli Martin.'

Cart was silent for so long that Pat had to look up at him. He was staring at her with an intense bitterness. But when he spoke, it was with gentleness. 'You can't be serious. The Judge is an old man, your father's closest friend. And he wouldn't have been able to sit on this case, anyway. But I was elected to this office only a short time ago. I took an oath that means something to me. I hate to sound like some stuffed shirt of a politician looking for votes—'

'Oh, but you do!' flared Pat.

'If Jim's innocent, he'll go free. If he's guilty—you wouldn't want him to go free if he's guilty, would you?'

'He's *not* guilty!'

'That's something the jury will have to decide.'

'You've decided already! In your own mind, you've condemned him to death!'

'Dakin and I have had to collect the facts, Pat. We've *had* to. Don't you understand that? Our personal feelings can't interfere. We both feel awful about this thing . . .'

Pat was near tears now, and angry with herself for showing it. 'Doesn't it mean anything to you that Nora's whole life is tied up in this "thing", as you call it? That there's a baby coming? I know the trial can't be stopped, but I wanted *you* on our side, I wanted you to help, not hurt!' Cart ground his teeth together. 'You've said you love me,' cried Pat. 'How could you love me and still—' Horrified, she heard her own voice break and found herself sobbing. 'The whole town's against us. They stoned Jim. They're slinging mud at us. Wrightsville, Cart! A Wright founded this town. We were all born here—not only us kids, but Pop and Muth and Aunt Tabitha and the Bluefields and . . . I'm not the spoiled brat you used to neck in the back of your lizzie at the Grove in Wrightsville Junction on Saturday nights! The whole world's gone to pot, Cart—I've grown old watching it. Oh, Cart, I've no pride left—no defenses—say you'll help me! I'm afraid!' She hid her face, giving up the emotional battle. Nothing made any sense—what she'd just said, what she was thinking. Everything was drowning, gasping, struggling in tears.

'Pat,' said Cart miserably. 'I can't. I just can't.'

That did it. She was drowned now, dead, but there was a sort of vicious other-life that made her spring from the chair and scream at him. 'You're nothing but a selfish, scheming politician! You're willing to see Jim die and Pop, and Mother, and Nora, and me, and everyone suffer, just to further your own career! Oh, this is an *important* case. Dozens of New York and Chicago and Boston reporters to hang on your every word! Your name and photo—Young Public Prosecutor Bradford—brilliant— says this—my duty is—yes—no—off the record . . . You're a hateful, shallow *publicity hound!*'

'I've gone all through this in my mind, Pat,' Cart replied with a queer lack of resentment. 'I suppose I can't expect you to see it my way—'

Pat laughed. 'Insult to injury!'

'If I don't do this job—if I resign or step out—someone else will. Someone, who might be a lot less fair to Jim. If I prosecute, Pat, you can be sure Jim will get a square deal—'

She ran out.

And there, on the side of the corridor opposite the Prosecutor's door, waiting patiently, was Mr Queen.

'Oh, *Ellery!*'

Ellery said gently: 'Come home.'

21. *Vox Pops*

'AVE, CAESAR!' wrote Roberta Roberts at the head of her column under the date line of March fifteenth.

> He who is about to be tried for his life finds even the fates against him. Jim Haight's trial begins on the Ides of March before Judge Lysander Newbold in Wright County Courthouse, Part II, Wrightsville, U.S.A. This is chance, or subtlety . . . Kid Vox is popping furiously, and it is the impression of cooler heads that the young man going on trial here for the murder of Rosemary Haight and the attempted murder of Nora Wright Haight is being prepared to make a Roman Holiday.

And so it seemed. From the beginning there was a muttering undertone that was chilling. Chief of Police Dakin expressed himself privately to the persistent press as 'mighty relieved' that his prisoner didn't have to be carted through the streets of Wrightsville to reach the place of his inquisition, since the County Jail and the County Courthouse were in the same building. People were in such an ugly temper you would have imagined their hatred of the alleged poisoner to be inspired by the fiercest loyalty to the Wrights. But this was odd, because they were equally ugly towards the Wrights. Dakin had to assign two county detectives to escort the family to and from the Courthouse. Even so, jeering boys threw stones, the tires of their cars were slashed mysteriously and the paint scratched with nasty words; seven unsigned letters of the 'threat' variety were delivered by a nervous Postman Bailey in one day alone. Silent, John F. Wright turned them over to Dakin's office; and Patrolman Brady himself caught the Old Soak, Anderson, standing precariously in the middle of the Wright lawn in bright daylight, declaiming not too aptly to the unresponding house Mark Antony's speech from Act III, Scene 1 of *Julius Caesar*. Charlie Brady hauled Mr Anderson to the town lockup hastily, while Mr Anderson kept yelling 'O parm me thou blee'n' piece of earth that I am meek an' zhentle with theshe—hup!—bushers!'

Hermy and John F. began to look beaten. In court, the family sat together, in a sort of phalanx, with stiff necks if pale faces; only occasionally Hermy smiled rather pointedly in the direction of Jim Haight, and then turned to sniff and glare at the jammed courtroom and toss her head, as if to say: 'Yes, we're all in this together—you miserable rubbernecks!'

There had been a great deal of mumbling about the impropriety of Carter Bradford's prosecuting the case. In an acid editorial Frank Lloyd put the *Record* on record as 'disapproving'. True, unlike Judge Eli Martin, Bradford had arrived at the fatal New Year's Eve party *after* the poisoning of Nora and Rosemary, so he was not involved either as participant or as witness. But Lloyd pointed out that 'our young, talented, but sometimes emotional Prosecutor has long been friendly with the Wright family, especially one member of it; and although we understand this friendship has ceased as of the night of the crime, we still question the ability of Mr Bradford to prosecute this case without bias. Something should be done about it.'

Interviewed on this point before the opening of the trial, Bradford snapped: 'This isn't Chicago or New York. We have a close-knit community here, where everybody knows everybody else. My conduct during the trial will answer the *Record*'s libelous insinuations. Jim Haight will get from Wright County a forthright, impartial prosecution based solely upon the evidence. That's all, gentlemen!'

Judge Lysander Newbold was an elderly man, a bachelor, greatly respected throughout the state as a jurist and trout fisherman. He was a square, squat, bony man who always sat on the Bench with his black-fringed skull sunk so deeply between his shoulders that it seemed an outgrowth of his chest. His voice was dry and careless; he had the habit, when on the Bench, of playing absently with his gavel, as if it were a fishing rod; and he never laughed.

Judge Newbold had no friends, no associates, and no commitments except to God, country, Bench, and the trout season. Everybody said with a sort of relieved piety

130

that 'Judge Newbold is just about the best judge this case could have.' Some even thought he was *too* good. But they were the ones who were muttering. Roberta Roberts baptized these grumblers 'the Jimhaighters'.

It took several days to select a jury, and during these days Mr Ellery Queen kept watching only two persons in the courtroom—Judge Eli Martin, defense counsel, and Carter Bradford, Prosecutor. And it soon became evident that this would be a war between young courage and old experience. Bradford was working under a strain. He held himself in one piece, like a casting; there was a dogged something about him that met the eye with defiance and yet a sort of shame. Ellery saw early that he was competent. He knew his townspeople, too. But he was speaking too quietly, and occasionally his voice cracked.

Judge Martin was superb. He did not make the mistake of patronizing young Bradford, even subtly; that would have swung the people over to the prosecution. Instead, he was most respectful of Bradford's comments. Once, returning to their places from a low-voiced colloquy before Judge Newbold, the old man was seen to put his hand affectionately on Carter's shoulder for just an instant. The gesture said: You're a good boy; we like each other; we are both interested in the same thing—justice; and we are equally matched. This is all very sad, but necessary. The People are in good hands. The People rather liked it. There were whispers of approval. And some were heard to say: After all, old Eli Martin—he *did* quit his job on the Bench to defend Haight. Can't get around that! Must be pretty convinced Haight's innocent . . . And others replied: Go on. The Judge is John F. Wright's best friend, that's why . . . Well, I don't know . . . The whole thing was calculated to create an atmosphere of dignity and thoughtfulness, in which the raw emotions of the mob could only gasp for breath, and gradually expire.

Mr Ellery Queen approved. Mr Queen approved even more when he finally examined the twelve good men and true. Judge Martin had made the selections as deftly and surely as if there were no Bradford to cope with at all. Solid, sober male citizens, as far as Ellery could determine. None calculated to respond to prejudicial appeals, with one possible exception, a fat man who kept sweating; most seemed anxiously thoughtful men, with higher than average intelligence. Men of the decent world, who might be expected to understand that a man can be weak without being criminal.

For students of the particular, the complete court record of *People* v *James Haight* is on file in Wright County—day after day after day of question and answer and objection and Judge Newbold's precise rulings. For that matter, the newspapers were almost as exhaustive as the court stenographer's notes. The difficulty with detailed records, however, is that you cannot see the tree for the leaves. So let us stand off and make the leaves blur and blend into larger shapes. Let us look at contours, not textures.

In his opening address to the jury, Carter Bradford said that the jury must bear in mind continuously one all-important point: that while Rosemary Haight, the defendant's sister, was murdered by poison, her death was not the true object of defendant's crime. The true object of defendant's crime was to take the life of defendant's young wife, Nora Wright Haight—an object so nearly accomplished that the wife was confined to her bed for six weeks after the fateful New Year's Eve party, a victim of arsenic poisoning.

And yes, the State freely admits that its case against James Haight is circumstantial, but murder convictions on circumstantial evidence are the rule, not the exception. The only direct evidence possible in a murder case is an eyewitness's testimony as to having witnessed the murder at the moment of its commission. In a shooting case, this would have to be a witness who actually saw the accused pull the trigger and the victim fall dead as a result of the shot. In a poisoning case, it would have to be a witness who actually saw the accused deposit poison in the food or drink to be swallowed by the victim, and moreover who saw the accused hand the poisoned food or drink *to* the victim. Obviously, continued Bradford, such 'happy accidents' of persons witnessing the Actual Deed must be few and far between, since murderers understandably try to avoid committing their murders before an audience. Therefore nearly all prosecutions of murder are based on circumstantial rather than direct evidence; the law has wisely provided for the admission of such evidence, otherwise most murderers would go unpunished.

But the jury need not flounder in doubts about *this* case; here the circumstantial evidence is so clear, so strong, so indisputable, that the jury must find James Haight guilty of the crime as charged beyond any reasonable doubt whatsoever. 'The People will prove', said Bradford in a low, firm tone, 'that James Haight planned the murder of his wife a minimum of five weeks before he tried to accomplish it; that it was a cunning plan, depending upon a series of poisonings of increasing severity to establish the wife as subject to attacks of "illness", and supposed to culminate in a climactic poisoning as a result of which the wife was to die. The People will prove', Bradford went on, 'that these preliminary poisonings did take place on the very dates indicated by the schedule James Haight had prepared with his own hand; that the attempted murder of Nora Haight and the accidental murder of Rosemary Haight did take place on the very date indicated by the same schedule.

'The People will prove that on the night under examination, James Haight and James Haight alone mixed the batch of cocktails among whose number was the poisoned cocktail; that James Haight and James Haight alone handed the tray of cocktails around to the various members of the party; that James Haight and James Haight alone handed his wife the poisoned cocktail from the tray, and even urged her to drink it; that she did drink of that cocktail, and fell violently ill of arsenic poisoning, her life being spared only because at Rosemary Haight's insistence she gave the rest of the poisoned cocktail to her sister-in-law after having merely sipped . . . a circumstance James Haight couldn't have foreseen.

'The People will prove,' Bradford went on quietly, 'that James Haight was in desperate need of money, that he demanded large sums of money of his wife while under the influence of liquor and, sensibly, she refused; that James Haight was losing large sums of money gambling; that he was taking other illicit means of procuring money; that upon Nora Haight's death her estate, a large one as the result of an inheritance, would legally fall to the defendant, who is her husband and heir-at-law.

'The People,' concluded Bradford, in a tone so low he could scarcely be heard, 'being convinced beyond reasonable doubt that James Haight did so plan and attempt the life of one person in attempting which he succeeded in taking the life of another an innocent victim—the People demand that James Haight pay with his own life for the life taken and the life so nearly taken.' And Carter Bradford sat down to spontaneous applause, which caused the first of Judge Newbold's numerous subsequent warnings to the spectators.

In that long dreary body of testimony calculated to prove Jim Haight's sole Opportunity, the only colorful spots were provided by Judge Eli Martin in cross-examination. From the first the old lawyer's plan was plain to Ellery: to cast doubt, doubt, doubt. Not heatedly. With cool humor. The voice of reason ... Insinuate. Imply. Get away with whatever you can, and to hell with the rules of cross-examination. Ellery realized that Judge Martin was desperate.

'But you can't be *sure?*'

'N-no.'

'You didn't have the defendant under observation *every moment?*'

'Of course not!'

'The defendant *might* have laid the tray of cocktails down for a moment or so?'

'No.'

'Are you *positive?*'

Carter Bradford quietly objects: the question was answered. Sustained. Judge Newbold waves his hand patiently.

'Did you *see* the defendant prepare the cocktails?'

'No.'

'Were you in the living room *all* the time?'

'You know I was!' This was Frank Lloyd; and he was angry. To Frank Lloyd, Judge Martin paid special attention. The old gentleman wormed out of the newspaper publisher his relationship with the Wright family—his 'peculiar' relationship with the defendant's wife. He had been in love with her. He had been bitter when she turned him down for James Haight. He had threatened James Haight with bodily violence. Objection, objection, objection. But it managed to come out, enough of it to reawaken in the jury's minds the whole story of Frank Lloyd and Nora Wright—after all, that story was an old one to Wrightsville and everybody knew the details!

So Frank Lloyd became a poor witness for the People, and there was a doubt, a doubt. The vengeful jilted 'other' man. Who knows? Maybe—

With the Wright family, who were forced to take the stand to testify to the actual events of the night, Judge Martin was impersonal—and cast more doubts. On the 'facts'. Nobody actually *saw* Jim Haight drop arsenic into the cocktail. Nobody could be sure ... of anything.

But the prosecution's case proceeded and, despite Judge Martin's wily obstructions, Bradford established: that Jim alone mixed the cocktails; that Jim was the only one who could have been certain the poisoned cocktail went to Nora, his intended victim, since he handed each drinker his or her cocktail; that Jim pressed Nora to drink when she was reluctant.

And the testimony of old Wentworth, who had been the attorney for John F.'s father. Wentworth had drawn the dead man's will. Wentworth testified that on Nora's marriage she received her grandfather's bequest of a hundred thousand dollars, held in trust for her until that 'happy' event.

And the testimony of the five handwriting experts, who agreed unanimously, despite the most vigorous cross-examination by Judge Martin, that the three unmailed letters addressed to Rosemary Haight, dated Thanksgiving, Christmas, and New Year's, and announcing far in advance of those dates the 'illness' of Nora Haight, the third actually announcing her 'death'—agreed unanimously that these damning letters were in the handwriting of the defendant, beyond any doubt whatever. For several days the trial limped and lagged while huge charts were set up in the courtroom and Judge Martin, who had obviously boned up, debated the finer points of handwriting analysis with the experts . . . unsuccessfully.

Then came Alberta Manaskas, who turned out a staunch defender of the public weal. Alberta evinced an unsuspected volubility. And, to judge from her testimony, her eyes, which had always seemed dull, were sharper than a cosmic ray; and her ears, which had merely seemed large and red, were more sensitive than a photoelectric cell. It was through Alberta that Carter Bradford brought out how, as the first letter had predicted, Nora took sick on Thanksgiving day; how Nora had another, and worse, attack of 'sickness' on Christmas Day. Alberta went into clinical detail about these 'sicknesses'.

Judge Martin rose to his opportunity. Sickness, Alberta? Now what kind of sickness would you say Miss Nora had on Thanksgiving and Christmas?

Sick! Like in her belly. (*Laughter.*)

Have *you* ever been sick like in your—uh—belly, Alberta? Sure! You, me, everyone. (*Judge Newbold raps for order.*)

Like Miss Nora?

Sure!

(*Gently*): *You've* never been poisoned by arsenic, though, have you, Alberta?

135

Bradford, on his feet. Judge Martin sat down smiling. Mr Queen noticed the sweat fringing his forehead.

Dr Milo Willoughby's testimony, confirmed by the testimony of Coroner Chic Salemson and the testimony of L.D. ('Whitey') Magill, State Chemist, established that the toxic agent which had made Nora Haight ill, and caused the death of Rosemary Haight, was arsenious acid, or arsenic trioxid, or arsenious oxid, or simply 'white arsenic' —all names for the same deadly substance. Henceforth prosecutor and defence counsel referred to it simply as 'arsenic'.

Dr Magill described the substance as 'colorless, tasteless, and odorless in solution, and of a high degree of toxicity.'

Q. (*by Prosecutor Bradford*)—It is a powder, Dr Magill? *A.*—Yes, sir.

Q.—Would it dissolve in a cocktail, or lose any of its effectiveness if taken that way? *A.*—Arsenic trioxid is very slightly soluble in alcohol, but since a cocktail is greatly aqueous it will dissolve quite readily. It is soluble in water, you see. No, it would lose none of its toxicity in alcohol.

Q.—Thank you, Dr Magill. Your Witness, Judge Martin.

Judge Martin waives cross-examination.

Prosecutor Bradford calls to the stand Myron Garback, proprietor of the High Village Pharmacy, Wrightsville. Mr Garback has a cold; his nose is red and swollen. He sneezes frequently and fidgets in the witness chair. From the audience Mrs Garback, a pale Irishwoman, watches her husband anxiously. Being duly sworn, Myron Garback testifies that 'sometime' during October of 1940—the previous October—James Haight had entered the High Village Pharmacy and asked for 'a small tin of Quicko'.

Q.—What exactly is Quicko, Mr Garback? *A.*—It is a preparation used for the extermination of rodents and insect pests.

Q.—What is the lethal ingredient of Quicko? *A.*—Arsenic trioxid. (*Sneeze. Laughter. Gavel.*)

Mrs Garback turns crimson and glares balefully about.

Q.—In highly concentrated form? *A.*—Yes, sir.

Q.—Did you sell the defendant a tin of this poisonous preparation, Mr Garback? *A.*—Yes, sir. It is a commercial preparation, requiring no prescription.

Q.—Did the defendant ever return to purchase more Quicko? *A.*—Yes, sir, about two weeks later. He said he'd mislaid the can of stuff, so he'd have to buy a new can. I sold him a new can.

Q.—Did the defendant—I'll rephrase the question. What did the defendant say to you, and what did you say to the defendant, on the occasion of his first purchase? *A.*—Mr Haight said there were mice in his house, and he wanted to kill them off. I said I was surprised, because I'd never heard of house mice up on the Hill. He didn't say anything to that.

Cross-examination by Judge Eli Martin:—

Q.—Mr Garback, how many tins of Quicko would you estimate you sold during the month of October last? *A.*—That's hard to answer. A lot. It's my best-selling rat-killer, and Low Village is infested.

Q.—Twenty-five? Fifty? *A.*—Somewhere around there.

Q.—Then it's not unusual for customers to buy this poisonous preparation—purely to kill rats? *A.*—No, sir, not unusual at all.

Q.—Then how is it you remembered that Mr Haight purchased some—remembered it *for five months?* *A.*—It just stuck in my mind. Maybe because he bought two tins so close together, and it was the Hill.

Q.—You're positive it was two cans, two weeks apart? *A.*—Yes, sir. I wouldn't say it if I wasn't.

Q.—No comments, please; just answer the question. Mr Garback, do you keep records of your Quicko sales, listed by customer? *A.*—I don't have to, Judge. It's legal to sell—

Q.—Answer the question, Mr Garback. Have you a written record of James Haight's alleged purchases of Quicko? *A.*—No, sir, but—

Q.—Then we just have your word, relying on your memory of two incidents you allege to have occurred five months ago, that the defendant purchased Quicko from you?

Prosecutor Bradford: Your Honor, the witness is under oath. He has answered Counsel's question not once, but several times. Objection.

Judge Newbold: It seems to me witness has answered, Judge. Sustained.

Q.—That's all, thank you, Mr Garback.

Alberta Manaskas is recalled to the stand. Questioned by Mr Bradford, she testifies that she 'never seen no rats in Miss Nora's house.' She further testifies that she 'never seen no rat-killer, neither.'

On cross-examination, Judge Martin asks Alberta

Manaskas if it is not true that in the tool chest in the cellar of the Haight house there is a large rat trap.

A.—Is there?

Q.—That's what I'm asking you, Alberta *A.*—I guess there is, at that.

Q.—If there are no rats, Alberta, why do you suppose the Haights keep a rat trap?

Prosecutor Bradford: Objection. Calling for opinion.

Judge Newbold: Sustained. Counsel, I'll have to ask you to restrict your cross-examination to—

Judge Martin (humbly): Yes, Your Honor.

Emmeline DuPré, under oath, testifies that she is a Dramatic and Dancing Teacher residing at Number 468 Hill Drive, Wrightsville, 'right next door to Nora Wright's house.'

Witness testifies that during the previous November and December she 'happened to overhear' frequent quarrels between Nora and James Haight. The quarrels were about Mr Haight's heavy drinking and numerous demands for money. There was one markedly violent quarrel, in December, when Miss DuPré heard Nora Haight refuse to give her husband 'any more money'. Did Miss DuPré 'happen to overhear' anything to indicate why the defendant needed so much money?

A.—That's what shocked me so, Mr Bradford—

Q.—The Court is not interested in your emotional reactions, Miss DuPré. Answer the question, please. *A.*—Jim Haight admitted he'd been gambling, and losing plenty, and that's why he needed money, he said.

Q.—Was any name or place mentioned by either Mr or Mrs Haight in connection with the defendant's gambling? *A.*—Jim Haight said he'd been losing a lot at the *Hot Spot,* that scandalous place on Route 16—

Judge Martin: Your Honor, I move that this witness's entire testimony be stricken out. I have no objection to give-and-take in this trial—Mr Bradford has been extremely patient with me, and it is an admittedly difficult case, being so vaguely circumstantial—

Mr Bradford: May I ask Counsel to restrict his remarks to his objection, and stop trying to influence the jury by characterizing the case?

Judge Newbold: The Prosecutor is right, Counsel. Now what is your objection to this witness's testimony?

Judge Martin: No attempt has been made by the People to fix the times and circumstances under which witness allegedly overheard conversations between defen-

138

dant and wife. Admittedly witness was not present in the same room, or even in the same house. How, then, did she 'overhear'? How can she be sure the two people *were* the defendant and his wife? Did she see them? Didn't she see them? I hold—

Miss DuPré: But I heard all this with my own ears!

Judge Newbold: Miss DuPré! Yes, Mr Bradford?

Mr Bradford: The People have put Miss DuPré on the stand in an effort to spare defendant's wife the pain of testifying to the quarrels—

Judge Martin: That's not my point.

Judge Newbold: No, it is not. Nevertheless, Counsel, I suggest you cover your point in cross-examination. Objection denied. Proceed, Mr Bradford.

Mr Bradford proceeds, eliciting further testimony as to quarrels between Jim and Nora. On cross-examination, Judge Martin reduces Miss DuPré to indignant tears. He brings out her physical position relative to the conversationalists—crouched by her bedroom window in darkness listening to the voices floating warmly across the driveway between her house and the Haight house—confuses her in the matter of dates and times involved, so that she clearly contradicts herself several times. The spectators enjoy themselves.

Under oath, J.P. Simpson, proprietor of Simpson's Pawnshop in the Square, Wrightsville, testifies that in November and December last James Haight pledged various items of jewelry at Simpson's Pawnshop.

Q.—What kind of jewelry, Mr Simpson? *A.*—First one was a man's gold watch—he took it off his chain to pawn it. Nice merchandise. Fair price.

Q.—Is this the watch? *A.*—Yes, sir. I remember givin' him a fair price—

Q.—Placed in evidence.

Clerk: People's exhibit thirty-one.

Q.—Will you read the inscription on the watch, Mr Simpson? *A.*—The what? Oh. 'To—Jim—from—Nora.'

Q.—What else did the defendant pawn, Mr Simpson? *A.*—Gold and platinum rings, a cameo brooch, and so on. All good merchandise. Very good loan merchandise.

Q.—Do you recognize these items of jewelry I now show you, Mr Simpson? *A.*—Yes, sir. They're the ones he pawned with me. Gave him mighty fair prices—

Q.—Never mind what you gave him. These last items are all women's jewelry, are they not? *A.*—That's right.

Q.—Read the various inscriptions. Aloud. *A.*—Wait till I fix my specs. 'N.W.'—'N.W.'—'N.W.H.'—'N.W.'

Nora's jewelry is placed in evidence.

Q.—One last question, Mr Simpson. Did the defendant ever redeem any of the objects he pawned with you? *A.*—No, sir. He just kept bringing me new stuff, one at a time, an' I kept givin' him fair prices for 'em.

Judge Martin waives cross-examination.

Donald Mackenzie, President of the Wrightsville Personal Finance Corporation, being duly sworn, testifies that James Haight had borrowed considerable sums from the PFC during the last two months of the preceding year.

Q.—On what collateral, Mr Mackenzie? *A.*—None.

Q.—Isn't this unusual for your firm, Mr Mackenzie? To lend money without collateral? *A.*—Well, the PFC has a *very* liberal loan policy, but of course we usually ask for collateral. Just business, you understand. Only, since Mr Haight was Vice-President of the Wrightsville National Bank and the son-in-law of John Fowler Wright, the company made an exception in his case and advanced the loans on signature only.

Q.—Has the defendant made any payments against his indebtedness, Mr Mackenzie? *A.*—Well, no.

Q.—Has your company made any effort to collect the moneys due, Mr Mackenzie? *A.*—Well, yes. Not that we were worried, but—well, it was five thousand dollars, and after asking Mr Haight several times to make his stipulated payments and getting no satisfaction, we—I finally went to the bank to see Mr Wright, Mr Haight's father-in-law, and explained the situation, and Mr Wright said he hadn't known about his son-in-law's loan but of course he'd make it good himself, and I wasn't to say anything about it—to keep it confidential. I would have, too, only this trial and all—

Judge Martin: Objection. Incompetent, irrelevant—

Q.—Never mind that, Mr Mackenzie. Did John F. Wright repay your company the loan in full? *A.*—Principal and interest. Yes, sir.

Q.—Has the defendant borrowed any money since January the first of this year? *A.*—No, sir.

Q.—Have you had any conversations with the defendant since January the first of this year? *A.*—Yes. Mr Haight came in to see me in the middle of January and started to explain why he hadn't paid anything on his loan—said he'd made some bad investments—asked for

140

more time and said he'd surely pay back his debt. I said to
him that his father-in-law'd already done that.

Q.—What did the defendant say to that? A.—He didn't
say a word. He just walked out of my office.

Judge Martin cross-examines.

Q.—Mr Mackenzie, didn't it strike you as strange that
the Vice-President of a banking institution like the
Wrightsville National Bank, and the son-in-law of the
President of that bank, should come to *you* for a loan?
A.—Well, I guess it did. Only I figured it was a confiden-
tial matter, you see—

Q.—In a confidential matter, without explanations or
collateral, on a mere signature, you still advanced the sum
of five thousand dollars? A.—Well, I knew old John F.
would make good if—

Mr Bradford: Your Honor—

Judge Martin: That's all, Mr Mackenzie.

Not all the evidence against Jim Haight came out in the
courtroom. Some of it came out in Vic Carlatti's, some in
the Hollis Hotel Tonsorial Parlor, some in Dr Emil
Poffenberger's dental office in the Upham Block, some in
Gus Olesen's *Roadside Tavern,* and at least one colorful
fact was elicited from the bibulous Mr Anderson by a
New York reporter, the scene of the interview being the
pedestal of the Low Village World War Memorial, on
which Mr Anderson happened to be stretched out at the
time.

Emmeline DuPré heard the Luigi Marino story
through Tessie Lupin. Miss DuPré was having her permanent done in the Lower Main Beauty Shop where
Tessie worked, and Tessie had just had lunch with her
husband Joe, who was one of Luigi Marino's barbers. Joe
had told Tessie, and Tessie had told Emmy DuPré, and
Emmy DuPré ...

Then the town began to hear the other stories, and the
old recollections were raked over for black and shining
dirt. And when it was all put together, Wrightsville began
to say: Now there's something funny going on. Do you
suppose Frank Lloyd was right about Carter Bradford's
being the Wrights' friend and all? Why doesn't he put
Luigi and Dr Poffenberger on the stand? And Gus Olesen?
And the others? Why, this all makes it plain as day that
Jim Haight wanted to kill Nora! He *threatened* her all
over town!

Chief Dakin was tackled by Luigi Marino before court
opened one morning when the Chief came in for a quick

shave. Joe Lupin listened from the next chair with both hairy ears. 'Say, Chefe!' said Luigi in great excitement. 'I been lookin' all over for-a you! I just remember something hot!'

'Yeah, Luigi? Once over, and take it easy.'

'Las' Novemb'. Jim-a Haight, he come in here one day for I should cut-a his hair. I say to Mist' Haight, "Mist' Haight, I feel-a fine. You know what? I'm-a gonna get hitched!" Mist' Haight he say that's-a good, who's-a the lucky gal? I say: "Francesca Botigliano. I know Francesca from the ol' countree. She been workin' by Saint-a Louey, but I propose-a in a lett' an' now Francesca she's-a comin' to Wrights-a-ville to be Mrs Marino—I send-a her the ticket an' expense-a mon' myself. Ain't that something?" You remember I get-a married, Chefe . . .'

'Sure, Luigi. Hey, take it easy!'

'So what-a does Mist' Haight say? He say: "Luigi, nev' marry a poor gal! There ain't-a no per-cent-age in it!" You see? He marry that-a gal Nora Wright for her mon'! You get-a Mist' Bradford put me on-a stand. I'll tell-a dat story!'

Chief Dakin laughed. But Wrightsville did not. To Wrightsville it seemed logical that Luigi's story should be part of the trial testimony. It would show that he married Nora Wright for her money. If a man would marry a woman for her money, he'd poison her for it, too . . . Those ladies of Wrightsville who were so unfortunate as to have lawyers in the family heard a few pointed remarks about 'admissible' testimony.

Dr Poffenberger had actually gone to Prosecutor Bradford before the trial and offered to testify. 'Why, Haight came to me last December, Cart, suffering from an abscessed wisdom tooth. I gave him gas, and while he was under the influence of the gas he kept saying: "I'll get rid of her! I'll get rid of her!" And then he said: "I need that money for myself. I want that money for myself!" Doesn't that prove he was planning to kill her, and why?'

'No,' said Bradford wearily. 'Unconscious utterances. Inadmissible testimony. Go way, Emil, and let me work, will you?'

Dr Poffenberger was indignant. He repeated the story to as many of his patients as would listen, which was practically all of them.

Gus Olesen's story reached the Prosecutor's ears by way of Patrolman Chris Dorfman, Radio Division (one car). Patrolman Chris Dorfman had 'happened' to drop into

142

Gus Olesen's place for a 'coke' (*he* said), and Gus, 'all het up', had told him what Jim Haight had once said to him, Gus, on the occasion of a 'spree'. And now Patrolman Chris Dorfman was all het up, for he had been wondering for weeks how he could muscle into the trial and take the stand and get into the papers.

'Just what is it Haight is supposed to have said, Chris?' asked Prosecutor Bradford.

'Well, Gus says Jim Haight a couple of times drove up to the *Tavern* cockeyed and wanting a drink, and Gus says he'd always turn him down. Once he even called up Mrs Haight and asked her to come down and get her husband, he was raisin' Cain, plastered to the ears. But the thing Gus remembers that I think you ought to get into your trial, Mr Bradford, is when one night Haight was in there, drunk, and he kept ravin' about wives, and marriage, and how lousy it all was, and then said: "Nothin' to do but get rid of her, Gus. I gotta get rid of her quick or I'll go nuts. She's drivin' me nuts!" '

'Statements under the influence of liquor,' groaned Cart. 'Highly questionable. Do you want me to lose this case on reversible error? Go back to your radio car!'

Mr Anderson's story was simplicity itself. With dignity he told the New York reporter: 'Sir, Mr Haight an' I have quaffed the purple flagon on many an occasion together. Kindred spirits, you understand. We would meet in the Square an' embrace. Well do I recall that eventful evening in "dark December", when "in this our pinching cave," we discoursed "the freezing hours away"! *Cymbeline*, sir; a much-neglected master work . . .'

'We wander,' said the reporter. 'What happened?'

'Well, sir, Mr Haight put his arms about me and he said, Quote: "I'm going to kill her, Andy. See 'f I don't! I'm going to kill her dead!" '

'Wow,' said the reporter, and left Mr Anderson to go back to sleep on the pedestal of the Low Village World War Memorial.

But this luscious morsel, too, Prosecutor Bradford refused; and Wrightsville muttered that there was 'something phony', and buzzed and buzzed and buzzed.

The rumors reached Judge Lysander Newbold's ears. From that day on, at the end of each court session, he sternly admonished the jury not to discuss the case with anyone, not even among themselves.

It was thought that Eli Martin had something to do with calling the rumors to Judge Newbold's attention. For

143

Judge Martin was beginning to look harried, particularly in the mornings, after breakfast with his wife. Clarice, who served in her own peculiar way, was his barometer for readings of the temper of Wrightsville. So a fury began to creep into the courtroom, and it mounted and flew back and forth between the old lawyer and Carter Bradford until the press began to nudge one another with wise looks and say 'the old boy is cracking.'

Thomas Winship, head cashier of the Wrightsville National Bank, testified that James Haight had always used a thin red crayon in his work at the bank, and produced numerous documents from the files of the bank, signed by Haight in red crayon.

The last exhibit placed in evidence by Bradford—a shrewd piece of timing—was the volume Edgcomb's *Toxicology*, with its telltale section marked in red crayon . . . the section dealing with arsenic. This exhibit passed from hand to hand in the jury box, while Judge Martin looked 'confident' and James Haight, by the old lawyer's side at the defence table, grew very pale and was seen to glance about quickly, as if seeking escape. But the moment passed, and thenceforward he behaved as before—silent, limp in his chair, his gray face almost bored.

At the close of Friday's session, March the twenty-eighth, Prosecutor Bradford indicated that he 'might be close to finished', but that he would know better when court convened the following Monday morning. He thought it likely the People would rest on Monday. There was an interminable conversation before the Bench, and then Judge Newbold called a recess until Monday morning, March the thirty-first.

The prisoner was taken back to his cell on the top floor of the Courthouse, the courtroom emptied, and the Wrights simply went home. There was nothing to do but wait for Monday . . . and try to cheer Nora up. Nora lay on the chaise longue in her pretty bedroom, plucking the roses of her chintz window drapes. Hermy had refused to let her attend the trial; and after two days of tears, Nora had stopped fighting, exhausted. She just plucked the roses from the drapes.

But another thing happened on Friday, March the twenty-eighth. Roberta Roberts lost her job. The newspaper woman had maintained her stubborn defence of Jim Haight in her column throughout the trial—the only reporter there who had not already condemned 'God's silent man', as one of the journalistic wits had dubbed him, to

144

death. On Friday Roberta received a wire from Boris Connell in Chicago, notifying her that he was 'yanking the column'. Roberta telegraphed a Chicago attorney to bring suit against News & Features Syndicate. But on Saturday morning there was no column.

'What are you going to do now?' asked Ellery Queen.

'Stay on in Wrightsville. I'm one of those pesky females who never give up. I can still do Jim Haight some good.'

She spent the whole of Saturday morning in Jim's cell, urging him to speak up, to fight back, to strike a blow in his own defence. Judge Martin was there, quite pursy-lipped, and Ellery; they heard Roberta's vigorous plea in silence. But Jim merely shook his head, or made no answering gesture at all—a figure bowed, three-quarters dead, pickled in some strange formaldehyde of his own manufacture.

22. *Council of War*

THE WHOLE week end stood between them and Monday. So on Saturday night Nora invited Roberta Roberts and Judge Eli Martin to dinner to 'talk things over' with the family. Hermione wanted Nora to stay in bed, because of her 'condition'; but Nora said: 'Oh, Mother, it will do me lots more good to be up on my feet and going through some motions!' So Hermy wisely did not press the point.

Nora was beginning to thicken noticeably about the waist; her cheeks were puffy and unhealthy-looking suddenly, and she walked about the house as if her legs were stuffed with lead. When Hermione questioned Dr Willoughby anxiously, he said that 'Nora's getting along about as well as we can expect, Hermy.' Hermy didn't dare ask him any more questions. But she rarely left Nora's side, and she would go white if she saw Nora try to lift so much as a long biography.

After dinner, which was tasteless and uneasy, they all went into the living room. Ludie had tightly flapped the blinds and lit a fire. They sat before it with the uncomfortable stiffness of people who know they should say something, but cannot think of what. There was no solace anywhere, not even in the friendly flames. It was impossible to relax—Nora was too much there. 'Mr Smith, you haven't said much tonight,' remarked Roberta Roberts at last.

Nora looked at Ellery beseechingly; but he avoided her eyes. 'There hasn't been too much to say, has there?'

'No,' the newspaper woman murmured. 'I suppose not.'

'As I see the problem before us, it's not intellectual, or emotional, but legal. Faith isn't going to acquit Jim, although it may bolster his spirits. Only facts can get him off.'

'And there aren't any!' cried Nora.

'Nora dearest,' moaned Hermy. 'Please. You heard what Dr Willoughby said about getting upset.'

'I know, Mother, I know.' Nora glanced eagerly at Judge Eli Martin, whose long fingers were bridged before his nose as he glowered at the fire. 'How does it look, Uncle Eli?'

'I wouldn't want to deceive you, Nora.' The old jurist shook his head. 'It looks just as bad as it possibly can.'

'You mean Jim hasn't got a chance?' she wailed.

'There's always a chance, Nora,' said Roberta Roberts.

'Yes,' sighed the Judge. 'You never can tell about a jury.'

'If there was only something we could *do*.' said Hermy helplessly.

John F. burrowed more deeply into his smoking jacket.

'Oh, you people!' cried Lola Wright. 'Moaning the blues! I'm sick of this sitting around, wringing our hands—' Lola flung her cigarette into the flames with disgust.

'So am I,' said Pat between her teeth. 'Sick as the devil.'

'Patricia darling,' said Hermy, 'I'm sure you'd better stay out of this discussion.'

'Of course, Momsy,' said Lola with a grimace. '*Your* baby. You'll never see Pat as anything but a long-legged brat who wouldn't drink her nice milk and kept climbing Emmy DuPré's cherry tree!'

Pat shrugged. Mr Ellery Queen regarded her with suspicion. Miss Patricia Wright had been acting peculiarly since Thursday. Too quiet. Over-thoughtful for a healthy extrovert. As if she were brewing something in that fetching skullpan of hers. He started to say something to her, but lit a cigarette instead. The Gold Rush of '49, he thought,

146

started with a battered pan in a muddy trickle of water. Who knows where the Fact may be found?

'Ellery, what *do* you think?' pleaded Nora.

'Ellery's been mulling over the case looking for a loophole,' Pat explained to Judge Martin.

'Not legally,' Ellery hastened to explain as the Judge's brows went up. 'But I've been handling crime facts so long in fiction that I've—uh—acquired a certain dexterity in handling them in real life.'

'If you juggle *these* with any success,' growled the old lawyer, 'you're a magician.'

'Isn't there *anything?*' Nora cried.

'Let's face it, Nora,' said Ellery grimly. 'Jim's in a hopeless position. You'd better prepare yourself . . . I've gone over the whole case. I've sifted every grain of evidence in the hopper, I've weighed every known fact. I've re-examined each incident a dozen times. And I haven't found a loophole. There's never been so one-sided a case against a defendant. Carter Bradford and Chief Dakin have built a giant, and it will take a miracle to topple it over.'

'And I,' said Judge Eli dryly, 'am no Goliath.'

'Oh, I'm prepared all right,' said Nora with a bitter laugh. She twisted about violently in her chair and dropped her face on her arms.

'Sudden movements!' said Hermy in an alarmed voice. 'Nora, you've *got* to be careful!' Nora nodded without raising her head. And silence entered, to fill the room to bursting.

'Look here,' said Ellery at last. He was a black man against the flames. 'Miss Roberts, I want to know something.'

The newspaper woman said slowly: 'Yes, Mr Smith?'

'You've lost your column because you chose to buck public opinion and fight for Jim Haight.'

'This is still a free country, thank God,' said Roberta lightly. But she was sitting very still.

'Why have you taken such a remarkable interest in this case—even to the point of sacrificing your job?'

'I happen to believe Jim Haight is innocent.'

'In the face of all the evidence against him?'

She smiled. 'I'm a woman. I'm psychic. That's two reasons.'

'No,' said Ellery.

Roberta got to her feet. 'I'm not sure I like that,' she said clearly. 'What are you trying to say?' The others were

147

frowning. There was something in the room that crackled more loudly than the burning logs.

'It's too beautiful,' mocked Mr Queen. 'Too, too beautiful. Hard-boiled newspaper woman renounces livelihood to defend total stranger who—all the facts and all the world agree—is guilty as Cain. There's an excuse for Nora—she's in love with the man. There's an excuse for the Wrights—they want their son-in-law cleared for the sake of their daughter and grandchild. But what's yours?'

'I've told you!'

'I don't believe you.'

'You don't. What am I supposed to do—care?'

'Miss Roberts,' said Ellery in a hard voice, 'what are you concealing?'

'I refuse to submit to this third degree.'

'Sorry! But it's plain you do know something. You've known something from the time you came to Wrightsville. What you know has *forced* you to come to Jim's defence. *What is it?*'

The newspaper woman gathered her gloves and silver-fox coat and bag. 'There are times, Mr Smith,' she said, 'when I dislike you very much . . . No, please, Mrs Wright. Don't bother.' She went out with a quick step.

Mr Queen stared at the space she had just vacated. 'I thought,' he said apologetically, 'I might be able to irritate it out of her.'

'I think,' said Judge Martin reflectively, 'I'll have a heart-to-heart talk with that female.'

Ellery shrugged. 'Lola.'

'Me?' said Lola surprised. 'What did I do, teacher?'

'You've concealed something, too.'

Lola stared. Then she laughed and lit a cigarette. 'You *are* in a Scotland Yard mood tonight, aren't you?'

'Don't you think the time has come,' smiled Mr Queen, 'to tell Judge Martin about your visit to the back door of Nora's house just before midnight New Year's Eve?'

'Lola!' gasped Hermy. 'You were *there?*'

'Oh, it's nothing at all, Mother,' said Lola impatiently. 'It hasn't a thing to do with the case. Of course, Judge, I'll tell you. But as long as we're being constructive, how about the eminent Mr Smith getting to work?'

'At what?' asked the eminent Mr Smith.

'My dear Smarty-Pants, you know a lot more than you've let on!'

'Lola,' said Nora, in despair. 'Oh, all this wrangling—'
148

'Don't you think,' cried Pat, 'that if there were something Ellery could do, he'd do it?'

'I dunno,' said Lola critically, squinting at the culprit through her cigarette smoke. 'He's a tough 'un to figure.'

'Just a minute,' said Judge Martin. 'Smith, if you know anything at all, I want to put you on the stand!'

'If I thought going on the stand for you would help, Judge,' protested Ellery, 'I'd do it. But it won't. On the contrary, it would hurt—a lot.'

'Hurt Jim's case?'

'It would just about cement his conviction.'

John F. spoke for the first time. 'You mean you *know* Jim is guilty, young man?'

'I didn't say that,' growled Ellery. 'But my testimony would make things look so black against him—it would establish so clearly that no one but Jim could have poisoned that cocktail—that you wouldn't be able to shake it with the Supreme Court to help you. *I musn't take the stand.*'

'Mr Smith.' Chief Dakin, alone . . . 'Sorry to bust in this way, folks,' said the police chief gruffly, 'but this was one subpoena I had to serve myself.'

'Subpoena? On me?' asked Ellery.

'Yes, sir. Mr Smith, you're summoned to appear in court Monday morning to testify for the People in the case of People Against James Haight.'

PART FIVE

23. *Lola and the Check*

'I GOT one, too,' murmured Lola to Ellery Queen in the courtroom Monday morning.

'Got one what?'

'A summons to testify today for the beloved People.'

'Strange,' muttered Mr Queen.

'The pup's got something up his sleeve,' said Judge Martin. 'And what's J.C. doing in court?'

'Who?' Ellery loked about.

'J.C. Pettigrew, the real estate man. There's Bradford whispering to him. J.C. can't know anything about this case.'

Lola said in a strangled voice: 'Oh, nuts,' and they stared at her. She was very pale.

'What's the matter, Lola?' asked Pat.

'Nothing. I'm sure it can't possibly—'

'Here's Newbold,' said Judge Martin, hastily standing up. 'Remember, Lola, just answer Carter's questions. Don't volunteer information. Maybe,' he whispered grimly as the bailiff shouted to the courtroom to rise, 'maybe I've got a trick or two myself on cross-examination!'

J.C. Pettigrew sat down in the witness chair shaking and swabbing his face with a blue polka-dot handkerchief, such as the farmers around Wrightsville use. Yes, his name is J.C. Pettigrew, he is in the real estate business in Wrightsville, he's been a friend of the Wrights for many years—his daughter Carmel is Patricia Wright's best friend. (Patricia Wright compresses her lips. Her 'best friend' has not telephoned since January first.)

There was an aqueous triumph about Carter Bradford this morning. His own brow was slick with perspiration, and he and J.C. kept up a duet of handkerchiefs.

Q.—I hand you this cancelled check, Mr Pettigrew. Do you recognize it? *A.*—Yep.

Q.—Read what it says. *A.*—The date—December thirty-first, nineteen-forty. Then it says: Pay to the order of cash, one hundred dollars. Signed J.C. Pettigrew.

Q.—Did you make out this check, Mr Pettigrew? *A.*—I did.

Q.—On the date specified—the last day of last year, the day of New Year's Eve? *A.*—Yes, sir.

Q.—To whom did you give this check, Mr Pettigrew? *A.*—To Lola Wright.

Q.—Tell us the circumstances of your giving Miss Lola Wright this check for a hundred dollars, please. *A.*—I sort of feel funny about . . . I mean, I can't help it . . . Well, last day of the year, I was just cleaning up at my office in High Village when Lola came in. Said she was in a bad spot, and she'd known me all her life, and could I let her have a hundred dollars. I saw she was worried—

Q.—Just tell us what she said and you said. *A.*—Well, that's all, I guess. I gave it to her. Oh, yes. She asked for cash. I said I didn't have any cash to spare, and it was past banking hours, so I'd give her a check. She said: 'Well, if it can't be helped, it can't be helped.' So I made out a check, she said thanks, and that's all. Can I go now?

Q.—Did Miss Wright tell you what she wanted the money for? *A.*—No, sir, and I didn't ask her.

The check was placed in evidence, and when Judge Martin, who had been about to demand the deletion of all J.C.'s remarks, turned the check over and saw what was written on the other side, he blanched and bit his lip. Then he waved his hand magnanimously and declined to cross-examine. J.C. stumbled and almost fell, he was so anxious to get off the stand. He sent Hermy a sickly smile. His face was steaming, and he kept swabbing it.

Lola Wright was nervous as she took the oath, but her gaze was defiant, and it made Carter Bradford flush. He showed her the check in evidence. 'Miss Wright, what did you do with this check when you first received it from J.C. Pettigrew on December thirty-first last?'

'I put it in my purse,' said Lola. There were titters. But Judge Martin frowned, so Lola sat up straighter.

'Yes I know,' said Carter, 'but to whom did you give it?'

152

'I don't remember.'

Foolish girl, thought Ellery. He's got you. Don't make things worse by being difficult. Bradford held the check up before her. 'Miss Wright, perhaps this will refresh your memory. Read the endorsement on the back, please.'

Lola swallowed. Then she said in a low voice: ' "James Haight." ' At the defence table James Haight unaccountably seized that instant to smile. It was the weariest smile imaginable. Then he sank into apathy again.

'Can you explain how James Haight's endorsement appears on a check you borrowed from J.C. Pettigrew?'

'I gave it to Jim.'

'When?'

'That same night.'

'Where?'

'At the house of my sister Nora.'

'At the house of your sister Nora. Have you heard the testimony here to the effect that you were not present at the house of your sister Nora during the New Year's Eve party?'

'Yes.'

'Well, were you or weren't you?'

There was something in Bradford's voice that was a little cruel, and Pat writhed in her seat in front of the rail, her lips saying: 'I hate you!' almost aloud.

'I did stop at the house for a few minutes, but I wasn't at the party.'

'I see. Were you invited to the party?'

'Yes.'

'But you didn't go?'

'No.'

'Why not?'

Judge Martin objected, and Judge Newbold sustained him. Bradford smiled. 'Did anyone see you but your brother-in-law, the defendant?'

'No. I went around to the back door of the kitchen.'

'Then did you *know* Jim Haight was in the kitchen?' asked Carter Bradford quickly.

Lola grew pink. 'Yes. I hung around outside in the back yard till I saw, through the kitchen window, that Jim came in. He disappeared in the butler's pantry, and I thought there might be someone with him. But after a few minutes I decided he was alone, and knocked. Jim came out of the pantry to the kitchen door, and we talked.'

'About what, Miss Wright?'

Lola glanced at Judge Martin in a confused way. He made as if to rise, then sank back.

'I gave Jim the check.' Ellery was leaning far forward. So that had been Lola's mission! He had not been able to overhear, or see, what had passed between Jim and Lola at the back door of Nora's kitchen that night.

'You gave him the check,' said Bradford courteously. 'Miss Wright, did the defendant ask you to give him money?'

'No!'

Ellery smiled grimly. Liar—of the genus white.

'But didn't you borrow the hundred dollars from Mr Pettigrew for the purpose of giving it to the defendant?'

'Yes,' said Lola coolly. 'Only it was in repayment of a debt I owed Jim. I owe everybody, you see—chronic borrower. I'd borrowed from Jim some time before, so I paid him back, that's all.'

And Ellery recalled that night when he had trailed Jim to Lola's apartment in Low Village, and how Jim had drunkenly demanded money and Lola had said she didn't have any . . . Only it wasn't true that on New Year's Eve Lola had repaid a 'debt'. Lola had made a donation to Nora's happiness.

'You borrowed from Pettigrew to pay Haight?' asked Carter, raising his eyebrows. (*Laughter.*)

'The witness has answered,' said Judge Eli.

Bradford waved. 'Miss Wright, did Haight ask you for the money you say you owed him?'

Lola said, too quickly: 'No, he didn't.'

'You just decided suddenly, on the last day of the year, that you'd better pay him back—without any suggestion from him?' Objection. Argument. At it again.

'Miss Wright, you have only a small income, have you not?' Objection. Argument. Heat now. Judge Newbold excused the jury. Bradford said sternly to Judge Newbold: 'Your Honor, it is important to the People to show that this witness, herself in badly reduced circumstances, was nevertheless somehow induced by the defendant to get money for him, thus indicating his basic character, how desperate he was for money—all part of the People's case to show his gain motive for the poisoning.' The jury was brought back. Bradford went at Lola once more, with savage persistence. Feathers flew again; but when it was over, the jury was convinced of Bradford's point, juries being notoriously unable to forget what judges instruct them to forget.

But Judge Martin was not beaten. On cross-examination he sailed in almost with joy. 'Miss Wright,' said the old lawyer, 'you have testified in direct examination that on the night of New Year's Eve last you called at the back door of your sister's house. What time was that visit, do you recall?'

'Yes. I looked at my wrist watch, because I had a—a party of my own to go to in town. It was just before midnight—fifteen minutes before the New Year was rung in.'

'You also testified that you saw your brother-in-law go into the butler's pantry, and after a moment or two you knocked and he came out to you, and you talked. Where exactly did that conversation take place?'

'At the back door of the kitchen.'

'What did you say to Jim?'

'I asked him what he was doing, and he said he was just finishing mixing a lot of Manhattan cocktails for the crowd—he'd about got to the maraschino cherries when I knocked, he said. Then I told him about the check—'

'Did you see the cocktails he referred to?'

The room rustled like an agitated aviary, and Carter Bradford leaned forward, frowning. This was important—this was the time the poisoning must have taken place. After that ripple of sound, the courtroom was very still. 'No,' said Lola. 'Jim had come from the direction of the pantry to answer the door, so I know that's where he'd been mixing the cocktails. From where I was standing, at the back door, I couldn't see into the pantry. So of course I couldn't see the cocktails, either.'

'Ah! Miss Wright, had someone sneaked into the kitchen from the main hall or the dining room while you and Mr Haight were talking at the back door, would you have been able to see the person?'

'No. The door from the dining room doesn't open into the kitchen; it leads directly into the pantry. And while the door from the hall does open into the kitchen and *is* visible from the back door, I couldn't see it because Jim was standing in front of me, blocking my view.'

'In other words, Miss Wright, while you and Mr Haight were talking—Mr Haight with his back to the rest of the kitchen, you unable to see most of the kitchen because he was blocking your view—someone *could* have slipped into the kitchen through the hall door, crossed to the pantry, and retraced his steps without either of you being aware of what had happened or who it had been?'

'That's correct, Judge.'

'Or someone could have entered the pantry through the dining room during that period, and neither you nor Mr Haight could have seen him?'

'Of course we couldn't have seen him. I told you that the pantry is out of sight of—'

'How long did this conversation at the back door take?'

'Oh, five minutes, I should think.'

'That will be all, thank you,' said the Judge triumphantly.

Carter Bradford climbed to his feet for a redirect examination. The courtroom was whispering, the jury looked thoughtful, and Carter's hair looked excited. But he was very considerate in manner and tone. 'Miss Wright, I know this is painful for you, but we must get this story of yours straight. *Did* anyone enter the pantry either through the kitchen or the dining room while you were conversing at the back door with Jim Haight?'

'I don't know. I merely said someone could have, and we wouldn't have known the difference.'

'Then you can't really say that someone *did?*'

'I can't say someone did, but by the same token I can't say someone didn't. As a matter of fact, it might very easily have happened.'

'But you *didn't* see anyone enter the pantry, and you *did* see Jim Haight come out of the pantry?'

'Yes, but—'

'And you saw Jim Haight go back into the pantry?'

'No such thing,' said Lola with asperity. 'I turned around and went away, leaving Jim at the door!'

'That's all,' said Carter softly; he even tried to help her off the stand, but Lola drew herself up and went back to her chair haughtily.

'I should like,' said Carter to the Court, 'to recall one of my previous witnesses. Frank Lloyd.'

As the bailiff bellowed: 'Frank Lloyd to the stand!' Mr Ellery Queen said to himself: 'The build-up.'

Lloyd's cheeks were yellow, as if something were rotting his blood. He shuffled to the stand, unkempt, slovenly, tightmouthed. He looked once at Jim Haight, not ten feet away from him. Then he looked away, but there was evil in his green eyes. He was on the stand only a few minutes. The substance of his testimony, surgically excised by Bradford, was that he now recalled an important fact which he had forgotten in his previous testimony. Jim Haight had not been the only one out of the living room during the time he was mixing the last batch of cocktails before midnight. There had been one other.

Q.—And who was that, Mr Lloyd? *A.*—A guest of the Wrights'. Ellery Smith.

You clever animal, thought Ellery admiringly. And now I'm the animal, and I'm trapped . . . What to do?

Q.—Mr Smith left the room directly after the defendant? *A.*—Yes. He didn't return until Haight came back with the tray of cocktails and started passing them around.

This is it, thought Mr Queen. Carter Bradford turned around and looked directly into Ellery's eyes. 'I call,' said Cart with a snap in his voice, 'Ellery Smith.'

24. *Ellery Smith to the Stand*

As MR Ellery Queen left his seat, and crossed the courtroom foreground, and took the oath, and sat down in the witness chair, his mind was not occupied with Prosecutor Bradford's unuttered questions or his own unuttered answers. He was reasonably certain what questions Bradford intended to ask, and he was positive what answers he would give. Bradford knew, or guessed, from the scene opened up to him by Frank Lloyd's delayed recollection, what part the mysterious Mr 'Smith' had played that bitter night. So one question would lead to another, and suspicion would become certainty, and sooner or later the whole story would have to come out. It never occurred to Ellery that he might frankly lie. Not because he was a saint, or a moralist, or afraid of consequences; but because his whole training had been in the search for truth, and he knew that whereas murder will not necessarily out, the truth must. So it was more practical to tell the truth than to tell the lie. Moreover, people expected you to lie in court, and therein lay a great advantage, if only you were clever enough to seize it.

No, Mr Queen's thoughts were occupied with another question altogether. And that was: How turn the truth, so damning to Jim Haight on its face, to Jim Haight's ad-

157

vantage? That would be a shrewd blow, if only it could be delivered; and it would have the additional strength of unexpectedness, for surely young Bradford would never anticipate what he himself, now, on the stand, could not even imagine.

So Mr Queen sat waiting, his brain not deigning to worry, but flexing itself, exploring, dipping into its deepest pockets, examining all the things he knew for a hint, a clue, a road to follow.

Another conviction crept into his consciousness as he answered the first routine questions about his name and occupation and connection with the Wright family, and so on; and it arose from Carter Bradford himself. Bradford was disciplining his tongue, speaking impersonally; but there was a bitterness about his speech that was not part of the words he was uttering. Cart was remembering that this lean and quiet-eyed man theoretically at his mercy was, in a sense, an author of more than books—he was the author of Mr Bradford's romantic troubles, too. Patty's personality shimmered between them, and Mr Queen remarked it with satisfaction; it was another advantage he held over his inquisitor. For Patty blinded young Mr Bradford's eyes and drugged his quite respectable intelligence. Mr Queen noted the advantage and tucked it away and returned to his work of concentration while the uppermost forces of his mind paid attention to the audible questions.

And suddenly he saw how he could make the truth work for Jim Haight! He almost chuckled as he leaned back and gave his whole mind to the man before him. The very first pertinent question reassured him—Bradford was on the trail, his tongue hanging out.

'Do you recollect, Mr Smith, that we found the three letters in the defendant's handwriting as a result of Mrs Haight's hysterical belief that you had told us about them?'

'Yes.'

'Do you also recall two unsuccessful attempts on my part that day to find out from you what you knew about the letters?'

'Quite well.'

Bradford said softly: 'Mr Smith, today you are on the witness stand, under oath to tell the whole truth. I now ask you: Did you know of the existence of those three letters before Chief Dakin found them in the defendant's house?'

And Ellery said: 'Yes, I did.'

Bradford was surprised, almost suspicious. 'When did you first learn about them?'

Ellery told him, and Bradford's surprise turned into satisfaction. 'Under what circumstances?' This was a rapped question, tinged with contempt. Ellery answered meekly.

'Then you knew Mrs Haight was in danger from her husband?'

'Not at all. I knew there were three letters saying so by implication.'

'Well, did you or did you not believe the defendant wrote those letters?'

Judge Martin made as if to object, but Mr Queen caught the Judge's eye and shook his head ever so slightly.

'I didn't know.'

'Didn't Miss Patricia Wright identify her brother-in-law's handwriting for you, as you just testified?'

Miss Patricia Wright, sitting fifteen feet away, looked murder at them both impartially.

'She did. But that did not make it so.'

'Did you check up yourself?'

'Yes. But I don't pretend to be a handwriting expert.'

'But you must have come to some conclusion, Mr Smith?'

'Objection!' shouted Judge Martin, unable to contain himself. 'His conclusion.'

'Strike out the question,' directed Judge Newbold.

Bradford smiled. 'You also examined the volume belonging to the defendant, Edgcomb's *Toxicology*, particularly pages seventy-one and seventy-two, devoted to arsenic, with certain sentences underlined in red crayon?'

'I did.'

'You knew from the red-crayon underlining in the book that if a crime *were* going to be committed, death by arsenic poisoning was indicated?'

'We could quarrel about the distinction between certainty and probability,' replied Mr Queen sadly, 'but to save argument—let's say I knew; yes.'

'It seems to me, Your Honor,' said Eli Martin in a bored voice, 'that this is an entirely improper line of questioning.'

'How so, Counsel?' inquired Judge Newbold.

'Because Mr Smith's thoughts and conclusions, whether certainties, probabilities, doubts, or anything else, have no conceivable bearing upon the facts at issue.'

159

Bradford smiled again, and when Judge Newbold asked him to limit his questions to events and conversations, he nodded carelessly, as if it did not matter. 'Mr Smith, were you aware that the third letter of the series talked about the "death" of Mrs Haight as if it had occurred on New Year's Eve?'

'Yes.'

'During the New Year's Eve party under examination, did you keep following the defendant out of the living room?'

'I did.'

'You were keeping an eye on him all evening?'

'Yes.'

'You watched him mix cocktails in the pantry?'

'Yes.'

'Now do you recall the last time before midnight the defendant mixed cocktails?'

'Distinctly.'

'Where did he mix them?'

'In the butler's pantry off the kitchen.'

'Did you follow him there from the living room?'

'Yes, by way of the hall. The hall leads from the foyer to the rear of the house. He entered the kitchen and went into the pantry; I was just behind him but stopped in the hall, beside the door.'

'Did he see you?'

'I haven't the faintest idea.'

'But you were careful not to be seen?'

Mr Queen smiled. 'I was neither careful nor careless. I just stood there beside the half-open hall door to the kitchen.'

'Did the defendant turn around to look at you?' persisted Bradford.

'No.'

'But *you* could see *him?*'

'Clearly.'

'What did the defendant do?'

'He prepared some Manhattan cocktails in a mixing glass. He poured some into each of a number of clean glasses standing on a tray. He was reaching for the bottle of maraschino cherries, which had been standing on the pantry table, when there was a knock at the back door. He left the cocktails and went out into the kitchen to see who had knocked.'

'That was when Miss Lola Wright and the defendant had the conversation just testified to?'

'Yes.'

'The tray of cocktails left in the butler's pantry were visible to you all during the period in which the defendant conversed with Lola Wright at the kitchen back door?'

'Yes, indeed.'

Carter Bradford hesitated. Then he asked flatly: 'Did you see anyone go near those cocktails between the time the defendant left them in the pantry and the time he returned?'

Mr Queen replied: 'I saw no one, because there wasn't anyone.'

'The pantry remained absolutely empty during that period?'

'Of organic life—yes.'

Bradford could scarcely conceal his elation; he made a brave but unsuccessful effort. On the mourners' bench inside the railing the Wrights turned stone-faced. 'Now, Mr Smith, did you see the defendant return to the pantry after Lola Wright left?'

'I did.'

'What did he do?'

'He dropped a maraschino cherry from the bottle into each cocktail, using a small ivory pick. He picked up the tray in both hands and carefully walked through the kitchen toward the door at which I was standing. I acted casual, and we went into the living room together, where he immediately began distributing the glasses to the family and guests.'

'On his walk from the pantry to the living room with the tray, did anyone approach him except yourself?'

'No one.'

Ellery waited for the next question with equanimity. He saw the triumph gather in Bradford's eyes.

'Mr Smith, wasn't there something else you saw happen in that pantry?'

'No.'

'Nothing else happened?'

'Nothing else.'

'Have you told us *everything* you saw?'

'Everything.'

'*Didn't you see the defendant drop a white powder into one of those cocktails?*'

'No,' said Mr Queen. 'I saw nothing of the sort.'

'Then on the trip from the pantry to the living room?'

'Both Mr Haight's hands were busy holding the tray. He dropped no foreign substance of any kind into any of the

161

cocktails at any time during their preparation or while he carried the tray into the living room.'

And then there was an undercurrent jabber in the room, and the Wrights glanced at one another with relief while Judge Martin wiped his face and Carter Bradford sneered almost with sound. 'Perhaps you turned your head for two seconds?'

'My eyes were on that tray of cocktails continuously.'

'You didn't look away for even a second, eh?'

'For even a second,' said Mr Queen regretfully, as if he wished he had, just to please Mr Bradford.

Mr Bradford grinned at the jury—man to man; and at least five jurors grinned back. Sure, what could you expect? —a friend of the Wrights'. And then everybody in town knew why Cart Bradford had stopped seeing Pat Wright. This Smith bird had a case on Patty Wright. So . . .

'And you didn't see Jim Haight drop arsenic into one of those cocktails?' insisted Mr Bradford, smiling broadly now.

'At the risk of seeming a bore,' replied Mr Queen with courtesy, 'no, I did not.' But he knew he had lost with the jury; they didn't believe him. He knew it, and while the Wrights didn't know it yet, Judge Martin did; the old gentleman was beginning to sweat again. Only Jim Haight sat unmoved, unchanged, wrapped in a shroud.

'Well, then, Mr Smith, answer this question: Did you see anyone else who had the *opportunity* to poison one of those cocktails?'

Mr Queen gathered himself, but before he could reply Bradford snapped: 'In fact, did you see anyone else who *did* poison one of those cocktails—anyone other than the defendant?'

'I saw no one else but—'

'In other words, Mr Smith,' cried Bradford, 'the defendant James Haight was not only in the *best* position, but he was in the *only* position, to poison that cocktail?'

'No,' said Mr Smith. And then *he* smiled. You asked for it, he thought, and I'm giving it to you. The only trouble is, I'm giving it to myself, too, and that's foolishness. He sighed and wondered what his father, Inspector Queen, no doubt reading about the case in the New York papers and conjecturing who Ellery Smith was, would have to say when he discovered Mr 'Smith's' identity and read about this act of puerile bravado.

Carter Bradford looked blank. Then he shouted: 'Are you aware that this is perjury, Smith? You just testified that no one else entered the pantry! No one approached the

162

defendant while he was carrying the cocktails into the living room! Allow me to repeat a question or two. *Did* anyone approach the defendant during his walk to the living room with the tray?'

'No,' said Mr Queen patiently.

'*Did* some else enter the pantry while the defendant was talking to Lola Wright at the back door?'

'No.'

Bradford was almost speechless. 'But you just said——! Smith, who but James Haight *could* have poisoned one of those cocktails, by your own testimony?'

Judge Martin was on his feet, but before he could get the word 'Objection' out of his mouth, Ellery said calmly: '*I could.*' There was a wholesale gasp before him and then a stricken silence. So he went on: 'You see, it would have been the work of ten seconds for me to slip from behind the door of the hall, cross the few feet of kitchen to the pantry unobserved by Jim or Lola at the back door, drop arsenic into one of the cocktails, return the same way . . .'

And there was Babel all over again, and Mr Queen looked down upon the noise makers from the highest point of his tower, smiling benignly. He was thinking: It's full of holes, but it's the best a man can do on short notice with the material at hand.

Over shouting, and Judge Newbold's gavel, and the rush of reporters, Carter Bradford bellowed in triumph: *Well, DID you poison that cocktail, Smith?'*

There were several instants of quiet again, during which Judge Martin's voice was heard to say feebly: 'I object——' and Mr Queen's voice topped the Judge's by adding neatly: 'On constitutional grounds——'

Then hell broke loose, and Judge Newbold broke his gavel off at the head, and roared to the bailiff to clear the damn courtroom, and then he hog-called a recess until the next morning and practically ran into his chanbers, where it is presumed he applied vinegar compresses to his forehead.

25. *The Singular Request of Miss Patricia Wright*

BY THE next morning several changes had taken place. Wrightsville's attention was temporarily transferred from one Jim Haight to one Ellery Smith. Frank Lloyd's newspaper came out with a blary edition reporting the sensational facts of Mr Smith's testimony; and an editorial which said, in part:—

> The bombshell of Mr. Smith's testimony yesterday turns out to be a dud. There is no possible case against this man. Smith has no possible motive. He had not known Nora or James Haight or any of the Wrights before he came to Wrightsville last August. He has had practically no contact with Mrs. Haight, and less than that with Rosemary Haight. Whatever his reason for the quixotic nature of his farcical testimony yesterday—and Prosecutor Bradford is to be censured for his handling of the witness, who obviously led him on—it means nothing. Even if Smith were the only other person aside from Jim Haight who could have poisoned the fatal cocktail on New Year's Eve, he could not possibly have been sure that the one poisoned cocktail would reach Nora Haight, whereas Jim Haight could have and, in effect, did. Nor could Smith have written the three letters, which are indisputably in the handwriting of James Haight. Wrightsville and the jury can only conclude that what happened yesterday was either a desperate gesture of friendliness on Smith's part or a cynical bid for newspaper space by a writer who is using Wrightsville as a guinea-pig.

The first thing Bradford said to Ellery on the stand the next morning was:—'I show you the official transcript of your testimony yesterday. Will you please begin to read?'

Ellery raised his brows, but he took the transcript and read:

' "Question: What is your name? Answer: Ellery Smith—" '

164

'Stop right there! That *is* what you testified, isn't it—that your name is Ellery Smith?'

'Yes,' said Ellery, beginning to feel cold.

'Is Smith your real name?'

Ho hum, thought Ellery. The man's a menace. 'No.'

'An assumed name, then?'

'Order in the court!' shouted the baliff.

'Yes.'

'What is your real name?'

Judge Martin said quickly: 'I don't see the point of this line of questioning, Your Honor. Mr Smith is not on trial—'

'Mr Bradford?' said Judge Newbold, who was looking curious.

'Mr Smith's testimony yesterday,' said Bradford with a faint smile, 'raised a certain logical question about what the People allege to have been the defendant's unique opportunity to poison the cocktail. Mr Smith testified that he himself was in a position to have poisoned the cocktail. My examination this morning, then, must necessarily include an examination of Mr Smith's character—'

'And you can establish Mr Smith's character by bringing out his true name?' asked Judge Newbold, frowning.

'Yes, Your Honor.'

'I think I'll allow this, Counsel, pending testimony.'

'Will you please answer my last question,' said Bradford to Ellery. 'What is your real name?'

Ellery saw the Wrights looking bewildered—all but Pat, who was biting her lip with vexation as well as perplexity. But it was quite clear to him that Bradford had been busy through the intervening night. The name 'Queen' carried no theoretical immunity against a charge of murder, of course; but as a practical measure its revelation would banish from the minds of the jury any notion that its well-known bearer could have had anything to do with the crime. The jig was up. Ellery Queen sighed and said: 'My name is Ellery Queen.'

Judge Martin did his best, under the circumstances. The punctuality of Bradford's timing became evident. By putting Ellery on the stand Bradford had given the defence a handhold to an important objective. But the objective was lost in the revelation of Ellery's true identity. Judge Martin hammered away at the anvil of one point. 'Mr Queen, as a trained observer of criminal phenomena, you were interested in the possibilities of this case?'

'Immensely.'

'That is why you kept James Haight under unrelaxing observation New Year's Eve?'

"That, and a personal concern for the Wright family.'

'You were watching for a possible poisoning attempt on Haight's part?'

'Yes,' said Ellery simply.

Did you see any such attempt on Haight's part?'

'I did not!'

'You saw James Haight make no slightest gesture or motion which might have concealed a dropping of arsenic into one of the cocktail glasses?'

'I saw no such gesture or motion.'

'And you were watching for that, Mr Queen?'

'Exactly.'

'That's all,' said Judge Martin in triumph.

The newspapers all agreed that Mr Ellery Queen, who was in Wrightsville seeking material for a new detective story, had seized upon this hell-sent opportunity to illuminate the cause of dark letters with some national publicity. And Bradford, with a grim look, rested for the People.

The week end intervened, and everybody involved in the case went home or to his hotel room or, as in the case of the out-of-town newspaper people, to their cots in the lobby of the Hollis; and all over town people were agreeing that it looked black for Jim Haight, and why shouldn't it—he did it, didn't he? The roadhouses and taverns were jammed over the week end, and there was considerable revelry. On Friday night, however, the unofficial committee for the defence of James Haight met again in the Wright living room, and the atmosphere was blue with despair. Nora said to Ellery, to Judge Martin, to Roberta Roberts: 'What do you think?'—painfully and without hope; and all they could do was shake their heads.

'Queen's testimony would have helped a great deal more,' growled old Judge Eli, 'if that jury weren't so dad-blamed set on Jim's guilt. No, Nora, it looks bad, and I'm not going to tell you anything different.' Nora stared blindly into the fire.

'To think that you've been Ellery Queen all along,' sighed Hermy. 'I suppose there was a time when I'd have been thrilled, Mr Queen. But I'm so washed-out these days—'

'Momsy,' murmured Lola, 'where's your fighting spirit?'

Hermy smiled, but she excused herself to go upstairs to bed, her feet dragging. And after a while John F. said:

166

'Thanks, Queen,' and went off after Hermy, as if Hermy's going had made him a little uneasy.

And they sat there without speaking for a long time, until Nora said: 'At least, Ellery, what you saw confirms Jim's innocence. That's something. It ought to mean *something*. Heavens,' she cried, 'they've got to believe you!'

'Let's hope they do.'

'Judge Martin,' said Roberta suddenly. 'Monday's your day to begin howling. What are you going to howl about?'

'Suppose you tell me,' said Judge Martin.

Her glance fell first. 'I have nothing to tell that could help,' she said in a faint voice.

'Then I *was* right,' murmured Ellery. 'Don't you think others might make better judges—' Something crashed. Pat was on her feet, and the sherry glass from which she had been sipping lay in little glittery fragments in the fireplace, surrounded by blue flames.

'What's the matter with *you?*' demanded Lola. 'If this isn't the screwiest family!'

'I'll tell you what's the matter with me,' panted Pat. 'I'm through sitting on my—sitting around and imitating Uriah Heep. I'm going to *do* something!'

'Patty,' gasped Nora, looking at her younger sister as if Pat had suddenly turned into a female Mr Hyde.

Lola murmured: 'What in hell are you babbling about, Patticums?'

'I've got an idea!'

'The little one's got an idea,' grinned Lola. 'I had an idea once. Next thing I knew I was divorcing a heel and everybody began to call me an amptray. Siddown, Snuffy.'

'Wait a moment,' said Ellery. 'It's possible. What idea, Pat?'

'Go ahead and be funny,' said Pat hotly. 'All of you. But I've worked out a plan, and I'm going through with it.'

'What kind of plan?' demanded Judge Martin. 'I'll listen to anyone, Patricia.'

'Will you?' jeered Pat. 'Well, I'm not talking. You'll know when the time comes, Uncle Eli! You've got to do just one thing—'

'And that is?'

'To call me as *the last witness for the defence!*'

The Judge began in bewilderment: 'But what—?'

'Yes, what's stewing?' asked Ellery quickly. 'You'd better talk it over with your elders first.'

'There's been too much talk already, Grandpa.'

167

'But what do you think you're going to accomplish?'

'I want three things.' Pat looked grim. 'Time, last crack at the witness stand, and some of your new Odalisque Parfum, Nora . . . Accomplish, Mr Queen? *I'm going to save Jim!*' Nora ran out of the room, using her knitting as a handkerchief. 'Well, I will!' said Pat, exasperated. And she added, in a gun-moll undertone: 'I'll show that Carter Bradford!'

26. *Juror Number 7*

'WE WILL take,' said old Eli Martin to Mr Queen in the courtroom Monday morning, as they waited for Judge Newbold to enter from chambers, 'what the Lord provides.'

'Meaning what?' asked Ellery.

'Meaning,' sighed the lawyer, 'that unless providence intercedes, my old friend's son-in-law is a fried squab. If what I've got is a defence, may God help all petitioners for justice!'

'Legally speaking, I'm a blunderbuss. Surely you've got some sort of defence?'

'Some sort, yes.' The old gentleman squinted sourly at Jim Haight, sitting near by with his head on his breast. 'I've never had such a case!' he exploded. 'Nobody tells me anything—the defendant, the Roberts woman, the family . . . why, even that snippet Patricia won't talk to me!'

'Patty . . .' said Ellery thoughtfully.

'Pat wants me to put her on the stand, and I don't even know what for! This isn't law, it's lunacy.'

'She went out mysteriously Saturday night,' murmured Ellery, 'and again last night, and she came home very late both times.'

'While Rome burns!'

'She'd been drinking Martinis, too.'

'I forgot you're something of a sleuth. How did you find that out, Queen?'

'I kissed her.'

Judge Martin was startled. 'Kissed her? You?'

168

'I have my methods,' said Mr Queen, a whit stiffly. Then he grinned. 'But this time they didn't work. She wouldn't tell me what she'd been doing.'

'Odalisque Parfum,' sniffed the old gentleman. 'If Patricia Wright thinks a sweet *odeur* is going to divert young Bradford . . . He looks undiverted to me this morning. Doesn't he to you?'

'An immovable young man,' agreed Mr Queen uneasily.

Judge Martin sighed and glanced over at the row of chairs inside the railing, where Nora sat with her little chin raised high and a pallid face between her mother and father, her gaze fixed beggingly upon her husband's motionless profile. But if Jim was conscious of her presence, he made no sign. Behind them the courtroom was jammed and whispery.

Mr Queen was furtively scanning Miss Patricia Wright. Miss Patricia Wright had an Oppenheim air this morning—slitted eyes, and a certain enigmatic expression about the mouth Mr Queen had kissed in the interests of science the night before . . . in vain. Perhaps not quite in vain . . .

He became aware that Judge Eli was poking his ribs. 'Get up, get up. You ought to know something about courtroom etiquette! Here comes Newbold.'

'Good luck,' said Ellery absently.

The first witness Judge Martin called to testify in defence of Jim Haight was Hermione Wright. Hermy crossed the space before the Bench and mounted the step to the witness chair if not quite like royalty ascending the throne, then at least like royalty ascending the guillotine. On being sworn, she said 'I do' in a firm, if tragic, voice. Clever, thought Ellery. Putting Hermy on the stand. Hermy, mother of Nora. Hermy, who of all persons in the world except Nora should be Jim Haight's harshest enemy—Hermy to testify for the man who had tried to kill her daughter! The courtroom and jury were impressed by the dignity with which Hermy met all their stares. Oh, she was a fighter! And Ellery could detect the pride on the faces of her three daughters, a queer shame on Jim's, and the faint admiration of Carter Bradford.

The old lawyer led Hermione skilfully through the night of the crime, dwelling chiefly on the 'gaiety' of the occasion, how happy everyone had been, how Nora and Jim had danced together like children, and incidentally how much Frank Lloyd, who had been Bradford's chief witness to the events of the evening, had had to drink; and the Judge contrived, through Hermy's helpless, 'confused'

169

answers, to leave the impression with the jury that no one there could possibly have said for certain what had happened so far as the cocktails were concerned, let alone Frank Lloyd—unless it was Mr Ellery Queen, who'd had only one drink before the fatal toast to 1941.

And then Judge Martin led Hermione around to a conversation she had had with Jim shortly after Jim and Nora returned from their honeymoon—how Jim had confided in his mother-in-law that Nora and he suspected Nora was going to have a baby, and that Nora wanted it to be kept a secret until they were 'sure', except that Jim said he was so happy he couldn't keep it in any longer, he had to tell someone, and Hermy wasn't to let on to Nora that he'd blabbed. And how ecstatic Jim had been at the prospect of being father to Nora's child—how it would change his whole life, he said, give him a fresh push towards making a success of himself for Nora and the baby—how much he loved Nora . . . more every day.

Carter Bradford waived cross-examination with almost a visible kindliness. But there was a little whiff of applause as Hermy stepped off the witness stand.

Judge Martin called up a roll of character witnesses as long as Judge Newbold's face. Lorrie Preston and Mr Gonzales of the bank, Brick Miller the bus driver, Ma Upham, young Manager Louie Cahan of the Bijou, who had been one of Jim's bachelor cronies, Miss Aikin of the Carnegie Library—that *was* a surprise, as Miss Aikin had never been known to say a kind word about anybody, but she managed to say several about Jim Haight despite the technical limitations of 'character' testimony—chiefly, Ellery suspected, because Jim had patronized the Library in the old days and broken not a single one of Miss Aikin's numerous rules . . . The character witnesses were so many, and so socially diversified, that people were surprised. They hadn't known Jim Haight had so many friends in town. But that was exactly the impression Judge Martin was trying to make. And when John F. clambered to the stand and said simply and directly that Jim was a good boy and the Wrights were behind him heart and soul, people remarked how old John F. looked—'aged a lot these past couple of months, John F. has'—and a tide of sympathy for the Wrights began to creep up in the courtroom until it was actually lapping Jim Haight's shoes.

During the days of this character testimony, Carter Bradford maintained a decent respect for the Wrights—

just the proper note of deference and consideration, but a little aloof, as if to say: 'I'm not going to badger your people, but don't expect my relationship with your family to influence my conduct in this courtroom one iota!'

Then Judge Martin called Lorenzo Grenville. Lorenzo Grenville was a drippy-eyed little man with hourglass cheeks and a tall Hoover collar, size sixteen, out of which his neck protruded like a withered root. He identified himself as a handwriting expert.

Mr Grenville agreed that he had sat in the courtroom from the beginning of the trial, that he had heard the testimony of the People's experts regarding the authenticity of the handwriting in the three letters alleged to have been written by the defendant; that he had had ample opportunity to examine said letters, also undisputed samples of the defendant's true handwriting; and that in his 'expert' opinion there was grave reason to doubt James Haight's authorship of the three letters in evidence.

'As a recognized authority in the field of handwriting analysis, you do not believe Mr Haight wrote the three letters?'

'I do not.' (The Prosecutor leers at the jury, and the jury leers back.)

'Why don't you believe so, Mr Grenville?' asked the Judge.

Mr Grenville went into punctilious detail. Since he drew almost exactly opposite conclusions from the identical data which the jury had heard the People's experts say proved Jim Haight *had* written those letters, several jurymen were not unnaturally confused; which contented Judge Martin.

'Any other reasons for believing these letters were not written by the defendant, Mr Grenville?'

Mr Grenville had many which, edited, became a question of composition. 'The phrasing is stilted, unnatural, and is not like the defendant's ordinary letter style at all.' Mr Grenville cited chapter and verse from Haight letters in evidence.

'Then what is your opinion, Mr Grenville, as to the authorship of the three letters?'

'I am inclined to consider them forgeries.'

Mr Queen would have felt reassured, but he happened to know that a certain defendant in another case *had* written a check which Mr Lorenzo Grenville just as solemnly testified to be a forgery. There was no slightest doubt in Ellery's mind about the Haight letters. They *had*

171

been written by Jim Haight, and that's all there was to it. He wondered what Judge Martin was up to with the unreliable Mr Grenville.

He found out at once. 'Is it your considered opinion, Mr Grenville,' purred Judge Eli, 'that it would be easy, or difficult, to forge Mr Haight's handwriting?'

'Oh, very easy,' said Mr Grenville.

'Could *you* forge Mr Haight's handwriting?'

'Certainly.'

'Could you forge Mr Haight's handwriting *here and now?*'

'Well,' said Mr Grenville apologetically, 'I'd have to study the handwriting a while—say two minutes!'

Bradford was on his feet with a bellow, and there was a long, inaudible argument before Judge Newbold. Finally, the Court allowed the demonstration, the witness was provided with pen, paper, ink, and a photostatic copy of one of Jim Haight's acknowledged samples of handwriting—it happened to be a personal note written to Nora by Jim on the Wrightsville National Bank stationery, and dated four years before—and the courtroom sat on the edge of its collective seat. Lorenzo Grenville squinted at the photostat for exactly two minutes. Then, seizing the pen, he dipped it into the ink, and with a casual air wrote swiftly on the blank paper. 'I'd do better,' he said to Judge Martin, 'if I had my own pens to work with.'

Judge Martin glanced earnestly at what his witness had written, and then, with a smile, passed the sheet around the jury box, together with the photostat of Jim's undisputed handwriting. From the amazement on the jurors' faces as they compared the photostat with Grenville's forgery, Ellery knew the blow had told.

On cross-examination, Carter had only one question to ask the witness. 'Mr Grenville, how many years has it taken you to learn the art of forging handwriting?'

It seemed Mr Grenville had spent his whole life at it.

Victor Carlatti to the stand. Yes, he is the owner of a roadhouse on Route 16 called the *Hot Spot*. What sort of establishment is it? A night club.

Q.—Mr Carlatti, do you know the defendant, James Haight? *A.*—I've seen him around.

Q.—Has he ever visited your night club? *A.*—Yeah.

Q.—Drinking? *A.*—Well, a drink or two. Once in a while. It's legal.

Q.—Now, Mr Carlatti, there has been testimony here that James Haight allegedly admitted to Mrs Haight that he had 'lost money gambling' in your establishment. What do you know about this? *A.*—It's a dirty lie.

Q.—You mean James Haight has never gambled in your night club? *A.*—Sure he never. *Nobody* ever—

Q.—Has the defendant borrowed any money from you? *A.*—He nor nobody else.

Q.—Does the defendant owe you a single dollar? *A.*—Not a chip.

Q.—As far as you know, has the defendant ever 'lost' any money in your establishment? Gambling or any other way? *A.*—Maybe some broad may have took him to the cleaners while he was feeling happy, but he never shelled out one cent in my place except for drinks.

Q.—You may cross-examine, Mr Bradford.

Mr Bradford murmurs, 'With pleasure,' but only Judge Eli hears him, and Judge Eli shrugs ever so slightly and sits down.

Cross-examination by Mr Bradford:—

Q.—Carlatti, is it against the law to operate a gambling parlor? *A.*—Who says I operate a gambling parlor? Who says?

Q.—Nobody 'says', Carlatti. Just answer my question. *A.*—It's a dirty frame. Prove it. Go ahead. I ain't gonna sit here and take no double-cross—

Judge Newbold: The witness will refrain from gratuitous remarks, or he will lay himself open to contempt. Answer the question.

A.—What question, Judge?

Q.—Never mind. Do you or do you not run roulette, faro, craps, and other gambling games in the back of your so-called 'night club'? *A.*—Am I supposed to answer dirty questions like that? It's an insult, Judge. This kid ain't dry behind the ears yet, and I ain't gonna sit here and take—

Judge Newbold: One more remark like that—

Judge Martin: It seems to me, Your Honor, that this is improper cross. The question of whether the witness runs a gambling establishment or not was not part of the direct examination.

Judge Newbold: Overruled!

Judge Martin: Exception!

Mr Bradford: If Jim Haight did owe you money lost at your gambling tables, Carlatti, you'd have to deny it, wouldn't you, or face prosecution on a charge of running a gambling establishment?

Judge Martin: I move that question be stricken—

A.—What is this? All of a sudden all you guys are

getting angels. How do you think I been operating—on my sex appeal? And don't think no hick judge can scare Vic Carlatti. I got plenty of friends, and they'll see to it that Vic Carlatti ain't going to be no fall guy for some old goat of a judge and some stinker of a D.A.—

Judge Newbold: Mr. Bradford, do you have any further questions of this witness?

Mr Bradford: I think that will be quite sufficient, Your Honor.

Judge Newbold: Clerk, strike the last question and answer. The jury will disregard it. The spectators will preserve the proper decorum or the room will be cleared. Witness is held in contempt of court. Bailiff, take charge of the prisoner.

Mr Carlatti puts up his dukes as the bailiff approaches, roaring: 'Where's my mouthpiece? This ain't Nazzee Goimany!'

When Nora took the oath and sat down and began to testify in a choked voice, the court was like a church. She was the priestess, and the people listened to her with the silent unease of a sinning congregation confronted by their sins . . . Surely the woman Jim Haight had tried to do in would be against him? But Nora was not against Jim. She was for him, every cell in her. Her loyalty filled the courtroom like warm air. She made a superb witness, defending her husband from every charge. She reiterated her love for him and her unquestioning faith in his innocence. Over and over. While her eyes kept coming back to the object of her testimony, those scant few feet away, who sat with his face lowered, wearing a dull red mask of shame, blinking at the tips of his unpolished shoes.

'The idiot might be more cooperative!' thought Mr Queen angrily.

Nora could give no factual evidence to controvert the People's case. Judge Martin, who had put her on the stand for her psychological value, did not touch upon the two poisoning attempts preceding New Year's Eve; and in a genuine act of kindness, Carter Bradford waived cross-examination and the opportunity to quiz her on those attempts. Perhaps Bradford felt he would lose more in good will by grilling Nora than by letting her go.

Mr Queen, a notorious sceptic, could not be sure.

Nora was to have been Judge Martin's last witness; and indeed he was fumbling with some papers at the defence table, as if undecided whether to proceed or not, when Pat signalled him furiously from inside the railing, and the

174

old gentleman nodded with a guilty, unhappy look and said: 'I call Patricia Wright to the stand.' Mr Queen sat forward in the grip of a giant tension he could not understand.

Obviously at a loss where to begin, Judge Martin began a cautious reconnaissance, as if seeking a clue. But Pat took the reins out of his hands almost at once. She was irrepressible—deliberately, Ellery knew; but why? What was she driving at?

As a defence witness, Pat played squarely into the hands of the People. The more she said, the more damage she did to Jim's cause. She painted her brother-in-law as a scoundrel, a liar—told how he had humiliated Nora, stolen her jewelry, squandered her property, neglected her, subjected her to mental torment, quarrelled with her incessantly . . . Before she was half through, the courtroom was sibilating. Judge Martin was perspiring like a coolie and trying frantically to head her off, Nora was gaping at her sister as if she were seeing her for the first time, and Hermy and John F. slumped lower and lower in their seats, like two melting waxworks.

Judge Newbold interrupted Pat during a denunciation of Jim and an avowal of her hatred for him. 'Miss Wright, are you aware that you were called as a witness for the defence?'

Pat snapped: 'I'm sorry, Your Honor. But I can't sit here and see all this hush-hush going on when we all know Jim Haight is guilty—'

'I move—' began Judge Martin in an outraged bellow.

'Young woman—' began Judge Newbold angrily.

But Pat rushed on. 'And that's what I told Bill Ketcham only last night—'

'What!'

The explosion came from Judge Newbold, Eli Martin, and Carter Bradford simultaneously. And for a moment the room was plunged in an abyss of surprise; and then the walls cracked, and Bedlam piled upon Babel, so that Judge Newbold pounded with his third gavel of the trial, and the bailiff ran up and down shushing people, and in the press row someone started to laugh as realization came, infecting the whole row, and the row behind that. 'Your Honor,' said Judge Martin above the din, 'I want it to go on record here and now that the statement made by my witness a moment ago comes to me as an absolute shock. I had no faintest idea that—'

'Just a moment, just a moment, Counsel,' said Judge Newbold in a strangled voice. 'Miss Wright!'

'Yes, Your Honor?' asked Patty in a bewildered way, as if she couldn't imagine what all the fuss was about.

'Did I hear you correctly? Did you say you told *Bill Ketcham* something last night?'

'Why, yes, Your Honor,' said Pat respectfully. 'And Bill agreed with me—'

'I object!' shouted Carter Bradford. 'She's got it in for me! This is a put-up job——!'

Miss Wright turned innocent eyes on Mr Bradford.

'One moment, Mr Bradford!' Judge Newbold leaned far forward on the Bench. 'Bill Ketcham agreed with you, did he? What did he agree with you about? What else happened last night?'

'Well, Bill said Jim was guilty, all right, and if I'd promise to—' Pat blushed—'well, if I'd promise him a certain something, he'd see to it that Jim got what was coming to him. Said he'd talk to the others on the jury, too—being an insurance man, Bill said, he could sell anything. He said I was his dream girl, and for me he'd climb the highest mountain—'

'Silence in the court!' bellowed Judge Newbold.

And there was silence. 'Now, Miss Wright,' said Judge Newbold grimly, 'are we to understand that you had this conversation last night with the William Ketcham who is Juror Number 7 in this trial?'

'Yes, Your Honor,' said Pat, her eyes wide. 'Is anything wrong with that? I'm sure if I had known—' The rest was lost in uproar.

'Bailiff, clear the room!' screamed Judge Newbold.

'Now, then,' said Judge Newbold. 'Let's have the rest of it, if you please!'—so frigidly that Pat turned *café au lait* and tears appeared in the corners of her eyes.

'W-we went out together, Bill and I, last Saturday night. Bill said we oughtn't to be seen, maybe it wasn't legal or something, so we drove over to Slocum to a hot spot Bill knows, and—and we've been there every night since. I said Jim was guilty, and Bill said sure, he thought so too—'

'Your Honor,' said Judge Martin in a terrible voice, 'I move—'

'Oh, you do!' said Judge Newbold. 'Eli Martin, if your reputation weren't . . . You there!' he roared at the jurist. 'Ketcham! Number 7! Get up!'

176

Fat Billy Ketcham, the insurance broker, tried to obey, half hoisted himself, fell back again, and finally made it. He stood there in the rear row of the jury box, swaying a little, as if the box were a canoe.

'William Ketcham,' snarled Judge Newbold, 'have you spent every evening since last Saturday in the company of this young woman? Did you promise her to influence the rest of the jury—Bailiff! Chief Dakin! *I want that man!*'

Ketcham was trapped in the main aisle after knocking over two fellow jurors and scattering the people inside the rail like a fat tom charging a brood of chicks.

When he was hauled up before Judge Newbold, he chattered: 'I didn't m-mean any harm, J-Judge—I d-didn't think I was doing wrong, Judge—I s-swear to you—everybody knows the s-sonofabitch is guilty—'

'Take this man in custody,' whispered Judge Newbold. 'Bailiff, station guards at the doors. There will be a five-minute recess. Jury, remain where you are. No one now present is to leave the courtroom!' And Judge Newbold groped for his chambers.

'That,' said Mr Queen while they waited, 'is what comes of not locking juries in. It's also,' he added to Miss Patricia Wright, 'what comes of scatterbrained brats meddling in grown-up people's affairs!'

'Oh, Patty, how could you?' wept Hermione. 'And that impossible Ketcham man, too! I warned you he'd make improper advances if you encouraged him. You remember, John, how he used to pester Patty for dates—'

'I also remember,' said John F. wildly, 'where my old hairbrush is!'

'Look,' said Pat in a low voice. 'Jim was in a bad spot, wasn't he? All right! So I worked on Fat Billy, and he drank a lot of Martinis, and I let him make a pass or two at me . . . Go ahead and l-look at me as if I were a loose woman!' And Miss Wright began to cry. 'Just the same, I did something none of *you* has been able to do—watch and see!'

'It's true,' said Ellery hastily, 'that we had nothing to look forward to but a conviction.'

'If only . . .' began Nora, a great bright hope on her pale face. 'Oh, Patsy, you're mad, but I love you!'

'And is Cart's face r-red,' blubbered Pat. 'Thinks he's smart . . .'

'Yes,' pointed out Mr Queen dryly. 'But look at Judge Martin's.'

Old Eli Martin came over to Pat and he said: 'Patricia,

177

you've placed me in the most embarrassing position of my life. I don't care about that, or the ethics of your conduct, so much as I do about the fact that you probably haven't helped Jim's chances, you've hurt them. No matter what Newbold says or does—and he really hasn't any choice—everybody will know you did this deliberately, and it's bound to bounce back on Jim Haight.' And Judge Martin stalked away.

'I suppose,' said Lola, 'you can't scratch an ex-judge without stuffiness leaking out. Don't you worry, Snuffles! You gave Jim a zero-hour reprieve—it's better than he deserves, the dumb ox!'

'I wish to state in preamble,' said Judge Newbold coldly, 'that in all my years on the Bench I have encountered no more flagrant, disgraceful example of civic irresponsibility. William Ketcham!' He transfixed Juror Number 7, who looked as if he were about to faint, with a stern and glittering eye. 'Unfortunately, there is no statutory offense with which you can be charged, unless it can be shown that you have received property or value of some kind. For the time being, however, I order the Commissioner of Jurors to strike your name from the panel of jurors, and never so long as you are a resident of this State will you be permitted to exercise your privilege of serving on a jury.'

William Ketcham's expression said that he would gladly relinquish many more appreciated rights for the privilege of leaving the courtroom that very instant.

'Mr Bradford—' Carter looked up, thin-lipped and black-angry—'you are requested to investigate the conduct of Patricia Wright with a view toward determining whether she willfully and deliberately sought to influence Juror Number 7. If such intention can be established, I ask you to draw an indictment charging Patricia Wright with the appropriate charge—'

'Your Honor,' said Bradford in a low voice, 'the only conceivable charge I can see would be corrupting a juror, and to establish corruption it seems to me necessary to show consideration. And in this case it doesn't seem as if there was any consideration—'

'She offered her body!' snapped Judge Newbold.

'I did not!' gasped Pat. 'He asked for it, but I didn't—'

'Yes, Your Honor,' said Bradford, blushing, 'but it is a moot point whether that sort of thing constitutes legal consideration—'

'Let's not get entangled, Mr Bradford,' said Judge New-bold coldly. 'The woman is clearly guilty of embracery if she attempted to influence a juror improperly, whether she gave any consideration or not!'

'Embracery? What's that?' muttered Pat. But no one heard her except Mr Queen, who was chuckling inside.

'Also,' continued Judge Newbold slamming a book down on a heap of papers, 'I shall recommend that in future trials coming under the jurisdiction of this court, juries shall be locked in, to prevent a recurrence of this shameful incident.

'Now.' He glared at Billy Ketcham and Pat, and then at the jury. 'The facts are clear. A juror has been influenced in a manner prejudicial to the rights of the defendant to a fair trial. This is by the admission of both parties involved. If I permitted this trial to continue, it could only bring an appeal to a superior court which must, on the record, order a new trial. Consequently, to save further and needless expense, I have no choice. I regret the inconvenience and waste of time caused the remaining members of the jury; I deplore the great expense of this trial already incurred by Wright County. Much as I regret and deplore, however, the facts leave me no recourse but to declare People Against James Haight a mistrial. I do so declare, the jury is discharged with the apology and thanks of the Court, and the defendant is remanded to the custody of the Sheriff until the date of a new trial can be set. Court is adjourned!'

27. *Easter Sunday:*
Nora's Gift

THE INVADING press retreated, promising to return for the new trial; but Wrightsville remained, and Wrightsville chortled and raged and buzzed and gossiped until the very ears of the little Buddha clock on Pat's dresser were ringing.

William Ketcham, by a curious inversion, became the

179

town hero. The 'boys' stopped him on the street corners to slap his back, he sold five insurance policies he had long since given up, and, as confidence returned, he related some 'details' of his relationship with Miss Patricia Wright on the critical nights in question which, when they reached Pat's ears by way of Carmel Pettigrew (who was phoning her 'best friend' again), caused Miss Wright to go downtown to Mr Ketcham's insurance office in the Bluefield Block, grasp Mr Ketcham firmly by the collar with the left hand, and with the right slap Mr Ketcham's right cheek five ringing times, leaving assorted marks in the damp white flesh.

'Why five?' asked Mr Queen, who had accompanied Miss Wright on the excursion and had stood by, admiring, while she cleansed her reputation.

Miss Wright flushed. 'Never mind,' she said tartly. 'It was—exact—retribution. That lying, bragging—!'

'If you don't watch out,' murmured Mr Queen, 'Carter Bradford will have another indictment to draw against you—this one for assault and battery.'

'I'm just waiting,' said Pat darkly. 'But he won't. He knows better!' And apparently Cart did know better, for nothing more was heard from him about Pat's part in the debacle.

Wrightsville prepared for the Easter holidays. The Bon Ton did a New York business in dresses and spring coats and shoes and underwear and bags, Sol Gowdy put on two 'extras' to help in his Men's Shop, and the Low Village emporia were actually crowded with mill and factory customers.

Mr Ellery Queen shut himself up in his quarters on the top floor of the Wright house and, except for meals, remained incommunicado. Anyone looking in on him would have been puzzled. He was doing exactly nothing visible to the uninitiated eye. Unless it was to consume innumerable cigarettes. He just sat still in the chair by the window and gazed out at the spring sky, or patrolled the room with long strides, head bent, puffing like a locomotive. Oh, yes. If you looked hard, you could see a mass, of notes on his desk—a mess of a mass, for the papers were scattered like dead leaves in autumn. And indeed the wind of Ellery's fury had scattered them so. They lay there discarded, and a mockery.

So there was nothing exciting in *that* direction. Nor anywhere else, except possibly in Nora's. It was strange about Nora. She had stood up so gallantly under the stresses of the arrest and trial that everyone had begun taking her for granted. Even Hermione thought of nothing but Nora's 'condition' and the proper care of the mother; and there old Ludie was of infinitely more practical use. Old Ludie said a woman was a woman, and she was made to have babies, and the less fuss you made over Nora's 'condition' the better off they'd both be—Nora *and* the little one. Eat good plain food, with plenty of vegetables and milk and fruit, don't go gallivantin', go easy on the candy and do plenty of walking and mild exercise, and the good Lord would do the rest. Ludie had incessant quarrels about it with Hermione, and at least one memorable tiff with Dr Willoughby.

But the pathology of the nervous system was so much Sanskrit to Ludie; and while the others were better informed, only two persons close to Nora suspected what was going to happen, and at least one of them was helpless to avert the catastrophe. That was Mr Queen; and he could only wait and watch. The other was Doc Willoughby, and the doctor did all he could—which meant tonic and daily examinations and advice, all of which Nora ignored.

Nora went to pieces of a sudden. On Easter Sunday, just after the family had returned from church, Nora was heard laughing in her bedroom. Pat, who was fixing her hair in her own room down the hall and was the nearest, got there first, alarmed by a queer quality in Nora's laughter. She found her sister in a swollen heap on the floor, rocking, laughing her head off while her cheeks changed from red to purple to yellow-ivory. Her eyes were spumy and wild, like a sea storm.

They all ran in then, and among them managed to drag Nora onto the bed, and loosen her clothes, while she laughed and laughed as if the tragedy of her life were the greatest joke in the world. Ellery telephoned Dr Willoughby, and set about with the assistance of Pat and Lola to arrest Nora's hysteria. By the time the doctor arrived, they had managed to stop the laughter, but Nora was shaking and white and looked about her with frightened eyes.

'I can't—understand—it,' she gasped. 'I was—all right. Then—everything . . . Ooh, I *hurt*.'

Dr Willoughby chased them all away. He was in Nora's room for fifteen minutes. When he came out he said harshly: 'She's got to be taken to the hospital. I'll arrange it myself.'

181

And Hermy clutched at John F., and the girls clung to each other, and nobody said anything while a big hand took hold of them and squeezed.

The Wrightsville General Hospital was understaffed for the day, since it was Easter Sunday and a holiday. The ambulance did not arrive for three quarters of an hour, and for the first time within the memory of John F. Wright, Dr Milo Willoughby was heard to swear—a long, loud, imagistic curse, after which he clamped his jaws together and went back to Nora. 'She'll be all right, Hermy,' said John F.; but his face was gray. If Milo swore, it was bad!

When the ambulance finally came, the doctor wasted no time in further anathema. He had Nora whisked out of the house and away, leaving his car at the Wright curb to accompany her in the ambulance. They glimpsed Nora's face for an instant as the interns carried her downstairs on a stretcher. The skin lay in coils that jerked this way and that, as if they had a life of their own. The mouth was twisted into a knot, and the eyes were opalescent with agony.

Mercifully, Hermione did not see that face; but Pat did, and she said to Ellery in flat horror: 'She's in horrible pain, and she's scared to death, Ellery! Oh, Ellery, do you think—?'

'Let's be getting over to the hospital,' said Ellery.

He drove them. There was no private pavilion at the Wrightsville General; but Doc Willoughby had a corner of the Women't Surgical Ward screened off and Nora put to bed there. The family was not admitted to the ward; they had to sit in the main waiting room off the lobby. The waiting room was gay with Easter posies and sad with the odor of disinfectant. It sickened Hermy, so they made her comfortable on a mission-wood settee, where she lay with tightly closed eyes. John F. just pottered about, touching a flower now and then, and saying once how nice it felt to have the spring here again. The girls sat near their mother. Mr Queen sat near the girls. And there was nothing but the sound of John F.'s shoes whispering on the worn flowered rug.

And then Dr Willoughby came hurrying into the waiting room, and everything changed—Hermy opened her eyes, John F. stopped exploring, the girls and Ellery jumped up.

182

'Haven't much time,' panted the doctor. 'Listen to me. Nora has a delicate constitution. She's always been a nervy girl. Strain, aggravation, worry, what she's gone through—the poisoning attempts, New Year's Eve, the trial—she's very weak, very badly run-down . . .'

'What are you trying to say, Milo?' demanded John F., clutching his friend's arm.

'John, Nora's condition is serious. No point in keeping it from you and Hermy. She's a sick girl.' Dr Willoughby turned as if to hurry away.

'Milo—wait!' cried Hermy. 'How about the . . . baby?'

'She's going to have it, Hermy. We've got to operate.'

'But—it's only six months!'

'Yes,' said Dr Willoughby stiffly. 'You'd better all wait here. I've got to get ready.'

'Milo,' said John F. 'If there's anything—money—I mean, get anybody—the best—'

'We're in luck, John. Henry Gropper is in Slocum visiting his parents over Easter; classmate of mine; best gynaecologist in the East. He's on his way over now.'

'Milo—' wailed Hermy. But Dr Willoughby was gone.

And now the waiting began all over again, in the silent room with the sun beating in and the Easter posies approaching their deaths fragrantly. John F. sat down beside his wife and took her hand. They sat that way, their eyes fixed on the clock over the waiting-room door. Seconds came and went and became minutes. Lola turned the pages of a *Cosmopolitan* with a torn cover. She put it down, took it up again.

'Pat,' said Ellery. 'Over here.'

John F. looked at him, Hermy looked at him, Lola looked at him. Then Hermy and John F. turned back to the clock, and Lola to the magazine.

'Where?' Pat's voice was shimmering with tears.

'By the window. Away from the family.' Pat trudged over to the farthest bank of windows with him. She sat down on the window seat and looked out. He took her hand. 'Talk.'

Her eyes filled. 'Oh, Ellery—'

'I know,' he said gently. 'But you just talk to me. Anything. It's better than choking on the words inside, isn't it? And you can't talk to *them*, because they're choking, too.' He gave her a cigarette, and held a match up, but she just fingered the cigarette, not seeing it or him. He snuffed the flame between two fingers and then stared at the fingers.

'Talk . . .' said Pat bitterly. 'Well, why not? I'm so confused. Nora lying there—her baby coming prematurely—Jim in jail a few squares away—Pop and Mother sitting here like two old people . . . *old*, Ellery. They *are* old.'

'Yes, Patty,' murmured Ellery.

'And we were so happy before,' Pat choked. 'It's all like a foul dream. It can't be us. We were—*everything* in this town! Now look at us. Dirtied up. Old. They spit on us.'

'Yes, Patty,' said Ellery again.

'When I think of how it happened . . . How *did* it happen? Oh, I'll never face another holiday with any gladness!'

'Holiday?'

'Don't you realize? Every last awful thing that's happened—happened on a holiday! Here's Easter Sunday—and Nora's on the operating table. When was Jim arrested? On St Valentine's Day! When did Rosemary die, and Nora get so badly poisoned? On New Year's Eve! And Nora was sick—poisoned—on Christmas Day, and before that on Thanksgiving Day . . .'

Mr Queen was looking at Pat as if she had pointed out that two plus two adds up to five. 'No. On that point I'm convinced. It's been bothering me for weeks. But it's coincidence. Can't be anything else. No, Patty . . .'

'Even the way it started,' cried Patty. 'It started on Hallowe'en! Remember?' She stared at the cigarette in her fingers; it was pulpy ruin now. 'If we'd never found those three letters in that toxicology book, everything might have been different, Ellery. *Don't* shake your head. It might!'

'Maybe you're right,' muttered Ellery. 'I'm shaking my head at my own stupidity—' A formless something took possession of his mind in a little leap, like a struck spark. He had experienced that sensation once before—how long ago it seemed!—but now the same thing happened. The spark died and he was left with a cold, exasperating ash which told nothing.

'You talk about coincidence,' said Pat shrilly. 'All right, call it that. I don't care what you call it. Coincidence, or fate, or just rotten luck. But if Nora hadn't accidentally dropped those books we were moving that Hallowe'en, the three letters wouldn't have tumbled out and they'd probably be in the book still.'

Mr Queen was about to point out that the peril to Nora

had lain not in the letters but in their author; but again a spark leaped, and died, and so he held his tongue.

'For that matter,' Pat sighed, 'if the most trivial thing had happened differently that day, maybe none of this would have come about. If Nora and I hadn't decided to fix up Jim's new study—if we hadn't opened that box of books!'

'*Box* of books?' said Ellery blankly.

'I brought the crate up myself from the cellar, where Ed Hotchkiss had put it when he cabbed Jim's stuff over from the railroad station after Jim and Nora got back from their honeymoon. Suppose I hadn't opened that box with a hammer and screwdriver? Suppose I hadn't been able to *find* a screwdriver? Or suppose I'd waited a week, a day, even another hour . . . Ellery, what's the matter?'

For Mr Queen was standing over her like the judgment of the Lord, a terrible wrath on his face, and Patty was so alarmed she shrank back against the window. 'Do you mean to sit there and tell me,' said Mr Queen in an awful quietude, 'that those books—the armful of books Nora dropped—those books were *not* the books usually standing on the living-room shelves?' He shook her, and she winced at the pressure of his fingers on her shoulder. 'Pat, answer me! You and Nora weren't merely transferring books from the living-room bookshelves to the new shelves in Jim's study upstairs? You're *sure* the books came from that box in the cellar?'

'Of course I'm sure,' said Pat shakily. 'What's the matter with you? A nailed box. I opened it myself. Why, just a few minutes before you came in that evening I'd lugged the empty wooden box back to the cellar, with the tools and wrapping paper and mess of bent nails—'

'It's . . . fantastic,' said Ellery. One hand groped for the rocker near Pat. He sat down, heavily.

Pat was bewildered. 'But I don't get it, Ellery. Why all the dramatics? What difference can it make?'

Mr Queen did not answer at once. He just sat there, pale, and growing perceptibly paler, nibbling his nails. And the fine lines about his mouth deepened and became hard, and there appeared in his silvery eyes a baffled something that he concealed very quickly—almost as quickly as it showed itself. 'What difference?' He licked his lips.

'Ellery!' Pat was shaking *him* now. 'Don't act so mysterious! What's wrong? Tell me!'

'Wait a minute.' She stared at him, and waited. He just sat. Then he muttered: 'If I'd only *known*. But I couldn't

have . . . Fate. The fate that brought me into that room
five minutes late. The fate that kept you from telling me
all these months. The fate that concealed the essential
fact!'

'But Ellery—'

'Dr Willoughby!'

They ran across the waiting room. Dr Willoughby had
just blundered in. He was in his surgical gown and cap, his
face mask around his throat like a scarf. There was blood
on his gown, and none in his cheeks.

'Milo?' quavered Hermione. 'Well, well?' croaked John
F. 'For God's sake, Doc!' cried Lola. Pat rushed up to
grab the old man's thick arm.

'Well,' said Dr Willoughby in a hoarse voice, and he
stopped. Then he smiled the saddest smile and put his arm
around Hermy's shoulder, quite dwarfing her. 'Nora's giv-
en you a real Easter present . . . Grandma.'

'Grandma,' whispered Hermy.

'The baby!' cried Pat. 'It's all *right?*'

'Fine, fine, Patricia. A perfect little baby girl. Oh, she's
very tiny—she'll need the incubator—but with proper care
she'll be all right in a few weeks.'

'But Nora,' panted Hermy. 'My Nora.'

'How is Nora, Milo?' demanded John F.

'Is she out of it?' Lola asked.

'Does she know?' cried Pat. 'Oh. Nor must be so happy!'

Dr Willoughby glanced down at his gown, began to
fumble at the spot where Nora's blood had splattered.
'Damn it all,' he said. His lips were quivering. Hermione
screamed.

'Gropper and I—we did all we could. We couldn't help
it. We worked over her like beavers. But she was carrying
too big a load. John, don't look at me that way . . .' The
doctor waved his arms wildly.

'Milo—' began John F. in a faint voice.

'She's dead, that's all!'

He ran out of the waiting room.

PART SIX

28. *The Tragedy on Twin Hill*

HE WAS looking at the old elms before the new Court-house. The old was being reborn in multitudes of little green teeth on brown gums of branches; and the new already showed weather streaks in its granite, like varicose veins. There is sadness, too, in spring, thought Mr Ellery Queen. He stepped into the cool shadows of the Court-house lobby and was borne aloft.

'No time for visitors to be visitin',' said Wally Planetsky sternly. Then he said: 'Oh. You're that friend of Patty Wright's. It's a hell of a way to be spendin' the Easter Sunday, Mr Queen.

'How true,' said Mr Queen. The keeper unlocked an iron door, and they trudged together into the jail. 'How is he?'

'Never saw such a man for keepin' his trap shut. You'd think he'd taken a vow.'

'Perhaps,' sighed Mr Queen, 'he has . . . Anyone been in today to see him?'

'Just that newspaper woman, Miss Roberts.' Planetsky unlocked another door, locked it carefully behind them.

'Is there a doctor about?' asked Ellery unexpectedly.

Planetsky scratched his ear and opined that if Mr Queen was feelin' sick . . .

'Is there?'

'Well, sure. We got an infirmary here. Young Ed Cros-by—that's Ivor Crosby the farmer's son—he's on duty right now.'

'Tell Dr Crosby I may need him in a very little while.'

The keeper looked Ellery over suspiciously, shrugged,

187

unlocked the cell door, locked it again, and shuffled away. Jim was lying on his bunk, hands crossed behind his head, examining the graph of sky blue beyond bars. He had shaved, Ellery noted; his clean shirt was open at the throat; he seemed at peace.

'Jim?'

Jim turned his head. 'Oh, hello, there,' he said. 'Happy Easter.'

'Jim—' began Ellery again, frowning.

Jim swung his feet to the concrete floor and sat up to grip the edge of his bunk with both hands. No peace now. Fear. And that was strange . . . No, logical! When you came to think of it. When you *knew*. 'Something's wrong,' said Jim. He jumped to his feet. 'Something's wrong!'

Ellery grimaced. This was the punishment for trespassing. This was the pain reserved for meddlers. 'I'm all for you, Jim—'

'What is it?' Jim made a fist.

'You've got a great deal of courage, Jim—'

Jim stared. 'She's . . . It's Nora.'

'Jim, Nora's dead.' Jim stared, his mouth open. 'I've just come from the hospital. The baby is all right. A girl. Premature delivery. Instruments. Nora was too weak. She didn't come out of it. No pain. She just died, Jim.'

Jim's lips came together. He turned around and went back to his bunk and turned around again and sat down, his hands reaching the bunk before he reached it.

'Naturally, the family . . . John F. asked me to tell you, Jim. They're all home now, taking care of Hermione. John F. said to tell you he's terribly sorry, Jim.'

Stupid, thought Ellery. A stupid speech. But then he was usually the observer, not a participant. How did one go about drawing the agony out of a stab to the heart? Killing without hurting—for as much as a second? It was a branch of the art of violence with which Mr Queen was unacquainted. He sat helplessly on the contraption which concealed Wright County's arrangement for the physical welfare of its prisoners, and thought of symbolism. 'If there's anything I can do—'

That wasn't merely stupid, thought Ellery angrily; that was vicious. Anything he could do! Knowing what was going on in Jim's mind! Ellery got up and said: 'Now Jim. Now wait a minute, Jim—'

But Jim was at the bars like a great monkey, gripping two of them, his thin face pressed as hard between two adjacent ones as if he meant to force his head through and

188

drag his body after it. 'Let me out of here!' he kept shouting. 'Let me out of here! Damn all of you! I've got to get to Nora! Let me out of here!' He panted and strained, his teeth digging into his lower lip and his eyes hot and his temples bulging with vessels. 'Let me out of here!' he screamed. A white froth sprang up at the corners of his mouth.

When Dr Crosby arrived with a black bag and a shaking Keeper Planetsky to open the door for him, Jim Haight was flat on his back on the floor and Mr Queen knelt on Jim's chest holding Jim's arms down, hard, and yet gently, too. Jim was still screaming, but the words made no sense. Dr Crosby took one look and grabbed a hypodermic.

Twin Hill is a pleasant place in the spring. There's Bald Mountain off to the north, almost always wearing a white cap on its green shoulders, like some remote Friar Tuck; there's the woods part in the gulley of the Twins, where boys go hunting woodchuck and jack rabbit and occasionally scare up a wild deer; and there are the Twins themselves, two identical humps of hill all densely populated with the dead.

The east Twin has the newer cemeteries—the Poor Farm burial ground pretty far down, in the scrub, the old Jewish cemetery, and the Catholic cemetery; these are 'new' because not a headstone in the lot bears a date earlier than 1805.

But the west Twin has the really old cemeteries of the Protestant denominations, and there you can see, at the very bald spot of the west Twin, the family plot of the Wrights, the first Wright tomb—Jezreel Wright's—in its mathematical center. Of course, the Founder's grave is not exposed to the elements—the wind off Bald Mountain does things to grass and topsoil. John F.'s grandfather had built a large mausoleum over the grave—handsome it is, too, finest Vermont granite, white as Patty Wright's teeth. But inside there's the original grave with its little stick of headstone, and if you look sharp you can still make out the scratches on the stone—the Founder's name, a hopeful quotation from the Book of Revelation, and the date 1723.

The Wright family plot hogs pretty nearly the whole top of the west Twin. The Founder, who seems to have had a nice judgment in all business matters, staked out enough dead land for his seed and his seed's seed to last for

189

eternity. As if he had faith that the Wrights would live and die in Wrightsville unto Judgment Day. The rest of the cemetery, and the other burial grounds, simply took what was left. And that was all right with everyone, for after all didn't the Founder found? Besides, it made a sort of show place. Wrightsvillians were forever hauling outlanders up to Twin Hill, halfway to Slocum Township, to exhibit the Founder's grave and the Wright plot. It was one of the 'sights'.

The automobile road ended at the gate of the cemetery, not far from the boundary of the Wright family plot. From the gate you walked—a peaceful walk under trees so old you wondered they didn't lie down and ask to be buried themselves out of plain weariness. But they just kept growing old and droopier. Except in spring. Then the green hair began sprouting from their hard black skins with a sly fertility, as if death were a great joke. Maybe the graves so lush and thick all over the hillside had something to do with it.

Services for Nora—on Tuesday, April the fifteenth—were private. Dr Doolittle uttered a few words in the chapel of Willis Stone's Eternal Rest Mortuary, on Upper Whistling Avenue in High Village. Only the family and a few friends were present—Mr Queen, Judge and Clarice Martin, Dr Willoughby, and some of John F.'s people from the bank. Frank Lloyd was seen skulking about the edge of the group, straining for a glimpse of the pure still profile in the copper casket. He looked as if he had not taken his clothes off for a week, or slept during that time. When Hermy's eye rested on him, he shrank and disappeared . . . Perhaps twenty mourners in all.

Hermy was fine. She sat up straight in her new black, eyes steady, listening to Dr Doolittle; and when they all filed past the bier for a last look at Nora, she merely grew a little paler, and blinked. She didn't cry. Pat said it was because she was all cried out. John F. was a crumpled, red-nosed little derelict. Lola had to take him by the hand and lead him away from the casket to let Mr Stone put the head section in place. Nora had looked very calm and young. She was dressed in her wedding gown. Just before they went out to the funeral cars, Pat slipped into Mr Stone's office. When she came back she said: 'I just called the hospital. Baby's fine. She's growing in that incubator like a little vegetable.' Pat's lips danced, and Mr Queen put his arm about her.

190

Looking back on it, Ellery saw the finer points of Jim's psychology. But that was after the event. Beforehand it was impossible to tell, because Jim acted his part perfectly. He fooled them all, including Ellery.

Jim came to the cemetery between two detectives, like an animated sandwich. He was 'all right'. Very little different from the Jim who had sat in the courtroom— altogether different from the Jim Ellery had sat upon in the cell. There was a whole despair about him so enveloping that he had poise, and self-control, even dignity. He marched along steadily between his two guards, ignoring them, looking neither to right nor to left, on the path under the aged trees up to the top of the hill where the newly turned earth gaped, like a wound, to receive Nora. The cars had been left near the gate.

Most of Wrightsville watched from a decent distance— let us give them that. But they were there, silent and curious; only occasionally someone whispered, or a forefinger told a story.

The Wrights stood about the grave in a woebegone group, Lola and Pat pressing close to Hermione and their father. John F.'s sister Tabitha had been notified, but she had wired that she was ill and could not fly to the funeral from California, and the Lord in His wisdom taketh away, and perhaps it was all for the best may she rest in peace your loving sister Tabitha. John F. made a wad out of the wire and hurled it blindly; it landed in the early morning fire Ludie had lit against the chill in the big old house. So it was just the immediate family group, and Ellery Queen, and Judge Eli Martin and Clarice and Doc Willoughby and some others; and, of course, Dr Doolittle. When Jim was brought up, a mutter arose from the watchers; eyes became very sharp for this meeting; this was very nearly 'the best part of it'. But nothing remarkable happened. Or perhaps it did. For Hermy's lips were seen to move, and Jim went over to her and kissed her. He paid no attention to anyone else; after that he just stood there at the grave, a thin figure of loneliness.

During the interment service a breeze ran through the leaves, like fingers; and indeed Dr Doolittle's voice took on a lilt and became quite musical. The evergreens and lilies bordering the grave stirred a little, too. Then, unbelievably, it was over, and they were shuffling down the walk. Hermy straining backward to catch a last glimpse of the casket which could no longer be seen, having been lowered into the earth. But the earth had not yet been rained upon it, for that would have been bestial; that could be done later, under no witnessing eyes but the eyes of the gravediggers, who were a peculiar race of people. So Hermy strained, and she thought how beautiful the evergreens and the lilies looked, and how passionately Nora had detested funerals.

The crowd at the gate parted silently. Then Jim did it.

One moment he was trudging along between the detectives, a dead man staring at the ground; the next he came alive. He tripped one of his guards. The man fell backward with a thud, his mouth an astonished O even as he fell. Jim struck the second guard on the jaw, so that the man fell on his brother officer and they threshed about, like wrestlers, trying to regain their feet. In those few seconds Jim was gone, running through the crowd like a bull, bowling people over, spinning people around, dodging and twisting . . .

Ellery shouted at him, but Jim ran on. The detectives were on their feet now, running too, revolvers out uselessly. To fire would mean hitting innocent people. They pushed through, cursing and ashamed.

And then Ellery saw that Jim's madness was not madness at all. For a quarter way down the hill, past all the parked cars, stood a single great car, its nose pointed away from the cemetery. No one was in it; but the motor had been kept running, Ellery knew, for Jim leaped in and the car shot forward at once. By the time the two detectives reached a clear space, and fired down the hill, the big limousine was a toy in the distance. It was careering crazily and going at a great speed. And after another few moments, the detectives reached their own car and took up the chase, one driving, the other still firing wildly. But Jim was well out of range by this time and everyone knew he had a splendid chance of escaping. The two cars disappeared.

For some moments there was no sound on the hillside but the sound of the wind in the trees. Then the crowd shouted, and swept over the Wrights and their friends, and automobiles began flying down the hill in merry clouds of dust, as if this were a paid entertainment and their drivers were determined not to miss the exciting climax.

Hermy lay on the living-room settee, and Pat and Lola were applying cold vinegar compresses to her head while John F. turned the pages of one of his stamp albums with great deliberation, as if it were one of the most important things in the world. He was in a corner by the window to

192

catch the late afternoon light. Clarice Martin was holding Hermy's hand tightly in an ecstasy of remorse, crying over her defection during the trial and over Nora and over this last shocking blow. And Hermy—Hermy the Great!—was comforting her friend!

Lola slapped a new compress so hard on her mother's forehead that Hermy smiled at her reproachfully. Pat took it away from her angry sister and set it right.

At the fireplace Dr Willoughby and Mr Queen conversed in low tones. Then Judge Martin came in from outdoors. And with him was Carter Bradford.

Everything stopped, as if an enemy had walked into camp. But Carter ignored it. He was quite pale, but held himself erect; and he kept from looking at Pat, who had turned paler than he. Clarice Martin was frankly frightened. She glanced quickly at her husband, but Judge Eli shook his hcad and went over to the window to seat himself by John F. and watch the fluttering pages of the stamp album, so gay with color.

'I don't want to intrude, Mrs Wright,' said Carter stiffishly. 'But I had to tell you how badly I feel about—all this.'

'Thank you Carter,' said Hermy. 'Lola, stop babying me! Carter, what about—' Hermy swallowed—'Jim?'

'Jim got away, Mrs Wright.'

'I'm *glad*,' cried Pat. 'Oh, I'm so very glad!'

Carter glanced her way. 'Don't say that, Patty. That sort of thing never winds up right. Nobody "gets away". Jim would have been better . . . advised to have stuck it out.'

'So that you could hound him to his death, I suppose! All over again!'

'Pat.' John F. left his stamp album where it was. He put his thin hand on Carter's arm. 'It was nice of you to come here today, Cart. I'm sorry if I was ever harsh with you. How does it look?'

'Bad, Mr Wright.' Carter's lips tightened. 'Naturally, the alarm is out. All highways are being watched. It's true he got away, but it's only a question of time before he's captured—'

'Bradford,' inquired Mr Queen from the fireplace, 'have you traced the getaway car?'

'Yes.'

'Looked like a put-up job to me,' muttered Dr Willoughby. 'That car was in a mighty convenient place, and the motor was running!'

'Whose car is it?' demanded Lola

'It was rented from Homer Findlay's garage in Low Village this morning.'

'Rented!' exclaimed Clarice Martin. 'By whom?'

'Roberta Roberts.'

Ellery said: 'Ah,' in a tone of dark satisfaction, and nodded as if that were all he had wanted to know. But the others were surprised.

Lola tossed her head. 'Good for her!'

'Carter let me talk to the woman myself just now,' said Judge Eli Martin wearily. 'She's a smart female. Insists she hired the car just to drive to the cemetery this morning.'

'And that she left the motor running by mistake,' added Carter Bradford dryly.

'And was it a coincidence that she also turned the car about so that it pointed down the hill?' murmured Mr Queen.

'That's what I asked her,' said Carter. 'Oh, there's no question about her complicity, and Dakin's holding her. But that doesn't get Jim Haight back, nor does it give us a case against this Roberts woman. We'll probably have to let her go.' He said angrily: 'I never did trust that woman!'

'She visited Jim on Sunday,' remarked Ellery reflectively.

'Also yesterday! I'm convinced she arranged the escape with Jim then.'

'What difference does it make?' Hermy sighed. 'Escape—no escape—Jim won't ever escape.' Then Hermy said a queer thing, considering how she had always claimed she felt about her son-in-law and his guilt. Hermy said: 'Poor Jim,' and closed her eyes.

The news arrived at ten o'clock that same night. Carter Bradford came over again and this time he went directly to Pat Wright and took her hand. She was so astonished she forgot to snatch it away. Carter said gently: 'It's up to you and Lola now, Pat.'

'What . . . on earth are you talking about?' asked Pat in a shrill tight voice.

'Dakin's men have found the car Jim escaped in.'

'*Found* it?'

Ellery Queen rose from a dark corner and came over into the light. 'If it's bad news, keep your voices down. Mrs Wright's just gone to bed, and John F. doesn't look as if he could take any more today. Where was the car found?'

194

'At the bottom of a ravine off Route 478A, up in the hills. About fifty miles from here.'

'Lord,' breathed Pat, staring.

'It had crashed through the highway rail,' growled Carter, 'just past a hairpin turn. The road is tricky up there. Dropped about two hundred feet—'

'And Jim?' asked Ellery.

Pat sat down in the love seat by the fireplace, looking up at Cart as if he were a judge about to pronounce doom. 'Found in the car.' Cart turned aside. 'Dead.' He turned back and looked humbly at Pat. 'So that's the end of the case. It's the end, Pat . . .'

'Poor Jim,' whispered Pat.

'I want to talk to you two,' said Mr Queen. It was very late. But there was no time. Time had been lost in the nightmare. Hermione had heard and Hermione had gone to pieces. Strange that the funeral of her daughter should have found her strong, and the news of her son-in-law's death weak. Perhaps it was the crushing tap after the heavy body blows. But Hermy collapsed, and Dr Willoughby spent hours with her trying to get her to sleep. John F. was in hardly better case: he had taken to trembling, and the doctor noticed it, and packed him off to bed in a guest room while Lola assisted with Hermy and Pat helped her father up the stairs . . . Now it was over, and they were both asleep, and Lola had locked herself in, and Dr Willoughby had gone home, sagging. 'I want to talk to you two,' said Mr Queen.

Carter was still there. He had been a bed of rock for Hermy this night. She had actually clung to him while she wept, and Mr Queen thought this, too, was strange. And then he thought: No, this is the rock, the last rock, and Hermy clings. If she lets go, she drowns, they all drown. That is how she must feel. And he repeated: 'I want to talk to you two.'

Pat was suspended between worlds. She had been sitting beside Ellery on the porch, waiting for Carter Bradford to go home. Limply and far away. And now Carter had come out of the house, fumbling with his disreputable hat and fishing for some graceful way to negotiate the few steps of the porch and reach the haven of night shadows beyond, on the lawn.

'I don't think there's anything you can have to say that I'd want to hear,' said Carter huskily; but he made no further move to leave the porch.

'Ellery—don't,' said Pat, taking his hand in the gloom.

Ellery squeezed the cold young flesh. 'I've got to. This man thinks he's a martyr. *You* think you're being a heroine in some Byronic tragedy. You're both fools, and that's the truth.'

'Good night!' said Carter Bradford.

'Wait, Bradford. It's been a difficult time and an especially difficult day. And I shan't be in Wrightsville much longer.'

'Ellery!' Pat wailed.

'I've been here much too long already, Pat. Now there's nothing to keep me—nothing at all.'

'Nothing . . . at all?'

'Spare me your tender farewells,' snapped Cart. Then he laughed sheepishly and sat down on the step near them. 'Don't pay any attention to me, Queen. I'm in a fog these days. Sometimes I think I must be pretty much of a drip.'

Pat gaped at him. 'Cart—*you?* Being humble?'

'I've grown up a bit these past few months,' mumbled Cart.

'There's been a heap of growing up around here these past few months,' said Mr Queen mildly. 'How about you two being sensible and proving it?'

Pat took her hand away. 'Please, Ellery—'

'I know I'm meddling, and the lot of the meddler is hard,' sighed Mr Queen. 'But just the same, how about it?'

'I thought you were in love with her,' said Cart gruffly.

'I am.'

'Ellery!' cried Pat. 'You never *once*—'

'I'll be in love with that funny face of yours as long as I live,' said Mr Queen wistfully. 'It's a lovely funny face. But the trouble is, Pat, that you're not in love with *me*.' Pat stumbled over a word, then decided to say nothing. 'You're in love with Cart.'

Pat sprang from the porch chair. 'What if I was! Or am! People don't forget hurts and burns!'

'Oh, but they do,' said Mr Queen. 'People are more forgetful than you'd think. Also, they have better sense than we sometimes give them credit for. Emulate them.'

'It's impossible,' said Pat tightly. 'This is no time for silliness, anyway. You don't seem to realize what's happened to us in this town. We're pariahs. We've got a whole new battle on our hands to rehabilitate ourselves. And it's just Lola and me now to help Pop and Muth hold their heads up again. I'm not going to run out on them now, when they need me most.'

'I'd help you, Pat,' said Cart inaudibly.

'Thanks! We'll do it on our own. Is that all, Mr Queen?'

'There's no hurry,' murmured Mr Queen.

Pat stood there for a moment, then she said goodnight in an angry voice and went into the house. The door huffed. Ellery and Carter sat in silence for some time.

'Queen,' said Cart at last.

'Yes, Bradford?'

'This isn't over, is it?'

'What do you mean?'

'I have the most peculiar feeling you know something I don't.'

'Oh,' said Mr Queen. Then he said: 'Really?'

Carter slapped his hat against his thighs. 'I won't deny I've been pigheaded. Jim's death has done something to me, though. I don't know why it should, because it hasn't changed the facts one iota. He's still the only one who could have poisoned Nora's cocktail, and he's still the only one who had any conceivable motive to want her to die. And yet . . . I'm not so sure any more.'

'Since when?' asked Ellery in a peculiar tone.

'Since the report came in that he was found dead.'

'Why should that make a difference?'

Carter put his head between his hands. 'Because there's every reason to believe the car he was driving didn't go through that rail into the ravine by accident.'

'I see,' said Ellery.

'I didn't want to tell that to the Wrights. But Dakin and I both think Jim drove that car off the road deliberately.'

Mr Queen said nothing.

'And somehow that made me think—don't know why it should have—well, I began to wonder. Queen!' Carter jumped up. 'For God's sake, tell me if you know! I won't sleep until I'm sure. *Did Jim Haight commit that murder?*'

'No.'

Carter stared at him. 'Then who did?' he asked hoarsely.

Mr Queen rose, too. 'I shan't tell you.'

'Then you do know!'

'Yes,' sighed Ellery.

'But Queen, you can't—'

'Oh, but I can. Don't think it's easy for me. My whole training rebels against this sort of—well, connivance. But I like these people. They're nice people, and they've been through too much. I shouldn't want to hurt them any more. Let it go. The hell with it.'

'But you can tell me, Queen!' implored Cart.

197

'No. You're not sure of yourself, not yet, Bradford. You're rather a nice chap. But the growing-up process— it's been retarded.' Ellery shook his head. 'The best thing you can do it forget it, and get Patty to marry you. She's crazy in love with you.'

Carter grasped Ellery's arm so powerfully that Ellery winced. 'But you've *got* to tell me!' he cried. 'How could I . . . knowing that anyone . . . any *one* of them . . . might be . . . ?'

Mr Queen frowned in the darkness. 'Tell you what I'll do with you, Cart,' he said at last. 'You help these people get back to normal in Wrightsville. You chase Patty Wright off her feet. Wear her down. But if you're not successful, if you feel you're not making any headway, wire me. I'm going back home. Send me a wire in New York and I'll come back. And maybe what I'll have to say to you and Patty will solve your problem.'

'Thanks,' said Carter Bradford hoarsely.

'I don't know that it will,' sighed Mr Queen. 'But who can tell? This has been the oddest case of mixed-up people, emotions, and events I've ever run across. Goodbye, Bradford.'

29. *The Return of*
Ellery Queen

THIS, THOUGHT Mr Ellery Queen as he stood on the station platform, makes me an admiral all over again. The second voyage of Columbus . . . He glanced moodily at the station sign. The tail of the train that had brought him from New York was just disappearing around the curve at Wrightsville Junction three miles down the line. He could have sworn that the two small boys swinging their dirty legs on the hand truck under the eaves of the station were the same boys he had seen—in another century!—on his first arrival in Wrightsville. Gabby Warrum, the station agent, strolled out to stare at him. Ellery waved and made hastily for Ed Hotchkiss's cab, drawn up on the gravel. As

Ed drove him 'uptown', Ellery's hand tightened in his pocket about the telegram he had received the night before. It was from Carter Bradford, and it said simply: 'COME. PLEASE.'

He had not been away long—a matter of three weeks or so—but just the same it seemed to him that Wrightsville had changed. Or perhaps it would be truer to say that Wrightsville had changed *back*. It was the old Wrightsville again, the town he had come into so hopefully the previous August, nine months ago. It had the same air of unhurried peace this lovely Sunday afternoon. Even the people seemed the old people, not the maddened horde of January and February and March and April. Mr Queen made a telephone call from the Hollis Hotel, then had Ed Hotchkiss drive him up the Hill. It was late afternoon and the birds were whizzing and chirping at a great rate around the old Wright house. He paid Ed off, watched the cab chug down the Hill, and then strolled up the walk. The little house next door—the house of Nora and Jim—was shuttered up; it looked opaque and ugly in its blindness. Mr Queen felt a tremor in his spine. That *was* a house to avoid. He hesitated at the front steps of the big house, and listened. There were voices from the rear gardens. So he went around, walking on the grass. He paused in the shadow of the oleander bush, where he could see them without being seen.

The sun was bright on Hermy, joggling a brand-new baby carriage in an extremely critical way. John F. was grinning, and Lola and Pat were making serious remarks about professional grandmothers, and how about giving a couple of aunts a chance to practise, for goodness' sake? The baby would be home from hospital in just a couple of weeks! Mr Queen watched, unobserved, for a long time. His face was very grave. Once he half turned away, as if he meant to flee once and for all. But then he saw Patricia Wright's face again, and how it had grown older and thinner since last he had seen it; and so he sighed and set about making an end of things. After five minutes of delicate reconnaissance he managed to catch Pat's eye while the others were occupied—caught her eye and put his finger to his lips, shaking his head in warning.

Pat said something casual to her family and strolled towards him. He backed off, and then she came around the corner of the house and flew into his arms. 'Ellery! Darling! Oh, I'm so *glad* to see you! When did you come? What's the mystery for? Oh, you bug—I *am* glad!' She

199

kissed him and held him close, and for a moment her face was the gay young face he had remembered.

He let her sprinkle his shoulder, and then he took her by the hand and drew her towards the front of the house. 'That's your convertible at the curb, isn't it? Let's go for a ride.'

'But Ellery, Pop and Muth and Lola—they'll be heart-broken if you don't—'

'I don't want to disturb them now, Patty. They look really happy, getting ready for the baby. How is she, by the way?' Ellery drove Pat's car down the Hill.

'Oh wonderful. Such a clever little thing! And do you know? She looks just like—' Pat stopped. Then she said quietly: 'Just like Nora.'

'Does she? Then she must be a beautiful young lady indeed.'

'Oh, she is! And I'll swear she knows Muth! Really, I mean it. We can't *wait* for her to come home from the hospital. Of course, Mother won't let *any* of us touch little Nora—that's her name, you know—when we visit her— we're there practically *all* the time! except that I sneak over there alone once in a while when I'm not supposed to . . . Little Nora is going to have Nora's old bedroom— ought to see how we've fixed it up, with ivory furniture and gewgaws and big teddy bears and special nursery wallpaper and all—anyway, the little atom and I have secrets . . . well, we do! . . . of course, she's out of the incubator . . . and she gurgles at me and hangs on to my hand for dear life and *squeezes*. She's so fat, Ellery, you'd laugh!'

Ellery laughed. 'You're talking like the old Patty I knew—'

'You think so?' asked Pat in a queer voice.

'But you don't *look*—'

'No,' said Pat. 'No, I don't. I'm getting to be an old hag. Where are we going?'

'Nowhere in particular,' said Ellery vaguely, turning the car south and beginning to drive towards Wrightsville Junction.

'But tell me! What brings you back to Wrightsville? It must be us—couldn't be anyone else! How's the novel?'

'Finished.'

'Oh, grand! Ellery, you never let me read a word of it. How does it end?'

'That,' said Mr Queen, 'is one of my reasons for coming back to Wrightsville.'

200

'What do you mean?'

'The end,' he grinned. 'I've ended it, but it's always easy to change the last chapter—at least, certain elements not directly concerned with mystery plot. You might be a help there.'

'Me? But I'd love to! And—oh, Ellery. What am I thinking of? I haven't thanked you for that magnificent gift you sent me from New York. And those wonderful things you sent Muth, and Pop, and Lola. Oh, Ellery, you shouldn't have. We didn't do anything that—'

'Oh, bosh. Seeing much of Cart Bradford lately?'

Pat examined her fingernails. 'Oh, Cart's been around.'

'And Jim's funeral?'

'We buried him next to Nora.'

'Well!' said Ellery. 'You know, I feel a thirst coming on. How about stopping in somewhere for a long one, Patty?'

'All right,' said Pat moodily.

'Isn't that Gus Olesen's *Roadside Tavern* up ahead? By gosh, it is!' Pat glanced at him, but Ellery grinned and stopped the car before the tavern, and helped her out, at which she grimaced and said men in Wrightsville didn't do things like that, and Ellery grinned again, which made Pat laugh; and they walked into Gus Olesen's cool place arm in arm, laughing together; and Ellery walked her right up to the table where Carter Bradford sat waiting in a coil of knots, and said: 'Here she is, Bradford. C.O.D.'

'Pat,' said Cart, his palms flat on the table.

'Cart!' cried Pat.

'Good morrow, good morrow,' chanted a cracked voice; and Mr Queen saw old Anderson the Soak, seated at a nearby table with a fistful of dollar bills in one hand and a row of empty whisky glasses before him.

'Good morrow to you, Mr Anderson,' said Mr Queen; and while he nodded and smiled at Mr Anderson, things were happening at the table; so that when he turned back there was Pat, seated, and Carter seated, and they were glaring at each other across the table. So Mr Queen sat down, too, and said to Gus Olesen: 'Use your imagination, Gus.' Gus scratched his head and got busy behind the bar.

'Ellery.' Pat's eyes were troubled. 'You tricked me into coming here with you.'

'I wasn't sure you'd come, untricked,' murmured Mr Queen.

'*I* asked Queen to come back to Wrightsville, Pat,' said

Cart hoarsely. 'He said he'd—Pat, I've tried to see you, I've tried to make you understand that we can wipe the past out, and I'm in love with you and always was and always will be, and that I want to marry you more than anything in the world—'

'Let's not discuss *that* any more.' said Pat. She began making pleats in the skirt of the tablecloth. Carter seized a tall glass Gus set down before him; and Pat did, too, with a sort of gratitude for the diversion; and they sat in silence for a while, drinking and not looking at each other.

At his table old Anderson had risen, one hand on the cloth to steady himself, and he was chanting:—

> "I believe a leaf of grass is no less than the journey-work of the stars,
> And the pismire is equally perfect, and a grain of sand, and the egg of the wren,
> And the tree-toad is a chef-d'oeuvre of the highest,
> And the running blackberry would adorn the parlors of heaven—"

'Siddown, Mr Anderson,' said Gus Olesen gently. 'You're rockin' the boat.'

'Whitman,' said Mr Queen, looking around. 'And very apt.'

Old Anderson leered, and went on:—

> "And the narrowest hinge in my hand puts to scorn all machinery,
> And the cow, crunching with depressed head, surpasses any statue,
> And a mouse is miracle enough to stagger sextillions of infidels!"

And with a courtly bow the Old Soak sat down again and began to pound out rhythms on the table. 'I was a poet!' he shouted. His lips waggled. 'And 1-look at me now . . .'

'Yes,' said Mr Queen thoughtfully. 'That's very true indeed.'

'Here's your poison!' said Gus at the next table, slopping a glass of whisky before Mr Anderson. Then Gus looked very guilty and, avoiding the startled eyes of Pat, went quickly behind his bar and hid himself in a copy of Frank Lloyd's *Record*. Mr Anderson drank, murmuring to himself in his gullet.

'Pat,' said Mr Queen, 'I came back here today to tell you and Carter who was really responsible for the crimes Jim Haight was charged with.'

'Oh,' said Patty, and she sucked in her breath.

'There are miracles in the human mind, too. You told me something in the hospital waiting room the day Nora died—one little acorn fact—and it grew into a tall tree in my mind.'

' "And a mouse," ' shouted Mr Anderson exultantly, ' "is miracle enough to stagger sextillions of infidels!" '

Pat whispered: 'Then it wasn't Jim after all . . . Ellery, no! Don't! Please! No!'

'Yes,' said Ellery gently. 'That thing is standing between you and Cart. It's a question mark that would outlive you both. I want to erase it and put a period in its place. Then the chapter will be closed and you and Cart can look each other in the eye again with some sort of abiding faith.' He sipped his drink, frowning. 'I hope!'

'You hope?' muttered Cart.

'The truth,' said Ellery soberly, 'is unpleasant.'

'Ellery!' cried Pat.

'But you're not children, either of you. Don't delude yourselves. It would stand between you even if you married . . . the uncertainty of it, the not-knowing, the doubt and the night-and-day question. It's what's keeping you apart, and what has kept you apart. Yes, the truth is unpleasant. But at least it *is* the truth, and if you know the truth, you have knowledge; and if you have knowledge, you can make a decision with durability . . . Pat, this is surgery. It's cut the tumor out, or die. Shall I operate?'

Mr Anderson was singing 'Under the Greenwood Tree' in a soft croak, beating time with his empty whisky glass. Patty sat up perfectly straight, her hands clasped about her glass. 'Go ahead . . . Doctor.' And Cart took a long swallow, and nodded.

Mr Queen sighed. 'Do you recall, Pat, telling me in the hospital about the time I came into Nora's house—last Hallowe'en—and found you and Nora transferring books from the living room to Jim's new study upstairs?' Pat nodded wordlessly. 'And what did you tell me? That the books you and Nora were lugging upstairs you had just removed from a *nailed box*. That you'd gone down into the cellar just a few minutes before I dropped in, seen the box of books down there all nailed up, exactly as Ed Hotchkiss had left it when he cabbed it from the

203

station weeks and weeks before . . . *seen the box intact and opened it yourself.*'

'A box of books?' muttered Carter.

'That box of books, Cart, had been part of Jim's luggage which he'd shipped from New York to Wrightsville when he came back to Wrightsville to make up with Nora. He'd checked it at the Wrightsville station, Cart. It was at the station all the time Jim and Nora were away on their honeymoon; it was brought to the new house only on their return, stored down in the cellar, and on Hallowe'en Pat found that box still intact, still nailed up, still unopened. That was the fact I hadn't known—the kernel fact, the acorn fact, that told me the truth.'

'But how, Ellery?' asked Pat, feeling her head.

'You'll see in a moment, honey. All the time, I'd assumed that the books I saw you and Nora handling were merely being transferred from the living-room bookshelves to Jim's new study upstairs. I thought they were *house books*, books of Jim's and Nora's that had been in the house for some time. It was a natural assumption—I saw no box on the living-room floor, no nails—'

'I'd emptied the box and taken the box, nails, and tools down to the cellar just before you came in,' said Pat. 'I told you that in the hospital that day.'

'Too late,' growled Ellery. 'When I came in, I saw no evidence of such a thing. And I'm no clairvoyant.'

'But what's the point?' frowned Carter Bradford.

'One of the books in the wooden box Patty opened that Hallowe'en,' said Ellery, 'was Jim's copy of Edgcomb's *Toxicology.*'

Cart's jaw dropped. 'The marked passage about arsenic!'

'Not only that, but it was from between two pages of that volume that the three letters fell out.'

This time Cart said nothing. And Pat was looking at Ellery with deep quotation marks between her eyebrows.

'Now, since the box had been nailed up in New York and sent to General Delivery, Wrightsville, where it was held, and the toxicology book with the letters in it was found by us directly after the box was unpacked—the letters fell out as Nora dropped an armful of books quite by accident—then the conclusion is absolutely inescapable: *Jim could not possibly have written those three letters in Wrightsville.* And when I saw that I saw the whole thing. The letters *must* have been written by Jim in New York—*before* he returned to Wrightsville to ask Nora for

204

the second time to marry him, *before* he knew that Nora would accept him after his desertion of her and his three-year absence!'

'Yes,' mumbled Carter Bradford.

'But don't you see?' cried Ellery. 'How can we now state with such fatuous certainty that the sickness and death Jim predicted for his 'wife' in those three letters *referred to Nora?* True, Nora was Jim's wife when the letters were found, *but she was NOT his wife, nor could Jim have known she would BE his wife, when he originally wrote them!*'

He stopped and, even though it was cool in Gus Olesen's taproom, he dried his face with a handkerchief and took a long pull at his glass. At the next table, Mr Anderson snored.

Pat gasped: 'But Ellery, if those three letters didn't refer to Nora, then the whole thing—the whole thing—'

'Let me tell it my way,' said Mr Queen in a harsh voice. 'Once doubt is raised that the "wife" mentioned in the three letters was Nora, then two facts that before seemed irrelevant simply shout to be noticed. One is that the letters bore *incomplete dates.* That is, they marked the month, and the day of the month, *but not the year.* So the three holidays—Thanksgiving, Christmas, and New Year's—which Jim had written down on the successive letters as marking the dates of his "wife's" illness, more serious illness, and finally death, might have been the similar dates of one, two, or even three years before! Not 1940 at all but 1939, or 1938, or 1937 . . .

'And the second fact, of course, was that not once did any of the letters refer to *the name Nora;* the references were consistently to "*my wife.*"

'If Jim wrote those letters in New York—before his marriage to Nora, before he even knew Nora would marry him—then Jim could not have been writing about *Nora's* illness or *Nora's* death. And if we can't believe this—an assumption we all took for granted from the beginning of the case—then the whole structure which postulated *Nora* as Jim's intended poison victim collapses.'

'This is incredible,' muttered Carter. 'Incredible.'

'I'm confused,' moaned Patty. 'You mean—'

'I mean,' said Mr Queen, 'that Nora was never threatened, Nora was never in danger . . . *Nora was never meant to be murdered.*'

Pat shook her head violently, and groped for her glass. 'But that opens up a whole new field of speculation!'

205

exclaimed Carter. 'If Nora wasn't meant to be murdered—ever, at all—'

'What are the facts?' argued Ellery. 'A woman did die on New Year's Eve: Rosemary Haight. When we thought Nora was the intended victim, we said Rosemary died by accident. But now that we know Nora *wasn't* the intended victim, surely it follows that Rosemary did NOT die by accident—*that Rosemary was meant to be murdered from the beginning?*'

'Rosemary was meant to be murdered from the beginning,' repeated Pat slowly, as if the words were in a language she didn't understand.

'But Queen—' protested Bradford.

'I know, I know,' sighed Ellery. 'It raises tremendous difficulties and objections. But with Nora eliminated as the intended victim, it's the only logical explanation for the crime. So we've got to accept it as our new premise. Rosemary was *meant* to be murdered. Immediately I asked myself. Did the three letters have anything to do with Rosemary's death? Superficially, no. The letters referred to the death of Jim's wife—'

'And Rosemary was Jim's sister,' said Pat with a frown.

'Yes, and besides Rosemary had shown no signs of the illnesses predicted for Thanksgiving Day and Christmas Day. Moreover, since the three letters can now be interpreted as two or three years old or more, they no longer appear necessarily criminal. They can merely refer to the natural death of a previous wife of Jim's—not Nora, but *a first wife whom Jim married in New York* and who died there some New Year's Day between the time Jim ran out on Nora and the time he came back to marry Nora.'

'But Jim never said anything about a first wife,' objected Pat.

'That wouldn't prove he hadn't had one,' said Cart.

'No,' nodded Ellery. 'So it all might have been perfectly innocent. Except for two highly significant and suspicious factors: first, that the letters were written but never mailed, as if no death *had* occurred in New York; and second, that a woman did actually die in Wrightsville on New Year's Day of 1941, as written by Jim in his third and last letter a long time before it happened. Coincidence? My gorge rises at the very notion. No, I saw that there must be *some* connection between Rosemary's death and the three letters Jim wrote—he did write them, of course; poor Judge Eli Martin's attempt to cast doubt on

206

their authenticity during the trial was a brave but transparent act of desperation.'

Mr Anderson woke up, looking annoyed. But Gus Olesen shook his head. Mr Anderson tottered over to the bar. ' "Landlord," ' he leered, ' "fill the flowing bowl until it does run over!" '

'We don't serve in bowls, and besides, Andy, you've had enough,' said Gus reprovingly. Mr Anderson began to weep, his head on the bar; and after a few sobs, he fell asleep again.

'What connection,' continued Mr Queen thoughtfully, 'is possible between Rosemary Haight's death and the three letters Jim Haight wrote long, long before? And with this question,' he said, 'we come to the heart of the problem. For with Rosemary the intended victim all along, the use of the three letters can be interpreted as a stupendous blind, a clever deception, *a psychological smoke-screen to conceal the truth from the authorities!* Isn't that what happened? Didn't you and Dakin, Bradford, instantly dismiss Rosemary's death as a factor and concentrate on Nora as the intended victim? But that was just what Rosemary's murderer would want you to do! You ignored the actual victim to look for murder motives against the ostensible victim. And so you built your case around Jim, who was the only person who could possibly have poisoned *Nora*, and never for an instant sought the real criminal—*the person with the motive and opportunity to poison Rosemary.'*

Pat was by now so bewildered that she gave herself up wholly to listening. But Carter Bradford was following with a savage intentness, hunched over the table and never taking his eyes from Ellery's face. 'Go on!' he said. 'Go on, Queen!'

'Let's go back,' said Mr Queen, lighting a cigarette. 'We now know Jim's three letters referred to a hidden, a never-mentioned, a first wife. If this woman died on New Year's Day two or three years ago, why didn't Jim mail the letters to his sister? More important than that, why didn't he disclose the fact to you or Dakin when he was arrested? Why didn't Jim tell Judge Martin, his attorney, that the letters didn't mean Nora, for use as a possible defence in his trial? For if the first wife were in all truth dead, it would have been a simple matter to corroborate— the attending physician's affidavit, the death certificate, a dozen things. *But Jim kept his mouth shut.* He didn't by so much as a sober word indicate that he'd married another

207

woman between the time he and Nora broke up almost four years ago and the time he returned to Wrightsville to marry her. Why? Why Jim's mysterious silence on this point?'

'Maybe,' said Pat with a shiver, 'because he'd actually planned and carried out the murder of his first wife.'

'Then why didn't he mail the letters to his sister?' argued Cart. 'Since he'd presumably written them for that eventuality?'

'Ah,' said Mr Queen. 'The very counterpoint. So I said to myself: Is it possible that the murder Jim had planned of his first wife *did not take place at the time it was supposed to?*'

'You mean she was alive when Jim came back to Wrightsville?' gasped Pat.

'Not merely alive,' said Mr Queen; he slowly ground out the butt of his cigarette in an ash tray. 'She followed Jim here.'

'The first *wife?*' Carter gaped.

'She came to *Wrightsville?*' cried Pat.

'Yes, but not as Jim's first wife. Not as Jim's any-wife.'

'Then who—?'

'*She came to Wrightsville,*' said Ellery, '*as Jim's sister.*'

Mr Anderson came to life at the bar, and began: 'Landlord—!'

'Go home,' said Gus, shaking his head.

'Mead! Nepenthe!' implored Mr Anderson.

'We don't carry that stuff,' said Gus.

'As Jim's sister,' whispered Pat. 'The woman Jim introduced to us as his sister Rosemary *wasn't his sister at all?* She was his *wife?*'

'Yes.' Ellery motioned to Gus Olesen. But Gus had the second round ready. Mr Anderson followed the tray with gleaming eyes. And no one spoke until Gus returned to the bar.

'But Queen,' said Carter, dazed, 'how in hell can you know *that?*'

'Well, whose word have we that the woman who called herself Rosemary Haight was Jim Haight's sister?' demanded Ellery. 'Only the word of Jim and Rosemary, and they're both dead . . . However, that's not how I know she was his first wife. I know that because I know who really killed her. And knowing who really killed her, it just isn't possible for Rosemary to have been Jim Haight's sister. The only person she could have been, the only person

208

against whom the murderer had motive, was Jim's first wife; as you'll see.'

'But Ellery,' said Pat, 'didn't you tell me yourself that day, by comparing the woman's handwriting on Steve Polaris's trucking receipt with the handwriting on the flap of the letter Jim received from "Rosemary Haight", that that proved the woman *was* Jim's sister?'

'I was wrong,' said Mr Queen, frowning. 'I was stupidly wrong. All that the two signatures proved, really, was that *the same woman had written them both*. That meant only that the woman who showed up here was the same woman who wrote Jim that letter which disturbed him so. I was misled by the fact that on the envelope she had signed the name "Rosemary Haight". Well, she was just using that name. I was wrong, I was stupid, and you should have caught me up, Patty. Let's drink?'

'But if the woman who was poisoned New Year's Eve was Jim's first wife,' protested Carter, 'why didn't Jim's real sister come forward after the murder? Lord knows the case had enough publicity!'

'If he had a sister,' mumbled Patty. 'If he had one!'

'Oh, he had a sister,' said Ellery wearily. 'Otherwise, why should he have written those letters to one? When he originally penned them, in planning the murder of his then-wife—the murder he didn't pull off—he expected those letters to give him an appearance of innocence. He expected to send them to his real sister, Rosemary Haight. It would have to be a genuine sister to stand the searchlight of a murder investigation, or he'd really be in a mess. So Jim had a sister, all right.'

'But the papers!' said Pat. 'Cart's right, Ellery. The papers were full of news about "Rosemary Haight, sister of James Haight", and how she *died* here in Wrightsville. If Jim had a real sister Rosemary, surely she'd have come lickety-split to Wrightsville to expose the mistake?'

'Not necessarily. But the fact is—Jim's sister *did* come to Wrightsville, Patty. Whether she came to expose the mistake I can't say; but certainly, after she'd had a talk with her brother Jim, she decided to say nothing about her true identity. I suppose Jim made her promise to keep quiet. And she'd kept that promise.'

'I don't follow, I don't follow,' said Cart irritably. 'You're like one of those fellows who keep pulling rabbits out of a hat. You mean the real Rosemary Haight's been in Wrightsville all these months, calling herself by some other name?'

Mr Queen shrugged. 'Who helped Jim in his trouble? The Wright family, a small group of old friends whose identities, of course, are unquestionable, myself, and . . . one other person. And that person a woman.'

'Roberta!' gasped Pat. *'Roberta Roberts, the newspaper woman!'*

'The only outsider of the sex that fits,' nodded Ellery. 'Yes, Roberta Roberts. Who else? She "believed" in Jim's innocence from the start, she fought for him, she sacrificed her job for him, and at the end—in desperation—she provided the car by which Jim escaped his guards at the cemetery. Yes, Roberta's the only one who *could* be Jim's sister, from the facts; it explains all the peculiarities of her conduct. I suppose "Roberta Roberts" has been her professional name for years. But her real name is Rosemary Haight!'

'So that's why she cried so at Jim's funeral,' said Pat softly. And there was no sound but the swish of Gus Olesen's cloth on the bar and Mr Anderson's troubled muttering.

'It gets clearer,' growled Cart at last. 'But what I don't understand is why Jim's first wife came to Wrightsville *calling* herself Jim's sister.'

'And why,' added Pat, 'Jim permitted the deception. It's mad, the whole thing!'

'No,' said Ellery, 'it's frighteningly sane, if you'll only stop to think. You ask why. I asked why, too. And when I thought about it, I saw what must have happened.' He drank deeply of the contents of the frosty glass. 'Look. Jim left almost four years ago on the eve of his wedding to Nora, as a result of their quarrel about the house. He went to New York, I should suppose desperately unhappy. But remember Jim's character. An iron streak of independence—that's usually from the same lode as stubbornness and pride. They kept him from writing to Nora, from coming back to Wrightsville, from being a sensible human being; although of course Nora was as much to blame for not understanding how much standing on his own feet meant to a man like Jim. At any rate, back in New York, Jim's life—as he must have thought—blasted, Jim ran into this woman. We all saw something of her—a sultry, sulky wench, quite seductive . . . especially attractive to a man licking the wounds of an unhappy love affair. On the rebound, this woman hooked Jim. They must have been miserable together. Jim was a good solid boy, and the woman was a fly-by-night, selfish and capable of

210

driving a man quite mad with exasperation. She must have made his life intolerable, because Jim wasn't the killing type and still he did finally plan to kill her. The fact that he planned each detail of her murder so carefully, even to writing those letters to his sister *in advance*—a silly thing to do!—shows how obsessed he became with the necessity of being rid of her.'

'I should think,' said Pat in a sick voice, 'that he could have divorced her!'

Ellery shrugged again. 'I'm sure that if he could have, he would. Which leads me to believe that, at first, she wouldn't give him a divorce. The leech, genus homo, sex female. Of course, we can't be sure of anything. But Cart, I'm willing to lay you odds that if you followed the trail back you'd discover (a) that she refused to give him a divorce, (b) that he then planned to murder her, (c) that she somehow got wind of his plans, was frightened, ran away from him, causing him to abandon his plans, and (d) that she later informed him that she had got a divorce!

'Because what follows makes all that inevitable. We know that Jim was married to one woman—we know that subsequently he came rushing back to Wrightsville and asked *Nora* to marry him. He would only have done that if *he thought he was free of the first*. But to think so, she must have given him reason. So I say she told him she'd got a divorce.

'What happened? Jim married Nora; in his excited emotional state he completely forgot about those letters which had been lying in the toxicology book for heaven knows how long. Then the honeymoon. Jim and Nora returned to Wrightsville to take up their married life in the little house . . . and the trouble began. Jim received a letter from his "sister". Remember that morning, Patty? The postman brought a letter, and Jim read it and was tremendously agitated, and then later he said it was from his "sister" and wouldn't it be proper to ask her to Wrightsville for a visit . . .' Pat nodded.

'The woman who turned up claiming to be Jim's sister— and whom he accepted as his sister and introduced as his sister—was, we now know, not his sister at all but his first wife.

'But there's a more factual proof that the letter was from the first wife . . . the busines of the identical signatures on the charred flag of the letter Jim received and on Steve Polaris's receipt for the visitor's luggage. So it *was* the first wife who wrote to Jim, and since Jim could

211

scarcely have relished the idea of her coming to Wrightsville, it must have been *her* idea, not his, and that's what her letter to him was about.

'But why did she write to Jim and appear in Wrightsville as Jim's sister at all? In fact, why did Jim permit her to come? Or, if he couldn't keep her from coming, why did he connive at the deception after her arrival and keep it a secret until her death and *still* afterward? There can be one reason: *she had a powerful hold over him.*

'Confirmation of that? Yes. Jim was "squandering" lots of money—and mark that his squandering habits coincided in point of time with the arrival of his first wife in Wrightsville! Why was he pawning Nora's jewelry? Why did he borrow five thousand dollars from the Wrightsville Personal Finance Corporation? Why did he keep bleeding Nora for cash? Why? Where did all that money go? Gambling, you said, Cart. And tried to prove it in court—'

'But Jim himself admitted to Nora that he gambled the money away, according to the testimony,' protested Carter.

'Naturally if his secret wife was blackmailing him, he'd have to invent an excuse to Nora to explain his sudden appetite for huge sums of cash! The fact is, Cart, you never did *prove* Jim was losing all that money gambling in Vic Carlatti's *Hot Spot*. You couldn't find a single eyewitness to his gambling there, or you'd have produced one. The best you could get was an eavesdropper who overheard *Jim* say to Nora that he'd been gambling! Yes, Jim drank a lot at the *Hot Spot*—he was desperate; but he wasn't gambling there.

'Still, that money was going somewhere. Well, haven't we postulated a woman with a powerful hold on him? Conclusion: *He was giving Rosemary that money*—I mean, the woman who called herself Rosemary, the woman who subsequently died on New Year's Eve. He was giving it on demand to the cold-blooded creature he had to continue calling his sister—the woman he'd actually been married to!'

'But what could the hold on him have been, Ellery?' asked Pat. 'It must have been something terrific!'

'Which is why I can see only one answer,' said Ellery grimly. 'It fits into everything we know like plaster of Paris into a mold. Suppose the woman we're calling Rosemary—the first wife—*never did get a divorce?* Suppose she'd only fooled Jim into believing he was free? Perhaps by showing him forged divorce papers? Anything can be procured for money! Then the whole thing makes sense. Then Jim, when he'd married Nora, had committed bigamy. Then he was in this woman's clutches for good . . . She warned Jim in advance by letter and then came to Wrightsville posing as his sister so that she could blackmail him on the spot without exposing her true identity to Nora and the family! So now we know why she posed as his sister, too. If she exposed her real status, her power over Jim was gone. She wanted money, not revenge. It was only by holding a *threat* of exposure over Jim's head that she would be able to suck him dry. To do that she had to pretend to be someone else . . . And Jim, caught in her trap, had to acknowledge her as his sister, had to pay her until he went nearly insane with despair. Rosemary knew her victim. For Jim couldn't let Nora learn the truth—'

'No,' moaned Pat.

'Why not?' asked Carter Bradford.

'Once before, when Jim ran out on her, he'd humiliated Nora frightfully in the eyes of her family and the town—the town especially. There are no secrets or delicacies, and there is much cruelty, in the Wrightsvilles of this world; and if you're a sensitive, inhibited, self-conscious Nora, public scandal can be a major tragedy and a curse to damn your life past regeneration. Jim saw what his first defection had done to Nora, how it had driven her into a shell, made her over into a frightened little person half crazy with shame, hiding from Wrightsville, from her friends, even from her family. If a mere jilting at the altar did that to Nora, what wouldn't the shocking revelation that she'd married a bigamist do to her? It would drive her mad; it might even kill her.

'Jim realized all that . . . The trap Rosemary laid and sprung was Satanic. Jim simply couldn't admit to Nora or let her find out that she was not a legally married woman, that their marriage was not a true marriage, and that their coming child . . . Remember Mrs Wright testified that Jim knew almost as soon as it happened that Nora was going to have a baby.'

'This,' said Carter hoarsely, 'is damnable.'

Ellery sipped his drink and then lit a fresh cigarette, frowning at the incandescent end for some time. 'It gets more difficult to tell, too,' he murmured at last. 'Jim paid and paid, and borrowed money everywhere to keep the

213

evil tongue of that woman from telling the awful truth which would have unbalanced Nora, or killed her.'

Pat was close to tears. 'It's a wonder poor Jim didn't embezzle funds at Pop's bank!'

'And in drunken rages Jim swore he'd "get rid of her"—that he'd "kill her"—and made it plain that he was speaking of his "wife". Of course he was. He was speaking of the only legal wife he had—the woman calling herself Rosemary Haight and posing as his sister. When Jim foolishly made those alcoholic threats *he never meant Nora at all.*'

'But it seems to me,' muttered Cart, 'that when he was arrested, facing a conviction, to keep quiet *then*—'

'I'm afraid,' replied Mr Queen with a sad smile, 'that Jim in his way was a great man. He was willing to die to make up to Nora for what he had done to her. And the only way he could make up to her was to pass out in silence. He unquestionably swore his real sister, Roberta Roberts, to secrecy. For to have told you and Chief Dakin the truth, Cart, Jim would have had to reveal Rosemary's true identity, and that meant revealing the whole story of his previous marriage to her, the divorce-that-wasn't-a-divorce, and consequently Nora's status as a pregnant, yet unmarried, woman. Besides, revealing the truth wouldn't have done *him* any good, anyway. For Jim had infinitely more motive to murder Rosemary than to murder Nora. No, he decided the best course was to carry the whole sickening story with him to the grave.'

Pat was crying openly now.

'And,' muttered Mr Queen. 'Jim had still another reason for keeping quiet. The biggest reason of all. A heroic, an epic, reason. I wonder if you two have any idea what it is.' They stared at him, at each other. 'No,' sighed Mr Queen. 'I suppose you wouldn't. The truth is so staggeringly simple that we see right through it, as if it were a pane of glass. It's two-plus-two, or rather two-minus-one; and those are the most difficult calculations of all.'

A bulbous organ the color of fresh blood appeared over his shoulder; and they saw that it was only Mr Anderson's wonderful nose. '*O vita, misero longa! felici brevis!*' croaked Mr Anderson. 'Friends, heed the wisdom of the ancients . . . I suppose you are wondering how I, poor wretch, am well-provided with lucre this heaven-sent day. Well, I am a remittance man, as they say, and my ship has touched port today. *Felici brevis!*' And he started to fumble for Patty's glass.

214

'Why don't you go over there in the corner and shut up, Andy?' shouted Cart.

'Sir,' said Mr Anderson, going away with Pat's glass, ' "the sands are number'd that make up my life; Here must I stay and here my life must end." ' He sat down at his table and drank quickly.

'Ellery, you can't stop now!' said Pat.

'Are you two prepared to hear the truth?'

Pat looked at Carter, and Carter looked at Pat. He reached across the table and took her hand. 'Shoot,' said Carter.

Mr Queen nodded. 'There's only one question left to be answered—the most important question of all: who really poisoned Rosemary? The case against Jim had shown that he alone had opportunity, that he alone had motive, that he alone had control of the distribution of the cocktails and therefore was the only one who could have been positive the poisoned cocktail reached its intended victim. Further, Cart, you proved that Jim had bought rat poison and so could have had arsenic to drop into the fatal cocktail. All this is reasonable and, indeed, unassailable— *if* Jim meant to kill Nora, to whom he handed the cocktail. But now we know Jim never intended to kill Nora at all!—that the real victim from the beginning was meant to be Rosemary, and only Rosemary!

'So I had to refocus my mental binoculars. Now that I knew *Rosemary* was the intended victim, was the case just as conclusive against Jim as when Nora was believed to be the victim? Well, Jim still had opportunity to poison the cocktail; with Rosemary the victim he had infinitely greater motive; he still had a supply of arsenic available. BUT—with Rosemary the victim, did Jim control the *distribution* of the fatal cocktail? Remember, he handed the cocktail subsequently found to contain arsenic to *Nora* . . . Could he have been sure the poisoned cocktail would go to *Rosemary?*

'*No!*' cried Ellery, and his voice was suddenly like a knife. 'True, he handed Rosemary a cocktail previous to that last round. But that previous cocktail had not been poisoned. In that last round *only Nora's cocktail*—the one that poisoned both Nora and Rosemary—had arsenic in it! If *Jim* had dropped the arsenic into the cocktail he handed Nora, how could he know that *Rosemary* would drink it?

'He couldn't know. It was such an unlikely event that he couldn't even dream it would happen . . . imagine it, or

215

plan it, or count on it. Actually, *Jim was out of the living room*—if you'll recall the facts—*at the time Rosemary drank Nora's cocktail*. So this peripatetic mind had to query: Since *Jim* couldn't be sure Rosemary would drink that poisoned cocktail, who *could* be sure?'

Carter Bradford and Patricia Wright were pressing against the edge of the table, still, rigid, not breathing.

Mr Queen shrugged. 'And instantly—two minus one. Instantly. It was unbelievable, and it was sickening, and it was the only possible truth. Two minus one—one. Just one ... Just one other person had opportunity to poison that cocktail, for just one other person handled it before it reached Rosemary! Just one other person had motive to kill Rosemary and could have utilized the rat poison for murder which Jim had bought for innocent, mice-exterminating purposes ... perhaps at someone else's suggestion. Remember he went back to Myron Garback's pharmacy a second time for another tin, shortly after his first purchase of Quicko, telling Garback he had "mislaid" the first tin? How do you suppose that first tin came to be "mislaid"? With what we now know, isn't it evident that it wasn't mislaid at all, but stolen and stored away by the only other person in Jim's house with motive to kill Rosemary?'

Mr Queen glanced at Patricia Wright and at once closed his eyes, as if they pained him. And he stuck the cigarette into the corner of his mouth and said through his teeth: *'That person could only have been the one who actually handed Rosemary the cocktail on New Year's Eve.'*

Carter Bradford licked his lips over and over. Pat was frozen. 'I'm sorry, Pat,' said Ellery, opening his eyes. 'I'm frightfully, terribly sorry. But it's as logical as death itself. And to give you two a chance, I had to tell you both.'

Pat said faintly: 'Not Nora. Oh, *not Nora!*'

30. *The Second Sunday in May*

'A DROP too much to drink,' said Mr Queen quickly to Gus Olesen. 'May we use your back roon, Gus?'

'Sure, sure,' said Gus. 'Say, I'm sorry about this, Mr Bradford. That's good rum I used in those drinks. And she only had one—Andy took her second one. Lemmy give you a hand—'

'We can manage her all right, thank you,' said Mr Queen, 'although I do think a couple of fingers of bourbon might help.'

'But if she's sick—' began Gus, puzzled. 'Okay!'

The Old Soak stared blindly as Carter and Ellery helped Pat, whose eyes were glassy chips of agony, into Gus Olesen's back room. They set her down on Gus's old horsehair black leather couch, and when Gus hurried in with a glass of whisky Carter Bradford forced her to drink. Pat choked, her eyes streaming; then she pushed the glass aside and threw herself back on the tufted leather, her face to the wall. 'She feels fine already,' said Mr Queen reassuringly. 'Thanks, Gus. We'll take care of Miss Wright.' Gus went away, shaking his head and muttering that that was good rum—he didn't serve rat poison like that chiseling greaseball Vic Carlatti over at the *Hot Spot*.

Pat lay still. Carter stood over her awkwardly. Then he sat down and took her hand. Ellery saw her tanned fingers go white with pressure. He turned away and strolled over to the other side of the room to examine the traditional Bock Beer poster. There was no sound at all, anywhere.

Until he heard Pat murmur: 'Ellery.' He turned around. She was sitting up on the couch again, both her hands in Carter Bradford's; he was holding on to them for dear life, almost as if it were he who needed comforting, not she. Ellery guessed that in those few seconds of silence a great battle had been fought, and won. He drew a chair over to the couch and sat down facing them. 'Tell me the rest,' said Pat steadily, Her eyes in his. 'Go on, Ellery. Tell me the rest.'

'It doesn't make any difference, Patty darling,' mumbled Cart. 'Oh, you know that. You know it.'

'I know it, Cart.'

'Whatever it was, darling—she was sick. I guess she was always a neurotic, always pretty close to the borderline.'

'Yes, Cart. Tell me the rest, Ellery.'

'Pat, do you remember telling me about dropping in to Nora's a few days after Rosemary arrived, in early November, and finding Nora "trapped" in the serving pantry?'

'You mean when Nora overheard Jim and Rosemary having an argument?'

'Yes. You said you came in at the tail end and didn't hear anything of consequence. And that Nora wouldn't tell you what she'd overheard. You said Nora had the same kind of look on her face as that day when those three letters tumbled out of the toxicology book.'

'Yes . . .' said Pat.

'That must have been the turning point, Pat. That must have been the time when Nora learned the whole truth—by pure accident, she learned from the lips of Jim and Rosemary themselves that Rosemary wasn't his sister but his wife, that she herself was not legally married . . . the whole sordid story.' Ellery examined his hands. 'It . . . unbalanced Nora. In a twinkling her whole world came tumbling down, and her moral sense and mental health with it. She faced a humiliation too sickening to be faced. And Nora was emotionally weakened by the unnatural life she'd been leading for the years between Jim's sudden desertion and her marriage to him . . . Nora slipped over the line.'

'Over the line,' whispered Pat. Her lips were white.

'She planned to take revenge on the two people who, as her disturbed mind now saw it, had shamed her and ruined her life. She planned to kill Jim's first wife, the hated woman who called herself Rosemary. She planned to have Jim pay for the crime by using the very tools he'd manufactured for a similiar purpose years before and which were now, as if by an act of providence, thrust into her hand. She must have worked it out slowly. But work it out she did. She had those three puzzling letters that were puzzling no longer. She had Jim's own conduct to help her create the illusion of his guilt. And she found in

218

herself a great strength and a great cunning; a talent, almost a genius, for deceiving the world as to her true emotions.'

Pat closed her eyes, and Carter kissed her hand.

'Knowing that we knew about the letters—you and I, Pat—Nora deliberately carried out the pattern of the three letters. She deliberately swallowed a small dose of arsenic on Thanksgiving Day so that it would seem to us Jim was following his schedule. And recall what she did immediately after showing symptoms of arsenic poisoning at the dinner table? She ran upstairs and gulped great quantities of milk of magnesia which, as I told you later that night in my room, Pat, is an emergency antidote for arsenic poisoning. Not a well-known fact, Patty. *Nora had looked it up.* That doesn't prove she poisoned herself but it's significant when you tack it onto the other things she did.

'Patty, must I go on? Let Carter take you home—'

'I want the whole thing,' said Pat. 'This moment, Ellery. Finish.'

'That's my baby,' said Carter Bradford huskily.

'I said "the other things she did",' said Ellery in a low tone. 'Recall them! If Nora was as concerned over Jim's safety as she pretended, would she have left those three incriminating letters to be found in her hatbox? Wouldn't any wife who felt as she claimed to feel about Jim have burned those letters instantly? But no—*Nora saved them* . . . Of course. She knew they would turn out to be the most damning evidence against Jim when he was arrested, and she made sure they survived to be used against him. As a matter of cold fact, how *did* Dakin eventually find them?'

'Nora . . . Nora called our attention to them,' said Cart feebly. 'When she had hysterics and mentioned the letters, which we didn't even know about—'

'Mentioned?' cried Ellery. 'Hysterics? My dear Bradford, that was the most superb kind of acting! She pretended to be hysterical, she pretended that *I* had already told you about the letters! In saying so, she established the existence of the letters for your benefit. A terrible point, that one. But until I knew Nora was the culprit, it had no meaning for me.' He stopped and fumbled for a cigarette.

'What else, Ellery?' demanded Pat in a shaky voice.

'Just one thing. Pat, you're sure—You look ill.'

'What else?'

'Jim. *He was the only one who knew the truth,* although

Roberta Roberts may have guessed it. Jim knew *he* hadn't poisoned the cocktail, so he *must* have known only Nora could have. *Yet Jim kept quiet.* Do you see why I said before that Jim had a more sublime reason for martyrizing himself? *It was his penance, his self-imposed punishment.* For Jim felt himself to have been completely responsible for the tragedy in Nora's life—indeed, for driving Nora into murder. So he was willing to take his licking silently and without complaint, as if that would right the wrong! But agonized minds think badly. Only . . . Jim couldn't *look* at her. Remember in the courtroom? Not once. He wouldn't, he couldn't look at her. He wouldn't see her, or talk to her, before, during, or after. That would have been too much. For after all she *had*—' Ellery rose, 'I believe that's all I'm going to say.'

Pat sank back on the couch to rest her head against the wall. Cart winced at the expression on her face. So he said, as if somehow it softened the blow and alleviated the pain: 'But Queen, isn't it possible that Nora and Jim together, *as accomplices*—?'

Ellery said rapidly: 'If they'd been accomplices, working together to rid themselves of Rosemary, would they have deliberately planned the crime in such a way that Jim, one of the accomplices, would turn out to be the only possible criminal? No. Had they combined to destroy a common enemy, they would have planned it so that *neither* of them would be involved.'

And then there was another period of quiet, behind which tumbled the water of Mr Anderson's voice in the taproom. His words all ran together, like rivulets joining a stream. It was pleasant against the malty odor of beer.

And Pat turned to look at Cart; and oddly, she was smiling. But it was the wispiest, lightest ghost of a smile.

'No,' said Cart. 'Don't say it. I won't hear it.'

'But Cart, you don't know what I was going to say—'

'I do! And it's a damned insult!'

'Here—' began Mr Queen.

'If you think,' snarled Cart, 'that I'm the kind of heel who would drag a story like this out for the edification of the Emmy DuPrés of Wrightsville, merely to satisfy my sense of "duty", then you're not the kind of woman I want to marry, Pat!'

'I couldn't marry you, Cart,' said Pat in a stifled voice. 'Not with Nora—not my own sister—a . . . a . . .'

'She wasn't responsible! She was sick! Look here, Queen, drive some sense into—Pat, if you're going to take that stupid attitude, I'm through—I'll be damned if I'm not!' Cart pulled her off the sofa and held her to him tightly. 'Oh, darling, it isn't Nora, it isn't Jim, it isn't your father or mother or Lola or even you I'm really thinking of . . . Don't think I haven't visited the hospital. I—I have. I saw her just after they took her out of the incubator. She glubbed at me, and then she started to bawl, and—damn it, Pat, we're going to be married as soon as it's decent, and we're going to carry this damn secret to the grave with us, and we're going to adopt little Nora and make the whole damn thing sound like some impossible business out of a damn book—that's what we're going to do! Understand?'

'Yes, Cart,' whispered Pat. And she closed her eyes and laid her cheek against his shoulder.

When Mr Ellery Queen strolled out of the back room he was smiling, although a little sadly.

He slapped a ten-dollar bill down on the bar before Gus Olesen and said: 'See what the folks in the back room will have, and don't neglect Mr Anderson. Also, keep the change. Goodbye, Gus. I've got to catch the train for New York.'

Gus stared at the bill. 'I ain't dreaming, am I? You ain't Santa Claus?'

'Not exactly, although I just presented two people with the gift of several pounds of baby, complete down to the last pearly toenail.'

'What is this?' demanded Gus. 'Some kind of celebration?'

Mr Queen winked at Mr Anderson, who gawped back. 'Of course! Hadn't you heard, Gus? Today is Mother's Day!'

Ⓞ

SIGNET Thrillers by Mickey Spillane

- [ ] **THE BIG KILL** (#E9383—$1.75)
- [ ] **BLOODY SUNRISE** (#W8977—$1.50)
- [ ] **THE BODY LOVERS** (#E9698—$1.95)
- [ ] **THE BY-PASS CONTROL** (#E9226—$1.75)
- [ ] **THE DAY OF THE GUNS** (#E9653—$1.95)
- [ ] **THE DEATH DEALERS** (#J9650—$1.95)
- [ ] **THE DEEP** (#E8688—$1.75)
- [ ] **THE DELTA FACTOR** (#Y7592—$1.25)
- [ ] **THE ERECTION SET** (#E9944—$2.50)
- [ ] **THE GIRL HUNTERS** (#J9558—$1.95)
- [ ] **I, THE JURY** (#J9652—$1.95)
- [ ] **KILLER MINE** (#W8788—$1.50)
- [ ] **KISS ME DEADLY** (#Q6492—95¢)
- [ ] **THE LAST COP OUT** (#J9592—$1.95)
- [ ] **THE LONG WAIT** (#J9651—$1.95)
- [ ] **ME, HOOD** (#Q5964—95¢)
- [ ] **MY GUN IS QUICK** (#J9791—$1.95)
- [ ] **ONE LONELY NIGHT** (#J9697—$1.95)
- [ ] **THE SNAKE** (#W9005—$1.50)
- [ ] **SURVIVAL . . . ZERO** (#E9281—$1.75)
- [ ] **THE TOUGH GUYS** (#E9225—$1.75)
- [ ] **THE TWISTED THING** (#Y7309—$1.25)
- [ ] **VENGEANCE IS MINE** (#J9649—$1.95)

Recommended Reading from SIGNET

Buy them at your local
bookstore or use the coupon
on the last page for ordering